Grow Where They Fall

Grow Where They Fall

MICHAEL DONKOR

FIG TREE
an imprint of
PENGUIN BOOKS

FIG TREE

UK | USA | Canada | Ireland | Australia
India | New Zealand | South Africa

Fig Tree is part of the Penguin Random House group of companies
whose addresses can be found at global.penguinrandomhouse.com

Penguin
Random House
UK

First published 2024
001

Copyright © Michael Donkor, 2024

The moral right of the author has been asserted

Set in 13.5/16pt Garamond MT
Typeset by Falcon Oast Graphic Art Ltd
Printed and bound in Great Britain by Clays Ltd, Elcograf S.p.A.

The authorized representative in the EEA is Penguin Random House Ireland,
Morrison Chambers, 32 Nassau Street, Dublin DO2 YH68

A CIP catalogue record for this book is available from the British Library

ISBN: 978-0-241-65685-3

www.greenpenguin.co.uk

MIX
Paper | Supporting
responsible forestry
FSC® C018179

Penguin Random House is committed to a
sustainable future for our business, our readers
and our planet. This book is made from Forest
Stewardship Council® certified paper.

For Moses Donkor and Patrick Netherton

August 1997

Kwame took a big deep breath in and clutched the paper. He wriggled his toes and knocked on the door. Hopefully a good start: as soon as they heard the sound, Mummy and Daddy stopped the scratchy shouting they'd been doing for half an hour that had brought him down from his room.

'Kwame?' Mummy's voice came through the frosted-glass panel. 'We disturbed him, Akwesi. Don't you feel ashame?'

'You put that one on me? Adwoa? I say –'

'Kwame, come. Come and enter here, eh.'

So Kwame twisted the sticky handle. Usually when his parents were cross with each other, if Akua was out and couldn't do her tough-talk refereeing, he found ways of distracting them. He'd tell them, for example, a fact about Jupiter he'd learned from the encyclopaedias they'd bought for him. Or ask them a really hard question about what cavemen ate. Because you had to keep them distracted. You had to work hard to put their attention where you wanted it to be.

He had done it well last week when the hi-fi had started making crunchy noises. Mummy had said Daddy should have replaced it last year when she told him to. They kept on going like that, Mummy jumping whenever Daddy came near her as if he were made of electric shocks. But then Kwame had explained to them about the different types of triangles until Mummy realized it was time to make dinner, and everything was fine for the rest of the evening. But, because the roaring had been so strong tonight – two dragons, neither willing to accept defeat – Kwame's knees were shy and he was unsure he could do it this time.

The kitchen door opened. The usual smell of kontomire wafted out. The scene in there made Kwame feel even less brave: Mummy was on one side of the table, Daddy on the other. Mummy's face was horribly covered with snot and tears, her chest going like she had run the whole of Garratt Lane without stopping. Daddy's eyes had burning red in them. He was angrier than Michael Jackson in the main screaming bit of 'Earth Song' when it's windy and he grabs hold of the spindly trees.

'Look.' Kwame made his voice calm and normal, to encourage his parents to be calm and normal too. He lifted the collage poster he held. The paper was bumpy because he'd used PVA to give it shine. 'I hope you think it's nice. I hope Mrs Gilchrist will too. It's my summer-holiday assignment. I'm nearly finished but not quite. You, you can see what I've been doing ever since we broke up from school. A diary in pictures, is what she said to do. I have to not get the corners bent because' – he tried to remember the strict word miss had used – 'she might put it on *prominent* display if it shows enough effort.' He pointed. 'Here are some of the characters from the books I've read and reread. So there's Mildred Hubble and there's Fantastic Mr Fox. And then I put in the ticket from when we went to the cinema. And herrrrrre I did the soul-singer ladies from the vases in *Hercules*. That was quite difficult, their swirly hair especially. And then therrrrrre's a drawing of ice creams from the fair at Figges Marsh.' Daddy's crunched forehead was smoothing out. Another good sign. 'I used furry pipe cleaners to do the 99p Flake in the ice cream.' Kwame wriggled his toes. 'Would either of you like to touch? You have to be careful, though.'

Mummy walked towards him. She pulled his earlobe, which was always nice. 'Is good. Very good. We have a Mona Lisa genius in our house, isn't it, Akwesi?'

Kwame let her take the work from him and saw her noticing details: the swatch of snipped Ankara from Tooting Market; the sketch of a football he made at the Rec, when he was watching Marcel and the other older Richmond Court boys playing, and was so relieved that they never asked him to join in. Now Daddy took the sheet from Mummy – not snatching but polite. Another good sign. Daddy laughed with a shaking head.

'A Mona Lisa artist is correct. And Mona Lisa artists need proper rest and recuperations if they are to keep on making masterpieces, isn't it?'

'Yes, Daddy. They do.'

'So you return to your room, eh?' He passed the poster back to Kwame. The red in Daddy's eyes was still there but it was fading. Or maybe Kwame just found it less frightening and burning because his parents were standing side by side now, Mummy's cardigan brushing Daddy's overalls, Mummy wiping her face with the end of her sleeve. 'You sleep well. The house is good only for your sound sleep. Wa te? Go back.'

Kwame looked from Daddy to Mummy and back again, nodded slowly, went up the stairs.

In his bedroom, at the desk he had begged for and amazingly actually got last Christmas, he moved his Pokémon albums to one side. Setting down the collage, happy again with the effect of the shiny foil he had used for the dodgems, he tried to imagine how he could fill the remaining blank patch in the bottom-right-hand corner.

The wondering didn't last long. Soon he heard the farty noise of the 57 resting at the bus stop, then a slam and something cracking. Mummy and Daddy were even louder this time, as if they were refreshed after the little break they'd had to chat to him. Every sentence was jagged, cutting through the floorboards like a saw. Mummy repeated how they couldn't feed anyone else. There was no space in the flat for this cousin from back home in Ghana. She was already working too hard. Daddy was working all God's hours at the sorting office *and* at the warehouse. Daddy came back stronger, said Akua's room was going to be empty soon so Mummy was being unreasonable.

Kwame checked the pencils in his pot. He sharpened the blunter ones as Mummy moaned that when one relative comes, they all do. This Yaw cousin person who she had never heard of would come over here and drain them out of house and home. Why hadn't he spoken to her of it before? She wanted no part in his kalabule immigration business, wanted nothing to do with the dodginess of getting this Yaw boy's papers sorted. There was another slam and Daddy said Mummy was selfish and they had a duty to help their own. Had she forgotten they were once like Yaw: needing a bit of help to come over, to get started?

Even though Kwame really wanted to know what 'kalabule immigration business' was, he darted beneath his duvet, squeezing the pillow over his head, because Mummy's scream was reaching up higher. Like she might even punch.

He curled himself tight – chin jammed against chest – keeping everything still, even though his heart and his mind jumped like the stormiest waves.

September 2017

'So I'd like to make a toast' – Kwame lifted his drink, hoping the slight tremor in his voice would go undetected – 'on the occasion of my thirtieth birthday. To arriving!'

'To arriving!' He let the echoed word settle. The darkness flickered with camera flashes, raised beers. Kwame gulped the last of the Margarita, slid the notecards into his pocket with tingling fingers. Applause rained and 'Ziggy Stardust' – Edwyn's choice? Wasn't it supposed to be TLC now? – started up.

He made his way down from the pub's stage, bursting for the loo, accepting Lloyd's pats on the back and Akua's hug. Milo's wobbling lower lip and running mascara made Kwame laugh. The applause swept on as he moved forward, and the swelling sound confirmed what he had sensed: his speech had balanced sentimentality and sass; gratitude to loved ones had landed sincerely. Edwyn's last-minute interventions about where to be braver with emphasis and when to maintain eye contact had worked. His footsteps soft, smiling his thanks, Kwame felt warmth spread to his stomach as he batted away balloons and watched Natalie's boozy grin veer to the left.

'Properly *bravo*.' Her voice – trained to strike fear into the hearts of Year 9s – easily overcame the music. 'You had everyone spellbound, babe. Wasn't all that hard, was it?' She took his empty glass, lurching towards the bar before

Kwame could respond. The last time he had been on stage like that, or anywhere near one, was in rehearsals for the Winter Show in Year 5 at Thrale. He knew standing at the whiteboard every day was a version of public speaking. But it was different when the audience were expectant – quietly judgemental? – family, peers. And so the run-up to his birthday speech had been marked by sickly anticipation.

Even though delivering it hadn't been as tough as he'd imagined – no heckling, no outrage – and even though Lloyd's brother was offering a celebratory fist bump now, a more solid relief still remained out of reach. He rubbed a palm over his buzzcut. The praise kept coming: Mummy cooing, an unknown presence shoving a party hat on his head. He high-fived, he feigned modesty at the complimenting of his Liberty shirt.

Daddy swayed in front of him. He reached for Kwame's lapels.

'The, the last of your speech? The final part? This your talking of your tutor group?'

'Daddy?'

'The students saying nice things about your youngish face? This Black-don't-crack stuff, as if you don't have to spend any time to worry on ageing –'

'Daddy –'

'Is not a laughing matter. You, you stand there for ten good minutes and not a word on precisely what your aims, your ambitions, what your next will be.' Daddy released the lapels. 'This classroom teaching is all well and good but, but is tiring. And is small, small in the grand scheme, eh? So what of something more . . . managerial? Head of department in a year? Principal, three years after that? And homeowner soon. Can't be on this mate's rates renting or whatever forever.' He opened his arms. 'This here land-mark birthday showed that time was marching and waits for no man, oh. So what is it? What are you wanting, eh? Eh? Because life has to be bigger, wa te?'

Daddy's eyebrows and the vibrating floor urged Kwame to speak. But no witty appeal to his father's lighter side or playful suggestion that a party mightn't be the ideal place for sermonizing came to mind. Just leaden silence. And Daddy was waiting. Kwame's jaw felt fuller. The stupid hat squeezed his temples.

'I mean, Daddy, I know what you're – it's not –'

Edwyn's shimmying into the gap between the two of them meant that Kwame had to take an awkward pace back and then right his balance. Daddy's questions hung in the air, and Kwame found his friend's canny disruption both merciful and frustrating. Edwyn grabbed Daddy's shoul-ders, sighed. 'Mr Akromah, you've got moves: will you help me start the conga?'

'What is conga? From Congo? I am a Ghanaian, not – we are Ghanaian, not –'

'Needs a man of your authority to get this lot in order, I'd say.' Kwame watched Edwyn's hands steer Daddy away. 'And I reckon it'll be thirsty work herding them, so de-finitely worth a Guinness on me once we're done.'

'I do enjoy a Guinness, Edwyn.'

'I know, Mr Akromah, I know.'

So Edwyn nudged Daddy further and started corralling guests – the bouncer and the barmaid too – into a messy single file, his laugh darting through objections, embarrass-ment, awkwardness. He sent Akua to the DJ to change the track, he twinkled as he fulfilled his Best Friend duties with the usual vigour, he turned to blow Kwame a kiss. But the kiss only glanced off the intended cheek. Kwame was squinting at a hunched back slipping through the crowd. He was almost sure of it: the familiar FUBU logo moving towards the rear door, that loping stride. The backs of Kwame's knees were tight. He couldn't move.

Thankfully, there had been only a couple of these unnerving, fleeting 'sightings' over the years. The first happened on A-level results day, just before Kwame whiteyed on Wandsworth Common. Everyone else was all sweaty abandon and booming jokes, but Kwame's attention had snagged on a tall black figure, his two earrings making glinting trails, vanishing between trees. The second, when Kwame was walking back from work, Balham High Road dense with returning commuters, galloping wind, sizzling rain. By the Moon Under Water, something had made him check the misted upper windows of the 249 at the crossing. And Kwame had seen him there, that face, the cheekbones, the questioning smile, searching the crowds, below. But then beeps came and the traffic was freed and the moment snapped, was gone.

Kwame knew, if he looked longer and more calmly now, he'd find nothing in the space ahead. Just the barman rearranging ketchups. Smokers locating fags and lighters. It was all a trick of the light, a trick of the tequila. Nostalgia works in mysterious ways.

The messy conga line weaved by, he joined it halfheartedly, his eyes pulled again and again to the green glow of the exit sign.

September 1997

He steadied himself by looking at the things nearby: the Calor gas heater in the corner, the smiling picture of Nkrumah and girls in kente and waving Ghanaian flags, the photos of him and Akua.

After counting to three he slipped the needle into his thumb, just beneath the surface of the skin, trying to chase out the splinter lodged there as he slid his hand down the banister, rushing to be in time for their Saturday ritual. But he pushed the needle in too fast, too far, too hard, and blood gathered in a full stop between thumb and index finger. Tears welled up while he sucked at the pain.

'It hurts, Mummy!'

He flapped to get her attention, but, on the other side of the living room, Mummy tucked two of her braids behind her ears and did not shift her eyes from the coloured, racing balls on the television or the pink slip she clutched. Kwame flapped more.

'Kwame, I've shown you how to do it before, isn't it? Eh henn. So then you know how is done. Be a big, strong boy.'

'It's really deep, deep down and sore, Mummy. Can you do it?'

'Making too much noise and whining. For what? Do it quickly so we can watch in peace. Don't you want to know if we are millionaires?'

Kwame nodded. He tried again with the needle, working

more patiently this time until – 'Mummy!' With pride, Kwame held up the tiny chip of wood. She scooped him into a hug and he pressed himself against the smells of her – cocoa butter, palm oil, nutmeg – before turning himself around in her lap so he faced the screen. Bob Monkhouse was saying well done and never mind to a ginger man who had missed out on the chance to win thousands of pounds. His face was long and grumpy; Kwame didn't blame him. If Kwame mentioned 'the Yaw guest' arriving in forty-five minutes' time, Mummy probably would be as grumpy as that. He licked his thumb again because more blood was coming out.

Kwame bounced and thought about what the Yaw cousin might be like. Since the big argument, no one had mentioned him, so Kwame had to fill in the blanks to stop himself worrying too much. He imagined that, if he was a relative of Daddy's, he would be short because Daddy wasn't the tallest of men. It would be great if the Yaw cousin were short – it would make him seem much friendlier. The age of the Yaw cousin was another unknown. Probably the man would be quite young; there was no way he would have a family because he wouldn't want to leave his children behind in Ghana, would he? And how strong would cousin Yaw's Ghanaian accent be? Of course, Mummy and Daddy sounded quite different from Kwame: he tried to speak like Mrs Gilchrist from school because her voice was neat and important; their voices were a fun mixture of the African man Matthew from the old barbershop programme *Desmond's* and the cockney of Mrs Jones who lived at 535. Kwame spoke more finely than the older boys on the block, like Marcel and Jermaine. They dropped the letters at the end of words and tried to be a bit Jamaican even though this was Tooting.

On the TV, Natalie Imbruglia was talking to Bob Monkhouse before she got to press the button on Lancelot and start the Big Draw, but it wasn't exciting because Natalie Imbruglia was everywhere you looked these days and so Kwame got even more distracted. His swinging legs nearly hit Mummy's shins. He stopped and stared ahead at the frosted windows. Even though Mummy didn't want the visitor to come, she had still made an effort with things. The brown carpet had been hoovered, the usual cluttering piles of bills and copies of the Yellow Pages had been moved. She had wiped the marks from the coasters and washed the doilies. He wanted to ask her why, if she hated the idea of the man coming so much, she had wasted her time.

'Here we go!' said Bob Monkhouse.

'Is coming. Let's cross our fingers.'

Mummy clutched the ticket tighter and Kwame did as he was told, but soon enough, because the numbers on the screen and on the ticket did not match, Mummy kissed her teeth and tapped Kwame's thighs: the signal for him to get up. She waddled out of the room, chuckling in a tired way.

'Same time next week, my dreamer-friend?'

Nodding, happy to have the remote control to himself for a few minutes, he pressed all the buttons, bringing a colourful mess to the screen. An explosion on a bridge, Gary Barlow, Cilla, two fighting gorillas, the Queen, Lenny Henry making everyone laugh.

For some reason Mummy had put the safety lock on, so the sound of the jangling chain and Daddy's angry confusion at not being able to enter the flat easily was Kwame's first realization that they had arrived. Kwame shouted for Mummy and ran to let them in. There was Daddy's hurried hello, hello, hello to Mr O'Shea, who had poked his head out of 436, and to Valeria, who was going into 437 – and then Daddy's complaining about the cold before he finally bustled through the corridor with two heavy suitcases. He nearly pushed over Kwame, but Kwame kept his balance and shot out his hand, ready to give Yaw his firmest handshake.

The man behind Daddy pulled back his hood to reveal a dark, pointy face. The cheekbones were the most noticeable thing. They looked so in charge. His hair was a high-top, and the curly tips were a kind of gingery-blond colour. His moustache was very tidy and pointed, almost like Jafar's in *Aladdin* but not quite as mean. The lips were different too: a deep pink, like a lady wearing make-up. Perhaps the man was twenty or so. He tilted his long head up and around, to take in the patterns of the brown wallpaper, and the big bump of his Adam's apple became clearer.

With his arm still thrust out, Kwame waited as the man pulled off his gloves and rested them on the pine side table. He eventually took Kwame's hand. The roughness to the touch was unusual.

'So you are the famous ten-year-old little kraakye your father told me of? The one and only Kwame Akromah. Your daddy says you will be the first Black prime minister of this United Kingdom. Is it so?'

Kwame didn't nod. His cheeks heated up.

'The prime minister at the moment is quite new. He's called Tony Blair. The one before him was John Major. He always looked ill. I think that's what happens to you if you're prime minister. It's too hard so you get sick.'

Yaw laughed. He had lots of teeth, bright against the darkness of his skin, so much darker than Kwame's. 'Yes. Wise. Power is a corrupting thing. Is a lesson you gotta hold on to.'

'I think the first president of Ghana was called Kwame Nkrumah. Daddy said he was a hero and that's why he lives on the wall of our living room. I'll show you later. The president of Ghana who is on the throne right now today is called Jerry Rawlings. Daddy told me he was half Scottish. Which is a surprise.' Kwame found he was jiggling like he needed a wee, and stopped still.

'We've got plantain and oxtail stew for dinner. Do you like that? *I* asked for a McDonald's because I thought it would be a good welcome, but Mummy said no.'

'Maybe we can have McDonald's another time. Is a good American food, isn't it? I will like to try that one soon.'

'Sounds nice. Thank you.'

Yaw smiled a slow smile, like he had a secret everyone wanted to know but he kept to himself. 'Such a smart little kraakye.'

'I, I know it's good if you collect your guests' coats when they arrive, so let me have yours now, please.' Yaw pulled off his puffer and took it from him carefully.

'We haven't got any space on the hooks down here so I'll lay it on Akua's bed upstairs. Neatly. That's where you'll sleep. It's quite a good room: Akua saved up money from her Saturday job at Superdrug to put in nice new curtains different from the others in the flat. I hope you'll like it. Akua's my sister, by the way. Did my daddy tell you? She left for university last week. Manchester. It's really far from here. She's doing Accounting and Economics, which I think is a bit like maths. I hate maths even though I'm doing well at it.'

Mummy bustled through with greetings and questions, and Yaw answered politely but started yawning too. And Kwame watched and couldn't stop watching as the man's arms and whole body stretched and Yaw's fists grazed the woodchipped ceiling. His jumper rode up. A slither of dark, tight stomach peeked through.

March 2018

'Was I TALKING to YOU? Was I, though? NO, FAM! Did I ask for you to give any opinion? NO. So sit down. I said, DAEQUAN, SIT YOURSELF DOWN, then.'

Princess rolled her big eyes, relishing the action. 'With your dusty cornrows trying to chat like dat to me. Foo-lish-ness. I said fix up your picky cornrows AND DON'T CHAT TO ME!'

Initially, it was only the girls sitting closest to Princess that were thrilled by her waving hands and flicking weave. They clapped, collapsing into one another, such was the hilarity, the shock of Princess's belittling of DaeQuan. But, as it always did, the laughter spread, rippling out around DaeQuan to those behind Princess and her faithful, all the way to the furthest corners of the classroom, where the sleepy Colombian boys sat. Soon all thirty kids – even silent Thom and Liberty – were chuckling.

'Year. 9. Year 9!'

Standing by the whiteboard, Mr Kwame Akromah flicked his purple lanyard, then rapped the marker against his knuckles. Javonne's and Stefan's eyes were streaming with tears. Tanvir was rocking on his chair with delight, swishing his purple blazer, and Hortense thought that was brilliant too. Princess glowed, absorbing the adulation.

The South London Academy, which had only been open for two and a half years, had a protocol to deal with

'Infractions' like this. The kids – especially this group, who were part of the school's first intake of students – knew that protocol like the backs of their sticky hands. Kwame would have been well within his rights to send Princess down to the Unit. There, in a cold room at the back of the shiny Sports Hall that Linford Christie had opened, Princess would have a stern dressing-down from Head of Behaviour. She would be left to complete her work 'in isolation', flanked by other miscreants – perhaps moody Ahmed from Year 13, sly Laverne from Year 12 – each in their own cramped white booth. But relying on the Unit was a cop-out. It was not, and would never be, Kwame's style – and the class knew it.

So, waiting for calm, Kwame shifted his weight from left foot to right. He had often been commended for this supposed poise; it was, apparently, a strength of his 'practice'. Recently he wondered whether it was apathy rather than a calculated move; whether, eight years into the trade, he just cared a little less.

Tanvir was getting up from his seat at the front of the class and heading for the back rows, no doubt to cause more trouble, so Kwame understood that shock tactics were required. He stood in a wide-legged pose and lobbed his marker pen through the classroom. It sailed past Kamila and Jasmine until it met the bin near Princess with a smack. Kwame brought his feet closer together, crossed his arms, maintained an unfazed expression. Princess clutched imaginary pearls to her chest.

'I swear down that's against Health and Safety. I swear you can lose your job now.'

'Shut up, Princess!' shouted Chyna.

'Yeah. *As iiiiif* I don't wanna get an education. Foolishness.

Listen to Mr Akromah and let him do the ting or move. Disrespec'ful. Coming on like you're bigger,' said Ravelle.

'Man's up there working hard and what you doing? Chatting fraff. You're a waste, Princess,' said Benji.

'Yeah.'

'He's one of the safe ones as well.'

'Yeah, Princess, hush up.'

'Zackly.'

Their flimsy loyalties still surprised and amused him – the students' split-second decisions to turn on each other. For a time, there was peace. Chastened Princess arranged her rubbers around the ridiculous straw boaters the girls had to wear: the quaint garb of public schools, it had been decided by SLA's governors, should be available to inner-city kids too. Kwame unfolded his arms.

'Good. So we'll continue, then.'

He pressed the clicker. An image appeared on the screen: a busy shopping street. A Sue Ryder shop with its splashy eighties cardigans, a Polski Sklep, a Snappy Snaps, an Odeon.

'That's Streatham High Road!' Zane said from the third row.

'A million and one points for that, genius.'

A titter from the middle of the row. Kwame rubbed his hands together. Time to summon up clarity and conviction. 'I see you lot. You never notice me, but I see you. All the time. I'm like a creepy spy or weird ghost.'

'What?'

'After school, on the weekends, when you walk down Streatham High Road, chatting your silly chat, shovelling chips into your greasy mouths, and you've got your earphones in and it's Bieber in your eardrums –'

'Bieber?!'

'Listening to Bieber is, like, haram, sir. Get me?'

'The thing I notice most about you lot,' Kwame continued, 'is that you're checking your phones and barely noticing the other people on the pavement, so you bump into everyone. And then everyone tells you that you're the rudest generation known to man, right?'

Another titter.

'You rarely notice what's going on up, up, up.'

Kwame pressed the clicker again. The image on the screen changed. Now Year 9 were presented with a picture of the redbrick world above the garish shop frontages: the Victorian windows above Lidl, Cash Converters, Boots. He showed them the camp turrets he often noticed, bold against the pewter sky. Then he clicked again to reveal ornate chimneys, elegant helixes twisting up. A close-up of a once-copper-now-green dome, a scoop of mint on the bland roof of the library building. He pressed the clicker once more. The screen showed bullet points, instructions.

'I want you to grab a fresh sheet of paper, my friends. I want you to imagine yourself walking along our beloved thoroughfare –'

'Thorough-who?'

'But this time, cast your thoughts *up*. What catches your attention there?' He passed around worksheets that reiterated the guidance on the screen. 'And let's try doing that thing we chatted about last week: use similes and metaphors and all that good stuff, but let's not be too reliant on them.'

He passed around another handout clarifying the task, its illustrations drawn with his own fair hand at the dinner table last night while Edwyn multitasked: complimented

Kwame's eye for design, attended to Grindr, complained about the thinness of his carbonara's sauce, consoled himself with another glass of Gavi.

'Thirty minutes and counting, my friends. Jot down initial ideas.'

Year 9 settled. Many frowned and turned to the ceiling for help. Their faces, when concentrating like this, were very beautiful, and vulnerable in a way that was almost painful for Kwame to watch for too long. In these seconds, the self-awareness usually present as they moved through the battlefield of early teenagedom was absent. The posher ones and the poorer ones. The detached and the super-keen. Maddie's thinking gaze, and Princess drumming her fingers as she tried to create. He neatened the stack of *Tess of the D'Urbervilles* on his desk.

He'd known this group since the school had opened for its first batch of Year 7s and its first batch of Year 12s, amid much pomp, two and a half years ago. It was a day when the headteacher – who, for no discernible reason, the pupils, staff and parents had to call Madame Evans, *never* Mrs Evans – made big promises. Madame Evans told them to think about Martin Luther King and the Pankhursts and William Wilberforce. After she stepped down from the podium, the new Year 7s, many of whom now sat before Kwame, delivered a screechy but determined performance of Gabrielle's 'Dreams', belting out each note with all the energy their nervous bodies could muster.

'Mr Akromah?' Kwame stopped shuffling the books and met Benji's stare. 'Like, sir, is disappear double *s* or not? Tanvir says it is double *s* and I say it's not. I always get so confused and I end up making a mistake and you circle it in my book. I beg you write it proper big on the board and finish off this fight.' Benji turned to his left. 'Watch me shame you up, Tanvir. Watch.'

After the bell had rung for the end of that day's last lesson – a wandering session with Year 12 – Kwame dragged himself through the empty classroom over to the messy desks. He collected the photocopies about Hardy's use of animal imagery that students should have taken away to help with their homework. Each sheet was decorated with doodles: Amara's drawings were the most impressive, including an accurate portrait of Kwame, where she had worked hard to convey the vigilance of his small eyes, the breadth of his nostrils, the fullness of his top lip; Elise and Elaine had been playing noughts and crosses on their sheet; mute Anton's offerings were unsurprising in their blandness, tiny square after square after square. But, in minute handwriting in the bottom-left-hand corner, Anton had become existential: *What the fuck are we all even doing here?* Feeling a kind of sympathy with the question, especially given the prospect of the long Parents' Evening that lay ahead, Kwame sighed.

It was an understatement to say that the Year 7 Parents' Evening, due to begin at half five, generated mixed emotions. Loosened tie swinging about his chest, Kwame gathered the bits from his desk that he'd need for his meetings with what surely had to be London's most varied and, often, most exacting parents. He sighed again, and tried to remind himself of the delights that might be on offer too.

Among the fortysomething, early-fiftysomething dads of South London, there were some delicious favourites. The Sporty Ones were a real treat: they showed up to Parents'

Evenings perfectly groomed – clever beardy-topiary, slicked short back and sides – fresh from the gym, decked in tasteful athleisurewear. Kwame could sense these men kickboxed and had PTs or had been told by mates they should 'look into becoming' PTs themselves. The Middle Management Dads had their charms too, although perhaps not quite so many. They were as coiffured as their sporty counterparts, but more Hugo Boss-suited and Armani-booted. It was usually a Middle Management Dad who, on first meeting Kwame in September, might firmly ask how long Mr Akromah had been teaching. Where had he taught before SLA? Where had Mr Akromah gone to university? What were Mr Akromah's views on recent curriculum reform? Conversations that moved discussion away from chatting about Mabel's, Matthew's, Matilda's work. Conversations that brought the odd sense that Kwame had to – but most likely would never – meet some ineffable criteria. Conversations that made Kwame press down his voice with care.

He clicked the option to shut down his computer and wiped at a smear of something shiny on the screen. He could hear groaning coming from the echoey corridor. He opened the door and, in the distance, saw the tiny frame of Natalie Collins. Natalie – Head of Geography and Head of Middle School – leaned against Year 13's Government and Politics Noticeboard. She clutched a clipboard to her chest. Softly, Natalie banged her forehead against the poster about Proportional Representation. Her braids flopped with each strike. Kwame approached her and she turned to him.

'Eugh.'

'I know, Natalie.'

'Three whole hours of dry chat? I wanna go *home* and chill on my sofa. Even if bloody Marina will be in, chewing wasps as bloody per.'

'I take it that things between you and your darling flatmate haven't improved?'

'If I see her dirty nail clippings on the coffee table one more time, no one – I said *no one* – can hold me responsible for any actions I might committeth.'

It was this silliness that pupils loved about Natalie, which meant that when Kwame received a class after they had been with Miss Collins for an hour – learning about erosion in zingy ways – they found Kwame's dissections of iambic pentameters lame.

She pouted at him. 'You know that because it's Year 7 tonight I'll have to see Alina Reynolds's mater?'

'Thoughts and prayers, pal, I –'

'Do you know how many emails she's sent me in the past two days? Thirty-eight! I'm not joking! I'm convinced all the woman does is sit at her laptop and email me. No breaks for food, water, pissing – just emailing poor innocent me. And for why, Kwame? For why?'

'Yeah. I've heard on the grapevine that one can be quite . . . *communicative.*'

'Fuck me, Kwame, you're always so careful with what you say: she's a certifiable loon, mate.'

The door of the History Office swung open and Mrs Antwi, the most senior of SLA's band of wearied Ghanaian cleaners, hobbled forward.

'Do I hear my son's joyful, joyful laughing, ohhhhh?'

The old woman put her stubby arms around Kwame's stomach. She stood like that for a full minute, purring.

'You getting a bit fatter,' she said. 'Not quite fat enough, yet. Not full fat. But is an improvement.'

'Thanks?'

While Natalie pulled her shoulders back, Kwame offered Mrs Antwi his imperfect Twi. As usual, she mocked the poverty of his speech and switched to English, making her voice more sympathetic to ask about the health of his mother and father, even though she had never met them. This exchange of pleasantries, which happened every few weeks, whenever Kwame stayed late to mark essays or put up displays, had never before had an audience. The whole thing seemed to deeply please Natalie. Mrs Antwi hobbled back, putting a chamois into her pocket.

'And, my son,' Mrs Antwi shouted without turning round, 'straighten your collar and things or else you will be looking like a disgrace in front of the parents, and I don't want that.' She closed the door.

'God, I *love* her.' Natalie squeezed Kwame's forearm hard. 'Reminds me of my nan. The Antiguan one, not the Irish one. Proper woman of the world; them women have seen it all. And more.'

When Kwame had first met Mrs Antwi, she had been quick to tell Kwame her name, and almost as quick to identify Kwame as one of her 'countrymen'. Apparently, his forehead had given away his Asante origins. Although his un-Asante tallness had momentarily made her question her first hunch – perhaps he was an Ewe? – the proud forehead was too Asante for him to be anything else. Kwame confirmed her suspicions and thought that would be the end of things, but the news that Kwame was indeed an Asante filled Mrs Antwi's face with so much light. And

24

then Mrs Antwi had started swiping through photos of her daughter on her phone: Serwaa had a degree in Marketing from Birmingham, was a good girl, had nice manners like Kwame, was *unmarried and ready*, very juicy in the behind, look at this: her in Cyprus, you like the bikini, isn't it? The red bikini? She looks well, isn't it? I have more snaps here, check them close . . . Kwame had returned the Samsung to Mrs Antwi. He told her that he was, in fact, gay.

Mrs Antwi loosened her grip on the mop in the wheeled bucket by her feet. She patted his chest three times. The fourth time she patted, she inhaled and left her hand against him. Some kind of prayer? The ridding of supposed sin? He had started to chew the corner of his lower lip, but then, without warning, Mrs Antwi was yanking her face into a smile, the rouge on her cheeks seeming thinner, more powdery.

'My son, tomorrow I will prepare you the sweetest kelewele your mouth has ever tasted.' She did a chef's kiss and set about peeling off her Marigolds. 'Or, or are you one of these like some of Maame Serwaa's friends who wear kente scarves and say they want to save their earnings to build a large house in Kumasi, yet they won't touch their home food?'

Even though she was calling him 'son'; even though he twerked his way through Brighton Pride with Edwyn every year; even though his parents were more sanguine about his sexuality these days; and even though he would never deny that he loved the saltiness between a man's balls and crack – as he had stood before Mrs Antwi that afternoon, his neck had felt hotter, his desire to be anywhere else stronger and stronger.

'How many times have you been back home, my son?

And are you excited about the new terminal they will finish in Accra soon?'

Mrs Antwi's words had continued to leap and bob. Kwame answered her questions fully and methodically so that she had had to call him a 'good boy', a 'fine boy' who 'spoke soooo well'. 'Wa ya die paa,' she told him.

Though Kwame's neck and vanity were satisfied by the compliments, a deeper part of him was still unsettled, remained unsettled even now. He didn't want to, but he always doubted her enthusiasm. He knew Ghanaians could be experts in silence – his own family so skilled at it that Yaw's name had, without blips or drama, been kept out of their mouths for two decades. And so he couldn't help but worry that, underneath Mrs Antwi's jolly fussiness, perhaps a more critical note lay, quieted. Something bitter and disgusted that let itself out in rages over fufu dinners with her husband or at the nail salon with Serwaa: 'They, they even have us cleaning the classroom of gays. Me, a good Christian woman? Working for gays? Is a disgrace.'

But she probably never felt like that. Her warmth, Kwame thought – as he and Natalie walked past the Nurse's Office and Natalie guessed Mrs Antwi's age – was probably derived from the simple pleasure of finding a fellow Ghanaian. Just that. Nothing more. But it was, undeniably, the prickling uncertainty about it all that saddened Kwame most.

'She's wrong about your waistline, though,' Natalie said, heading towards the staff room. 'I'd say the exact opposite, Kwame. If anything, you're very trim, very svelte right now. It's like you're disappearing.' She pinched her stomach and frowned. 'What's your secret?'

*

26

When the SLA first opened, the architects who created it by transforming the old primary on Weir Road into a 'state-of-the-art learning and ideas space' delivered a presentation about the features of the site to the new staff. There was bold talk of 'creativity zones' and 'breakout mezzanines'. The architects had ended their 'show and tell' with a slide called 'Piece de Resistance!' It had shown shiny images of the expansive staff room. The staff had oohed and ahhed.

It *was* an impressive space. Kwame especially liked the row of dramatic windows that let in the sunset's deepening tones. Kwame watched rich purple spread across the central table where laminated posters about the next week's canteen menu were stacked. Purple light glinted against the tea urn too, where the Maths Department tutted: the instructions about the classrooms that teachers had been designated for this evening's meetings were confusing. The light also washed over Head of English, as she ransacked her locker looking for her mark book – fretting, spitting feathers. The photocopier ground on, and Kwame remembered Anton's scrawled musing – *What the fuck are we all even doing here?* Making himself smile a small smile, he looked forward to getting back to the flat later, no doubt for extensive discussion of Edwyn's exciting day up in town, helping Claridge's head sommelier update their selection of champagnes. It was a stupidly camp gig that Edwyn had dreamed of since their Durham days.

Kwame's first sighting of Edwyn had been in the third week of the first term. Kwame had been walking from his new room to the JCR for more shuffling around the pool table, more half-hearted joining-in with limp analyses of Super Hans's unique appeal.

But through an open door by the vending machines, a loud voice curled out towards the corridor's ceiling beams. It was describing, in detail, a 'capricious little Sauternes'. Kwame liked the silly adjectives the voice used: 'dancerly . . . nimble . . . luminous'. He peered in. Busy in there. Soft candlelight. Long table with olives and cheese. Jazzy tune playing in the background. There was a crowd, a circle, noses in little glasses, swilling and puckering of lips. White name labels on chests: Flozz, Big T, Milo. Tiny pencils scratching against tiny pads. In the middle of it all, the crown of a head was visible, topped with curly, chestnut hair. Its voice told the gileted-and-charm-braceleted crew to notice the wine's astringent masculinity too. The voice went throatier when it said 'masculinity'. Everyone laughed at that with jiggling shoulders. The circle opened out, the volume of the jazz crept up. There was more sniffing until Kwame understood that the tall, thin boy now reaching for another bottle was the owner of the voice and those curls. He had such pale skin, such showy cheekbones. He turned to face the door.

'Oh, *great*! Oh, *welcome, welcome welcome*! Bit late. But clever to come when things are flowing and miss my admin preamble about membership fees.' He walked towards Kwame, offering a thimble of amber liquid. There was something coiled about this long boy's physicality. As if he were always moving on the balls of his feet. 'Whack your chops round that. Give us a rundown, what you make of it, etc. Everyone else has.'

Kwame tipped his head back, drank. And as a honeyed flavour expanded, Richmond Court rose before him. The trellises on the balcony of 436, the tiny flowers Mr O'Shea

28

waited for, so nervously, every year. Was it the clarity of that memory that made it easy to speak? Or the bold stare of the man in charge?

'Spring. Gardens in the spring. There's a . . . jasminey thing . . . going on. I think. Yeah. Jasmine. But springtime is mostly what I'm thinking of. Droplet of sunshine.' He wanted to lick his lips but did not. He met the man's stare and made his shoulders soften. 'It's nice. Delicious, actually.'

The man – whose label said 'Wyn' – beckoned Kwame further in. He closed the door with a balletic roundhouse kick, which led to more laughs with jiggling shoulders. 'Instinctive.' Wyn poured more into Kwame's glass. 'Such a real and instinctive take that is so bang on the money. Brilliant that we'll be getting a different perspective up in here. Right, guys? Could learn a lot from him.' Nods, slight raising of glasses, hands sliding into chino pockets. 'Now, Vin Santo! We roll on to the new.'

That gleam of being favourably singled out twinkled. Kwame took steps towards the circle as Edwyn talked about wooden caskets and alchemy.

Disrupting his quiet pre-Parents' Evening marking in the staff room, Barbara, the bosomy, chirpy TA, plonked herself in the seat next to Kwame's. He shifted to make room. 'Just the man I was after. It's a total pain, but you know Ahmed Hussen in your Year 13 group?' Kwame nodded. 'Can you make sure to email him the resources you'll use in your next lesson? He'll be away for a few days. There's "family stuff afoot".' She looked exhausted.

Kwame clucked his tongue and flattened his tie against his shirt. Before he could tell Barbara he'd actually noticed more focus in Ahmed of late and more willingness to share ideas in discussion, the top dogs processed into the staff room and stationed themselves by the pigeonholes.

The entry of the senior management team brought the staff's gentle milling around the hot desks to an end. Kwame watched Head of Behaviour, Head of Progress and Head of Vision all line up behind the headteacher. Bedecked in varied greys, all standing with the same stance, they were like some very unremarkable band. *Madeline and the Mediocres.* Natalie would like that. He'd tell her when she came back from the loo.

An unlikely lead singer, Madame Evans put her left foot forward like she was about to dash off somewhere, jolting her Aztec-y statement necklace.

'You know' – Madame Evans swung her grey bob around – 'colleagues, I am excited. This is an extraordinary place of learning. *We* make it remarkable. And on evenings like this we get to re-engage with those who also bring real brilliance to our community – the parents.' She started walking through the staff. 'Admittedly there is often . . . how shall we put it . . . a handful of tricky customers on occasions like these, but, in the main, these evenings are *celebrations.* Parents' Evenings are an opportunity for collective back-patting. Because those parents queuing out there are doing a magnificent job of raising the extraordinary young people who grace our classrooms. And, you educators in here' – Kwame watched her try to make eye contact with as many teachers as she could, and wasn't sure how he felt when she didn't meet his gaze – 'you *equally* magnificent, pioneering, brave educators are – are –'

Given that she was a relatively compact woman, the noise Madame Evans's body made as she crumpled to the floor

30

was loud. It was a thudding blow felt underfoot. The lights above suddenly seemed far too bright, stinging almost. There were gasps, and Kwame heard a glassy scream from somewhere behind him, before lots of frenzied movement. Head of Drama scaled the sofa with a leap, swooped in to check for breathing. Head of PE touched the side of the headteacher's face, pulled at her chin to still her snagging, juddering mouth. Then Head of Behaviour produced a walkie-talkie from his pocket, shouted for an ambulance. Head of Progress, his fingers wide and palms assertive, told everyone to move back, back, back – get back! – but Kwame turned to see Natalie frozen on the spot and NQTs who were comforting each other frozen in place as well. And all the while Madame Evans's right hand kept reaching up in fits and starts, desperate to get at the colourful ovals lying slack on her chest.

September 1997

On the tenth morning of Yaw's stay, Kwame was scrubbing at his shoes, getting caked mud out of the whirling grips on the soles and making them glisten. After Mummy shouted goodbye up the stairs and closed the front door, Kwame heard grunting coming from somewhere. He stepped into the corridor and, through the ajar door to Akua's – *Yaw's* – room, he saw Yaw skipping in circles, punching at an imaginary enemy. Yaw's expression was furious, like he wanted to kill. And his movements were so fast. If someone tried to photograph it, there would be only blurs: a flashing white of his vest, the swinging gold of his fine crucifixes.

Kwame climbed the stairs and thought again about how Yaw was a man with odd habits. He spoke with a sort of American accent even though he had never been to America. He ate heavy meals of yam and stew at strange hours. He drummed his cutlery during dinnertimes when you were supposed to eat or talk about your day, not drum your cutlery. And often he put the cutlery to one side – wanted to eat absolutely everything with his hands. He spent ages taking care of his black puffer jacket, carefully picking pink lint off the big, wonky FUBU letters stitched on the back. He slept with his bedroom door wide open and the lamp on throughout the night. He sang hymns as he moved around the flat. He wore a baggy T-shirt with Tupac on it, and neither Mummy nor Daddy complained – usually they changed the station if hip-hop came on. Even though Yaw did these quite weird things, Kwame tried to bear in mind what he'd learned in a Circle Time last year when lovely Mrs Gilchrist taught them that making snap judgements never helped anyone, and might also stop you from learning new things. Still, Kwame wished Akua was around, because she would have thought Yaw's skipping and punching stuff were one hundred per cent different and properly crazy. Standing in the doorway to the room, Kwame knew Akua would also be annoyed because it no longer smelled of her CK One but of Yaw's lemony Versace Blue Jeans instead.

'Boxing. What are you doing that for?'

A surprised Yaw bent over, stood up and caught his breath. Out of nowhere, he jabbed in Kwame's direction. It was hard not to blink or flinch.

'Keeping on top of my fitness, kraakye. Gotta stay strong and a stèp ahead.' Yaw jabbed again, then let his arms hang at his sides. 'My father, in our town, Atonsu, he keeps a, a . . . gymnasium. Is like a yard, behind our house, and he has put some weights there. And some guys in the local area, they come and pay him few cedis to use the equipments to maintain their strength. There are only a few weights. Is not the best. But still everyone likes to come. He gets the boys and we do fights, and people place small bets to guess who the victor will be. Many of the boys take it seriously but I kinda don't care so much. Is only for fun.'

To show that his speech had come to an end, Yaw nodded a firm nod. He started hitting the air again.

'Do you miss A-ton-su yet? Am, am I saying it right – Atonsu?'

'Uh huh, uh huh, uh huh, yep you got it.' Yaw did some star jumps. 'And, no, sir, no, man. I said my bye byes when I left. Me, I'm just very excited to see what's next. Your, your pa has been good so far and shown me the important things like this Tooting Broadway Tube Station and those shops you guys got out here. But I wanna start *livin*, you know? Prayin your daddy comes through and soon I'll get my papers fixed and someone's NI to use, and I'll get hustlin on.' Jab. Jab. Jab. 'Need to make that cash money *double quick* – you feel me?'

'Erm, a bit. Yeah, a bit. But what's an NI? And what, what job do you think you'll do? Something like Mummy in the clinic reception? Or like Daddy in the sorting office? Or are those jobs too old for a twenty-two-year-old? Maybe a paper round is a good idea because you'll have to walk around a lot so then you'll get to know the local area well so it becomes like second nature.'

'Bro, I dunno. Not up to me. It's down to your pop and the Almighty.' Yaw paused, then quickly started doing more invisible punching. The veins on his muscles came out. Every now and then Yaw shuffled towards the window, where Kwame had once seen angry Akua crying and smoking a cigarette disgustingly after she had tried to stop Mummy and Daddy arguing and Daddy had told her to stop pressing 'her nose in all the time'. Yaw shuffled back the way he came, with tiny hops and sharp punches, often shooting Kwame a glance between each movement. Then he dropped and did press-ups. Kwame could see Yaw's sweaty armpit hair as he pumped against the floor. The press-ups continued, and after each five Yaw smiled up at Kwame with a gritted, glittery smile. Kwame nodded in the certain

34

way Yaw had done to bring things to an end, and made his way back downstairs.

Did Yaw win the fights his dad arranged in Atonsu? Yaw's limbs were long and wiry, not chunky like Frank Bruno's or Reece Campbell's from school, but he was still probably a very excellent fighter. There was a slinkiness in the way he moved, and so he was probably great at dodging, swerving, protecting himself. Kwame wasn't sure whether defence or attack was bravest. Being brave mattered, but you had to use bravery wisely. Everyone said Matthew Da Souza in Year 6 was brave because he shoplifted Double Deckers from Mr Agrawal's corner shop even though everyone knew Mr Agrawal protected his stock with two angry terriers, and they had growled at Matthew but that didn't put off Matthew from darting into the shop, grabbing, running away with the chocolate in his pocket and dashing into everyone's applause. Kwame thought there had to be better ways to use bravery than stealing from a poor Indian man who never did anything wrong to anybody.

In the kitchen he watered the row of spider plants on the window ledge as he did every few days. It was a job that made him calm and safe. It made him feel like that because of its end results. Mummy and Daddy always said they wanted their little patch of greenery thriving, wanted it full and healthy so Alan Titchmarsh was jealous. So whenever they stroked the leaves and did a hats-off to Kwame for his care and green fingers, there was no chance of raised voices or complaining. And the healthiness of the plants kept them thinking he was a good boy – a good and ordinary boy, trying his best – and nothing else.

The morning light's sluggishness was like Daddy, who

now sat at the table and chomped away on Frosties with a tired, rolling jaw and eyes on the picture of Elton John and candles in the newspaper. The difference between the enthusiastic tiger on the cereal box and Daddy's hard, beardy face was funny. Kwame collected his favourite yellow bowl with the sun at the bottom and poured in Frosties, milk.

'I'm sorry to disturb you but will you explain to me how Yaw and I are related? I know you haven't got loads of time —'

While Kwame took a mouthful Daddy stood, pulled one of the yellow writing pads from the drawer with the rubbish in it: batteries, vouchers, elastic bands. He plonked it on his newspaper.

'Nice to see you taking an interest in your history. Is good.'

Kwame moved to the other side of the table to watch Daddy draw stretching branches and write names Kwame didn't recognize and knew would be harder to pronounce than A-ton-su. Daddy wrote Mummy's name, ADWOA AKROMAH, and Kwame wanted Daddy to draw a big sparkling flower near her to show that Mummy was special to him, but Daddy didn't do that. Instead, he quickly wrote M. 1978. Kwame knew the *m* was for married. He also knew that Mummy and Daddy had married in Wandsworth Register Office. He'd seen the old photos. He loved Daddy's silly outfit in the pictures: the shirt with peach ruffles running down its middle, and the massive Afro that reduced the size of his cheerful face. Mummy's dress was hilarious too: a lime-green ballgown with frills matching Daddy's. The best picture was the one in which Mummy was sitting on Daddy's lap. Mummy's Afro was even bigger than Daddy's, and almost blocked him out. Mummy was glowing like the wine glasses of those around them: Ghanaians with their huge headwraps and flapping white handkerchiefs, all seeming to love Mummy and Daddy's closeness.

Daddy wrote his own name, AKWESI AKROMAH, near Mummy's and then wrote DADDY/ANDY, making sure to include the English name that he told people at work to call him. Kwame saw himself appear on the page beneath that, as Daddy bordered his name with asterisks which were almost pretty. More squiggles and arrows grew. Daddy did not stop to check details or question himself as the diagram spread, lines everywhere, notes and dates added to the left and right. Maybe the sheet wouldn't be big enough, long enough, wide enough, to fit in Yaw.

'Our people. Scattered to your four winds,' Daddy muttered as he noted down where the different people lived – USA, Canada, Germany, Italy. 'They land, but do they grow where they fall?'

The question sounded half dreamy, half sad, but, before Kwame had a chance to ask what the matter was, Daddy put Yaw's name in the top-right-hand corner of the page, circled it and did the asterisk thing again. Even though there were some confusing squiggles, overall the effort deserved a round of applause, so Kwame clapped and Daddy smiled, and Kwame's stomach felt warm.

'You follow, kraakye? He is a kind of . . . very, very distant cousin. But I know you will treat him like he is your very real brother, isn't it?' Kwame nodded. 'Eh henn. *Good.* So, so tell me what they will have you do in your Thrale School today, eh? What learnings are to come?'

Kwame finished his last gulp of cereal. He told Daddy

about designs they were doing for the playground garden, and the haikus about trust and respect they were writing up. Above them, in the bathroom, Yaw had started running a shower and making loud relaxed noises as the water hissed away. Kwame imagined the steam and the tightness in Yaw's arms calming down after the boxing exercises, the veins quietening now they didn't have to work hard. Kwame wanted to run his finger along those veins, up and down.

After break time, Mrs Gilchrist arranged the class in a line to walk into the headteacher's assembly and said Kwame should stand behind Ravi. Most of the class muffled a laugh unsuccessfully, until Mrs Gilchrist tapped her foot and everyone shut up. Doing as he was told, Kwame moved along and, as soon as Mrs Gilchrist's back was turned, pulled up the collar of his jumper so it covered his nose. As they marched in single file, nearby David Siddon gave Kwame a thumbs-up. He puffed out his cheeks and then pretended he was going to throw up, before smiling and pulling up his own shirt over his face too.

Everyone hated sitting next to Ravi Akbar. Though it was mean to admit it, Kwame knew it was true: Ravi Akbar smelled. Badly. He always had. In Year 1, David Siddon had called Ravi 'Paki Le Pew' to his face. The whole playground had clenched. Ravi had been silent for two whole days after that. Once, when they were in Year 3, Mrs Gilchrist had helped Ravi mix green and yellow to get the right colour for a Granny Smith, and Kwame could have sworn he saw Mrs Gilchrist screw up her nose. As Kwame tied himself into his apron and settled down to start his own painting, he wondered why Mrs Gilchrist hadn't told

Ravi or Mrs Akbar that Ravi needed to wash himself or his clothes more, that he was ruining his chances of having an easier time. She would have done it kindly, as if it were nothing to be upset about, her freckles making Ravi feel better.

As Kwame waited in the hall, his grin inside his top matched David Siddon's. The smile soon drooped because Ravi frowned at him – but for other reasons too. Kwame understood the importance of David Siddon congratulating him for doing what you were supposed to in these situations, but why David Siddon got to do the congratulating and why David Siddon – rather than anyone else – could decide how you behaved around Ravi troubled Kwame's stomach.

Breathing through his mouth, Kwame knew David Siddon's face explained why he was the boss of Year 5. David Siddon's was a cheeky face: underneath floaty blond curls, his twinkly eyes got everyone's attention and his round cheeks glowed with pinkness. Mums loved to pinch them at Home Time while doing the 'Ahhhh!' noises audiences made when puppies jumped around on *Pets Win Prizes*. It was the kind of face you could only love or be jealous of. Staring ahead at the empty stage, Kwame was certain – even though he quite liked the friendly width of his own nose and the way his eyelashes curled – that his face didn't have the same magic as David's. He was also sure that when David Siddon grew up he would be richer than Kwame would ever be, because grown-up David Siddon could go into any place with wealthy people and they would see all the light gleaming off him and think, 'I have to give this nice man everything I own because then maybe he'll like me back and some of his shine will rub off on me.'

Mrs Gilchrist lifted, then dropped her hand, and they all sat, with a scrunching sound. When she caught Kwame's eyes, his stomach became even more troubled. The mime she did – removing something from over her mouth – was slow and strict. Immediately understanding what she meant, Kwame lowered his collar.

The fire doors flew open and Mr Plumstead walked in, clickety-clacking as he entered. Mrs Ashton, the school nurse who also had some musical skills and ran the school's little library too, followed behind him. Kwame saw that the headteacher held a rolled-up tube of card under his arm, and as Mr Plumstead marched by the other staff they laughed like they would never stop.

He climbed the steps up to the stage. 'My boys and girls, good morning to you!'

'Good morning, Mr Plumstead. Good morning, everyone.'

'Boys and girls, can you tell how excited I am today? Hey? Shall I let them in on the secret, Mr Bell?'

The Year 6 teacher that everyone hated wrinkled his long nose. 'I'm not sure, Mr Plumstead, do you *really* think they're all sitting up as beautifully as possible?'

'You're right, Mr Bell. I'm not so certain. They're still a tad scruffy.'

The whole school crossed their arms and legs even more tightly, and put their fingers over their lips to show they would never dream of speaking when Mr Plumstead had something to say, and eventually, with slow-motion movements, Mr Plumstead unrolled the tube. Everyone in the hall leaned forward, paperclips drawn to a magnet. When Mr Plumstead finished unrolling, a massive piece of card showed a snowman grinning with coal teeth. He had two stars where eyes should have been. In one of his snow-man hands, he held a top hat, in the other a cane. He had one snowman leg kicked out at a happy angle, in front of a backdrop of shimmering dots. Above his head, arranged in an arch, were the words THRALE'S WINTER SHOW 1997 and underneath the snow-clown: PREPARE FOR FESTIVE AMAZE-MENT! Kwame recognized the style of the cartoony drawing as Mrs Gilchrist's.

'Boys and girls, I am *thrilled* to share something so ex-citing with you.' He jogged on the spot, his knees bashing against the bottom of the poster. 'Now it seems a long way off, but Christmas will be upon us before you can say "mince pies" . . .'

The hall said 'Mmmmm', and people patted their tum-mies. The poster was passed to Mrs Ashton, who stood at the back of the stage with it.

'Now we love our hymns and our carols, don't we, Thrale?'

'Yes, Mr Plumstead!'

'And we're often thinking about Christianity at Christmas. Suppose that sounds silly, eh? But what I'm getting at is that lots of us celebrate different things at that time of year, don't we? Hanukkah for example. Can our Jewish friends put their hands up?' Ben Tansey and Sarah Levy did as they were told. 'And, over in America, there's *Kwaanza*' – Kwame listened to him say that funny word in a special, amazed way – maybe like when you say *abracadabra* – 'for African Americans, and that's taking off in a big way, so I've no doubt it will be taken up on our shores by our Afro-Caribbean . . . brothers and sisters too.'

Mr Plumstead looked like he had confused himself.

41

'And for some people there's no religious celebration at all. Atheists. We've got lots of Jehovah's Witnesses here too, haven't we? For some people, the end of the year is simply a great time for catching up with family and for being thankful. And we've got lots to be thankful for, haven't we, Thrale?'

'Yes, Mr Plumstead!'

'My point is that Christmas, well, it's about *more* than just Christmas. So, rather than a good old-fashioned nativity play which concentrates on telling only the story of Jesus's birth, we – your teachers, the PTA, myself – want to put on a different kind of show – a *Winter* Show – that celebrates, *yes*, the important Christian festival but so much else besides. It'll have the carols we all love but also songs from the charts – a bit of the Spice Girls' – the whole hall tried its best to keep calm but Mr Plumstead had to speak louder – 'and a few numbers from musicals too, plus some new ones written by our very own Mrs Ashton and Mrs Gilchrist' – they both waved – 'and the real treat will be some of you lovely lot doing solo performances. It'll come together to tell a glorious story of wintery wonder and family joy, and celebrate our school community.'

Now the hall couldn't help but chat furiously. Some, like Lottie Wren, were on the verge of excited tears. Some, like David Siddon, were sniggering. Kwame didn't join in, even though Francis Baker tugged his elbow. Kwame was busy picturing himself doing one of the solos, throwing the snow-clown's top hat and cane high in the air, somersaulting, then catching the hat and cane as if it were the easiest thing known to humankind.

*

After school, at the dining table, Kwame watched Mummy reading her post in silence. She pinned red pages to the fridge with the talking-drum magnet, positioning them in the middle of all the other bills. A deep clicking rose from the back of her throat. She handed Kwame a letter from Akua (the handwriting told him his sister was obviously the sender) and a proper Wagon Wheel from her pocket. Yessss! A real one! Not Own Brand!

Even though Mummy's black eyes were heavy, heavy like Kwame's sometimes felt, she stroked the top of his ear, then she stepped to the sink to do the dishes. He took his first bite.

'Don't let —'

'I won't let any crumbs fall, Mummy. You're not living with some kind of hooligan.'

The drain burped.

'Is best, sometimes, for it to be only us two. A bit of peace without all this noisy men rampaging about the place.' She did a slow laugh. 'Me and my sweet son. Just a time to think about what can be done to manage things. Even when you know truly nothing can be done.' The laugh again. 'Wa te?'

She turned the taps so that more water gushed.

'Yes, Mummy.'

The thought of the heavy eyes and the long laughs were too much, so Kwame concentrated on wiping clean his chocolatey fingers and flipping the envelope, front and back. He was amazed, as usual, by how tangled Akua's words were. It was actually a ginormous surprise the post-man had even known where to deliver the letter. Kwame would never let his writing get like that: as mysterious as ancient hieroglyphics.

43

Neither Mummy nor Daddy could ever work out the meaning of Akua's messy writing. Kwame could. He liked that. After a bit of determination, he always translated: notes saying she and Valeria were at Centre Court shopping, notes about after-school revision sessions. He ate another real Wagon Wheel and enjoyed the pattern his teeth had made in its surface. Would Yaw have the same special translating talent too? Maybe. Maybe not. Maybe the reason Kwame could do it was because Akua and he were brother and sister, were right next to each other on a branch of the tree Daddy had drawn. Even if Akua could be quite bossy, quite close to rudeness, being brother and sister meant you had a magical connection no matter what because of the shared flesh and bones. Everyone said they looked alike. You couldn't deny it.

The card Akua had chosen was a fun choice. He'd give it eight out of ten. On the front was a picture of Eevee – the most underrated Pokémon and probably the cutest one, but he couldn't say that to Reece or David when they exchanged stickers. Eevee was standing against a sea of swirling orangey yellow. Kwame opened the card: Akua had covered both sides.

Pips,

I know how excited you get when your own post lands on the doormat – plus I don't want to waste my phonecard on dry chat with you (your sis is cheeky) so here's this little note.

What's Manc like, I hear you ask? Pipsqueak, everything is WICKED. It's fun being in halls because your friends are around you 24/7, like a sleepover the whole time. And actually the lectures (which are like Story Time but waaaaay longer) are pretty interesting. Apart from Dr Pointin's.

He actually made <u>himself</u> fall asleep last week while he was chatting. I've been doing loads of dancing too (the clubs are dope) and I have soooo many STUPID new moves to embarrass you with/force you to learn at Christmas.

But I want your news, really. I actually miss Richmond Court sometimes but I had to break freeeeeeee! And (oh my days!) what's Yaw like? I keep asking Mummy and Daddy, but you know skimping on details is their superpower. My girl Valeria said she sees the two of you hanging out, which is sweet – amazing that you found someone else who can tolerate your bad breath (I am on FIRE with these jokes, Kwame). How's school? Are you doing that River Wandle Challenge yet? Or is that in Year 6? And how far through reading all them encyclopaedias have you got? Be my pen pal, I beg! Make me a card with your Crayolas, something for my dead, dead noticeboard, tell me everything.

And don't forget what I <u>told you</u> that last night before I left. I know you were sort of emotional, sad to see me go and everything, so perhaps it didn't sink in enough, but, like I said, you properly being a kid is important. You are allowed to and should properly play. It was hard for me to explain, but, just trust me, you having fun matters so much more than it does for so many of the other kids in your class. They'll grab it any chance they get. You need a nudge, I reckon. Because the world is lit up when you smile, Kwame. Honestly. Don't bother with anyone or anything – <u>worrying</u> or whatever else – that stops that fun for you.

Okay, literally no space left. I did not start off this thing thinking I was gonna get all preachy and whatever. But we are where we are.

Hope you're missing me tooooooooo, Pips.
Peace out,
Axxxx

Kwame closed the card. He took a big final chomp of the biscuit. Of course he remembered Akua's last night. She had whispered into his ear weirdness about, yes, fun and joy and that whoever he wanted to be and however he wanted to be was okay and was actually great and that he should let himself have adventures and dreams. And, even though the instructions and the hug, he assumed, were supposed to be helpful, they made him want to break away. In her arms, he felt hot, unsafe, was frightened of what she might know about his thoughts. She clung to him harder so he had to work to push out of her arms. When he managed it at last, he did a big thumbs-up. That was all. He closed the door of his bedroom, curled up under the duvet, knees pressed up high so those two hills were all he needed to focus on.

'You ate that Wheelie fast!' Mummy said, her hands covered with dripping bubbles, pointing towards the table with her wrists.

'Yes. Thank you very kindly for the treat.' He pulled back the chair, scooped the wrapper from the table and poured crumbs into the bin, staring at its black emptiness, which pulled him like gravity.

March 2018

On the radio, Theresa May started warbling smugly about the transition period. Kwame was pleased when Edwyn reached up to turn it off. He went back to raking his spoon over Edwyn's homemade granola, then stopped to rest the handle against the bowl's rim.

'You'd better have an appetite.' Edwyn was getting water for the two of them, was a little irritated that the temperamental tap splashed his tie-dyed T-shirt. 'I've made loads.'

'Have you done that thing again?'

'What?'

'That thing where you add weird saffron and cumin to –'

'I prepare this spread and you're looking for faults?'

Edwyn sat, and Kwame accepted the offered glass.

A banquet had indeed been laid out, their first proper breakfast in the new flat since they'd moved in a fortnight ago. Plates of kiwi, mango; Greek yoghurt swirled with honey; bowls heaped with blueberries and pumpkin seeds; dark tiles of rye bread; steaming jasmine tea. Kwame scooped granola into his mouth, clamped it shut and chewed, understanding what motivated the grandness of the feast. It was a generosity that had been present from the moment he'd told Edwyn about Madame Evans's seizure. For the last few days, Edwyn had been fussy and mothering, concerned at the impact seeing such a thing might have on his friend – and also drawn to the inherent drama of the situation: flashing blue lights, heroic paramedics.

Every half-hour since it had happened, Kwame's phone lit up with Edwyn's texts. How was Kwame bearing up? Did he need a chat? Was he looking after himself – properly resting at break times, not marking or doing planning? Because, Edwyn insisted, a lot of people would find the whole business quite traumatic. Was Kwame feeling traumatized? *Did he need a chat?* How was Natalie? How were they going to explain it all to the kids? And all this despite the prognosis for Madame Evans's recovery seeming positive, and an acting headteacher had been appointed to cover what, the staff room had been assured, would be the short period of Madame Evans's convalescence.

Each time his iPhone displayed Edwyn's heated enquiries, Kwame smiled. He liked Edwyn's attentiveness. So he made the replies to his friend's messages vague: a thumbs-up, a smiley face, a sun half hidden behind clouds, and Edwyn's concern, and Kwame's feeling of having caught Edwyn, lasted a while longer.

To be fair, Kwame's woolliness when asked if he was still in shock wasn't wholly fabricated. He didn't know what he needed. Absolution? Because it was awful that, even when he had been inches from her as she clawed the air, dribbled, struggled to breathe, he was thinking about her words almost three years earlier when she had given him the job at SLA. She had told him she thought the 'vibrant and varied' student body would find him 'unique', 'refreshing', 'relatable', a 'role model the likes of which they won't have previously encountered'. He had not found those descriptions novel.

As the phone call went on, he'd endured her self-satisfied references to 'diversity' and 'inclusion', banal words but strung like baubles meant to please; words intended to show that Madame Evans was 'forward-thinking', to reassure him that she was one of the good ones.

In response, Kwame had said thank you, had swallowed the questions he really wanted to ask: if she would have talked to a successful white candidate in that same tone, using those same terms? Was it *awful* that those words – and his anger – were on his mind as Mrs Greene again asked staff to stand back from where Madame Evans lay?

As soon as Head of Behaviour had cancelled the Parents' Evening and dismissed the parents, Kwame had thought about calling Mummy and Daddy. The pace of their conversation would be plodding and steady, and might have calmed the bitty sentences zapping across his mind. Mummy might talk about the Okolies: maybe they had painted their front door a colour she hated. She would ask Kwame when he had last spoken to his sister, suggest he call her too. He would make non-committal hums. In the background, Daddy might grumble until Mummy passed over the receiver. Once he had it, he might ask Kwame to tell him if he and Edwyn had settled in to Edwyn's new place? Did he and Edwyn need any DIY help? Shelves? He'd do it! Didn't care what his arthritis had to say! But Kwame had not called them.

He painfully ground his way through the last spoonful of Edwyn's disgusting, spicy cereal and was thrilled to see Edwyn couldn't hide his own strained expression.

'Perhaps *some* fine-tuning might be needed.' Edwyn coughed, gulped water, tried to keep a straight face. 'Wants even more cumin, TBH. Think it's too subtle.'

49

'You're a silly prick sometimes.'

'Why do you love chatting about my dick so much? You're obsessed with it. It's *oppressive*.' Kwame threw his napkin across the table lightly. 'A real big-time prick.'

'By the end of the day, I shall not be just your common or garden prick, I will be a *painted* prick.' Edwyn wrinkled his nose as if about to sneeze. The sneeze did not arrive. 'You're still coming, right? Moral support?'

In the communal corridor, behind the door to the flat of their downstairs neighbour Hanna, Kwame could hear her singing to herself. Waiting for Edwyn to finish looping his scarf round his long neck and to slide into a battered Barbour, he acknowledged the reproduction of Henry Scott Tuke's *A Bathing Group* on the wall. The print had been a 'housewarming treat' from Edwyn's mother. When Phyllida had brought the painting round, along with various things wrapped in artisanal brown paper – ranunculi, champagne – Kwame had thought that the large deposit she and Edwyn's father had given their son for the flat was surely enough of a present.

The central figure in the painting was a semi-naked, alabaster-skinned young man fresh from a swim. He locked eyes with a crouching boy in the foreground, a squashed thing in the corner with his back turned towards the viewer. Kwame liked something about the quietness of the brushstrokes, the green flecks of light shaping the swimmer's thighs, the texture of the almost-indigo towel preserving most of the swimmer's modesty. There was a self-possession about this young man that Kwame was drawn to.

Edwyn patted his pockets to check he had his keys. 'The studio's fifteen minutes from here. Not far.'

'Where?' Kwame buttoned up his fleece. 'I've never noticed it.'

'Apparently, it's a very *queer* studio – all the inkers are dykes. Or maybe trans. Or both. Can't remember.'

'Do they call themselves inkers?'

'Probably. Think so. Don't know. Sounds good, though, doesn't it? Inkers? Edgy. Subcultural.'

'Do tattooists have to be edgy? I mean, like, is there some niche place in . . . *Stoke Newington* where all the . . . *inkers* aren't hard but are, like, cutesy and speak in baby voices and wear – I don't know – pink aprons and have pink ribbons in their hair, and their hair's in pigtails and –'

'Or do you reckon there might be a *well-being-focused* tattoo place somewhere? Breathing techniques before –'

Edwyn unclicked the Chubb. They clung to each other's forearms as the sharp gusts of wind made their eyes start to stream.

After they had trotted up Fernlea Road, at his insistence Kwame took them into the Italian greasy spoon on Balham High Road for espressos. Its stubborn outdatedness charmed Kwame. Glass cases held sturdy cannoli. A belt of smudged, mirrored glass ran around the middle of the room. Above this, magnolia paint was plastered with posters of Lazio players; blurry family photos; Italian and EU flags. The puce floor tiles had a strange film on them that made Edwyn's Hunters screech. The noise set Kwame's teeth on edge as he ordered from the whiskery man at the till. He drew out his wallet from his jeans' back pocket. 'I'm paying.'

'No, fuck off, I am – to say thank you for accompanying me to my torture chamber.'

'*I'm paying.*'

But, zippily quick, Edwyn shoved a fiver into the whiskery man's hand and Kwame could only puff an exasperated breath. Edwyn always did that – paid for things. It was unnecessary and illogical, even when your sums included what Edwyn called the 'stipend' from Phyllida and Gibson's coffers that took care of rent – or, rather, *mortgage repayments* – on the new flat now. Edwyn's freelance wine-writing income was probably still a bit less than Kwame's teaching salary, so it was Kwame who should be shelling out.

But Kwame left it at that, at a simple, huffy exhalation of annoyance. He reasoned with himself that it was only a fiver. He didn't want to make a big scene because they had clearly already made scene enough, had made quite the impression. As they walked back across that slippery floor, portly old men, in once-white shirts with their *Sun on Sunday*s and a couple of Pomeranians, eyed Kwame, eyed Edwyn, as they left.

It was one of those spring days when winter tried to re-emerge, seize control. The stern wind surged through the trees and telephone wires undulated.

'Do you think I'll be brave, Kwame? When the needle's lowered?'

'Heroically so.'

'Or do you think I'll chicken out at the last minute? Maybe I'll puke.' Edwyn coughed. 'I think it'll probably be fine –' Edwyn led them over a crossing. 'But I'm not going to pretend. If I want to scream, I'll scream. I reckon the whole process might actually hurt *more* if I try to pretend I'm all okay when I'm not, right?'

Kwame sipped. 'Have you ever had an injection in your bum?'

'What? No.'

'I think it was the first time we went to Ghana. I was about . . . eleven, twelve. Yeah. About two years after –' He paused, steeled himself to say a name loaded with memories of that final night: shouting and hurting, a night when Kwame had been the biggest, strongest, wildest ten-year-old, capable of anything. 'All that stuff with *Yaw*. I told you about him?'

'Yeah, of course.' Edwyn swilled his espresso. 'That man. The cousin. The one you had the little crush on.'

The flippancy wrong-footed Kwame. So did the strength of his longing for Edwyn to handle delicate things with the delicateness that they deserved. Perhaps he was being overly sensitive. The breeze whipped and whipped, and Kwame chose to concentrate on the anticipation in Edwyn's face as he pushed back his curls.

So Kwame picked up again, hoped his bouncy tone didn't sound too forced. 'So I had to have this vaccination – I can't believe this has never come out before – I had to have this vaccination and my mum took me to St George's and there was this Scottish nurse, and she was like' – he wriggled his mouth to affect his best Morningside accent – '"I'm sorry to tell you this, young chappie, but this one here" – she'd pointed at Yellow Fever on this list – "this one'll have to be done in your jacksie." My mum laughed and I was so bloody ashamed about exposing my little brown arse I forgot about the whole scary-needle bit.'

'Hold on.'

Edwyn stopped by the homeless woman who always nestled in a broken tent outside the post office. He told her about the impending tattoo, then told her why he wanted one of a pine cone on his forearm. Giving her a two-pound coin, he promised her he would be heroically brave about the whole thing. Edwyn asked her if she had any tattoos and she mumbled a reply – eyes trained on this generous, willowy, Period Drama-y man. While Edwyn fished a Tracker bar out of his pocket and gave it to the woman, Kwame knew he should offer something too – but was stuck in that thought of Yaw, the strangeness of considering Yaw as a *man*. There had been something so boyish about him; a twinkling spirit that made Kwame stare and stare and stare.

He gulped coffee, and it helped with the dryness in his throat that came on the rare occasions when he let recollections of Yaw resurface. What was that dryness? What else might come loose after picking at those thoughts of a time it was useless to revisit? A ragged anger at his parents, stunted rage about how they had taken the shelter Yaw needed?

Then Edwyn was off, back up Balham High Road and breezing past the Devonshire, remembering the word 'jacksie' and trying to come up with other brilliant synonyms for 'arse'. That too was helpful for Kwame, comforting. Ahead, the studio – its window displaying a graffitied crow with a paintbrush in its beak – came into view.

'I'm a bit sad that you weren't up for getting one as well.' Edwyn pouted and pressed the button at the pedestrian crossing. 'It would have been cool – matching tatts.'

Kwame reached for brightness again, held on to it as securely as he could. 'Not my vibe, babe – but I cannot wait to see how yours turns out. This is the most exciting thing you've done since you sucked off that Venezuelan professional from *Strictly*.'

Thirty yards away from the banquette on which Kwame sat, Edwyn reclined on a sort of S and M version of a dentist's chair. Edwyn's left forearm was prone on a small platform, worked on by Larissa, an Australian with a tangled beehive. The purple walls around the three of them were the backdrop to neon creations: guitars intertwined with shoals of seahorses and scattered rose petals. The wiring in the sketch of a clown doing a cartwheel was faulty: it flickered so that the clown's airborne foot appeared, disappeared, appeared. Charged with two espressos now, to Kwame it was a visual assault. Larissa's laugh was even more aggressive; it brought to mind Natalie's giddy enthusiasm earlier in the week. En route to their lunch hall duty, she had rattled off gleaned insights about the man (or, apparently, Messiah) set to take on the acting head role while Madame Evans was recuperating. A pal from Natalie's PGCE cohort had worked under this *Marcus Felix* at a school in Archway, and had raved to Natalie about his foresight and passion. And how brilliant it was for the kids of colour at the school to finally see a Black man in a position of real seniority within the institution. In the hall, Natalie was making sure that the Year 8s were stacking their cleared plates, and Kwame was making sure that they thanked the dinner ladies before darting out to the playground, so his ability to be swept up in her chatter was limited. He predicted that this shiny Big Cheese would no doubt stomp in and want to prove himself: new directives would be issued here, new initiatives led there. Staff would limply introduce these to unreceptive classes, entirely un-convinced by the faddiness. Soon enough, everyone would be counting the days until Madame Evans and her vacuousness returned. Natalie had said that what she loved most about Kwame was his sunny disposition.

Kwame cracked then rubbed his knuckles, while Larissa pulled off her latex gloves, undid her surgical mask and walked to the other side of the room.

'Fuck off, mate. *Right off*,' she said to Edwyn. 'What do you have me down for? He's *never* your dad.'

'Kwame?'

He headed towards Edwyn slowly. In the two hours or so they'd been at Larissa's, Larissa had made light work of it: Kwame could see the pine cone was blossoming, if that's what pine cones did.

'Can you get my mobile? I'd do it myself but –' Edwyn glanced at his occupied arm. 'She needs photographic evidence, apparently.'

'Of?'

Over by the corner cabinet, Larissa stopped riffling through a selection of sharp things. 'This beautiful fella's dad isn't Gibson Bellamy?'

Kwame retrieved the iPhone from the Barbour, punched in the passcode and opened Photo Albums. He handed it over to Larissa, who then went through the summoned images: Gibson and Edwyn in deep embraces; Gibson and Edwyn in the middle of the richest laughs. Kwame tried to recall how many times he had witnessed it: the theatrical disbelief, the delight once the resemblance between father and son crystallized.

'*Maybe* I see it . . . in the . . . the chin?' She squinted harder.

'Fuck! Gibson Bellamy's your dad?! He's a total le-gend. His shows are *incredible*. Love the way he's, totally like, no BS.'

'Absolutely.'

'And the stuff is so frickin *easy* to cook but looks super-impressive. My Alana did the spicy lentils and pork medallions the other week. Know it?'

'Not off the top o—'

'It's epic.'

Larissa returned the whining needle to Edwyn's flesh, and Kwame returned to his seat. The conversation continued as Kwame expected it to. There followed a discussion about what it must be like for Edwyn to have such a famous father. *An Onion, Properly Sweated* was a classic. And how many series of *At Bellamy's Table* had there been now? And so amazing about the Michelin star. And could Edwyn help get them a cheeky reservation at Laleham? Because you couldn't get a booking for love nor . . .

She pursued her predictable lines of enquiry, and Edwyn answered questions about whether that bust-up between Gibson and Marco Pierre White was a publicity stunt for the French road-trip programme with the annoying narrator. There was a noble evenness to Edwyn's voice as he told Larissa about Laleham's waiting list, in his polite acceptance of Larissa's assertion that it had been Edwyn's father who had taught her how to cook. The bell above the door in the foyer tinkled, and Kwame heard Larissa's receptionist simper as she talked to geezer-ish-sounding men about their appointment times. Even though Edwyn's lips smiled thank-yous at Larissa's complimenting of Gibson, the enthusiasm didn't reach his eyes. Whenever Edwyn was required to be gracious as the general public gushed about his father,

Kwame sensed that his mind went to some solemn place; the green of his irises became muddy.

During those conversations, Edwyn seemed to do the kind of mournful thinking he fell into when the two of them were at Laleham for weekend stays at the Marjoram. Over the past decade, when visiting the cottage a stone's throw from the Bellamys' eighteenth-century manor house and Gibson's gemlike restaurant, the fire roared and the Rioja was plentiful. Never quite plentiful enough to loosen Kwame's tongue into describing the exact strangeness he experienced each time he was at Laleham. To name the chilly alienation and chillier fear that he was always on the verge of a faux pas would ruin the 'lovely time' he'd been gifted. To be uncomfortable wouldn't be suitably guestly behaviour, while actually expressing discomfort would be even worse. Laleham, with its dovecotes and crests, its outhouses and electric fences and discreet CCTV – a place more than a world away from Richmond Court.

Unaware, ever the life-and-soul, in the Marjoram Edwyn would start off with handsy hugs and slurred recognition of Kwame's kindness and patience. But, eventually, the opening of the third or fourth bottle would turn things maudlin. Kwame would fold into the armchair, Edwyn would station himself at Kwame's feet. Kwame would tousle his friend's hair and Edwyn would stare at the flames, woozily critiquing his own failures – laziness, inanity, indecisiveness – shredding himself with harsh words. Kwame would eyeball Phyllida's forebears on the walls, would not stand for Edwyn's nonsense. He would remind his friend how much he was loved by everyone he met, for his wonderful knack of brightening everything around him and bringing needed ease too. And Kwame would always, always be grateful for having a presence like that in his life.

Larissa was swearing, colour flooding her cheeks. 'It's not my problem those guys're fucking early. Not my shitting problem.'

Kwame's eyes followed her stomp into the foyer, where she shook her head at the geezers. They played with their rugby shirts and made noises about going back to the Devonshire: since there's time, squeeze in another half? One of them – messy, red hair, chunky bum – was exactly Edwyn's type. Kwame got up to tell Edwyn to steal a look, but, as he walked over, the labouring of Edwyn's breath made him approach with less glee.

'Is it really sore? I would've been yowling like the biggest pussy if –'

'It's, yeah, getting a bit stingy. Will you distract me? Tell me something, something funny that happened at school this week. What's, er, Princess been up to?'

'Erm . . .'

'Or, I don't know, sing some . . . Sade?'

'What?'

'Or make up something fantastical and great. Whatever.' He hissed: 'Quick.'

'I can't just –'

Edwyn's mouth dropped. 'Now you listen, guv'na, and you listen good. I don't ever, *ever* wanna hear you say anyfink, any rubbish about how you *can't* do *sumfink* – you hear me?'

'It still makes me . . .' Kwame did his most exaggerated thinking expression, 'uncomfortable when you appropriate that, like, cockney accent – nevertheless, Edwyn, I do have

59

to admit, since the last time you did it, your take on that voice has developed in its richness and depth. That being said, there is work to be done in terms of pronunciation. On this occasion –'

'Yes, yes, come on – I can't bear this tension!'

'It's going to be a six-point-five out of ten.'

'Are you joking me? Six-point-five. Is that it?'

'Take it,' Kwame said, affecting his own, much more convincing Danny Dyer voice, 'or you can fuckin leave it, mate.'

The straight boys had started singing 'And I Would Walk Five Hundred Miles', but Kwame's and Edwyn's laughter rose above it.

September 1997

Mummy was almost ready to leave for Aunty Charity's to get her old plaits rebraided cheaply. From the kitchen table, Kwame watched her, all flustered, weaving around Daddy, snapping that he was getting under her feet and would make her late. She spooned out waakye and then meat for patient Kwame, patient Yaw. It made him feel quite stressed, her noisy commotion. The Orangina he sucked through a pink straw was nicer. In his opinion, straws were more sophisticated than drinking straight from the bottle.

While Mummy kept darting around, folding kitchen towels to make napkins, Daddy seemed to get even slower and looked exhausted – was it like the hare and the tortoise? – washing his hands at the sink. Still concentrating on drinking but sucking quietly because to slurp wasn't right, Kwame wished Mummy would pat Daddy's cheek, call him her Prince Charming instead of kissing her teeth at him. Kwame wished Akua was around to give Mummy the chilly look that always made her think twice. But Akua was not there. The fizzing Orangina crackled against his cheeks.

It would be terrible if his Mummy and Daddy got lawyers in suits, got divorced, like Ruby Foley's in Year 6. When Ruby Foley was in Year 4, she randomly took weeks off school. Everyone thought it must be the worst flu ever. But then Jamila Roy's mother heard at Home Time that it was because Ruby's family was broken and unfixable. Ruby was being pulled between the parents. Then Jamila told absolutely everybody. As far as Kwame knew, Ruby's parents were the first in Thrale to split up like that. When Ruby came back to school and cried at the tuck shop because there was no Sunny Delight, everyone understood the truth behind the tears. People watched her weep and looked away.

It would make Kwame even more wrong to have parents who lived in separate houses, separate places, like Ruby's. It would be even more for him to deal with – too much to fit in his head. He just wished everything was quieter and would stay like that. Kwame wished his wishing and wishing actually worked.

Daddy left the room as Kwame focused on his food. 'Thank you, my dearest mummy, for this very delicious meal. It looks like we'll be fed very –'

But Mummy was too busy pointing at Yaw: 'Make sure you watch my son well when I'm gone, eh? Watch. Him. Well.'

Yaw stopped his greedy eating so he could flap his long fingers to show Mummy that watching Kwame would be super-easy-peasy. She seemed to like that gesture: her lips broke into the broadest grin.

'Eat all, my growing boys. You need to grow up and be big strong men – real men! And don't forget to check on my Lotto balls to see if victory is finally mine.'

Stew – oily and orange – swooped in a smear near Yaw's nose, and grains of rice clung to his moustache. Kwame didn't pick them out, even though he wanted to. As soon as Mummy was gone, Yaw started chanting the Tupac songs he muttered as he moved around the flat, this time the one about how God was the only one who can judge. He tap-tap-tapped the Motorola Daddy had shelled out for so they could know his whereabouts at all times.

Kwame pushed the millet stalks around his plate, then lifted the dish and traced the condensation the heat made on the plastic placemat. Yaw's noisy rapping and tapping irritated him; Kwame was also irritated because he had always been taught it was shameful manners to eat roughly, with elbows everywhere, and to have your busy phone out at the dinner table, which was a place for face-to-face adult conversations. If Yaw wasn't so busy with the mobile's tiny green screen, Kwame might have told him that he was mostly having a wonderful Saturday so far, thank you for asking.

On Friday, at Home Time, Francis Baker had suggested Kwame come round to his house the next day. It was the first time Kwame had been invited. Kwame had checked with Mummy and, while folding Daddy's blue shirts, she had said okay and, because she was covering Pam's Saturday-morning slot at the clinic, it would be a helping hand having someone take care of him.

Though only a ten-minute walk away – up by the Common, on Birchwood Road – Francis's house seemed so different from the flat. Thick black beams divided the white front wall and framed the windows and door. The front garden had bushes trimmed into perfect spheres. Gnomes with blushing cheeks protected pots of yellow flowers. The house looked small, cottagey and warm, so Kwame thought of *The Borrowers* – which was lovely – and it helped him not to be too scared about visiting somewhere new or too worried about accidentally breaking any of their things.

When you went inside? Not cottagey at all. The massivest place ever. Four floors. Mrs Baker greeted him with her red curls and in her Keep Fit sweaty leotard, excited to see Kwame. She helped him take off his coat, talking, talking, so much bouncier than Mummy or Daddy ever were. Mrs Baker told him to make himself at home, and her voice floated as he followed her through corridors. The kitchen was beautiful: polished wood, shiny taps. One of the bedrooms wasn't a bedroom but an office for Mrs Baker so she could run her business from home. She made wallpapers, or something like that. Kwame liked the office: the computer on the desk, the hundreds of labelled files, the fat fax machine in the corner.

Francis had joined Thrale in Year 3. Encouraged by David, Reece and Gary, most of the boys ignored him. Kwame understood why: Francis's lack of height. Though ten years old, and – like Kwame – one of the oldest in the year, Francis was even shorter than lots of the kids in Infants. He spoke quietly and wore an eyepatch that he covered with transfers of Disney characters. Carly Holling – the prettiest girl in Year 5, a few points ahead of mixed-race Martinique, according to the survey Reece had everyone fill out – complained that Francis Baker would say one single sentence to her and then say no more: such a scaredy cat. Some people said he looked a bit like Macaulay Culkin but mostly Francis was forgettable and so had to be a loner.

But Kwame liked talking to Francis when Mrs Gilchrist put them in groups according to maths or reading levels. If they needed to vote for a group leader, Francis picked Kwame without hesitating. And if people started butting in when the group had to make decisions, Francis tried to get people to pay attention to Kwame, and listened with the strictest concentration.

He and Francis had spent most of that Saturday doing fun stuff in the glass-ceilinged room that Mrs Baker called the conservatory. They spent ages on jigsaws of Van Gogh paintings. *Starry Night* was really difficult. In the afternoon, over hummus and celery and rice cakes and squash, they got excited about the Winter Show auditions. They moaned about Mr Bell. Kwame talked about Yaw, careful with the details about how he had arrived in London and how long he'd stay, just like Mummy had told him to be because it was a family matter and no one else's business so don't let people be nosy parkers, just keep shtum. Francis kept saying he thought it would be really cool to come from another country. Kwame just agreed.

At about half five, Kwame gathered his things to go home and was nervous Francis would ask if he could visit Richmond Court next time. Kwame never invited friends who didn't live on the block to come round to his. He didn't even really invite the local lot – Naveed from 235, Billie from 620 – to his either, because Daddy said they were too scruffy for their kraakye. Even though Kwame thought Francis might like to learn how to play Oware, and even though Yaw might teach Francis the Bogle, Kwame didn't want Francis at his place. He couldn't explain why, but the idea of Francis in the wet lift, in their bathroom with its chipped tiles, or at their wonky kitchen table, panicked him.

The nervousness that Francis might expect an invitation in return made him hotter as Kwame headed towards the Bakers' front door to leave. He struggled with his duffle's toggles as he thanked Francis's parents for their hospitality. But, after he hugged Francis, gathering Francis's body into his bigger one, he got nothing but a quiet, serious 'See you, then. It's been . . . really nice' from Francis. Kwame had gone into the purpling early evening feeling relieved, and ashamed of that relief. He had punched his pockets as he dashed downhill, almost willing himself to trip and gash his knees.

Yaw was clicking his fingers at his mobile, Muttley-cackling at it and wobbling the wonky table. Kwame could have asked Yaw what made the text messages so hilarious, but, with each new flash of the screen, Yaw became more hunched and guarded. Kwame stripped the goat meat from its bones until his gums ached.

Muttering to himself, Daddy was back in the kitchen, getting ready to go to Purley for his shift at the warehouse. Mustard-coloured overalls slumped over his big belly. Kwame scraped his chair back and, with the help of his fluffy sports socks, skidded across the lino, gliding over to near the sink. He riffled in the drawer there and eventually found and handed over the knobbly rubber gloves Daddy needed whenever he did nights. Daddy swiped a bit of Yaw's food, then pulled Yaw's ear.

'You will watch my son well, eh? By all means, yes? Watch. I said, *watch* him *well*.'

Yaw flapped his long fingers again to show that watching Kwame would be so super-easy.

'Ewurade!' Daddy shouted at the clock above the hob and scurried off.

Although it was sort of funny that Mummy and Daddy had said such similar things, now Kwame was too annoyed to be amused. Scrunching the serviette and throwing it on to his plate, he wanted to know why everyone was making out he was likely to do something naughty or wrong if he wasn't kept under 24/7 surveillance. It wasn't like this was the first time Yaw had babysat, as Mummy called it, although Kwame hated that word because it didn't respect his maturity. Why would Kwame need so much watching? Had he ever got a detention at school? No, sir. Did Mummy or Daddy ever have to raise their voices to get him to finish homework, yelling like Mrs Memet at 521? Not once in the living memory, thank you very much. So why did Mummy and Daddy act like he couldn't be trusted or might commit an offence? Like they knew or worried he was hovering on the edge of badness and care had to be taken to keep him safely on the right side?

'Your plate please, Yaw.'

'Cheers, Lil' G.'

Being called 'Lil' G' by Yaw was nice and made Kwame less annoyed. He didn't know what *G* meant or what it might stand for, but it was a secret, a special code.

Outside, the plane trees gave away the last of their leaves to the wind. Kwame washed the dishes and Yaw continued to do whatever on his phone, striding around behind Kwame's back, his Reeboks squeaking. Yaw's quick body shifted in the reflection in the window above the sink, downturned head, Bugs Bunny's eyes on his T-shirt wide and unbelieving. Yaw flipped up his mobile, punched towards the ceiling and did a sort of moonwalk on the spot. Kwame spun round too, flicked suds at Yaw.

'You,' Kwame giggled, between attempted splashes, 'are silly. I mean, *really* silly, actually. With your funny, weird dancing.'

'My friend, I am the slickest don. The wickedest and baddest don, and you cannot even come close to denying that one. Is a golden fact of law.' He stopped wriggling, kissed his phone and slid it into the pocket of his Kappa poppers. 'So how's it gonna go play out this eve, Lil' G? You want me to go through your winter-performance-audition thingy with you again? Happy to be at yo service, if needs be.'

Kwame smiled.

'What? What's that plan you scheming up, my man? Huh? Just us pair of sick bros here tonight so some kind of craziness is gonna go down, am I right?'

First, Kwame got Yaw to wipe the fake gingham tablecloth. While Yaw was busy with that, Kwame collected the pile of leaflets, magazines, photocopies and the old ice-cream box in which he kept his markers, paints, packets of beads, glue. He spread them out over the table.

'I'd like to do it with candlelight. I'm going to get the candles too.'

'Say what now?' Yaw scrunched up his face.

'It gives a better atmosphere, I think. Don't worry, I can sort it all out.'

'You even allowed to be messing with matches and all that stuff?'

'I'm not *messing*, Yaw. I'm very careful. I don't want to get third-degree burns.' Kwame took a lighter and tealights from the drawer you had to bang before it opened. He lit them and placed them in scattered patterns along the work surface before returning to the table.

'Time for business. We're going to make a collage about dinosaurs. We'll use this sugar paper I got from school. Your mission – and you have no choice, so you have to

68

accept it – is to sort through the pictures here' – Kwame gestured at the images splayed before them – 'to find the most exciting stuff. I've been collecting them for ages so we should have a good range – because, even though diplodocuses are my absolute favourite, Mrs Gilchrist says variety is important.'

'Naturally.'

'A few more things before you can start, Yaw, so you have to listen close.'

'Yowser. You ain't here to play.'

'We should have a tropical background for the dinosaurs to be living in, to show their natural habitat. So I got these catalogues from Homebase and they've got loads of pictures of ferns and palms. We can use them. And I thought we could create a border with the beads. That will be quite original and attractive –'

'Is our own *Art Attack*. Man, I am liking that Buchanan dude. He's mad clever with them toilet roll-tubes –'

'I planned to put it in my bedroom but, now I think about it, we should put it somewhere we can both see it whenever we want to.' Kwame shifted in his chair. 'Perhaps on the fridge. How does that sound?'

'You da boss, it's yo vision.'

Yaw started checking the pages in front of him with curious fingers. He didn't seem to mind taking orders at all, even from someone smaller and younger than him.

The candles flickered. The tap dripped. Outside, a motorcycle buzzed and someone turned up the volume on Mariah Carey. Lining up his felt-tip pens in order, from lightest to darkest, a coolness came over Kwame. He slipped the brown pen out of the rank, stared at the gap he had made.

'Probably this is the last thing you'd want to do on a Saturday night. Probably the most boring and most rubbish thing you've ever done.'

He reached for his safety scissors and snipped around the tail of a velociraptor.

'It's a'ight being in wit chu. Kinda like it. Is relaxing. And, and I owes your ma and pa a lot, you feel? I gots to give back.'

'That's true.' Kwame hoped fixing his attention on the scissors' blade might distract from the disappointment that it was, as he understood it, duty Yaw felt as they sat at the table passing the time together. He skimmed the glue stick over the back of the velociraptor and pressed the snarling thing on to the sugar paper. 'But what *would* be your ideal thing to do? If you could choose to do absolutely anything in the whole wide world, and you could be anywhere or do anything right here and right now. What would it be? Imagine.'

A long, whistling sound came through Yaw's teeth. The blackness of his irises seemed even deeper and more serious. 'Is gonna sound dumb, Lil' G.'

'I will be the judge of that. Go on.'

'I . . . Well. Like, I know ain't neva gon be some time when no man like me is up in space cos they ain't about to be allowing us up there. And I know it's dumb to say you wanna be an astronaut when you grow up, so that's not what I'm sayin neither. But I reckon if I was, you know, up there' – he pointed to the ceiling – 'Floating. Between all those stars. Me, myself and I. Free. Not tied to nothing. Not held back. Floating on. Reckon that'd be kinda nice.'

'You wouldn't find it lonely?'

'Nah, man. Coming through space like an angel. No stressin. Master of my own skies.' He sighed. 'I'm not about to get all sad for missing Ghana, because you know I'm livin the life right here in Tooting, but you see *stars* in Atonsu, man. Every night. Millions of droplets of God. Puttin on they best show. You only got a few here. Is all hidden by a smoke, street lamps. Sometimes I think you people need many more stars to look at and dream on. Pass that picture, please? Yeah, yeah that one. Thanks a mil.'

A silence came. In it, Yaw lowered his head and Kwame jiggled his legs.

'Your turn, Lil' G.'

'What?'

'While I'm up above and free from the cares, what you doing? What's your fantasy thing?'

Kwame found his glittery silver pen to add highlights to the triceratops' grey horns. He moved the nib with care. 'It's a past thing. Already happened in real life. But I'd like to do it again. Rewind? Does that count?'

'You's in charge.'

'Mummy had collected coupons from the newspaper. Once you got enough, you got a family coach ticket to Brighton. She collected for about three months and we all went. I was in Year 1. The coach journey was ages and a lot of the people on the bus were old and ponged of wee. I first of all thought I'd have to hold my breath for the whole journey, which I worried might lead to premature death. After a while I got used to the wee smell and it was fine. Mummy had fried chicken for the trip, so she handed out some of that. Me and Akua were sitting next to each other, and she gave me some of hers because she was doing dieting, which was unnecessary because she's actually slim and people say she's pretty, but anyway it meant I got the gift of her wings and drumsticks. *So tasty*. When we got to Brighton the sun was ruling the sky and ruling over everything. And –'

'Damn Mr Chat, Chat, Chatterbox –'

'And we had ice cream on our fingers and I got a balloon. Daddy even rolled up his trousers and ran into the sea – but not too far because everyone knows about Black people being frightened of proper swimming. We went to a Punch and Judy show as well, and, even though I know about sexism because of the Suffragettes and obviously we shouldn't laugh about the violence stupid Mr Punch does to his wife, it was still nice to watch every time because we were all laughing together and no one was thinking about anything else but the silly jokes and laughter. All four of us.'

'What the hell is a Punch and Judy?'

The pivot point of Kwame's scissors stiffened. He slipped his fingers out of the holes and searched his ice-cream tub for a replacement pair.

'You know what puppets are, right?'

'Yeah.'

'Punch and Judy are these sort of old-fashioned puppets. They're married. Punch has a squeaky voice, a bad temper and lacks any kind of common sense. He's always dropping his baby because it's too big for him. When he makes stuff go wrong, he blames it on Judy. I've seen it a few times, not only that time in Brighton. It's always the same story.' Kwame frowned. 'I'm not explaining it that well, but I think that might be a big reason for why people like it – because you always already know what Mr Punch is going to do and how Judy will react and knowing what will happen next is a comfort. So that was a lovely time. The opposite of yours because I had people in mine and you didn't.'

'That's cos we different. Moving different ways, branching out in our own ways even if we coming from the same tree.' Yaw caught Kwame's eyes. 'Ain't nothing wrong with that, friend. We all individuals. You a individual. Me too. Different things make us special from one another. Like fingerprints. Not even twins matching. Makes the world beautiful.'

Yaw's elbows looked dry. The chalky skin had dark lines, tiny cracks, running through it. Kwame's went like that, sometimes. He wanted to tell Yaw, like Mummy did to him, that he should take better care of himself, always use cocoa butter on those parts too. Never, never forget the little things.

The bell's ring was woozy; a drunk man messing up his words. Its batteries were running low. Again, it rang.

Yaw jumped. 'Expectin anyone?'

Kwame shook his head, played with his dungarees' straps and watched Yaw take soft footsteps out into the corridor. Because his jeans were rudely low, you could see a lot of his boxer shorts, orange with hundreds of exploding bombs raining down. The bell rang and rang.

Whatever evil Yaw thought lurked out there seemed to really frighten him. Kwame knew what it was like to be scared – of his family falling to pieces, of people getting a glimpse of his head or heart – but Yaw seemed even more petrified than any of that. He was crouching and then hiding like someone dreadful had found him and meant him harm. Kwame had never seen Yaw so panicked and jumpy, making his body small then big, looking like he was out of breath and putting his hand on his forehead like he hadn't a clue what to do, the Motorola shaky in his hand, looking all around like he wanted a secret fire escape to run to, so afraid of being caught and –

Kwame pressed his lips together as Yaw tilted himself forward to check the peephole. Then the stranger started really banging, attacking the letterbox, saying 'Big man, I'm brewin.'

'Marcel?! Chill, man!'

As soon as Yaw let in Marcel from 323, the flat seemed to shrink. Usually Marcel did cheeky smiles, showing his teeth, which were so straight since his braces had been taken off. Now his face folded in on itself. Because he was mixed race, you could see angry redness in his cheeks. Those usually friendly teeth were gritted. He stomped around the kitchen like he owned the place, and, when he banged the table, Kwame worried the two loose diplodocuses waiting to be glued might fall.

'Bro,' Yaw said, pulling three Supermalts from the fridge, 'be cool! Why, why you vexin so? What –'

'Fam, why you got bare séance witchcraft candles blazin in here?'

'Coming in here like some mental man crazing all over the show. Scared the life out of – could've upset Aunty, Uncle, and you worried about candles? What the hell?'

'Sorry, bruv, sorry. And sorry, Kwams. I' – Marcel took the offered drink, swigged – 'they jus get to me, yunnerstan?' He swigged again. 'Can't treat mans like this. I ain't no boy for you to be pullin me up on nuffink.'

'You're losing me for real –'

74

'Feds. I was jus sittin out on the bus stop, mindin my own, literally fully doin nothin jus havin a smoke – and not even reefer, jus some likkle Marlboro ting, and then the fuckin – the fuckin Feds all roll up arksin me, *me, you know*, what I'm doin. They started goin all rer rer rer, tellin me to mind my tone when I'm like, what, this is my yard, I was born here. Man's got the cheek to arks me for my address when I'm sayin to the brer, are you dumb, *are you dumb*, I live here. Then they start puttin their hands on me, pattin me down and whatever, arksin where I'm goin, if I've got the right fare.' He glugged again. Kwame watched a bubbling drip dribble down his chin and he licked it up quick. 'Dem mans all proper goin thru my pockets mad and puttin their dutty hands on my shit. And man's got the nerve and the balls to be tellin me bout loiterin and how I should use more appropriate language or whatever. I'm vex. Inappropriate? Is it fuckin appropriate to be botherin nex man when nex man is sittin on his jays doing no disturbin of no peace waitin for the fuckin 133 so I can go and link Andre?' Marcel slammed the bottle down by the micro-wave. 'White *dickheads*. All of dem. Pu-ssyholes. Pu-ssyclart, trus. Any time I see a Black officer I think, bruv, you mus be dead to be workin for dem pricks. They hate us. Always tryin to mess with us, still.'

'That shit's deep.' Yaw clapped Marcel's shoulder. 'Why they playin you like that?'

'They're round dees ends too much. Ain't nuffink goin on here for them. Dis place is calm. Ain't one of them rowdy yards. We're some likkle one block and most people here are ancient fam, not causin no trouble. So why the Feds all circlin like vultures day and night?'

Kwame pulled the label from his Supermalt loose. He didn't understand. Why did the policemen stop Marcel? Marcel wasn't bad. He played basketball, went to Mount Nod for sixth form, ate chips on the bench by the plane tree, sometimes throwing chips at Akua's friend Valeria from 437 to get her attention when she walked by. Why would the police bother him? Were the police not very busy? So why were they looking for something to pass the time? And why was Marcel calling the police horrible names? The police weren't evil. They were important heroes because they made things safe, risking their lives for ours. You were supposed to look at the ground when a police officer went by, and not make eye contact with them. Daddy said to do that; Daddy said it was a mark of respect.

Really, the worst thing about the police was how boring they were. When PC Hardie did the assemblies about 'Stranger Danger', Kwame found it almost impossible to stay awake; the man's voice had only one tone and his words were dry. Kwame spent the time imagining Mrs Gilchrist as a ten-year-old or using his fingers to spell out secret messages on the back of the person sitting in front of him. Why didn't Marcel just speak to the officer politely – perhaps ask how their day was and tell them about his – then they would have realized that he was not a menace to society. They would have lifted up their hats and gone on their merry way. Kwame was certain if *he* met any policeman and shook their hand and got them to discuss the weather, the policeman would think he was a fine and good young man. And why was Marcel going on about *Black* policemen? Even though being in the police was very low down on Kwame's list of jobs for the future – he didn't think he'd be able to cope with having to deal with frightening criminals – if he had wanted to do that job, it was his choice. No one should tell him off for it.

When might they be able to get back to the collage they were building?

Yaw and Marcel were talking more quietly, their heads leaning closer together. Yaw passed Marcel his Motorola and they high-fived.

'Yes, bruv!' Marcel said. 'Get dat, fam, GET DAT! GET DAT YAT now! Or, trust, I'm gonna get dat from you. That yat is fire.'

Watching the two boys – Marcel jutting his bottle at the phone, Yaw stepping back with crossed arms – deciding who was most handsome was hard. If you had a piece of paper and drew a line down the middle to work out which of the two was the best, on the Marcel side, the points in his favour were obvious: the nice colour of his mixed-race face, his powerful height and the muscles he got from going to the gym at Tooting Leisure Centre. On the other side, Yaw had the prettiness of his slanting eyes, the good jaw, the oval shape of his nostrils. The cackling boys shook their heads at the same time, like they couldn't believe something. Did they ever talk or argue about which of the two of them was better-looking? Kwame thought they probably didn't, they didn't care about stuff like that, and he ought to think about something else, something cleaner and simpler. He picked up his gold glitter-gel pen, drummed it on the table before turning to the boys.

'Yaw, we, we promised we'd check on Mummy's balls. We mustn't forget.'

Marcel and Yaw froze.

'Mummy's balls?' Marcel's eyebrows were high on his forehead. 'Mummy's balls,' he said, this time in a voice that was higher pitched and wobbly, meant to be an impression of Kwame's. Kwame gripped the pen tightly while the two older boys wheezed and screeched, steadying themselves against the worktop, 'Mummy's balls!', rocking with glee, holding one another like Kwame was no longer in the kitchen with them, Marcel's paler fingers squeezing Yaw's sleeve, the fabric getting rumpled and messy in his grasp, Yaw clapping his hand over that clasping one. It felt like it was happening very far away from Kwame, or like he was seeing them through the wrong end of a telescope. The feeling of being lost spread and spread, but Kwame did not want it, wanted to find some other way. He raised his eyebrows, pulled his shoulders back, waited until he had their attention again.

'Yes.' Kwame made his voice even posher now, more like Trevor McDonald's, as posh as he could go. He pinched his mouth, made his lips small. 'Mummy's. Balls. Mummy's balls.'

And then all three laughed, with Kwame's cackling not quite as huge as Marcel's, who was doubled over and clutching his knees. Between the catching of breath and the wiping of tears from eyes, Kwame noticed Yaw smiling straight at him.

March 2018

Kwame had a dim awareness, from what he'd overheard Head of Behaviour saying at the urinal once, and from Barbara's intimations, that there was 'trouble' in Ahmed Hussen's 'home life'. Ahmed qualified for the scant bursary the school offered sixth formers instead of the old EMAs. His Somali parents spoke very little English. There was a brother in prison, about to be sent to prison or coming home after a spell in prison – the precise details were guarded by senior management and disclosed only on a 'need to know' basis, and Kwame understood the thinking behind that confidentiality. But, that morning, sitting with Ahmed in the Data Hub – as they had been instructed to call a space that was clearly *a library* – the lack of intel on this Prince of Truanting was unhelpful. Kwame and Ahmed were squashed around one of the Data Hub's stylish but impractical desks. Their uncomfortable fidgeting broke the general hush. The librarian – Data Keeper? – wasn't best pleased.

Rather than making eye contact with his teacher, Ahmed decided to angle his bulk away from Kwame's small talk. The bearded six-foot-four man-boy – almost bursting out of his purple uniform – plucked at his blazer's cuff. He fixed on the huge photos between the windows opposite, images of the icons who gave the school's four 'houses' their names: Mandela, Seacole, Gandhi, Hawking. Trying yet again to get Ahmed to focus on the coursework plan that sat between the two of them, Kwame stabbed the page with his nib.

'So, if I were you, Ahmed, I would move *this* paragraph about the narrator and their purpose to the end? It makes for a more logical drawing-together of the points you've established earlier on.' Kwame dragged his pen up the page. 'And then maybe move *this one* up here?'

Continuing to ignore his teacher, Ahmed showed Kwame only half of his face: the grey swipe of sleeplessness under his left eye and a spotty cheek. Kwame could have told Ahmed that the precious minutes of this free period were slipping by and Ahmed would be wise to make the most of the insights Kwame was offering. They could push him up from a C to a B. Surely that was all Ahmed wanted? When Kwame was in Ahmed's position, on the cusp of starting university, he had sought out so much extra guidance to get the grades he needed. He had pestered teachers for extension reading, past papers and longer office hours, until Mr Wilcox had weirdly called him a 'too-hungry beast'. But Kwame was unwilling to take any chances with his place at Durham. He had to get himself away from his parents' focus on him as their only unifying business: hovering at his closed bedroom door with impromptu advice about avoiding 'smoking that everywhere weed' unless he wanted to become 'schizophrenic'; avoiding the Common late at night because 'God knows what bumping in the bushes goes on there'; their pointed interest in who he might take to the Leavers' Ball – a prying and edging closer to him that made him feel smaller. It was imperative that he step into that shiny next stage of his life.

Steadfast and true, Ahmed maintained his dismissiveness, playing with a thumbnail, flicking his purple tie. Kwame wanted to sigh, give up, make himself a tea. It was frustrating that Ahmed viewed this as punishment. It was supposed to be mature, productive collaboration. Kwame could have asked him: didn't Ahmed want to be treated like a grown-up? Someone who, in six months' time, would be fending for himself at Brunel?

A seasoned player at this game, Kwame turned the plan over, trying to gift the boy a little more space and time. At the chrome counter ahead of them, the moon-faced librarian tended to texts. She'd take a book from the pile on the left, open it, lick her forefinger, and turn to the title page before stamping it and placing it on a new pile on the right. She patted her accoutrements and the piles. For some reason, the pats seemed to widen her grin. Time to change tack.

'I cannot *stand* it when people do that.'

'What, sir?'

'The finger-licking thing she's doing. You know, like when you're on the Tube or whatever and the person next to you licks their finger to flick through the *Metro*. Eugh.'

'What's wrong with that?'

'I can't quite . . . oh, it gives me the creeps, Ahmed. Absolute creeps. Don't you have stuff like that? Pet hates, but everyone else is like "Oh that . . . that thing is totally *fine*, why are you making a big song and dance?" whereas you yourself cannot stand it? No?'

'I ain't no freak so I cannot relate.' Ahmed sat back in his chair and placed both hands on his stomach.

'So I'm a freak, am I, Mr Hussen?'

81

'If I say yes it's a Infraction, innit? So I'm gonna make my life calm and say no. Even though' – he pressed his temples – 'I could be thinkin somethin else altogether.'

'What do you think *I think* about *you*, Ahmed?'

'Not my concern, sir. I ain't worried about you.'

'No, I know, that's plain as day, babe.'

'Babe?'

'But humour me? What is going on in my headpiece' – Kwame pointed at his temples – 'when I'm trying to work with you and you're giving me . . . nothing?'

'Like . . . you're wishing I would nod and get on with it so you can go off and get some sort of egg-and-cress sandwich for your lunch, innit.'

'Egg and cress?' Now Kwame knew what he was doing. He took on Daddy's accent, outraged and incredulous. 'Egg and cress? I look to you like I'm an egg-and-cress man? Enjoying an egg and cress? Ewurade. No.' He thrust his thumb at the centre of his chest. 'I am an African. I go to seek out heat and spice. I have brought my own kelewele in Tupperware. I don't trust this white people's food – and don't tell me you do. I know your people, like mine, have a good common sense on these matters. The whites they don't know *fla-vour*.' Kwame harrumphed. 'Egg and cress.'

He again made a mental note to call home before Akua had to nudge him again.

Ahmed stroked his beard and almost smiled. 'Wallahi, on the DL you're a bit mad, innit, sir? Marbles gone.'

'What *I think* about *you*, Ahmed, is that you have immense potential. Immense potential you can use to help yourself. Or you can just hold yourself back. This essay plan –' Kwame flipped over the sheet.

'Is rubbish, sir, you've got me here to tell me how rubbish it is, innit? That's why it's got your red marks all over it.'

'I wrote on it because your ideas were giving me ideas! It's really interesting, Ahmed, what you're trying to say here.'

'*Trying?*'

'And, yes, there are a few shoddy bits needing more thinking through, and *entre nous* –'

'What?'

'*Entre nous* I reckon you wrote some of this on the bus on the way to school, and perhaps the top deck of the 50 isn't necessarily the best environment for rigorous academic study?'

'Small-minded of you, sir.'

'But I reckon this can be worked up into a meaningful piece you'll be proud of.'

Ahmed stared at his lap. This, Kwame knew, was the moment. Now he could walk through the gap he had teased open, guide Ahmed forward. Kwame would have to lead with gentle footsteps. His directions to Ahmed needed to be prefaced with quiet self-deprecations that, somehow, never undermined his ultimate control. Without knowing that this persuasion was happening, Ahmed would end up noting down Kwame's sage advice. Yes, Ahmed would hear wisdom. Ahmed would hear care. And he'd eventually, yes, nod in agreement with the tasks and targets set and leave the Data Hub with a keenness to succeed.

Ahmed mumbled something. Kwame sat forward a little to hear better. It was a thing countless Student Voice Questionnaires noted about his teaching: it was his listening that made the difference. And he never really told anyone that he had learned to listen, and understood

83

its power, by watching Yaw. When Yaw talked with the Richmond Court neighbours, or to Mummy or Daddy, and especially to Kwame himself, the way Yaw valued and was so curious about the words he heard made you want to keep opening and opening and opening. In the presence of his attention, all seemed possible and saying more felt important. Kwame dug his elbows into the desk. The sheets with Assessment Objectives and Grade Boundaries crunched.

Ahmed mumbled more.

'Tell me again, mate?'

'I SAID why did I even take English as a A level, man? It's *long*, FAM.'

'Ahmed –'

'What even is the point? In like, fifteen years' time, will I even remember this stupid coursework about flipping *Mayor of Casterbridge*? No. Is it gonna be useful for my life? No. Is this coursework gonna help me pay my way when I'm at uni? No. And the only reason you like some bits of my plan is cos those are what *you* told us to put in.' Ahmed used the pen to asterisk the smiley faces Kwame had drawn next to three paragraphs. 'These ain't from my brain. That's all you. And that's all you lot wanna hear and see. You wanna see us lot writing down what you've said. Following orders. I lie?'

Kwame turned away from Ahmed's hot and accusatory breathing. It was always disarming when the older kids 'called it', when their frustration reached such heights they could speak only truth about the teachers they studied for hours each week. Kwame acknowledged, rubbing his nail along the pen lid, that Ahmed wasn't far off the mark. Despite what Kwame perceived as his strict but ultimately approachable, ultimately likeable way with the kids, in all honesty he was a tyrant: life would be much easier if, in their essays, the kids repackaged exactly what he told them.

Bending the pen lid hard so that the blue plastic whitened under the pressure, Kwame knew his desire to keep things just so extended beyond the kids and their work. It shaped his presentation of himself to the world. He relaxed his force on the lid. How would he describe that presentation, that performance? A combination of decorum and . . . an appropriate kind of playfulness. *Appropriate*. His overriding aim was, you could reasonably say, that in whatever context he might find himself he was brilliantly *appropriate*. Kwame's wrists itched. Ahmed was singing something to himself, nodding a little. Kwame needed to be determined. He just needed to push a little harder. Tonight, he and Edwyn would celebrate surviving Monday by tucking into the Georgian wines with spiky names Edwyn was reviewing for *Waitrose Magazine*. Hanna from downstairs might pop round. There would be marvelling at Edwyn's tender tattoo. Perhaps even impromptu karaoke.

'Ahmed. You know the deadline passed ages ago and everyone else —'

'Everyone else can jog on.'

'Isn't all this a way of your avoiding actual graft?'

Ahmed gathered his rucksack from the floor. 'I will do this final-plan thing and do this essay thing when I'm ready, yeah? I know that deadline is a fake one, a school one anyway. Ain't set by the exam board. Ain't no real time pressure on me. So 'llow it.'

'Well —'

''Llow me, sir, yeah? I'm a man, sir, get me? Let me do

things my own way. You're the one said I've got potential or whatever. I beg you let *me* use it instead of telling me what to do the whole time. Coming on *so long.*'

'Ahmed —'

'I think we're done here. Give me another Infraction if you like. It's a minor in the grand scheme.'

Kwame turned to the Data Hub's doors. Flora and Abshir, head girl and head boy, stood there like sentinels. They beamed without explanation. Soon they were joined by three prefects who kept looking back down the corridor. They nodded at the librarian, who blushed, kept smoothing her blouse. Kwame finally cottoned on.

'Sit down, Ahmed,' he whispered. 'Now.'

'Scuse me?'

'Sit. And concentrate on the essay plan. Now!'

Ahmed followed Kwame's gaze to the opening doors. 'Oh. It's like *that.*'

Knowing, smiling, but, most importantly, obedient, Ahmed let the rucksack fall and returned to his desk. The senior management team, and the swiftly appointed acting headteacher, Marcus Felix, entered the Data Hub. It was the new head's first tour of the site, his first glimpse of the school he would run from the start of next term while Madame Evans recuperated.

While those around Marcus Felix fretted and appealed for his attention, he remained tranquil. His calmness seemed to change the ambient temperature, bring a chill. There was, Kwame noticed, a distinct sense of control in the way he angled his head to listen; a certain measuredness in his nods of understanding. Flora led them to the Modern Languages section, yards from where Kwame and Ahmed were stationed. In exaggeratedly plummy tones, she gushed about JSTOR access and Creative Learning.

'That girl is *proper jarring*, fam,' Ahmed said under his breath.

'One hundred per cent.'

'Sir, you can't agree! Unprofessional!'

'I just did. And what?'

'Liberties!' Ahmed yelped.

The delegation turned towards Kwame and the over-excited charge by his side, whose hands had flown up to his mouth. Kwame listened while, like a young Fiona Bruce, Flora pontificated about Mr Akromah's virtues. She went on about the extraordinary provision for one-to-one tuition that SLA teachers offered when their schedules allowed, and how grateful the students were for this kind of commitment. Marcus Felix did a discreet but definite salute with two fingers towards Kwame. Kwame watched, as those two, dark fingers hung in the air, poised and frozen for a moment. With his tongue oddly heavy in his mouth, Kwame found that he did nothing in response – nothing, except to continue watching as Marcus Felix folded those two fingers into his palm, dropped his hand, then slid it into his pocket. It was only then that Kwame made a tight smile, one that Marcus Felix returned in a brighter, more forceful form.

Flora clapped.

'The Sports Hall, yes?'

She escorted them out, gluing herself to the head-teacher's side again.

'Wow, that brother was looking slick, you know,' said Ahmed, reclaiming his bag. 'The suit was *swaggy*, sir, wasn't it? Jeeeeeeeeeesus.'

'I suppose it was. Swaggy.'

'And there's me thinking teachers get paid rubbish –'

'Well,' Kwame said, 'he's a *head*teacher, so. Yeah.'

'A *headteacher* and bussin Louis Vuitton or whatever.'

'I doubt it was Vuitton, actually.'

'How do you know? Were you in *Devil Wears Prada*, sir? Didn't think so.' Ahmed's eyes flashed. 'Sirsirsir – I bet you wish you wore Vuitton on the regs as well, innit? I bet you truly do.'

Much to Kwame's delight, Year 7 quickly settled down to the independent group task he set them, so there was plenty of time for him to sit at his desk and e-stalk the new head-teacher in peace. Battling against their hysteria about the imminent Easter holidays, he'd split the class into five clusters spread around his room, and each team was making an artwork to explore the definition of one of five Difficult Words they'd been given – *inauspicious, incandescent, indelible, ineffable, ineluctable* – a quintet Kwame had decided on as he took the register at the start of the lesson.

To begin with, the Year 7s had responded to the instructions with jadedness. But when he said they could use the MacBooks for research, could raid the craft cupboard for whatever they liked to give their posters extra pizazz, and then shown them the big sheets of sugar paper he wanted them to use – 'That's not even A3, that's A-one trillion, sir!' – they had become peppy.

The room hummed with productivity. Unsure why he was doing what he was doing, and what he hoped to discover, he typed 'Marcus Felix' into the URL bar.

'Sir?'

Kwame pushed the mouse away and looked up at Nosheen and her crossed arms. 'Sir, it's very serious.'

'I'm sure it is.'

'So, basically, I'm "incandescent".'

'Mmm.'

'And, basically, my idea is to draw a fat smiling clown. But not, like, a normal clown cos you told us to use our imaginations. So my idea of a clown is a clown with fire coming off of its head. Don't you think that's quite funny and clever? Fire is incandescent. I lie?'

'Well –'

'Anyway, Michelle says it's stupid –'

'Michelle' – Kwame threw his voice towards the jittery girl in the corner by the British Values posters – 'should know better than to use that sort of language.'

'That's not the point, sir. Basically, she wants to do some dry thing about a light bulb. And she wants to use some silver pen or whatever, yeah, to make it shiny and realistic. I think my plan is a hundred times better but she is being so stubborn as a mule. Tell her, sir!'

Kwame sucked in his laugh.

'Nosheen –'

'Yeah?'

'I know you like a challenge.'

'That's very true, Mr Akromah.'

'So my challenge to you, Nosheen – are you ready?'

The girl flashed a grin and rubbed her hands together. 'Yeah, yeah!'

'Is to *combine* your two brilliant ideas, mmm? Maybe mix the images somehow?'

'But –'

'I think you can do it, Nosheen. I think *you* can. And I bet you can do it in a way that's going to leave everyone in your group feeling really positive. Yeah? And then we'll stick your work up on the wall' – he gestured towards the back of the room – 'so everyone can admire it.'

'But a flaming clown and a light bulb? Those things cannot ever be friends. You know it and I know it. Michelle is chatting *bare* fraff.'

'Nosheen. *Try.*'

She looked at her trousers, screwing up her nose. 'Fine. But only because you're quite safe.' She started to walk back to Michelle and the others. '*Quite* safe,' she muttered, half smiling back at her teacher – and Kwame couldn't help but be touched by this tenderly begrudging approval. Perhaps he didn't need the kind of big, brassy dream that his father had insisted was vital at Kwame's thirtieth. Perhaps knowing that *most* of the young people he worked with valued his words and his efforts – perhaps that really was plenty.

Kwame turned to tell Raven to stop putting pens in his ears, to tell Eden to sit up properly and nodded praise when Katie showed how nicely the 'inauspicious' design – some sort of sad butterfly – was coming along. He returned to his desk and to what he pretended could be seen as valuable professional research.

Because it was a name as commonly Ghanaian as Peter Smith was commonly English, if you were to Google 'Kwame Akromah' the first few pages of results would have nothing to do with him. A businessman in Takoradi. A wedding caterer in Sunyani. An anaesthetist in Baltimore; immigrant done good. But, after clicking through, you might come across a handful of Kwame's articles from the *Palatinate*, the

Durham student rag. Florid pieces. One was on Edwyn's tenure as president of the university wine society. Another was about the directorial debut of their mutual friend Milo, the beginnings of his career in performance art; in a dilapidated bingo hall, he'd staged a one-man version of *A Streetcar Named Desire*, the action of the play transplanted, for no clear reason, to eighties Bethnal Green.

Marcus Felix MBE's impressive accomplishments were more easily accessible and thoroughly recorded, and they required less sleuthing to uncover. As the 'indelible' group struggled to get the Persil logo right, Kwame pored over the findings on screen. First, a glowing *Times* profile of his new boss, a piece with his physicist wife, Anastasia. *How on earth do you balance such demanding careers with family life? How do you make time for one another?* Next, a feature in the *Guardian*: Marcus Felix's pride in the history of his Trinidadian forebears. A clip from *The One Show* in which Marcus Felix promoted his first book, *From Small Acorns*, clutching the volume to his muscular chest. Kwame slipped in his earphones and listened to a snippet of Marcus Felix entrancing fellow guests with eloquence and bonhomie on *Question Time*. A small knot of tension formed between Kwame's eyebrows. He kept on scrolling through features about how Marcus Felix had dragged himself up from a 'sink estate' in Tottenham, got himself to university against all the odds and wound up as one of the nation's leading educators – at just forty-two years old! Kwame scrolled further. On panel events about resilience and gifted children and underperforming boys, Marcus Felix sat back in his chair, rattled off grand proposals. How unequivocal his broad white smile was. There was an imperial quality about this bald, Black man: convincing forehead; expectant hazel eyes; proud chin. Yes, you could imagine a face like his – in profile, shapely nose in the air – stamped on a coin, demanding subservience. A man who made few or no concessions but – beautifully tailored suits, soft dimples – could never be called bullying or brutish.

The throb between his eyebrows persisted, but Kwame clicked a picture from *The Times*, zoomed in on the headteacher's shapely nose. Narrower than you'd expect. Almost aquiline, like Edwyn's. Was Marcus Felix mixed? The pale eyes indicated that possibility, but the skin? Velvety, dark. Almost as dark as Joel's, the boy in Team Incandescent, now rubbing out his mistakes and reaching for a pencil sharpener. Kwame zoomed in on the eyes again. White grandparent? Slave master's seed making itself known, generations later? He zoomed out and got ready to tell the class they had ten minutes to go but was stopped in his tracks by Team Ineffable waiting before him.

'Sir,' Rebecca, their squat spokeswoman, began, 'can you draw God? Because I know, obviously, you're an English teacher so you're mostly about nouns, adjectives, verbs, but some of us' – Nadia and Robert nodded – 'thought you might have some other skills. Like, drawing God. Because we've spent most of this lesson trying to do it ourselves but, if we're honest' – Nadia and Robert wobbled their heads – 'it's quite difficult for us to do and we don't want to fail.'

'Fail? Bit of a very serious word to be using in relation to all this,' Kwame said, gesturing to the room. As if on cue, Nosheen pressed a gold star into the middle of Michelle's forehead. 'It's supposed to be fun.'

Rebecca and her troop were silent. They all blinked. He

shooed them to their table, followed in their wake. 'Let me horrify you with my artistic ineptitude.' After cracking his knuckles, he grabbed an HB and started.

'Ineptitude,' Rebecca pondered. 'That would have been *waaaaaay* easier to do than ineffable. I wish we'd been given that word. I would've drawn a life-sized portrait of my baby brother and – sir, are you making God . . . a, a woman? *Kind of* looks like you are.'

Kwame inspected his sketch, turning the sheet this way, then that, as if movement might improve the image. 'Not my intention but –'

'Nahnahnah! It's great, sir, congratulations. Feminism, innit? Girls can be gods. Why not? It's the modern day. Keep going, sir. The picture's gonna be so good. I can feel it' – she patted her stomach – 'in my waters.'

October 1997

Waiting in the corridor, balancing the sheet of lyrics on his palm, he stared at the smudged words. He knew them off by heart. He could probably even recite them backwards because Daddy helped him memorize them every morning over breakfast and Mummy did the same every evening straight after *Family Affairs*. Yaw did fun, surprise spot checks of random lines too – when they were in the lift or when they walked to the library – and Kwame always aced them because it would have been horrible and impossible to disappoint Yaw's hopeful smiling.

Looking at the floppy laces of his Clarks, he tried his very best to ignore the chatting group of Year 3 girls a few steps away. Ears and hands pressed flat against the fire doors, peering through the little windows even though Mr Plumstead had warned them not to, they listened to Rosa Tate's audition like her voice could make their dreams come true, and waited for her to finish so they could pet her. To Kwame's left, Francis didn't seem bothered: he sucked his thumb, sometimes pulling it out of his mouth to see its wet shine.

Rosa Tate was the tallest, blondest girl in Year 3. She was so annoying. She did tap dancing, ballet and jazz on the weekends and won lots of trophies. Her mum was on the PTA and helped the Eritrean pupils with their reading on Fridays because she had the time and so they always put photos of Rosa and her dance prizes in the school newsletter even though the prizes were nothing to do with anything she had learned at school. Rosa walked everywhere with one hand on her hip. When she talked to the boys in Year 1 and Year 2, she wiggled her head around like the angry women on *Jerry Springer*. But Rosa was most famous for doing cartwheels and handstands in the playground. When she did them, everyone screamed because they could see her knickers. Kwame had tried to get Francis to agree with his feelings about Rosa Tate when he'd visited the Bakers' house, but Francis had said Kwame was being bitchy. That sharp word embarrassed Kwame. Now, something about how the Year 3 girls were squealing and wriggling impatiently reminded him of when Esmerelda the class rabbit gave birth. Her fat body had grown a pink, jiggling border of tiny faces, legs, arms. Although Mrs Gilchrist called it the Miracle of Life, it was obviously the most disgusting thing on Planet Earth.

When Rosa Tate was done, everyone whooped. She swung through the doors and her name was chanted. Like the Pied Piper's followers, the Year 3 girls trailed after her along the corridor. Rosa walked past Kwame and said, 'They told me to tell you to come in whenever you're ready.' Before he could thank her, she was off, continuing her victory march.

Because his unpatched eye was really bright and round that day, Francis was like a cartoony good-luck mascot. But Kwame thought it might be weird or rude to say so, so he high-fived Francis instead. He went into the hall and stood on the *x* made from strips of duct tape. With his hands placed at the small of his back — near, he had learned in

Year 4, where we used to have tails – he waited, rocking on his heels.

About ten yards ahead of him, Mr Plumstead, Mrs Jordan, the deputy head, and Mrs Ashton sat behind a long table, in front of the huge rainbow painted by the Special Needs group. Whistling a tune Kwame didn't recognize, Mr Plumstead popped open the CD player's door and took out a disc while Mrs Ashton shuffled to the piano. Kwame laced his fingers together, unlaced them, then pulled at the bottom of his sweatshirt so it hung more snuggly over his shoulders. He wanted snugness, wanted someone to put their arms around him and tell him he would be wonderful, and remind him it was only an audition for a school play. No big deal.

'Aha! The marvellous Mr Akromah.' Mr Plumstead's shout made Kwame's insides flutter and struggle to pull themselves together.

'Hello, sir. Hello, miss. Hello, miss.'

'I have to tell you we are seeing some excellent singing today, Kwame.'

'Yes.' Mrs Ashton reached for her tea, slurped it. 'So much talent. Especially among the little 'uns. Do you know Rosa, in Year 3?'

'Yes, miss. She's good at skipping games and stuff.'

'Well,' Mrs Ashton chuckled, 'she's also *good* at singing, Mr Akromah. She did a very rousing version of "All by Myself". Do you know that song?'

Kwame shook his head.

'Ooh, it's a classic. Full of emotion. And Rosa did herself proud. The lungs on her! Voice of an angel. A Christmas angel!'

Outside, as it had been since the first bell, icy rain came down in slicing lines. The school's grumpy old central heating paid no attention and everyone had been wearing hats and gloves indoors. But, even though Kwame saw his breath steaming up the air around his face, his armpits and palms were damp, his forehead sweaty too. He wanted to get started.

Mrs Jordan coughed. 'In all seriousness, competition is stiff, Mr Akromah.'

'Yes, miss.'

'So if you don't get a chance to do a solo, you're not to be too upset, okay?'

'No, miss.'

'Because we know you can take things to heart some-times, can't you? I remember how sad you were when Jay pipped you to the post in that spelling bee. And you mustn't do that in this scenario, all right, my sweet pea? There will be lots of different ways you can contribute.'

Kwame's gentle dropping of his head to the side was a lie. The action was soft, but his mind was hardening. Why were they making him imagine defeat before he had even begun? *As if* he weren't going to make his parents proud, so proud they hugged each other and loved each other more. *As if* Mummy and Daddy wouldn't be so happy and have a million and one questions about the rehearsals and dance routines, so many that their minds would be too busy to see the wrong thoughts that could easily spill. And had the teachers forgotten the good reputation he had built since Reception? Why were they acting like he wouldn't succeed? He had practised and listened to Mrs Gilchrist's advice, memorized her instructions – stand like this, knees like this, chest like this – and yet they were making out that wouldn't be enough. He wanted to spit in their faces, and for the sick froth to drip down their noses, lips and chins. He shouldn't even have to audition! They should automatically give him the part he wanted as a big thank-you for his hard work and excellent behaviour; for being a good citizen for the younger years to see, and for being extra polite when the governors visited.

'Ready, dear? It's the first three verses, yes? Ready in a jiffy, sweet pea.'

As Mrs Ashton did some trills and then pressed the first note of his song over and over again as his signal to begin, his bubbling emotions annoyed him because he wanted to concentrate on giving it his best shot, like Yaw said he should.

Mrs Ashton pressed the note again. 'It is "Consider Yourself", isn't it? I've not mixed you up with someone else?'

'Yes, I . . . I . . . need one split second to compose myself. Bear with, please.'

He faced the doors he'd walked through a few seconds earlier and took in the biggest breath. Then he leaped up, spun round and landed on the ground in a squatting position, facing the judges. The piano plinkety-plonked along and his hands thumped at his bobbing knees. He made his face break into a smile, all his teeth glowing. He strutted left to get the laughs, then strutted right, not missing a beat, using Mrs Jones from 535's cockney accent to become the Artful Dodger, but still careful so each sound was crisp.

Mrs Jordan was really enjoying herself, tapping her biro along with Mrs Ashton's music, lifting her scary pencilled-on eyebrows when Kwame skipped at the end of each bar. Mr Plumstead seemed happy too, especially when Kwame got to the part when he had to switch between being the Dodger and Oliver, leaping from left to right to show the swapping of roles, pushing his voice up to high poshness for Oliver and down to poor lowness for the Dodger. Next in the routine, Kwame ran towards the judges, and they clutched their chests as if they were frightened when he got close. Like he had practised – but even better – he scooted back snakily, a bit like Yaw's Moonwalk.

Mrs Ashton's hopping white curls and Mr Plumstead's standing up to clap along were amazing. Even more amazing was how much Kwame was enjoying it. His voice was louder than it had ever been – no Mummy telling him to keep it down before Mr O'Shea in the flat next door complained. His throat almost hurt because of the volume he fought to reach. One, two, three, KICK, and one, two, three, KICK – his kicks were so hard and high he thought he might flick off his Clarks and they'd land on the judges' desk. That would be awful, but also quite hilarious. He kept on singing about friendship, about the moment when a friendship gets set in stone and is signed, sealed, delivered. And it was so joyful, getting each step right, each word perfect; every move deserving and achieving a long, red tick or beaming smiley face.

Still plinky-plonking, Mrs Ashton punched the air to remind him to get ready for the finale. He did not want the music to end. He did not want to do the last big note, a sound he'd have to throw out like a slap across Rosa Tate's too-pleased grin. He did not want the teachers to return to their seats and talk about the importance of taking part

99

above all else; he wanted to do it right. So he sprinted back to the *x* and stood with his feet wide apart. Hands cupped and moving upwards as if raising two ginormous beach balls, he shouted: ' . . . one of uuuuuuus!'

The 'us' evaporated. He threw back his head. Arms out wide. Fingers pointing and stretching up. Branches of the tallest, strongest tree. Breath squeezed out of him as he stared at the blurring lights above and the teachers' loud applause rolled and stretched.

'What an adorable creature you are.'

Kwame's breathing tried to return to normal. His legs cooled.

He didn't think what he had done was adorable. And he was not a creature. He felt like a big man.

April 2018

Above, in the flat, Edwyn stomped and collected crushed John Lewis packaging. In the communal passageway, Kwame stood by the Tuke and waited, the racket overhead getting louder. It was not unusual for Kwame's interest in the painting to lie with the figure in the foreground. Today, he was taken by the figure's hands. Bony things. Stepping closer to the painting, Kwame studied lighter patches denoting the boy's tense knuckles. They were more claws than hands, really, scrabbling over rock, desperately levering the boy up on to dryness.

Kwame reached for his fleece. Turning to the front door and seeing the glow of spring through the glass panels, he decided he didn't need it. The Easter holidays were beginning with brightness. He checked the weather app on his phone to see what the exact temperature was and noticed the date.

The scale of Edwyn's twenty-first at Laleham, ten years ago to the day, had been excessive, fantastical: the Moët; the squadrons of beaming waiting staff, Milo and Edwyn's friends from Marlborough, the peacocks; the 'welcome' fireworks display over the lake; the vividness of the cocktail dresses, the vividness of the cocktails; the names (Amethyst, Orazio); the adoring speeches about Edwyn's talents; the flickering lanterns, the Gin Bar; the crab; the orchard; the beehives; the Moët; the barbershop quartet's rendition of 'Baby, You're the Best'; the disappearance of Milo and three suspicious-looking Etonians; the veal; the being spirited away to do thick white lines with Edwyn off Phyllida's dresser; Edwyn gifting Kwame his very own sachet to dip into 'as and when'; the babas au rhum; the sprays of laughter each time Edwyn's illustrious father made a joke; the re-emergence of Milo and three suspicious-looking Etonians; Spin the Bottle; the bourbon; the girl slipping on the dancefloor, bashing her nose, which poured with blood, but insisting on staying until the end of 'Hey Ya!'.

All these things made it seem entirely reasonable that, at 2 a.m., the swaying thirtysomething man who had sat opposite Kwame at dinner would seek him out at the bonfire. He entertained the man's incoherent but flirtatious moves because he was pleased to be rescued: Edwyn had been boringly waxing lyrical about Springsteen's virtues for ages. Now, Bedalians were banging on about Bob Dylan. So, to the sound of Edwyn's applause, Kwame had let this man, Lex, lead him away. Damp grass compacted under each footstep. The sound of Edwyn's clapping propelled him, stronger than the crazed galloping of Kwame's heart as the man pressed him into one of the walls surrounding the walled garden and pushed his claiming lips into Kwame's neck. He slid his hand into Kwame's trousers, fingers straining against the belt Kwame fought to undo. The smell of him – the cigarettes, something peppery spritzed around his neck – filled Kwame up. His hands were on the man too, squeezing his arse. Even though he had never given a blow job before, it had been so easy for Kwame to ease off Lex's pants, sink to his knees and guide Lex's cock between his lips. His tongue seemed to know what to do, running itself over the head before taking harder gulps. And the weight – the particular weight and warmth – of a hard dick on Kwame's tongue was delicious. As was the tartness of the cum, which brought tears to his eyes that Lex stroked away.

Kwame returned his gaze to the painting – that clambering hand and struggling elbow, that difficulty and strain – but found himself smiling at the memory of a greener time, long ago. Then suddenly Edwyn was pounding down the stairs, bursting into the corridor, a little shiny with sweat, dragging his orange sack of flattened boxes.

'Sweet for you to want to get second-hand books for your geekiest students. Thanks for letting me tag along.'

'Sure, but you know the British Heart Foundation shop is, like, just full of chipped crockery? Somewhere like maybe . . . Portobello might be better if you're really set on a properly antique-y vibe for your side tables.'

'Hanna says it's a goldmine. And it'll be a lark: rootling around in crap with you. Maybe we can even get something for your bedroom walls – they are tragically bare, babe. Just your grim old timetable.'

Kwame unclicked the Chubb. Sunlight played on the stucco and the bay windows opposite. He stopped to tie the fuzzy laces of his old yellow Vans and then walked down the steps to open the wheelie bin. Edwyn flung the recycling in and did an impressively low plié.

Slowly, they walked up to the crossing by the Bedford Pub at the top of Fernlea Road. Though the spectre of having to write Year 9's reports soon and the prospect of Marcus Felix's tenure had the potential to overshadow things, Kwame wanted to be optimistic. He loved these times when Edwyn could enjoy the fruits of freelance life, and the lull in Edwyn's workflow coincided with Kwame's school holidays. They had already planned their annual trip to Chessington World of Adventures for the following week. Edwyn would moan about the long queues and the feral children in said queues; they'd conquer rides, eat candy floss, bitch. A Catarratto tasting in Hackney was lined up later in the week. Cocktails at Jake's had been pencilled in too, because Milo was over from Berlin for a bit – or Milo might come to see the new place instead.

Waiting for the lights to change from red to green, Edwyn showed Kwame pictures of the big Canadian doctor from Grindr he was hooking up with later that night. Both of them admired the Canadian's broad shoulders and then zoomed in to better inspect the promising bulge between the Canadian's legs. When the beeps came, they crossed over.

Edwyn put his phone away. 'I'm impressed by your tenacity.'

'What?'

'Your ban. Your Grindr ban. How long's it been, exactly?'

'About' – Kwame reflected – 'eight months now?'

'And you've really not fallen off the wagon once?'

'Not once.'

'No action with that Home Counties octogenarian?'

'Andrew, *as you know*, is way off eighty, you knob. He's hot and you're just jel–'

'Okay.com.'

'I've not been in touch with him for a while and he's not been in touch with me. I'm not fussed.' Kwame rubbed his wrist. 'It's always been caj with him, and right

had been no rolling through the mental Rolodex of IRL exes either. No hitting up Seth for rimming and reminiscing about how their thing had started: at that party where they watched the BRITs when Madonna fell on her face. No reaching out to PGCE Daniel, whose impeccable fingering technique almost compensated for his whining that Kwame drew their fights to a close too rapidly, that he never let arguments spiral down where they needed to. Apart from wanking with adolescent dedication, no, there had been nothing of note in those celibate months. Nothing except a blankness where Kwame might have expected to feel a more devastating kind of wanting after a decade of it all: some unremarkable hook-ups; some fucking delicious and unforgettable ones; reliable Andrew; two longer relationships and intermittent drier patches. Swinging his arms forward, sketching idleness, Kwame told himself there was a welcome relief that came from, temporarily, stepping away from the chase.

Edwyn found his composure. His stare cooled.

'Real talk now, though. Right?'

'Okay.'

'Lately, I do sometimes think I've seen a little hint of a thing like sadness . . . around your eyes?'

Kwame rubbed the insides of his pockets.

'You could, you *should* be out there, meeting fucking fit men, making human connection, making the most of your God-given body while it's still young and able. Am I wrong? Am I? Can I get an amen up in here?'

Edwyn was flushed. The concern, Kwame told himself, was well meaning. Kwame swept hair away from his friend's left eyebrow. 'For that top-quality sermon you can get an amen' – Kwame waved rejoicing palms to the sky – '*and* a hallelujah.'

They stopped at the florist's by the station because Edwyn was struck by the sight of jazzy orange tulips. Kwame breathed in – rich hyacinths – and rotated his face in the sun. A little red-haired girl was whizzing past the stall on a scooter, ignoring her mother's pleas for caution. Plucking purple irises, eucalyptus and calla lilies, Edwyn sought Kwame's approval for the masterpiece. Kwame did impressed eyebrows that made Edwyn beam and start buying more – a few lisianthus, yes? The florist slapped Edwyn on the back – his laugh was a wheeze – and Edwyn mimed a pratfall. The girl on the scooter was hurtling in wobbly circles.

'Those snapdragons look quite fun too, don't you think?'

Kwame had been quiet for a time, and Edwyn seemed to like Kwame's breezy suggestion. He pointed towards the bunch of pinkish things to be sure he was going for the ones Kwame wanted.

'Yeah, those,' Kwame said. 'Perfect.'

'They're pretty hard to look after.' The florist forced his hands into his money belt. He did not meet Kwame's eyes. 'And they don't go with what's already been selected.' The man faced Edwyn. 'But, yeah, by all means . . . What do I know? Go for it. It all keeps the coin coming in.'

The florist eyed Kwame slowly – scanning from head to toe – and crossed his arms tight across his chest. He tapped his heel and sharply turned to talk only to Edwyn, encouraging him to go for cornflowers instead. But Edwyn was unsure, stood with hand on hip, thought aloud about what vases he might use. He mulled over the virtues of the peonies instead. He told the florist they were his mother's favourite, and the florist seemed to find that touching. His own dear old mum had been more of a sweet pea gal, God rest her soul. That settled it: with a nod, Edwyn decided on some sweet peas too. Momentarily, the florist's eyes flicked back towards Kwame, seemingly discovered something distasteful, and then flicked away again. The florist bundled the flowers in paper that crackled too loudly and secured them with lengths of Sellotape that screeched their way out of the dispenser. He eyed Kwame again.

Was it racism? Was it? Could Kwame let the building adrenalin help him to raise his voice so he spoke without confusion about what he could see? Could Kwame withstand the vertiginousness as he spoke about disrespect? Did Kwame want to make that whooshing kid on the scooter do an abrupt about-turn because he had called out the florist's offensiveness, his disgusting *racism*? Did Kwame want to make that mother, waddling with her Sainsbury's bags, wince at the sight of an enraged florist demanding Kwame show proof of prejudice? Why should Kwame have to do that – explain what was plainly and painfully there?

Kwame pressed his heels into the pavement. He stared at Edwyn, as Edwyn asked the florist more detailed questions about plant food, direct sunlight, the need for misting. Eventually Kwame flipped up his hood, tersely told Edwyn to meet him at the charity shop. Walking away, he was determined not to look back – and then the red-haired girl stopped him to say how much she liked the colour of his trainers.

October 1997

Maybe they were too excited because of tomorrow's announcements about who had got what parts in the Winter Show. Maybe they'd had too much jam roly-poly at lunch and that was why they were so full of beans. Because when Mrs Gilchrist said that until Home Time it was going to be Arts and Crafts 'but with a difference', Year 5 screamed high-pitched screams, so loud Kwame had covered his ears. The classroom door was opened to reveal a complete stranger wearing baggy jeans held up by a rope.

'This is Zack, and he's from Wimbledon School of Art down the road. Say hello to Zack. He's going to be working with you all today.'

'Good afternoon, Zack. Good afternoon, everyone.'

'Hi, you guys,' said Zack's television smile, 'so great to meet you all.'

The day was a chilly one, the sky a big duvet of cloud blocking the sun, so Zack was right to wrap up warm. But his wrapping, Kwame thought, was so funny. The man's jumper was knitted, a collection of heavy black knots, and seeming to hold together some of these knots were about thirty fluffy orange and yellow balls, a bit like the bobbles on the tops of woolly hats.

Mrs Gilchrist tried to explain Zack's university project and something about outreach. It was difficult to take in because the talk of university made him think of Akua's card, which had made him feel weird and which he had stuffed into his desk drawer because he didn't want to think about her final message. It was also difficult because the ones with, in Kwame's opinion, some of the worst manners in the class (Loretta Cairney, Raquel Glass, Jack Krenshaw) were now running towards Zack madly, tugging the woolly balls, asking what they were for over and over again.

'Brilliant question.' Zack continued to smile. 'Do you know, I haven't got the faintest idea, guys. I just thought they were sort of pretty. Do you think they're pretty?'

Loretta shook her head.

'I like honesty.' Zack removed a ribbon from his ponytail and Kwame watched brown-blond flood across the man's shoulders. 'Does anyone here know what origami is?'

Ashamed that he didn't have a clue, Kwame scratched his chin like he could tickle the answer out. He went through some of the strangest *o* words he could remember from the encyclopaedias at home – *oligarch, oology, ornithology* – to see if that would give him inspiration. Nothing.

Jay stretched up his arm, long and proud like the flag poles explorers stick into the ground to claim a country. 'It's a Japanese art form.'

'Fab. Today, I'm going to show you a few origami tricks and techniques. And then you'll have a go yourselves?'

The class cheered and Mrs Gilchrist did as well.

The smugness of Jay's stupid face irritated Kwame, but Zack's voice, cool like melting vanilla ice cream as he explained the history of origami, was more important. As Zack talked, his conker-sized Adam's apple – smaller than Yaw's – moved constantly. Across the carpet, Kwame could see Francis paying close attention to everything Zack said as well. But Francis probably wasn't comparing who was most handsome out of Yaw, Marcel, David Siddon and Zack, because Kwame was sure Francis didn't play those sorts of secret and worrying games.

Zack beckoned for them to come closer. The class moved forward, and Reece Campbell pushed, shoved and trod on toes as he tried to get to the front, elbowing Lottie Wren and Ravi Akbar until they whined and got Mrs Gilchrist's attention.

'Reece Campbell! Corner! Now!' Her pointy finger was no joke. 'I am appalled. *A-ppalled*. Causing a fuss and hurting your classmates when we've got a visitor in, Reece! A visitor! What do you think Zack thinks of our school after seeing your hooligan behaviour? Hmm? Think he'll ever want to come back again? I wouldn't if I were him.'

Reece Campbell's brown hands became fists.

'Corner. Now.'

'But Mrs G—'

'Reece. Campbell. Do not make this worse. Move!'

Zack and the class watched Reece go over to the sink where you had to wash up your brushes after painting. Reece stood with his hands on his head — making a little roof for himself — and turned away from everyone.

While Mrs Gilchrist — arms cross and crossed — marched over to whisper angry words at Reece, Zack changed squares of green, yellow, blue paper into other things. Taking his time, Zack folded and pinched the corners of the paper, his bossy fingers turning the sheet into a square into a diamond into a yapping beak into a mean spike into a wizard's hat into a kite into a boat with pointy sails into a rosebud into a tiny crown —

'What's a crane?' Zack asked, licking the corner of his mouth. 'Do you guys know what a crane is?'

'Building sites!' Kwame spurted out before Jay could do anything. 'You find them on building sites.'

'That's right. And, if I were to tell you that those cranes were named after something natural, something from the natural world, any guesses what I might be going on about?'

The urging and encouraging in Zack's stretchy neck and Zack's soft face were so nice.

Kwame put his hand up this time. 'Are cranes a bird or something?'

'Bingo.' Zack balanced his creation on the table. It looked like a swan but the wings were sharper. 'And they are very special in Japanese culture.'

Zack gave everyone a crane to take home. He said he had prepared them earlier, like *Blue Peter*. Everyone sat the birds on their palms and stared at them like they were treasure.

'Time to get you lot doing some stuff. I'm going to put you all into groups. Is that all right, Mrs Gilchrist?'

'Fine by me.'

'Okay, patience and silence, guys, while I sort this out. Guys? I said silence and I *meant it*.'

'Very authoritative – you're a natural!'

Kwame watched as Zack wandered around the class, dividing everyone up. It felt weird that Kwame and the other Black boys in the class – Temi, Olu and Robel – were put together in one group, but it was okay, because, as Zack got ready to give out more instructions, he turned to Kwame and asked him to hand out paper. Zack asked *him*. With his head sky high, Kwame made sure everyone had what they were supposed to have, and saw Zack move over to Reece Campbell.

Zack got Reece to take his hands off his head and the roof tumbled down. The way Zack squeezed one of the baubles on his jumper at Reece, honking it like an impatient car, was funny and friendly. But Reece didn't respond, even after Zack gave him a green crane; he snatched the bird into his pocket, turned around to face the window, wall, sink. The roof went up again and the heel of Reece's right foot tapped madly, like Reece was trying to destroy the floor. It was sad, Kwame thought, how Zack stood there, waiting and looking to Mrs Gilchrist for help. She shook her head and carried on with her marking.

Part of Kwame imagined slapping Reece for the ungrate-fulness, his hand hitting Reece's cheek so hard that, like on *Looney Tunes*, his teeth would flip out and chatter on the carpet. A different part of Kwame wanted to walk over to the sink and teach Reece what to do; teach him to prom-ise never to do it again, tell him how to apologize just as Mummy and Daddy had shown him – with your eyes and your voice completely clear – even though he had never seen his parents following their own advice by nicely apolo-gizing to each other. He wanted to tell Reece how easy it could be to give Zack and Mrs Gilchrist what they wanted and needed: a few soft words. And, if Reece just did it – quietly, with dropped shoulders – he could be included again. That, Kwame knew, was a million times better than staring through the window down at the playground; the empty, silent hopscotch court; the empty, frozen swings.

*

Rain had made the fallen autumn leaves disgusting. They were supposed to be like beautiful flames, but they were mushed up on the pavements like cornflakes you've left in the milk for too long. Autumn, Kwame thought, as he did the two-minute walk from Thrale to Richmond Court, was his least favourite season. Waving goodbye to Naaisha Garg and her mum on the other side of Southcroft, he considered how he disliked autumn because everything was unsure of itself. On some days, especially in the morning, the sky was bright as if from a film. Other times, as now, the grey cold captured you and you had to hunch your shoulders as you walked past confused trees – half of them showing off their green and gold, half naked and skinny and embarrassed.

He picked up a twig and ran it along railings as he walked. He liked the lazy music he created, a flat tinkling that told pigeons to fly off. Maybe it wasn't only his noise which frightened them: as he got close to the block, he could hear loud crying. These sobs were coming from a deeper place and it sounded like it took loads of effort to wrench them out. The girl – he could tell it was a girl, because the noise had a featheriness to it – wheezed as if she smoked forty-a-day like Mrs Constanza in 132. He dropped the stick in a puddle and fiddled with his duffle's toggles.

At the gate, he worked out that the crier was Melodee from 503, sitting on the bench near the parking spaces. He knew Akua and Valeria didn't like Melodee, because the way she spelled her name was stupid, and Akua said Melodee was the kind of girl that put hearts above her *i*'s, but Kwame still said hello to Melodee if he saw her. He enjoyed her outfits and hairstyles when she wasn't in her boring Sainsbury's uniform: Melodee's favourite colour was pink and so lots of her clothes were pink or similar shades. Leather jackets, big boots, scarves. Blazing loud pink in the lift, or near the bins. She had pink streaks in her glossy weaves, and always had long pink nails and rosy cheeks. Her smell was pinkish too: sweet strawberries wafted by whenever she passed. But today, twisting her mouth into a tight flower, dragging her pink make-up all over the place in ugly lines, she only seemed mad – and not lovely at all, to be perfectly honest.

Going up the paved path between the weeds, Kwame searched his inside pocket for his keys, careful not to press against the crane he'd tucked in there too. The best idea would be to ignore Melodee, to leave her to it – go upstairs and cook Chicken Pot Noodles for him and Yaw – because Mummy said they shouldn't involve themselves in other people's business that was not their concern. Even though Kwame understood Mummy's rule, he also knew ignoring Melodee when she was upset was unkind. A good Samaritan would sit with her. Tell her a joke or a nice story, like how Zack had promised to come back to Thrale to see the Winter Show. He could sing 'Consider Yourself' to her until she calmed down. Scraping his feet on the pavement, he wasn't sure if he had the skills, if he was capable of cheering up Melodee. Something big must have happened to her to make her think it was fine to bawl her eyes out and show all her feelings in a place where anyone could see you.

'No respect for your elders now, Kwame?' Melodee shouted. He jumped. 'No hi. No nuffink.'

'Sorry. I, I was daydreaming. Got distracted. Also, you are an elder but not a proper, proper one. You're about Akua's age. Or Yaw's.'

Her eyes went massive, and she kissed her teeth and

shuddered. Kwame wished he could disappear away from her madness, but then she took in a deep breath, patted her thighs and seemed to become a bit less strange. 'Was it nice, then?'

'What?'

'Your dream, Kwame. Your daydream?'

'Sort of.'

'Anything to take you away from this shithole for a bit, innit?'

The swearing made his shoulders twitch.

'Forgot I need to watch my French around you with your posh self and dat.'

'Why do people always say French when they use foul language? Is French full of dirty words? It's supposed to be the language of love.'

'Love?!! Crack me up, fam. Chattin bout love.'

Melodee stomped through the spiky grass in her soft, poodle-y boots, and stood a few yards away from Kwame. The softness and the angriness didn't make sense together. Her usual strawberry smell was mixed with sweat and horrible cigarette smoke. One of her rows of fake eyelashes had slipped. Her lipstick was smudgy.

'Mandem say love, love, love and then they jus dash you out and dash you about like you're some likkle piece of nuffink.'

'I, I have to go inside and do my homework now. I hope you feel in a better mood soon.'

'Yeah, that's it. Run off. That's what you all do, innit? Go on, then. Go.'

For some reason, Kwame turned around and bowed.

'Such a freak, Akromah. Such a frickin freak.'

*

'Yaw?'

No answer.

Kwame ducked his head to get into the cupboard under the stairs so he could put his rucksack there, where Daddy couldn't go on about its getting in the way. Crouched low in the dusty dark, nestling the bag, Kwame thought about how he might describe what had happened with Melodee. It was an interesting story, so he definitely wanted to tell Yaw and wanted Yaw's opinions about her behaviour. Kwame would explain everything in detail, perhaps even do a loud impression of the sobbing. When Kwame talked about it, he would skip the ending. He didn't want the mean word 'freak' to stain the air.

'Yaw?'

Dropping his coat on the hook and whispering 'Good night' to the crane hidden in the pocket, Kwame could hear feet pattering, a thudding, a hissing. When he went into the living room, Yaw was not calmly enjoying another day at home waiting for a man to give him someone's NI card – whatever that meant – watching his grainy video of *Alien* again and getting popcorn on the side tables. Instead, Yaw was hopping around, a flying banshee, pulling out the sofa's cushions, plumping the cushions, spraying Glade Air Freshener everywhere, the one that smelled more like a launderette than like the forest pictured on the can. Yaw's top was on back to front. Maybe it was a new style. If it were, it probably wouldn't catch on because it looked quite silly, really. Yaw was moving so fast, *so fast*, the black durag tied to his head whipped around, a crazy black wave flicking with each step.

'Wow!' Kwame said, slipping off his Clarks and putting them in the corner.

'Yes – *wow*. You are so very prompt and so very on time, aren't you?' The sharpness of Yaw's voice changed to annoyed muttering as he carried on tidying. 'How come I can lose track of time but here you are punctual like clockwork?'

'Yep. Three forty-five on the dot. Unless I get distracted by going to the sweetshop for one or two treats, which I chose not to do today.'

Yaw flopped into the La-Z-Boy armchair with his legs wide apart, hot and angry. Sweat shone on his grumpy forehead – quite a lot of sweat. Flapping a tissue at him, Kwame padded over.

'It's clean. Take it. For your face. Messy. And your tracksuit bottoms too. All twisted round, and a bit dirty. Eugh! Look! On your tracksuit bottoms. What's that wet pat – have you wet – or is it just a splash of wat–'

'Will you give me some space, man? Quit it, seriously. Everywhere I look, there you be. Quit fussin.'

In four long bounces, Yaw was out of the room, and Kwame didn't know what he had done that had been so wrong. He didn't understand why everyone – Yaw, Melodee – was behaving like they were under a mad spell. Yaw slammed his door upstairs, turned on Tupac – the one called 'Ambitionz az a Ridah', which always puzzled Kwame, because he didn't understand why a rapper would do a song about a jockey. But, he thought, sneezing because Yaw really had been crazy with the Glade, now probably wasn't the time to ask about it. There would be an opportunity later, maybe over Mummy's okra stew, which he would eat greedily and Mummy would congratulate him for eating his greens. Kwame and Yaw would chat, and

Yaw would listen extra closely to every single last word Kwame said about Zack, Tupac, Melodee. Yaw would want to make up for the pain stinging Kwame's body as he stood alone in the middle of the living room, with only proud President Nkrumah watching as Kwame's foot pounded the carpet.

April 2018

The chill of dawn was at odds with his lethargy. The first morning back after the holidays was always godawful. Kwame plodded up the road, Thermos in hand, ears full of Billie Holiday, head full of the sentences he'd have to cobble together into reports before the 10 a.m. deadline. Wanting to kick the pavement like one of his naughtier Year 7s, yet again he cursed himself for not being diligent enough over the Easter break. Cyclists and cars flew by Kwame as he neared the entrance to the station, where the florist would set up shop soon.

When Kwame and Edwyn had been reunited at the British Heart Foundation shop, Edwyn had angled the vast bouquet away from his face, said, 'Well, *he* was a bit of an arsewipe, wasn't he?' and then encouraged Kwame to consider a pale blue seventies tea set. Though Kwame had found Edwyn galling and, in fact, had to wait until the tightening along his jawline settled, Edwyn's reaction was not unexpected in the slightest.

It was typical of the swift comebacks Edwyn offered as soon as those encounters were over: an attempt to draw things to a neat close. So many of them. That time when Edwyn's maître d' pal had pursued Kwame around a party, certain Kwame could hook him up with 'some pills, K — *anything, bruv*! Whatever you've got!' Waiters unstinting in their ignoring of Kwame and their addressing only Edwyn.

Or when Hanna revealed she thought gollywogs were cute. Or the frivolous occasions when they went first class on the train up to Laleham and the faces of elderly white passengers furrowed as Kwame boarded. Then, when at Laleham, years ago: Gibson asking Kwame's advice about how to motivate his lazy Senegalese kitchen porters, or Phyllida shouting across the dinner table to ask Kwame why rap artists had to speak so ludicrously fast. 'Why wouldn't they want to be understood? Hey?' Kwame had rested his fork on the side of his plate, sipped the Pouilly-Fuissé and thoughtfully commented on the relative complexity of Brahms. He understood and respected the term 'micro-aggressions', but he found it lacking too. Nothing felt 'micro' about any of these incidents and about what they seemed to ask of him, each and every time. It was effortful, tiring – and humiliating, this keeping feathers unruffled.

Pressing the Thermos into his pocket, he turned to walk alongside the council block so many of the SLA kids lived in. The flats' tiny balconies above him were colourful, bursting with potted plants and fluttering laundry.

Well, *he* was a bit of an arsewipe, wasn't he?

Through his earphones, Lady Day kept trying to lull with her talk of a blue moon while the white sun climbed higher above him. Kwame knew there was kindness in Edwyn's attempts to move him on from the discomfort those hostilities left him with. But, while those incidents unfolded – when Phyllida kept on and on, when the florist turned stony – Kwame couldn't help but entertain the flickering hope that Edwyn might *do* something. Just once, Edwyn might leap on to the proverbial soapbox, put his people right. Because so often – not always, but often – in those instances when overt or covert racism was thick in the air, Kwame felt a paralysis, an enclosing inability to act. That was the power and the loneliness of those encounters.

He pressed his warmed palms against his cold ears.

Expecting such defences from Edwyn or anyone but himself was unfair. Besides, how problematic to live in anticipation of salvation from a shiny white saviour. But – white, Black, whatever – in different ways, surely friends should do that for each other: save one another? And it wasn't as if there wasn't precedent. In those bitter months after graduation when Kwame had come out to his parents, Edwyn had provided Pinot Noir and easy shelter when staying at Richmond Court seemed impossible. At Richmond Court, threats were issued, arguments sputtered, in tears Akua tried and failed to broker peace. And, over another glass, another glass – let's just finish the bottle – Edwyn had impressed on Kwame his bright certainty that things would come right. Edwyn had faith that, in time, Kwame's parents would soften because any other outcome was wholly unjust, given Kwame's overall and indisputable loveliness. Why, Edwyn had insisted, would they want to live without his loveliness in their lives? Why would you shoot yourself in the foot like that? Madness. Impossible. And it had, in part, been Edwyn's refusal to accept the idea of Mummy and Daddy's frostiness lasting forever that enabled Kwame to keep going back to Richmond Court, determined they would see better. As Kwame had spoken to his parents, his eyes had been full of Edwyn's firmness each time Daddy sketched out the diminished life Kwame could expect if he continued 'down that chosen gay path'.

Maybe it was this distraction or maybe it was tiredness that made Kwame trip up as he turned into Weir Road that morning. He bent down, saw that he'd trodden on a toddler's trainer. Pink. Abandoned. Lost. Pined after, somewhere? Its tiny, once-white laces were grey and unkempt, a pattern of stars only hinted at by flaking glitter.

The speedy finishing of his reports – forty-five minutes, a personal best – was an achievement worthy of celebration. So, at a quarter to eight, the stairwells ringing with bursts of stretchy laughter, Kwame set off for the staff room. He'd reward himself with a handful of custard creams. Full of greedy abandon, he'd mash them into his face like the Cookie Monster. He'd delight in his messiness before dusting himself off and settling down to mark the essays he clutched.

For a second, Kwame considered the new Get Well Madame Evans message board by the boys' loos. The familiar hint of disinfectant hit the back of his throat: Mrs Antwi and her crack team of industrious Ghanaians had worked much harder than he had over the break. Then he passed the ugly papier mâché bust of Shakespeare, before pushing open the frosted-glass doors to the staff room. He acknowledged the keen crew of NQTs by the photocopier, and pitied himself for the smallness of the pleasures he was permitted in the working week: custard bloody creams. But then Kwame was struck by whom he saw panting on the sofa in front of him.

'Welcome to the South London Academy, Mr Felix. Wel–'
'Kwame! Yes, bro! Join me.'
Marcus Felix patted a seat as breath pounded through

him. He dropped his shiny bald head forward and held it in his hands like it was in danger of falling apart. His heaving shoulders, vest and shorts were covered in sweat. The veins on his dark shins were visible: routes on a map, the dusty knees a strange pair of landmarks. Kwame sucked in his stomach, lengthened his spine, thrust out his chin. He wanted to feel taller. Despite the headteacher's continued beckoning pats, Kwame remained standing.

'I am so rusty,' the headteacher said. 'It's dreadful.'

'Sorry?'

'Kwame, I finished my workout ages ago and I'm still sitting here, like this, in absolute agony. How the mighty fall.'

His voice, to Kwame's ear, seemed much less business-like than it had been on those YouTube clips. Looser. More . . . London? Kwame shifted on the spot and straightened his spine again. He shuffled the essays under his arm.

'How the mighty fall,' Marcus Felix repeated, and then he unfurled his big arms across the top of the sofa. The embossed tick that spread across the breadth of his chest highlighted his nipples. 'Did the Hackney Half a couple of summers back. Loved it. Thought I'd got the running bug for real. But I've been slack as hell since my fortieth. Which is *terrible*, man. For a guy of my age you only reap the benefits if you're consistent, if you keep pushing yourself – you know?'

'Nope, afraid I don't. Me and exercise have never been the best of friends.'

'But you look as if you're in *pretty* decent shape – you must run, or something?' Kwame shrugged. 'So you never use the staff gym, then?' Kwame shook his head. 'It is *swish*, my friend. None of my previous schools had anything like it, trust. And it *is* part of the benefits package –'

'Ah, well, Mr Felix, I'm not in this line of work for the perks. I think I've been in that place maybe . . . once?'

'You're missing out.' Marcus Felix pulled up his white socks. 'I was expecting to roll in there this morning and see a whole gang of you lot training together, burning off the Easter choccy and whatnot. Thought it might be a good way to start getting a sense of the rank and file. But no rank and file to be seen. I had to trudge on that treadmill with only Piers Morgan and his sunny sidekick woman on that massive widescreen for company. Poor me, right?'

Perhaps it was a failure of his imagination, but Kwame struggled to envisage this manspreading colleague taking strong swigs from his sports bottle, this man so fucking full of himself and yet pretending to be familiar and self-effacing, experiencing the disappointment he described – or any other kind of disappointment, for that matter.

Kwame moved his essays, stowed them under his other arm. 'Poor you, indeed. Piers Morgan is a right twa–. Let's just say, erm, he and I are on very different wavelengths.'

'What wavelength are you on, Kwame? And what's he on?'

He'd love it if Marcus Felix stopped calling him by his first name – Mr Akromah would be fine. How ridiculous for the sound of your own name to put you on edge.

Kwame cleared his throat, aimed for breeziness. 'I mean, Morgan, that Humphrys too – why do we have to start our days with angry old men roaring us awake? How can that be right? To begin things with so much – I don't know – hostility?'

'Is it hostility? Or is it force? Because force isn't always bad, Kwame. In the right context, it's got its uses, it's got its virtues. It's about channelling force properly.'

'If Jerome Linton from 8Q gets wind of that sort of thinking, he'll be in even more *virtuously forceful* fights this term than last.'

'Linton. Yeah, he's big on the "At Risk" register, isn't he?' Marcus Felix drained the last of his bottle. 'Madeline talked about him *a lot* when I saw her.'

'How is she?'

'Getting there, health-wise. Not *really* getting the hang of letting go of this place for a while. Insisted I come round for tea to be "briefed", as she put it. Beautiful home. Dulwich. Her old man's very proper. Very Sergeant Major. Made us a delicious Victoria sponge.' Madame Evans having a husband, and one who baked at that, was a very funny idea. 'She mentioned you too.' Marcus Felix pointed the bottle towards Kwame. 'Well, a bit.'

'Okay.'

'She said, she said you were "one to watch". Which I thought was an interesting sum-up, Kwame. And she didn't elaborate on it. It's interesting because, it's a sort of "That kid's gonna go far" type of statement, obviously. Or maybe, *maybe* it's an indication that someone's a loose cannon. Do you see what I mean? So are you a loose cannon or climbing the ladder? Eh? Or both?' The headteacher paused, flexed fingers as he wrapped them around his left bicep, released. 'Or maybe neither? Maybe you're much too innocuous for any of that? An entirely harmless type.' The fingers coiled again. 'Which is it, Kwame?'

Heat moved, in diagonal strokes, down from Kwame's temples. It seemed to quiver when it reached the corners of his mouth. He turned his flinching, his almost-grimacing, into a grin. '*Innocuous!* That's a brilliant one. My Year 7s would have loved it.'

'Eh?'

'Oh.' Kwame waved his essays, crossed one ankle over the other. 'I did this, this, er, vocabulary lesson with them before the hols. Interesting words that begin with the *in*-prefix? Yeah, they produced some gorgeous work, actually.' Kwame uncrossed his ankles, enjoyed experimenting with a wider stance and the helpful grounding feeling it gave. 'They really seemed to take to the openness and creativity of the task.' He took a step closer to the sofas. 'What I asked them to do was –'

The headteacher was pouting, his expression forlorn and longing. 'So that's it, eh? My juicy, searching questions go unanswered? My little attempts to get beneath the skin are completely ignored? Masterful swerving, Kwame.' The headteacher bobbed: up, down, left, right. 'Masterful ducking and diving away from what's tricky. Eh? One–nil to you.'

Frowning, Kwame focused on the square of bobbly carpet between himself and Marcus Felix. Then Kwame looked up: the headteacher's scrutiny was unwavering, felt too close. His gaze seemed to become more probing as the seconds passed, more intent on extracting *something* from Kwame, regardless of resistance – what if there were nothing to give or surrender? Until the headteacher smiled, shrugged, put out a fist. Kwame quickly bumped it with his own.

'Nice to chat, bruv. I'm off for a shower, a coffee and then a slew of meet-and-greets with stakeholders and governors and God knows who else. Observations and whatnot.' He squeezed his right thigh. 'What's your Monday looking like?'

'It's my six-period day,' he replied quickly. 'No breaks at all. Got a chat with one of my trickiest sixth formers at lunchtime, Ahmed Hussen. You'll probably get used to that name too. Then Homework Club until five.'

'Tough.'

'I'm used to it.'

'Good fella.' Marcus Felix clapped Kwame's tensed shoulder. 'And you're right about Piers Morgan. I was sat next to him at this Pride of Britain-charity-launch-dinner thing a few years back. Let me tell you, it's not an act for the cameras. One hundred per cent, through and through, the guy is a total' – Marcus Felix winked – 'twerp.'

'What a treat I've got in store for you, guys.' Kwame shook with dramatic disbelief. 'What a way to end the day!'

'What, Mr Akromah?! What is it? WHAT?'

'This has repeatedly proved to be your jam and will, again, prove to be so.' 8M fidgeted in their seats. Kwame sank an octave to sound more grave. 'What I want from you, this fine Period 4 . . . is a One Para Tale, folks.'

'Sick!'

Feet were stomped, howls were howled.

'So today's title is' – Kwame used biros to drum roll on Emir's desk – '"The Unusual Gift".'

He slowly wrote the phrase on the board and the class's gossipy imagining bubbled:

'A bomb is quite unusual for a present, isn't it?'

'So is a paperclip!'

'So is . . . a nun!'

'So is a . . . life-sized cardboard cutout of Trump!'

'Ugh, Trump!'

Kwame bent his knees a little, bounced. 'You know the drill but let's belt and brace this one and go over instructions mega fast.' He pointed dynamically – boyband choreography – to Arifa. It made her jump, then giggle. 'So, working individually, my peoples, fifteen minutes. Beginning, middle and end. One paragraph so we're maybe thinking three hundred words here? Really interested in you achieving a sense of resolution, yeah? As discussed, yeah? One para short story centred around this intriguing title about a strange, an unexpected, an out-of-the-ordinary gift.' Kwame extended the last word to maintain the building awe. It worked: Sara on the right widened her eyes. 'An extra challenge: if you can be thinking about the *symbolism* of the present, some underlying meaning it might have, what it might reveal about the relationship between the giver and the receiver? Well, that would be totes magnif, my friends' – Kwame bounced on the spot again – 'totes magnif.'

'Mr A?'

Kwame snapped his gaze to the front row again. The students giggled.

'Sir must be munchin bare Berocca.'

'Come throooooough my man on a Red Bull-gives-you-wings ting.'

'Sir?'

'Mr Malachi Justice Wright?'

'I like it when he calls me my full name. Mans seeing me like an equal, get me?'

'Mr Malachi Justice Wright, did you have an actual question for me? Or can we crack on?'

'Yeah.' The boy pushed back the dreadlock falling towards his nose. 'I'm curious: did you come up with that title yourself or did you get it online or did you steal it from some next place?'

'Steal?' Kwame was mock-horrified.

'Or like, *borrow*, then, if steal is too tonk a word?'

'No, Mr Malachi Justice Wright. I came up with it all by myself.'

'It's a good one, sir. You can take it lots of different ways. Really gets them cogs spinnin and –'

'Much as I love a chat, what I love even more is when I see my favourite group –'

'Don called us his favourite group! *Told you* he rated us! Told you!'

The class braaaped, Kwame raised his voice but not so much that its smile was drowned out.

'*What I love even more*, 8M, is when I see my favourite group working hard. So get to it' – he made his arm descend in twitches – 'time is marching on.'

Kwame returned to the whiteboard to write up the point about symbolism. Without fail, the kids assumed that when his back was turned he magically could not hear their prattling; Sophie asking Malachi if he liked Mr Akromah's zigzagged-patterned socks, Malachi saying he would rather be dead up than wear anything like that, Malachi muttering to Emir: 'But it's nice when sir's like this. When he's got that spicy spicy thing. Like, his energy comes through, over and into you and makes you proper energetic as well. Makes you want to write something good. And you kind of feel like you can do it too.'

'Seen. And it is actually quite a interesting task.'

It was tried-and-tested, this sideways entry into teaching the Carol Ann Duffy poem about a humble onion offered as a Valentine's present. How many times had he taught this text? For how many groups? Even if Head of English loved it, Kwame thought it had been dustily hanging around the curriculum too long, was dragged out too often. He had studied it himself at GCSE, in classes where he had trained his eyes on annotated pages to stop himself looking at Aidan Hall and the ginger fluff around his lip he so desperately wanted to lick.

Walking between the tables, Kwame encouraged Rahel when she got stuck. He stood by the filing cabinets, hands deep in pockets, whistling 'Side to Side', which delighted Azure. His forced peppiness had a stranger flavour this afternoon. It was both a tactic to keep 8M with him and also an attempt to counter the lingering feeling that had been there since the conversation with Marcus Felix earlier. Shame. Shame coupled with a spiky regret that, in the silence between them, Kwame hadn't shoved the head-teacher, hard, between his pecs. It would have been such a relief, albeit momentary, to push with the flat of his hand, to watch Marcus Felix fall on his big arse, maybe get a little hurt, suffer as Kwame had. Fucking innocuous. The absolute fucking cheek.

'Tick tock!' He clapped loudly. The class kept on writing, undisturbed, as if they hadn't noticed the sound at all.

October 1997

Everyone in Richmond Court loved Yaw.

Whenever Mummy sent Yaw to get shopping – usually because she forgot something on her way home and then complained about her old-woman brain – Kwame would often go with him. It was hard to keep up with Yaw's pace. He had such long strides that Kwame spent a lot of time staring at the back of Yaw's fake FUBU jacket, his 'prized possession'. Being out of the flat and in the world with the cold wind smacking their faces and making their noses run felt good. Even if the world was only Tooting, South London.

On their travels, when they bumped into neighbours – Mr Anandeswaran and his wife from 212; Valeria from 437; Laetitia and Kimberley from 302, whose dad rented out bouncy castles for a living – they beamed at Yaw. When it was Melodee they bumped into, she played around with her pointy fake nails and giggled so much you could almost forget about her mad crying. Yaw made everyone glowy-eyed, sugary and slow, like in a romantic comedy – although they never really let Black people on to rom coms. Even the boys Yaw played basketball with on the rec – Marcel, Jermaine – when they bumped into Yaw and Kwame, and Yaw did those complicated handshakes, even those serious and always watchful boys cheered up too. People treated Yaw like a celebrity, as if they wanted to make the most of the time they had with him before he went off to some exciting Hollywood awards show and left them to their ordinary lives. Yaw stopped to talk to everyone, to make a comment about the weather or the rubbish collection. If the unexpected chat happened in the stinky stairwell (it smelled no matter how often Mrs Eddy poured soapy water on the steps), Yaw didn't seem to mind. He was interested only in checking how Ms Memet's nieces enjoyed the aubergines she bought last week, or finding out about how Mr O'Shea's family used to own a farm in Wicklow. Their neighbours asked how Yaw was settling in, they complimented his English, they worried about how he dealt with the cold. They said it was 'bloody freezing' and the rudeness made Kwame a bit tense, but Yaw didn't seem to have any problems with it. Every now and again people quietly asked how Yaw coped with all Mr and Mrs Akromah's shouting. That made Kwame the most uncomfortable.

While these conversations with neighbours went on for what felt like twenty thousand years, Kwame enjoyed the opportunity to watch Yaw. What interested Kwame was how Yaw didn't behave like people were staring at him or acting like he was a god fallen to earth. Although it was obvious to Kwame – especially when it was Valeria, Melodee or Kimberley – that they thought Yaw was incredible, Yaw was never boastful; he smiled, and wished people well or good health.

Once Mr O'Shea, Melodee or whoever went on their way, Yaw would carry on talking to Kwame as if nothing had happened. As Yaw focused on him again, something tugged and tense inside Kwame eased. When they walked up Southcroft Road, past the identical houses with their pebbledash and BEWARE OF THE DOG stickers, Yaw would ask Kwame nice questions. About what it was like to be on the School Council, or about the Winter Show and the solo Kwame had been given.

Yaw told Kwame about Atonsu. Kwame had imagined Atonsu would be like a desert, or only huts. When Yaw talked about his life there, he said some people were very poor – very, *very* poor – in his stories of his home he also mentioned roads, cars, the local hospital, his old senior school, a church, a television. Yaw knew about Eddie Murphy and Denzel Washington. He had watched a lot of different fuzzy pirate DVDs at his friends' houses, kung fu and sci-fi movies, which maybe explained where his strange half-American accent came from. When Kwame heard all this, he was confused, impressed, sometimes embarrassed. Yaw even taught him a few naughty phrases in Twi: 'wa gime' was the best. Kwame repeated it in different voices as they walked back from Costcutter's, laden with Persil, Lenor and Galaxy.

On the Friday at the end of half-term, Daddy was complaining that he couldn't find his glasses anywhere and was blaming Mummy and Kwame, although it couldn't be their fault. Mummy wanted Yaw and Kwame to get tomato purée for that night's curry dinner. She promised it would be more delicious than the ones they made in the glittery restaurants on Upper Tooting Road; she promised she would make it extra hot because Yaw liked it that way, and because it made her laugh when Kwame coughed like a white man who couldn't handle the heat.

Outside, as they waited for the lift, the two of them were

quiet for a time. Kwame's eyes passed over the cracks on the passageway's grey tiles. He stared at his Reeboks. The ding came, the doors slid apart, and they got in.

'Yaw, can I ask your opinion about something?'

'For sure you can.'

'I think it might be personal and dangerous. Maybe quite grown-up. Maybe quite rude.'

'Sounds juicy. You're getting the suspense building up.'

'Don't sound so happy about it. I don't think it's a good thing.'

'I'm listening.'

Being in the lift was sometimes a bit like being in a prison cell. It was how it felt now, with the trapping weight of wondering if he should say what he wanted to pressing on Kwame. Weirdly, the thing that made the lift nice was the graffiti: a huge picture of *The Simpsons*. It stretched up on to the ceiling, covering everything. The best part was Lisa's saxophone: whoever had painted it managed to make the metal buttons on the sax seem so shiny. It must have taken ages.

The ding came again. They walked out of the block, careful of the three motorbikes speeding down the road.

'So? C'mon, Lil' G.'

'I want your opinion about Mummy and Daddy.'

'Okay.'

'Actually, it's not your opinion I want. I want to check something.'

'Shoot.'

'Do you think parents have to be friends with each other?'

'What you mean?'

'Do you, do you think parents have to like each other?'

Kwame scratched the fiver in his pocket. 'I don't think mine do – like each other. Not really. Not at all. But maybe that doesn't matter, so long as – what does Mummy say?' Kwame screwed up his face for a second until he remembered. 'They keep a roof over the heads and the wolves from the doors. And plus Akua used to always say that, even though Mummy and Daddy were sometimes cross with each other, they still cared about me and her a lot. So.' He paused. 'But what, what do you think?'

Kwame filled his cheeks with air and then slowly let it out. Yaw's expression stilled. His sideburns were so neatly shaped, his cheekbones so sure. They crossed over Salterford Road. In the gutter, a fat ginger cat rolled on its back. Two passing white girls slowly studied Yaw, from his head to his trainers and back again.

'This isn't the kind of thing you need to be worrying over. Is a adult business. You should chill.'

Kwame kicked the pavement. 'You're not even trying. I think "adult business" means you've got an idea but you're frightened of it. Are you a coward? Or, or maybe you don't like me enough to tell me what your idea is. And it's unfortunate and unfair because I thought we were supposed to be friends, and friends share, not hide.'

A 57 sailed by. Kwame saw teenagers on the upper deck pulling at one another's Afros, slapping each other's shoulders, laughing.

'What can I tell you, Lil' G? I've known Aunty and Uncle er' – Yaw checked the very fake Rolex on his wrist – 'like, about ten minutes? I can't tell you nothing about anything. People can be a mystery – and that's okay.' He shrugged one shoulder, paused. 'Look. Alls I know is, what, they been in marriage for twenty years plus? Maybe sometimes they is a bit hard on one another. Probably they too used to one another, that's all. And perhaps sometimes they find this parentin game kinda hard. Who can blame em, bro? Ain't no easy ride. But mostly they seem fine to me. They gettin along with their lives. So I think you gots no need for any kind of stress. They old. They workin hard and providin for you and your sister. That's where they focus at now. Period.'

'I'm not stressed, I only –' Kwame's tracksuit bottoms, usually soft, became scratchier with each step he took. 'I hate when everyone else knows something and I don't. I hate being . . . being on the outside.'

'It's the way of the world, man. We all gots to be outside one time or another. You just gotta keep your calm when you solo. You get back in the fold in good time. Bide your time, keep a ice-cool head.'

'How come sometimes when you speak it's as if you're a really old person? Like older than twenty-two and like you've got all sorts of wise sayings?'

'When you come from Africa like I do, when you live that life, that hustle, you can't help but be wise.'

'What's a hustle?'

'You livin the hustle, the struggle right now.'

'I don't get it. I –'

Kwame stopped talking when he caught sight of the man at the bus stop ahead.

Lit by the blinking tubes above, the man wore a big green parka coat. The hood was trimmed with pale fur, and the man himself had loads of wild, white hair frothing out of his head, the weirdest halo. When Kwame and Yaw passed by, his face became more visible: red and blotchy, the nose sore and even redder, like it had been chewed. The man did the most awful smile and made a kissing noise with his cracked lips, then opened his coat and spread his legs. In the darkness of his lap, out of a mess of more white scratchy hair: a long, pink willy. Bulging and disgusting like an alien monster.

'You a sick muthafuck, dawg. In front of a kid? A kid?' Yaw threw his hands up. 'What the *fuck*, man?'

Then Yaw pulled Kwame roughly to the other side of the road. The street lights, the traffic lights and the image of the man's penis made Kwame's head wobbly. He wanted Yaw to stop for a second. Yaw wouldn't. Why had the man done it to them – did he think they'd like it? Did he do it to frighten them? Even though Yaw's arm had come down on to his shoulder to wrap, hold and protect, Kwame was frightened. The man might chase after them and get them – then what? Even scarier was that some nasty curious part of Kwame almost wanted to see the man again because it had been exciting and interesting.

He had seen penises a few times before. Obviously, he met his own every day in the bath or when he did a wee. It was a boring thing. Mousy. No different from his arm or knuckle or toe – although you could show your arm or knuckle or toe to anyone who wanted to take a look. He had also seen drawings of penises in their Art class, when Mrs Gilchrist had shown them Michelangelo's *David* on the overhead projector. All the boys apart from Kwame had laughed because of the pretty, finger-like thing resting on David's balls. Mrs Gilchrist had told them to grow up and had smiled at Kwame.

When they were finally in Somerfield, Kwame wished Yaw would stop spitting crazy, repeated whispers about the sinfulness of white folks; the fat security guard who always followed them with his stupid, beady staring eyes was watching extra hard that day. Yaw suddenly stopped in the home-baking aisle, grabbed Kwame's cold chin and asked if he was all right. The chilly air had made Yaw's eyes water, and his eyelashes glittered. Yaw's gaze became calmer and quieter as soon as Kwame nodded, gave his biggest smile. It was nice to know you could change the way someone felt.

April 2018

Who winks? *Who?* Why, with all the other verbal and non-verbal tools available, had Marcus Felix chosen to wink at him in the staff room? Waiting in line outside the Royal Vauxhall Tavern, those questions that had often surfaced in Kwame's mind over the last fortnight rose again. There was something jarring about Marcus Felix's bigness and the delicacy of the action – and an unwelcome chumminess too. With a scraping sound, bouncers straightened the metal barriers to Kwame's right. He rubbed the back of his neck. Winks were . . . *creepy*, the kind of unnerving thing children's television presenters did.

A squat drag queen with a green beehive purred at Kwame. 'Oh, the agony, the anguish on your mug. You turn that frown upside down.' Kwame did as instructed, and the drag queen teetered off towards the muffled notes of 'La Isla Bonita' issuing from the club's entrance.

Edwyn was a full hour late now. Kwame's frenetic thumb scrolled through his phone and closed down the ten messages from Akua insisting that he call his parents, because it had been weeks since they'd heard from him. He sent Edwyn the red-faced swearing emoji and the clock emoji multiple times. A speedy reply said Edwyn was still twenty minutes away, but he was bringing the best of surprises.

Kwame tried to recall exactly when Edwyn's punctuality got so dreadful, struggled to imagine Edwyn changing his ways in response to Kwame's complaints about it. And, to make matters worse, the night was unseasonably cold *and* the queue for the RVT was ridiculously long. It cluttered the pavement, pissing off drunk pedestrians with dripping shawarmas. Under vast rainbow flags, Milo did the Macarena to entertain the section of the line dominated by his raggle-taggle coterie, the 'alternative' crowd from Edwyn and Milo's Marlborough days: matronly lesbians; haughty twinks; Art Gays wearing oversized tunics; winsome girls called Heloise or Figgy – all here for his farewell bash before he disappeared back to Berlin.

Bouncers asked those further ahead for IDs with voices both bored and demanding. Kwame was bored too, bored by himself, bored by waiting for Edwyn's arrival as the signal for him to have a good time. He wanted – now, right now – the crackle and quick gratification that happened in the paciest of his lessons. He spun on his heel. Three garrulous men queued behind him. Kwame scanned the tallest of the group, lifted his chin, pointed.

'Loving the necktie. Magenta works for you.'

The man, who perhaps had a touch of Andrew about him – the slope of the forehead, a steeliness in the eyes – launched into a shaggy-dog tale about the dearly departed, well-hung benefactor with terrible politics and even worse breath who'd lent him the cravat long ago.

'Smelled sort of . . . vinegary, didn't it?' the shortest one suggested cheerily, nudging their third musketeer, who was busy making rollies. 'And funny feet? Wasn't there a thing wrong with his feet too? Was one loads bigger than the other?'

The tallest one shook his head, making the neckerchief

waggle. 'You misremember. His feet were actually rather petite things.' He shrugged. 'No, he just had a liking for a *foot wanks*. Was the only way I could get him off. That was it. But, to be honest, nothing wrong with enjoying a foot wank.' He appealed to Kwame. 'Who passes up a lovely foot wank if it's offered? Not I. Not I, for sure.'

The three of them went on like that for a while, showing off for Kwame, and Kwame was eventually allowed a word in edgewise to introduce himself. He liked the way the men took pleasure from their shtick. Their archness loosened him. So did the miniature bottles of vodka they passed around and surreptitiously swigged from.

The queue moved forward and the shortest man clutched Kwame's shoulder. 'Can't hold it back any more: you've got such pillowy blow-job lips. The pillowiest I've ever seen.'

'Keep talking like that and I'll give you the snog of a lifetime in the loos later.'

'Kwame! Only a snog? The disappointing tameness and lameness.'

The track inside the club changed: the tongue pops of 'Drop It Like It's Hot' subsided, the trumpets of 'California Love' flourished. The men's noisy recollections that none of their teachers back in the day had been anywhere near as fit as Kwame – would have made Home Economics a bit more interesting – was something to focus on as the opening verses rolled out. Kwame knew Tupac's part was imminent.

Yaw had taught him those lyrics, around the wobbly kitchen table, with a tender coaxing so different to Tupac's pumped-up bragging. Each time Kwame proved to Yaw that he had committed a line to memory and could repeat it back without prompting, Yaw had jubilantly shaken him by the shoulders and the tiny kitchen had seemed to pulse with new energy. And throughout that strained Christmas when Kwame was ten, he had recited those same embedded words as he peeled clementines or helped Mummy wrap presents to be sent Back Home, until Mummy or Daddy shouted, anger no longer containable: how many times had they told him never to bring that Yaw's Tupac music under their roof again?

Shivering in line now, Kwame refused to be floored by the strength of feeling those memories brought. He could not always be at their mercy. It was fucking Saturday night. So he tried instead to control the speed of his heartbeat when Tupac's rapping came in, and interrupted the men's chatter. He stunned them with a beat-perfect rendition. It was full of all the strutting bravado he could muster. He shrugged his shoulders, snarled with menace. It was a performance that the shortest and now most excitable of the trio described, with gravelly sincerity, as the most erotic thing he had witnessed in some time. It was a performance that made Kwame's laughter at their praise rolling and wild.

Edwyn breezed into that laughter – a scrunch of hair and a dash of eyeliner – swaying his leather jacket's fringing, leaping to one side like an Irish dancer to reveal the navy blazered, grey chinoed Canadian standing behind him. Kwame noted that, in person, the Canadian seemed even sturdier, his tan deeper and skin smoother.

He stretched a long arm over the dividing barrier, said, 'Prescott,' and shook Kwame's hand. 'And so I'm guessing you're the one he's been speaking so highly of all day.' Kwame shrugged. 'Honestly, dude, we were in this gorgeous vineyard, trying all this gorgeous wine and, yes, he's teaching me stuff about barrels, acidity and pétillance, and, yes, he's making me buy this astronomically pricey case of Gamay –'

'He's good at that sort of encouragement. It's dangerous. Watch out.'

'But literally every other sentence was Kwame's brilliance this, Kwame's brain that, Kwame's sensitivity, Kwame's jokes, thank God I met Kwame in the first term at uni, you'll love Kwame . . .'

Kwame did a vomiting mime, smiled. It wasn't especially admirable, in fact it was something Kwame rather disliked about himself, but he always enjoyed that bit: when Edwyn's beaux repeated Edwyn's glittering hagiographies about him and a giddiness shot through his legs.

Edwyn and Prescott were smuggled into the line. They whispered giggled things into each other's ears and necks, seemed incapable of not touching each other. Kwame connected the way he felt watching Edwyn now with what it was like when he proofread one of Edwyn's articles. As Kwame's red pen floated over the phrases, he marvelled at the references his friend braided together, and at the suppleness of the prose. It would be reductive to say reading Edwyn's journalism let him see a different side of his old friend – that wasn't quite right. When he read Edwyn's paragraphs, and as he observed Edwyn now, Kwame knew it was beautiful to see someone you cared about in fullest flight, moving forward fearlessly – sentence by sentence or kiss by kiss. 'Nasty Girl' pounded out on to the street, and Kwame wondered when he himself was in fullest flight – wondered who helped him to ascend.

Edwyn whispered to Kwame that the tallest of the older queens had something of Andrew's look about him, and then turned to them all to apologize for stealing their places. He asked to try on the magenta neckerchief and, happy with their posh new toy, Kwame's three new friends assessed the styling in great detail and Edwyn absorbed their suggestions raptly.

'Thing is,' Prescott went on to Kwame, as Edwyn tied the cravat around his head at an angle, 'first glance at him you're like, you know, he's quite hipsterish and fancy, and you kinda expect he'll be a prick. But, I don't know, he was gentle with me all day when I asked my questions. He had this research to do for his piece or whatever, but he seemed to like that I was interested.' Coral blotches blossomed on Prescott's cheeks. 'It's always kind of hot to be in the presence of someone with a passion, who can't help but express it, share it?' He passed his hand over his stubble. 'I am renowned for my corniness after shitloads of Chardonnay. Apologies.'

'Not at all.'

The whole queue was wiggling along to the music, so Kwame joined in, encouraging Prescott to do the same, which he did with awkward clomps. Edwyn was busy arguing with the tallest man about possibilities for the legacy of *America's Next Top Model*, and Kwame understood he had been left to put Prescott at ease throughout the ritual of meeting some of Edwyn's pals for the first time – a responsibility Kwame knew well and excelled at. He gave Prescott a rundown of the principal players. He told Prescott about Milo and Edwyn in their student days: their contrived outrageousness, shouting about douching

146

as they clattered over the Elvet Bridge with Kwame looking on, fascinated by their frankness and determined to fashion a version of it for himself.

A sudden, pressing, bodily weight on and against Kwame was uncomfortable. He shifted: Edwyn was resting his chin on Kwame's shoulder and sliding arms round Kwame's waist.

'Aha!' Edwyn was triumphant. 'The two of you are *flirting*. Great stuff.'

All that 'California Love' confidence gone in an instant, Kwame frowned, felt belittled, noted a sting in Edwyn's mocking tone – as if the idea of his flirting with someone as desirable as Prescott was completely ludicrous. He escaped the embrace just as bouncers started clapping to get their attention, asking them all to turn out their pockets. Often, this was the point when Kwame prepared himself to be more robustly patted down than Edwyn or Milo, than any of the others. But the guards at this venue were always friendlier, less keen to shove their fingers inside his shoes, so soon they were ushered along. They parted with their cash at the door, and Kwame let a chatty girl stamp his hand with a grainy image, a little falling leaf.

November 1997

The sulking sky outside turned nastier, shooting down hailstones that pinged. Kwame noticed the living room's windows steaming up, getting streaky with water. He was smug about being indoors. Mummy swore their flat was so toasty-cosy because it absorbed the Okolies' central heating from the flat below and Mr O'Shea's from next door. Wriggling his toes, he sipped his hot Ribena and returned to his important work of pulling the newspaper apart, the ink leaving smudges on his fingertips.

He was careful about which pages he decided to lay down to protect the carpet, just as Mummy had shown him to do. In the *Sun*, in the *Express* – in fact, everywhere – there were still pictures of Dodi and Diana he didn't want to see. So many of the princes, with their tufty hair. The pictures reminded him of how – on the day the world had found out about the car crash – his first thought had been to write Harry a letter saying how sorry he was. Because for your mum to die – especially if your mum was beautiful and perfect – was the worst thing that could ever happen. He wanted Harry to know he was empathizing with him because they had learned about empathy (and why it was different from sympathy) in RE in Year 3.

Kwame sifted through the papers and made sure the ones with Diana and the poor African orphans, and Diana in her expensive dresses, were pushed to one side. He chose pages with easier stuff on them, like Manchester United and Pavarotti, and flattened the selected sheets against the carpet. Humming as he went, then he pressed PLAY on the VHS to watch the final episode of *Heartbreak High* that he'd missed. He pulled out his watercolours from the drawer underneath the TV stand and started his Paint by Numbers. It was a painting of a deserted island with parrots flying through the sky. The lone tree's knobbly trunk would be done first. As he worked, he was half concentrating on his brush – doing tiny movements so he wouldn't go over the lines – and half looking at the Australian teenagers on the telly standing on the tables in their school canteen.

There was a banging, a swishing and a banging again. He swivelled away from the telly, making the newspaper crackle and nearly knocking over his Ribena and the jam jar full of water. Yaw appeared in the doorframe with his hood up and stood with his back to Kwame as if he were hiding something or was ashamed. Big plastic bags rustled in his clenched hands. Dripping rainwater slid down his big FUBU logo until wetness pooled at his feet. He shivered and giggled. 'Aunty, Uncle, get in here. In the living room.'

'Yaw, why are you being a bit of a loon? Turn around.'

'What is going on here?' Mummy asked as she met him at the door, 'And what is in all these b–'

'Sit on the sofa, Aunty, sit. Come on, play along! Don't be a spoiling sport, okay?'

Yaw was still not facing Kwame, was still jiggling his bags around. It was surprising to see Mummy do what she was told, lowering herself on to the cushions and crossing her arms.

'Okay, you guys, you guys, everyone's gotta close their

eyes. Close your eyes, okay?' Yaw's breathing came out in fast spurts and he moved around a lot, sending silvery showers everywhere. 'You got it? Where's Uncle? Is he – no, it's his late shift. *Damn.* Still, you guys are here. That's plenty for me. Let's get us doing this thing, then, all right? Eyes closed, I said, Aunty!'

Kwame's heart beat fast. He didn't understand what Yaw was doing. It felt dangerous. Eyes closed as instructed, the thudding of Kwame's heart became faster and Yaw's breathing got madder. He heard Mummy's long, wide sigh.

'Yaw, what is –'

'You first, Aunty.' A crinkling, and then Yaw clearing his throat. 'You've been so nice. I wanted to show respect for that. So these are for you. I bought a vase as well because I checked down in the cupboards and I couldn't see one anywhere.'

Kwame flashed open one eye. Yaw handed Mummy a bunch of big white and yellow flowers, the kind you see in petrol stations wrapped in squeaky plastic. Mummy's face didn't know what to do with itself. Like origami but softer, it turned and stretched and tried to make nice shapes. Before Yaw noticed, Kwame closed the eye, went back to patience.

'And I put some electricity and gas on the key. Uncle told me how he does it at the post office on Amen Corner. So. There's food here too. Yams. Chickens for the freezer. Tinned tomatoes – the ones you say are best.'

'Yaw, these are – I can't remember the last time anyone – and that's very – kind of you. Yes. Very nice and kind. Thank you. But I hope you haven't poured all of your first wages into –'

'Benny at the garage says I put my back into it, so he gave

me an extra fifty pounds. Ain't like work for me: I like it there with the boys in the car wash. We have a laugh. That's what you say, isn't it? We kick it, chill together. Lads.'

'Eh henn, boys will be boys. Boys need to be boys!'

'I've put away the cash I need and already sent some back home. Like I promised. So you haven't any need for worrying. Okay?'

The flowers rustled again. 'Such pretty things, Yaw. Maybe I will take them into work. Put them on the front desk so when I get tired and is feeling all pointless I will turn to them and think: no, no, there is some gratefulness in the world.' But then Mummy shouted, 'Ey! The plantain is burning,' and her feet did a fast dash.

'And now for my Lil' G.'

Opening his eyes, Kwame offered his damp palm.

'Hang on –'

To begin with it was exciting, waiting for Yaw to pull out the mystery thing from his shopping. But soon Kwame was also a bit disgusted, because Yaw peeled back his damp hood to reveal two jewels stuck on his ears.

'Are they diamonds?' Kwame's voice came out more quietly than he thought it would. The rappers called them ice. 'Are they real diamonds? Your, your *ice*? How come you've got them in both ears? Jermaine and Marcel only have them in one. Is that why you got more – to outdo them? To, to be the best?'

Yaw kept on rummaging and Kwame's stomach twisted, angry that Yaw hadn't talked to him before making such a big decision. Piercings! Pier-cings! If they had talked beforehand, he would have convinced Yaw how silly an idea it was, because Mummy said piercings stopped men from looking sensible. Kwame supposed that at least they weren't eyebrow piercings: the absolute worst; the ones in boybands with eyebrow piercings were always his least favourite. Yaw's studs reminded him of what an old lady might wear to a special occasion, or what a princess in a panto might put on when she was getting ready to meet her Prince Charming. Watching them sparkle, Kwame was confused about how boys could be boys but also be happy to wear ladies' jewellery.

He flexed his fingers to show his enthusiasm for the gift he was about to receive, but also because he was uncomfortable. Those sparkling things made Yaw's small, gentle earlobes seem less friendly than usual. Kwame particularly liked Yaw's earlobes; they had a dimple in the centre, like when you pressed your finger into welcoming dough. Yaw didn't need to change anything about himself, so Kwame didn't know why he'd done it, or what it meant.

'It's here somewhere. Man, I bought way too much crap.'

There was a bright beeping as the smoke alarm went off. Mummy moaned. The Australian teenagers were still shouting at the fat principal about their rights on the TV. The hailstones were still hailing.

'Finally!' Yaw shouted. 'You like it? It's meant to bring a touch of class.'

In the small plastic box he was handed, Kwame saw a red bow tie covered with white spots. A sticky patch remained where Yaw had fought with and mostly peeled away a stubborn label.

'It's —'

'You hate it? *Aww, man*. A smart customer came in with his Porsche the other day. White guy. Sunglasses, even though you people don't have no proper sunshine here. Designer sharpest suit. I'm telling you this chale was very smoothest smooth. He was wearing one of these right here. And, and so was his kid, his son, sitting on the passenger side. The little guy looked all proper and staring at me like he's made it, and I thought – I want my kraakye to be like that. So I was, like, saying to this guy: "Yo, nice piece, nice tie, where'd you get it?" and he told me some Bond Street and he must of known I didn't comprenez-vous so he was, like, "There's an M&S on the Broadway." After I clocked off today, I sprinted down there and gots it for you. They had all types. Hard ones where you gotta tie it all up yourself with these complicated twists. But I thought, nah, let me make my Lil' G's life easier, so I got *pre-tied*. I thought it all out. But now' – Yaw's head hung low and the smoke alarm's noise pierced deeper – 'you ain't even down for it.'

Taking Yaw's emotions seriously was difficult, because of the sparkling studs, but Kwame did as best as he could.

'I like it very much, actually. I'm happy you bought me a gift. The generosity knows no abounds. I –' Kwame undid the box's flaps, shook out the gift and rested it on the back of his hand like it was some rare and magical butterfly that could flit away at any point. 'I don't know when I'll wear it but –'

'Any time you wanna feel like the bee's knees. When you're shaky, and like your bee's knees ain't strong and you need to be biggin yourself up. Let's try it out.'

Yaw moved behind him, Kwame thought he might flinch but was glad he stood completely frozen like Stuck in the Mud. The top Kwame wore – his yellow sweatshirt – wasn't right for a bow tie but he didn't mind. He handed the bow tie over to Yaw and kept his head held high as the thin belt of slippery fabric was looped round his neck, clipped into place, tightened. Kwame let Yaw spin him round so he could take a better look. They faced each other. The smoke alarm stopped.

'Fly, my bro. You da flyest.'

'Think so?' Kwame pushed Yaw aside so he could check himself in the mirror above the mantelpiece. He liked what he saw. It made him look so smart. And there was something Christmassy about it. Something very jolly; he couldn't imagine being sad while wearing it. He could imagine people being jealous of it and wanting it, which was a nice idea. He pulled it to straighten it, again and again, trying to get it right.

'The flyest.'

Kwame watched Yaw checking himself in the mirror too, enjoying the studs and nodding to himself.

'Was it – was it to impress girls, then? Is that the explanation for the jewels? Do, do *girls* like them? Are you trying to impress a girl? Valeria? Kimberley? Mel–'

'You crack me up and down and all around!'

That was not a good enough answer. Kwame searched Yaw's expression in the mirror, until the burnt smell grew almost unbearable and the alarm started up its annoying chirp again.

'Think we should help your ma?'

May 2018

Standing at the whiteboard, Kwame could see, through the little window in the classroom door, Natalie out in the corridor. She was doing her best to distract him, pulling faces even more hideous than those she had made in their first ever staff meeting at SLA when Head of Behaviour had droned on about the appropriate length of students' ties. Natalie was really going for it today: pressing her nose up to the glass and flaring her nostrils, crossing her eyes, baring her teeth, doing unspeakable things with her lips. Trying to keep his gaze forward, he pushed his laugh deep as his Year 9s noted down the last point he had made. But, for a second, while the class were fixed on their scrawling nibs, Kwame turned and poked his tongue out at her, wiggling his ears for good measure. Natalie nodded her satisfaction and swiftly disappeared. Kwame clapped to reset himself and signal to the class the lesson was moving on.

'So, to be clear, it's a persuasive letter that I want you to write, okay? Using the rhetorical devices you've learned, you need to present a convincing argument. Now DaeQuan' – Kwame turned towards the sleepy student – 'could you remind us what the letter is trying to achieve?'

DaeQuan lifted his head off the desk with agonizing slowness. 'Sir, allow man. *Allow*. You've told us what to do a million times, I swear. Why you arksin me to repeat what is already crystal clear?'

'Well, I'm definitely not doing this to test if you've been concentrating for the last ten minutes – ten minutes in which you've looked very *drowsy*?'

'I'm not drowsy!' Petulance made DaeQuan squeaky. Princess and her girls found it hilarious.

'Button it, Year 9. Button. It. *Thank you*. DaeQuan, apologies for Princess's disturbance. The floor is yours. Take it away.'

'Teachers can't help themselves going off on one with all your sarcasm, innit? From Period 1 till Home Time. Like, they think they should have been stand-up comedians on *BGT* but they're too scared and don't wanna face a proper heckling, so they just ended up here. It's like . . .'

A gently anarchic bit of Kwame – maybe the same part that sometimes wanted to take Edwyn to task for his blitheness or thoughtlessness dressed up as urbanity, maybe the same part of him that had thrown himself into the 'California Love' performance outside the RVT – wanted to see what ideas the boy might produce. The class were curious too: they had hushed themselves. Tanvir and Thom were doing eager smiles as DaeQuan played with an imaginary beard.

'Sir, it's like sarcasm ain't even *the one*, get me? Like, sarcasm is . . . being funny, but . . . only halfway? Sarcasm is, I dunno, making a joke but holding something back. Kinda safe and so kinda dry? Know what I mean? Like doing it halfly ain't any kinda life.'

The phrase floated and then settled in the air and, tugging his lanyard, Kwame wondered if it was always possible to tell if your life was half or whole.

Rubbing his temples, DaeQuan was sighing. 'Naw, I'm getting it twisted, sir. Can you explain it better, Mr A?'

'You're insulting me, and then you want my help?!'

'Aww, sir. I wasn't proper insulting you. I would never do that, fam. I'm playin, innit? Cat and mouse. Plus, we know you can take a bit of a jab jab, one two, one two. Things slide off you easy, innit. Water and the duck's back. Everyone clocked that about you from day. It's not like Mrs Jeffries. She starts bawlin every two seconds in our classes.'

The group's chuckles of recognition rose. When he had been their age, life had been so far from their loud looseness. Year 9 Kwame had beautifully perfected the art of moving conversation elsewhere or doing the uncanniest impression of a teacher whenever a Lidl pencil case or Lisa Maffia's hairline or the issuing of a whole class detention was casually decried as 'Gay, gay, GAY, MAN!'

Princess reminded the class of the time Abi accidentally said 'shit' in Year 7 when she got a papercut: Mrs Jeffries had gone red and looked like her head was going to pop off. Now *everyone* was in complete hysterics, so Kwame stepped forward, snatched Liberty's straw boater, tossed it in the air and leaped so it landed on his head at a comical angle. He lapped up the applause.

'So, with your persuasive writer's *hat* on' – the class groaned at the silly cheesiness – 'can you tell us, DaeQuan, like we were discussing as a class earlier, what youth centres contribute to society? For the letter? About the closure of your local youth centre? Hmm?'

Before DaeQuan could respond, the door opened and Marcus Felix stepped in. Kwame threw the hat back at Liberty. Well-trained students that they were, the class shot to their feet.

'Good afternoon, Mr Felix!' they chanted.

'Wonderful stuff, guys.' Marcus Felix gestured with his iPad. 'All of you. Very smart. Now sit, sit, sit – and, Mr Akromah, carry on as normal. Pretend I'm invisible.' Kwame half expected him to wink again. Instead, the head-teacher tiptoed to the back with slapstick exaggeration.

After being subjected to lesson observations for years now – scheduled or, like this one, infuriatingly impromptu – Kwame was well aware they were occasions during which he felt territorial about his classroom, wanted to hiss at the note-taking spy until they scurried off his patch.

In that lesson, monitoring his pupils' letters and correct-ing their eccentric paragraphing, Kwame refused to fawn to get Marcus Felix's praise. As he moved between the rows from student to student, he was annoyed at how easily the headteacher's presence had shifted his mood. He was sure he could feel Marcus Felix's gaze between his shoulder blades, as persistent as it had been when they'd discussed Piers Morgan. It was hard, but Kwame resisted the urge to turn around and check what those hazel eyes were thinking.

He sat himself next to Princess for a while. She glowed in response to the close and focused attention. Kwame con-gratulated her for writing an excellent point about keeping 'roadmen off road'. She didn't flinch at his circling of her unnecessary commas. When he got up to leave, she piled her braids on top of her head and asked if 'roadmen' was the best word to use in a serious letter. Kwame told her that was a wise question, one he was convinced she could answer for herself.

When there were five minutes of the lesson left, Kwame asked DaeQuan to read his work aloud. DaeQuan leaped up, checked if Marcus Felix was listening. He kept flattening down the ends of his cornrows and spoke with hesitancy, as if he didn't recognize the words as his own. Watching from the front of the classroom – attention on the speaking student, never slipping elsewhere – Kwame thought that DaeQuan's words were good, carefully chosen ones. There were, here and there, some inaccuracies, but, overall, there was a lot of fervour in the letter. The tentativeness of DaeQuan's reading lasted until he reached the beginning of what Kwame sensed was the final paragraph; a confident smile then broke out across his face.

'So, Mr Local MP, therefore, I think you'll have to concur that shutting down our club would be a disaster. Shutting down our club would be a tragedy. Shutting down our club would break the community's heart in two.'

DaeQuan closed his exercise book with a thwack. 'I did what you said, sir. That ending has got a tricolon. That's a rhetorical whachamacallit, innit?'

Kwame clapped, and then did the dabbing thing the kids were obsessed with. The class were so thrilled they almost didn't hear the bell.

Once they'd all hurried out, keen not to be late for Spanish – *you know, Señora Erdlington, don't mess with la puntualidad* – Kwame set about righting the furniture they had messed up during their manic exit. He tried to be as casual as he could, while noticing that Marcus Felix was squinting at his tablet's screen.

'So those,' Kwame said, retrieving an abandoned pencil sharpener, 'are my Year 9s. Really entertaining. Some pretty decent writers among them.'

After removing his jacket and draping it over the filing cabinet, the headteacher slotted himself next to Kwame and, bearing the weight together, they rearranged skewed desks. Kwame didn't need help, but Marcus Felix was adamant and made grumbles of exertion each time they lifted and lowered.

'Kwame,' the headteacher began, 'it's clear that you're a very good teacher. You help the kids enjoy learning, enjoy achieving, I see that. And you enjoy being up there, doing your thing. You're a natural.' He paused. 'And what is most *powerful* about your teaching, and is undeniable, is that the students trust you. Maybe more than that, Kwame, they *respect* what you have to say.'

'I'm not so sure. Those kids are generally pretty *spirited* more than respectful.'

'It'd be hypocritical for me to tell a young person not to be "spirited". Should've seen what I got up to at school.' The headteacher plonked himself on Kwame's desk. 'I was a nightmare. *Trust*, bruv. Spat in my form tutor's face a couple of times. That wasn't the worst of it.'

Kwame's instinct to baulk at the bragging was tempered by Marcus Felix's hangdog expression. He played with his salmon tie – idle and absent-minded flicking, perhaps he was lost in the pain or shame of remembering – and Kwame softened. But then with sudden energy Marcus Felix hopped up. 'What I really want to talk about, Kwame, is you. *You* and your excellent teaching.'

'It's always good to –'

'Do you mentor, Kwame?'

'What?'

'I guess you've been teaching maybe seven, eight years –'

'Pretty much.'

'And so how, over that time, you've developed the trust

that's integral to this space is knowledge you need to be passing on, my man. Share that excellence with newer colleagues. We need to raise each other up. The staff body is a community in need of what you've got.'

'How do –'

'And the last, last, last thing, then I'll be outta yo' hair.' Marcus Felix turned slightly so the light filtering through the blinds fell on his strong brow. 'Where are *you* in the classroom, Kwame? I mean, you were doing a lesson on writing about a live, real-life issue. Youth clubs, wasn't it?'

'Yep.'

'I hoped, perhaps, that you might, I don't know, relate that issue to yourself somehow? To give the kids a way into the subject matter, and to give them a greater sense of who you are. Some insight into your own youth they could latch on to, use as a springboard. Or as a way of you forging a deeper, more human connection with them. Cos that matters, doesn't it?'

'Of course. If you'll look at my lesson plan, you'll see that I –'

'I just get this' – the headteacher's wide hands coursed around each other, fingers outstretched, shaping a vast sphere – 'this vibe that, I don't know, the world has made you doubt yourself a bit? Made you doubt the validity of your presence in the world? Doubt the validity of what you've got to offer? All that shows up as a kind of constrained feeling in your teaching style.'

'I didn't know you had a degree in Psychotherapy, Mr Felix.'

Now the headteacher's hands were appealing for assent, cooperation. They received neither.

'Bruv, I'm here to tell you that you – *you*, my friend – are legit and you are worthy, and you need to be real and true and at the heart of all the action and discovery in this room. No constraining. Full-blooded. That's what the kids nee–'

'The learning is about *them*. Centre the student in –'

'You're sensitive and clever enough to frame things so it's not you being all ego, ego, ego. I'm not advocating narcissism, mate. Nah.' The headteacher's face lost its brightness and, after a pause, became more serious. 'I remember when my dad left. For good. Slammed the door. No tearful goodbye – gone. Mum was beside herself at the kitchen sink. Thought she might do herself a damage the way she was carrying on. Screaming. My sis too. *Wailing.* And me?' He shook his head. 'I breezed out, Kwame. Went to this bit of the estate by the swings where we used to mess around. My bredrins were there. I didn't need to tell them anything; they'd seen it, heard it before. So they took the piss out of me, dissed my trainers, which were always shit, to be fair. We talked crap about the gyaldem and whatnot and kicked a ball about. Smoked, whatever. Like normal.' Kwame watched him suck in his lips. 'That kind of bond you have when you're young? The kind of . . . vibe, when you're in a *youth club* and it's your whole world – and it's you and your crew, and you're having a laugh, but having a laugh means so much more. It's a deep thing, man.'

Kwame found himself remembering Marcel and Yaw, in Akua's room, playing with Marcel's Sega, the two of them laughing and cussing and nudging each other, him standing in the doorway, watching and placing one small foot gently on top of the other. He blinked.

'My point is if you show them *you*, you'll have them

forever.' Marcus Felix closed his hand in a tight grasp. 'It's an approach that really revolutionized my classes, brought about a lot of meaningful success and change.' The grasp relaxed. 'But, but it's a minor, *minor* quibble. Not even a quibble, more . . . a space for exciting growth.' The head-teacher scooped up his ivory-coloured blazer and picked imagined fluff from its shoulders.

Kwame could hear his Year 7s lining up outside the class-room, the chatter rising as heat ascended, spreading from his face to his scalp.

'I mean, I'm very open with them. I mean, like, the kids know I'm gay,' Kwame said, plainly. He pulled his lanyard. 'All of them. Yeah, I don't hide that from them. So.'

'That's great. *Great.* I'm glad you're able to do that, man. But that's not *exactly* what I was getting at? I'm just not sure if the kids know what's truly in the blood and bones of you?'

Kwame guffawed. 'Really sorry if I'm speaking out of turn but that sounds a bit simplistic to me.' He pressed his lanyard between his palms. 'I mean, that suggests there's some kind of settled, core self I'm meant to share. I – I just don't buy that idea that there's, like, some fixed, essential thing that I can serve up just like that. People aren't as even and solid as that. We're in flux. No one is –'

'That sounds like fancy theorizing to me. More deflect-ing.' Marcus Felix cocked his head to one side, seemed to bounce on the spot – spoiling for a fight? 'All I'm asking, all I'm *suggesting*, is that you don't hide so much of who you are when you're in the classroom. Right?'

'But I don't –'

'I reckon if you can crack that you'll move from being

an excellent teacher to being an astonishing one. Because you're full of promise, Kwame. Very nearly there, next to greatness.' Marcus Felix pulled at his right cuff, then the left.

'Sorry to rush you but my next class are here.'

Marcus Felix turned around.

'My collar looks okay here, yeah? This jacket is always such a pain. Fits weirdly, doesn't it?'

Kwame noticed how perfectly the vents of the beautifully tailored blazer fell over Marcus Felix's lower back, fell over his strong, full arse – Kwame pressed his heels into the carpet, hoped to dear fucking God that he wasn't about to get an erection, then told Marcus Felix that the collar looked completely normal to him, before showing the headteacher to the door with unnecessary formality.

'Oh, and Kwame, bruv – how would you like a bit of mentoring yourself?'

It was nearing half five and, with one strap of his rucksack slung over a shoulder, Kwame was about to turn off his classroom lights. But then Mrs Antwi appeared through the opening door, greeting him with a limp nod. Her other movements were laboured, stubby fingers more hindrance than help with the uncoiling of her hoover's winding lead, the screwing-on of its pointed nozzle.

'Let me do that, Aunty. Please. Pass it here.'

She raised a hand to hold him off and struggled on with the cord's tangles for a while longer. 'When you doing this cleaning for hours, sometimes the concentration can fall. Your mind can drift.' She kissed her teeth. 'Is been one of those days when I am only bad thoughts.' Kwame enjoyed the testing quality of her expression now. His impatience to get home was checked and he placed the bag on his desk. 'You haven't even a foggy clue what I'm saying, eh, my son?' Mrs Antwi scratched her cheek, deepened her smirk. 'Maame Serwaa always telling me summer holidays only round the corner. Telling me use meditation app, use Radox Bath Salts. But this is more than tiredness in the lower back. Is like when the old man and me we are watching these sports. You seeing the winners climb on the stage for their medals. The crowd they do Mo Farah's Mobot – even though last week they are probably thinking of him as pirate and terrorist. But all the clapping, beer-belly English men, they themselves have to admit they can't run even three footsteps. They see this Mo Farah's achievements as amazing. So everyone applauds and meets Mo only with the happiest looks because it wasn't a joke for him to collect gold.'

'Okay.'

She angled the vacuum against the filing cabinets. 'What I'm feeling, Kwame, is . . . is . . . almost a wanting to scream, as if to ask where is my own trophy of gold? Eh? Forty good years here of never complaining and pay the tax and go to the church and send the child to school, make sure they behave. To do this – forty good years, Kwame – is as big as any Mo Farah success. It is! But who even sees me to say: eh, that Agnes Antwi, she is not a joke, wa ya die oohhh, wa ya die paaaaa. Who? You think me I'm surprised by any Windrush? No! Why will I be shocked when all along they telling you to be old and Black means you don't count in anyone's book?' She rocked in her plimsolls, like the strength of her own words was charging her up – or like the kind of openness Marcus Felix was encouraging was moving her forward. And, in listening, in really listening, to Mrs Antwi, Kwame found a kind of a freedom from himself and his own smaller thoughts: Year 12 marking, would Edwyn want to rewatch that *Cybill* episode again.

'Can I say way ya die to you, Aunty? Does my saying it count for anything?'

Her laugh was soft. 'I admit, there is *good* in my life – we thank God for the child. Ampa. But even all the worrying for her is a dedication of life. Where the trophy for that? Maybe, maybe I should clock my own face in the tables I'm shining up and say congratulations. But doing it for yourself, that is another tough work. And all I want is a little peace, eh. I think to have my trying *known* by others, it will give me that peace.' She pulled at the Velcro on the side of her tabard. It made a crackling yawn before Mrs Antwi refastened, putting the sticky strip back into place with a flurry of little pats.

Taking a step forward, Kwame's legs were light. 'I'm glad that you, that you were able to tell me that, Aunty. Thank you. It sounds. What you're saying sounds really difficult, actually.'

She threw a Fisherman's Friend in her mouth and offered him one from the packet, which he declined. 'Is only grumble grumbling. And grumble grumbling doesn't do much, isn't it? So we quiet ourselves. Keep our heads down, nose clean and can only hope.'

'Well. Well, it's still –'

Mrs Antwi pressed the switch. The vacuum roared into noisy life. She pushed the nozzle into the tight space between the back of the book cupboard and the wall. 'And when last you saw your family, you passed on my well wishes, isn't it? How is your mother, Kwame? And your father? The sister also? The small nieces? You talk on them all so little.'

'I should probably call them, to be honest.' Kwame reached for his rucksack again. 'I've been naughty. Term time's always mental with reports and –'

'Naughty? You don't be naughty, wa te? Is not you! Call home fast. Is an order! And you know I don't come to play!'

November 1997

Some nights, Yaw returned from work quite late. Kwame had washed, changed into pyjamas, brushed his teeth and tucked himself into bed, and Yaw still hadn't come back with a story about what Valdis or Babou did to someone's VW during his shift at the car wash. In the mornings, over breakfast, no one ever told Yaw off for it, which was funny and surprising. If Akua had ever come home after 10 p.m., Daddy would have screamed until he got a sore throat and then Mummy would have taken over shouting and been so loud the windows would have shattered.

Tonight was one of those nights when all Kwame could do was to lie awake in bed, eyes searching the blue darkness, waiting for Yaw's sleepy voice to sail through the flat and into his ears. A breezy 'Wassup' and a clink of the letterbox; a quick 'Hey, fam' and his fake Timberlands climbing the stairs.

It wasn't as if, when Yaw did arrive, Kwame planned to throw off the covers, eager like it was Christmas morning, and run down to greet and question him. Kwame never did that. There were rules put in place for his own good: bedtime meant lights out, and so Kwame had to be in his bed until the alarm beeped the next morning. Kwame just liked knowing he fell asleep in the same space as Yaw, knowing that Yaw was or would soon be on the other side of the wall. That was why he waited for the voice, for Yaw's sleepy call, the signal Kwame could close his eyes and rest easy.

Turning over, punching his thin pillow, Kwame heard activity below – not Yaw returning but Mummy's and Daddy's separate sounds: Mummy moving trays, plates and glasses to the kitchen; Daddy arguing with the telly, shouting that all politicians were cut from the same dirty cloth, Mummy asking him if he was Michael Buerk to be offering his opinion – no? Then quiet and listen for a change. Soon enough, Daddy started to snore like he always did if he had a Heineken with dinner. Mummy's sigh sank into a groan, and then came her shuffling as she went to clean the front doorstep, thwacking the doormat, probably rearranging the tangled vines in their hanging baskets. She said hello to Mr O'Shea, asked about the council replacing his window.

The duvet over Kwame felt boring and stupid. He sat upright, his back squishing against the headboard. Straight ahead, the shadow of the bare plane tree was temporarily blocked by the shadow of a passing 57 as it moved along his wall, stretched and slanted. The light from the street lamp picked out the edges of his stacked CDs, toys from Happy Meals, his bow tie.

Even though Yaw's bow tie was kind and thoughtful, and Kwame was very grateful, really he wanted to wear Yaw's clothes, or clothes similar to Yaw's. The ideal thing would be the FUBU. How interesting and nice it would be to slip his arms into the massive sleeves of Yaw's jacket and to carry its enormous weight. In the huge coat, he would be surrounded by the smells of Yaw, smells stuck deep in the fabric: the tang of sweat, the sweetness of Versace Blue Jeans, the spiciness of Big Red gum. Or, even better, he'd like to wear one of Yaw's vests. Kwame saw Yaw wearing them in the mornings, under his stripy blue dressing gown, as he clomped around the flat hunting for socks or his work uniform. When Kwame looked up from his orange juice or from doing his laces, he would catch sight of whistling Yaw going about his business, catch a quick flash of the white scoop of the vest that dipped low and showed the beginning of the deep line between Yaw's pecs. Yaw often left his vests on the damp bathroom floor for Mummy to sling into the laundry basket. Kwame wanted to put one on himself, let it drop on to his shoulders, to have something that had been close to Yaw's skin close to his own. He could have done these things in secret: try on a vest in the quiet of the locked bathroom, maybe for a few minutes after a bath. But he was too scared. He worried he might enjoy Yaw's things so much that he screamed. And it seemed a bit like stealing, illegal and wrong.

Kwame rubbed the itchy big toe of his right foot with the heel of his left. Like all the other boys on the estate, Yaw had started to 'bop', as they called it – their lazy, sly way of walking which sometimes included a hop after every third or fourth step. Neither Yaw, Marcel, Jermaine – nor anyone else for that matter – ever explained why they moved so messily. Yaw's version of the walking style, Kwame thought, was ridiculous. Maybe the length of Yaw's legs made his bopping silly, gave his moves a lumpiness. It was often when around the other boys, and Marcel in particular, that Yaw's walk went super-slow-mo.

Kwame rocked in the bed and the mattress's springs cried. The boys' bopping was enjoyable too, though, because – and it was actually quite hard to explain it to himself, so he chewed the inside of his cheek – there was something sort of helpful about the slowness.

When Kwame imagined what the inside of his mind and body were like, a Catherine wheel seemed right: firing, whizzing. Especially when he was a bit scared, like if Mummy refused to make dinner for Daddy because she was too angry or when he couldn't stop thinking how lovely Marcel's shimmering smile was. When he was a bit scared, things got so fast, exactly like a Catherine wheel. Words and feelings streamed through his brain and he couldn't catch them. He hated those hot, fast-forward moments. Like once, when Rohima Begum asked him why he wasn't good at sports when boys were supposed to be excellent at them. Or when he thought Francis might want to come over to Richmond Court. Or when Jay Basir won the spelling championship and then apologized for beating him. In those spinning seconds, everything pressed down and Kwame worried he might fall over. Sometimes it helped to curl under the duvet and squeeze really tight as soon as he got home and got the chance. But it didn't always work.

It must feel good to be Yaw – to take your time, move and behave as if you didn't care about a single thing. Maybe Yaw slowed his body down to quiet his own whirring mind. Maybe, even though it never seemed like it, Yaw's thoughts troubled him too. Perhaps they yanked him between being excited by the new fun of London – Our Price and Woolworths – and everything he missed back home: his fat, clever friend Ibrahim, who wanted to be an engineer; the chickens he kept in hutches made with his own hands.

Tomorrow he would tell Yaw how grateful he was for everything he brought to their home. A brightness that could even sometimes make Mummy and Daddy unclench. Their home might not be special like Francis's, but their flat had Yaw in it. That was better than Sky TV, a big garden or two cars in the driveway. Yaw would love to hear that.

Passing his tongue over his teeth, Kwame tasted the last of the toothpaste's mintiness there. What would it be like if *he* started bopping too? He'd only do it around the block rather than at Thrale, because he was certain Mrs Gilchrist wouldn't approve. She'd call him 'slouchy sloth' or 'slouchy salamander'. Slow step. Slow step. Dragged step, slow step, bounce.

Another bus rumbled up Southcroft, headlights scoring the ceiling, showing the glow in the dark sticker of three Care Bears that the previous tenants had left behind. Neither Mummy nor Daddy ever talked about painting over or removing it. Kwame had often thought about how it got up there, and if it soothed the last boy or girl who lived here, helped them when monsters you couldn't give a name to kept them up at night. The bears' chunky smiles might have that power for a younger child, but not for Kwame and his monsters. He wanted the ceiling blank.

One day, he would ask Yaw for help. He could climb on to Yaw's shoulders and reach up, his fingers pulling at the sticker until it came loose. Yaw wouldn't mind being used like a tree. He'd say, 'Glad to be of service, Lil' G.' And Kwame would love being up there, held by Yaw's branching arms. He would enjoy looking at Yaw from a new angle, his eyes passing over Yaw's serious forehead, sliding all the way down to his long, thin feet.

May 2018

On the doorstep, clutching freesias, Prescott sceptically considered Kwame's Poundland haul of CONGRATULATIONS! banners and big foil balloons. Quickly, however, he proved to be more useful, more enthusiastic. Careful to avoid bashing the Tuke, Prescott lugged the bags into the flat, while Kwame knocked on Hanna's door to invite her up for the festivities later before remembering she'd told him she had plans. Once upstairs, the diligence continued: the surprisingly light-footed Canadian stood on a chair to string paperchains between the living room's corners; he wrapped a fuzzy length of tinsel around the telly, and laid out little dishes of baba ganoush and crackers on the side table. After an hour or so of tidying and finessing, he even remembered – Kwame had entirely forgotten – that they had put two bottles of Edwyn's favourite Pét-Nat in the freezer, and whipped them out before they turned to ice. They poured gin and tonics and slumped into the armchairs to wait for Edwyn's arrival, pleased with themselves and admiring the jolly, pompommed paper hats crowning their heads.

Watching Prescott attend to emails on his iPhone, Kwame had to acknowledge that Marcus Felix's assessment of him as remote or uptight in the classroom was still rankling, even though three days had passed. Kwame had tried to reason that the comments were an expression of professional judgement, a useful evaluation of his teaching style. But – perhaps it was the needling quality of the head-teacher's gaze as he spoke; perhaps it was the conspicuous ease of the headteacher's footsteps as he had left Kwame's classroom – it felt weightier. The headteacher had – again – cast judgement about Kwame as a *person*. He had been marked out as lifeless, mechanical, somehow – not in pos-session of the headteacher's own charisma and authenticity, traits that enabled him to make a story out of a family trauma for a colleague he barely knew.

After the headteacher had left and the Year 7s trotted in, Kwame had had to work hard to make sure his students, getting out their pens, were unable to see his discomfort. Throughout that class, and when he'd had lunch with Natalie later, Mrs Gilchrist's face kept coming to mind. In particular, the memory of how she had essentially told Kwame to lighten up when they were practising for the Winter Show. While Natalie savaged her chips and outlined her housemate's latest crimes, Kwame reflected that the headteacher's observation and Mrs Gilchrist's rehearsals – and his father's questioning at Kwame's thirtieth, come to think of it – spoke to one of his deeper concerns. No matter how precise the pronunciation of his *t*'s, how well he performed at university, how happy his students seemed to be, how palatable he might try to make himself to strangers or superiors, there would always be someone ready to tell him he wasn't *quite* enough. He knew it was cowardly – the response of a child as opposed to an adult maybe – but Kwame found himself unable to look at that fear for long. It produced nothing but a wrenching at the base of his spine and a need to be held, reassured.

Kwame collected Prescott's empty glass, rattled it so that

the ice cubes tinkled. 'Someone was *thirsty.*' Prescott's laugh in response was knowing. 'Another? Something else?'

The front door clicked open, and soon enough Edwyn, with bags of bottles, bolted into their standing ovation. Kwame watched Prescott pull him into an embrace, asking Edwyn what his dad had made of his performance on *This Morning*, and had he seen all the rave reviews on Twitter: #sexysommelier #buffboozeboi #boozebae #wouldntmindsqueezinghisgrapes? Edwyn shook his head: he had not looked at his phone since leaving the studio, had been walking around West London in a daze since he had 'wrapped'.

Prescott began to organize a takeaway from the Moroccan place at the end of the street. Kwame pulled the cork from the sparkling wine. Glasses were filled. Edwyn – flushed, foot tapping – drank deeply and started up.

'So Phillip very much has particular demands about where lights can go because he's afraid he'll look jowly. But Holly Willoughby's *gorgeous*, not nearly as basic as I thought she'd be, plus she loved the pine-cone tattoo and we compared notes: she's got a rather delicate little heron on her ankle.' With tightly closed eyes and tossed-back head, Edwyn drank more. His eyes snapped open. 'But that's not the best bit, Kwame. There was this *runner*, Kwame, called Kyle. Kissable Kyle. Ideal for you. Like, *idealisssimo.*'

'If you say so.'

'Seriously. Vital stats: twenty-nine, single, phenomenal arms, runs a film club for disadvantaged kids, so he's all worthy like you.'

Kwame laughed. 'Am I worthy?'

With purposeful elbows, Edwyn urged Kwame to look

up Kyle's Instagram: Kyle climbing Ben Nevis, Kyle slouching on a balustrade after 'a massive one' at Berghain.

'And how's school? Hmm, Kwame? Your Year 12s still struggling with *Tess*? Will you do an impression of that Anton for me? Or Malachi, adorable little Malachi? God, he always sounds just like the most brilliant livewire presence the way you talk about him. What do you reckon he might want to be when he's older? Has he told you? Are they too young for all that fucking careers-guidance crap yet? And, and, and is Mrs Antwi still monitoring your waistline? Oh. and Kwamekwamekwame don't forget your nieces' ninth birthday next Tuesday.'

'I –'

'I know the date's circled on the calendar on the fridge, but it's definitely the kind of thing you might forget, Kwame, and Akua will be livid if you do. It's funny, Holly was actually saying –'

'Babe, did they give you a celebratory bit of chang at the end of the show? Eh?' Kwame reached for Edwyn's chin, tilted him this way, then that. 'Your mouth isn't doing the usual slidey grimace, but wowwwww the radioactive energy coming off you and the need for you to *take an actual breath*!'

'I'm adrenalized, what of it?' Edwyn sipped again, slid away, pressed himself into Prescott's flank and started playing with his loosened collar. 'It's been a big day.'

Kwame realized he hadn't seen his friend in such a heightened state of nervousness for a while. Perhaps the last time was a couple of years ago: it was late, they'd been on the way home to the old flat in Norwood after an Arcade Fire gig. They were full of gin, euphoria, self-satisfaction. They had turned on to Chatsworth Way and a group of boys – maybe ten of them; some on bikes, others on foot – formed a circle. They demanded mobiles, wallets. Almost immediately, Edwyn started shaking his right leg, stuttered fragmentary apologies, tossed coins everywhere. Kwame had been more circumspect. He had known to stand taller, and to take on the words and tones of others to negotiate. He called the boys *bruv*. Encouraged them to *'llow it*. He appealed to their decency, their understanding *that man's jus tryin to get to yard in peace, get me?* It took time, it took persistence, but it worked. The boys agreed to head off with fifty quid, cycled away shouting *'Fassy!'* and all the rest. Edwyn and Kwame got to keep their phones, and yet this victory had not soothed Edwyn's twitchiness. It had remained as Kwame led him the rest of the way home, with Kwame increasingly uncomfortable each time Edwyn jabbered gratitude for Kwame knowing how to deal with those sorts of boys. It remained as Kwame became a little sickened while Edwyn went on about how Gibson had worried that *that* bit of South London mightn't be safe enough and somewhere like leafier Balham – closer to Clapham – might be more suitable.

And now, with similar jangliness, Edwyn undid more buttons on his linen shirt and roughed up Prescott's hair before darting back to Kwame. So Kwame pressed his palms into Edwyn's shoulders. He rested his forehead gently on Edwyn's and then stood back.

'I bet,' Kwame said. 'You were fucking brilliant. I bet you will light up the screen. Remember your speech at Phyllida's sixtieth? Fucking dazzling. All the puns and the callbacks and the call and response? It was brilliant. Audience were eating out of the palm of your etcetera, etcetera. It'll be just like that, no? The nation will be, will be calling you a national treasure by the end of the week.'

To begin with, Edwyn spoke to the flute in his hand. 'It's funny, I've never really been recorded like that. Not for, like, such a sustained period. With all the lights on and everyone shouting, telling you where to look. I don't know how Dad's stood it for all these years. Nightmare. There's this sense that you are definitely going to fuck up, and when you do fuck up it's on you to turn it into something charming and relatable. It's *intense*. All through my piece, even though I was meant to be outward and outgoing – that was literally what I was being paid for – I had this sort of double vision? I was chatting away about Franciacorta, but I was actually focused on what my hands were doing?' He bit his lip. 'I suppose I was trying to make sure I was giving the right kind of gay? Like, perfectly pitched gay. It's not like anyone specifically took me aside and said, you know, don't camp it up too much. But, yeah, I found myself being super-aware of my body's movements and how I was standing and holding bottles. It was like I was . . . undoing myself?' He massaged the back of his shoulder. 'Does that sound horribly overblown?' He poured more Pét-Nat. It shivered into the glass. 'I should probably shut the fuck up and count my lucky etcetera, etcetera.'

Kwame tore a sliver from the foil encasing the wine bottle's neck, pulled the sliver taut. 'I reckon you should drink, *revel* in your good fortune, and be excited about whatever might come from all this new fame.'

'Fame? Fuck. *You* slow down, Akromah.' Edwyn grabbed at his curls.

'Of course I know what you're getting at. Of course I

do. Totally. But I also know how talented, brave and fantastic you *always* are. So relax.' He traced a section of Edwyn's jawline with a finger. 'Plus it's a fucking party – and one in your bloody honour – so put on a fucking party face. Yeah? I said yeah?'

'Yeah.'

As Kwame squeezed Edwyn's hand, his friend's eyes began to lose more of their unnatural sheen. Prescott spread across the sofa and paused the show. The knowledge that Kwame could change the way his friend felt, that he could temper his friend's discomfort, that Kwame was needed and only Kwame had the right sentence to bring Edwyn back from some brink, rose, spread, settled.

An immobilized Edwyn – cheekbones and smile ready – filled the TV screen. The three men did a drum roll and pressed PLAY. By way of introducing their new vintner, Holly chirpily shared a long story about a disastrous family barbecue. On the sofa Edwyn stretched out, resting his head on Prescott's chest and draping his legs across Kwame. They laughed at the screen, groaned at Edwyn's cheesy dismissal of Phil's preference for lager as 'phil-istine'. Edwyn looked up to check whether Kwame had caught his subsequent clever fact about terroir and Kwame rested his palms on Edwyn's shins.

November 1997

The row of sunflowers the class had created from sweet wrappers wriggled up towards the ceiling. Their stems were thick as arms, golden petals flicked out like rude tongues. The puffy clouds between them were made from cotton wool. Kwame liked Mrs Gilchrist's wall displays a lot. Everyone knew hers were the most colourful in the whole school. A few of the lovely sunflowers were shorter than the rest or had drooping, rather than proud, lion-like heads. Sometimes it seemed like these smaller ones looked down on Year 5 in a sad way, like they knew that in Year 6 they would have Mr Bell as their teacher and not Mrs Gilchrist. Mr Bell, with his stupid shoes and evil, pointy fingernails. And long division.

Down there, beneath the pretend sunflowers, Year 5 gossiped on the carpeted bit of the Reading Corner. Robel picked dried glue from his palms. Francis sucked his thumb, not thinking about how David and Reece could see him doing something so babyish and would tell him off at break time. Cross-legged, Kwame sat with the straightest back, tall like he was being pulled up by a strict string, even though lispy Jill next to him was trying to get him to talk about tomorrow's rehearsals for the Winter Show. He was sitting smartly enough to be wearing Yaw's bow tie. Among them – also crossed-legged, with her scuffed trainers poking out from under floaty skirts – Mrs Gilchrist and the book on her lap waited for stillness.

'Reece, you seem to be taking an incredibly long time to get your act together. I'm disappointed by that. It's like you've forgotten it's Parents' Evening tonight. I don't want to have to tell someone's daddy that someone isn't very good at following important instructions.'

'Sorry, miss.'

Reece's apology didn't sound truthful. A laugh hid in the words. Everyone knew Mrs Gilchrist would be polite and girlish with Reece's dad, because Reece's dad was deep-voiced and had heaped muscles. A rumour had gone around since they were in Year 2 that Reece's dad had been in prison, and, when you saw him with his wide hands and the rough marks on his knuckles, it was very easy to believe the rumour was truth. Kwame hated it when, at Parents' Evenings or the carol concert, or if they happened to see each other at Amen Corner, Reece's dad tried to do a fist bump with his father. Daddy always got it wrong: went for a high-five or handshake, and Reece's dad shook his head like Daddy was pitiful and rubbish, and Kwame wanted to run home. But it was also okay too, because Reece's dad often ended things by pinching Kwame's cheek and telling Daddy he respected him for raising a decent son.

Kwame watched Mrs Gilchrist surveying the class as everyone shot up, changing from slouches into soldiers, their focus on Mrs Gilchrist's chilly blue eyes.

'Well done, Year 5. Spick and span. So, boys and girls, gents and princesses, who can tell me what story we had last time? Who can remember? What did I read to you yesterday?' Hands flew up. 'I'm going to aaaaaaaask . . . Naaisha, why don't you share with us?'

Naaisha stood, squeaked out a few sentences from the Cherokees' story about how they believed the world had come to be, and ended with the idea that got a big laugh yesterday: the first people were a brother and sister who didn't get on. The brother had hit his sister around the head with a big fish because he was bored and wanted her to produce children, friends for his entertainment.

'Can you imagine?!' Mrs Gilchrist's eyes heated with disbelief. 'What would you do, Naaisha, if your brother attacked you with a salmon! Hmm?'

'I would call the police on him, miss.'

'Good idea, Naaisha. And thank you for recalling that detail. Can we all clap for Naaisha?'

Applause rained.

'Now, I want to keep things fishy and of the sea, as it were, but I want to move away from creation stories to other kinds of myths.' Kwame watched Mrs Gilchrist's fingers dancing through the pages before coming to rest. 'This one is about a mythological character from Africa –' Mrs Gilchrist slid her glance around the class of thirty, from Temi at the back, to Olu and Vembi in the middle, over to Robel and Hawah, until the glance rested on him. He wanted to cough but sucked it down. 'This figure is well known in Central and West Africa, places like Nigeria and Ghana. That's where your family are from, isn't it, Kwame? And that's where your lovely name is from, right?'

Kwame smiled.

'Yes,' she went on, 'this goddess I'm going to read about today is a bit like Ariel from *The Little Mermaid*. We've all seen that, haven't we –' Everyone nodded, apart from Reece, David and Gary. 'Yep, it's one of my fave Disneys too. So, in Ghana and Nigeria, and other parts of Africa, they've got their own kind of Ariel, and she's called Mami Wata.'

Mrs Gilchrist walked to the flipboard. In her neat, girl's handwriting she wrote the name. 'I hope I'm saying that right! Am I, Kwame? Kwame, could you say it for the class? Do you mind? Stand up and say it for us.'

A sizzle buzzed behind his right ear as he got to his feet. Eyes were on him. He didn't want to disappoint but he had never heard of 'Mami Wata' before. Neither Mummy, Daddy nor Yaw – nor anyone – had ever mentioned her. He couldn't tell Mrs Gilchrist that, but he wasn't sure why she needed help to say the name. He didn't think it was such a difficult thing to pronounce. It seemed easy enough, almost like a baby's gibberish.

As much as a part of him was enjoying the class's attention, he also wished he could have decided when and why the spotlight was shone on him. Because it was as if Mrs Gilchrist had put a hot beam of light on his face. It was too bright and unfair. She was too close. He couldn't see.

'Ma-mi Wa-ta,' he said, exactly as Mrs Gilchrist had done. Because what else could he do? 'Mami Wata,' he repeated.

'That's such a big help. It's so good to have an expert in the room, Kwame.' She frowned. 'Erm, Year 5, why is there silence? Give him a clap, boys and girls. Have you forgotten your manners?' More rainy applause. 'That's better.'

Kwame returned to the carpet and Mrs Gilchrist explained about the part-woman, part-fish goddess-creature who tempted sailors, brewed sea storms, could live on land and water; a witchy sorceress trickster who could bring good fortune and disaster as she pleased. A shape-shifter, she was woman one day, man the next, young one day, ancient the next – charming, then deadly in the blink of an eye. The sentences came from Mrs Gilchrist's mouth with wonder. She turned the book round to face the class, surprised them with bright pictures of a frightening thing with thick hair and shells covering her breasts, pointing a fork at angry seas. Much more powerful and scary than Ariel.

When Mrs Gilchrist said, 'Mami Wata' again, she gave him a quick, secret wink. The sizzle moved from his ear, down his neck, down his back.

Kwame turned to the clouds drifting between the sunflowers. One of them hadn't been stapled on properly. He stared at it. The wilting, waving thing flapped in the slight breeze. It would soon fall.

At the Parents' Evening in the Assembly Hall, when Mrs Gilchrist greeted his parents, she winked at Kwame again. As they took their seats, Mummy patted his shoulder twice; Daddy patted the other one, more stiffly. Mummy placed her handbag on her knees and clutched it, the position of her hands reminding Kwame of a cartoon dog begging for treats. But Mummy didn't seem like she was begging anyone for anything: she had changed out of her white uniform into a dark blue jacket with matching skirt and squarish shoes. Pink powder had been dusted across her cheeks and her lips had been slicked with a serious red. Daddy had done the same smartening-up. He was wearing a brown, scratchy blazer that looked like it was from olden times.

On Kwame's left, near where they had folded back the rainbow-coloured climbing frame, Jason Greig's parents were queuing up to see Mr Bell. They had decided grey Adidas tracksuits were appropriate for the important occasion of discussing Jason's schoolwork. Slightly dirty tracksuits, like they had rolled straight from sloppy pizzas on the sofa to the school, splotchy, almost like Yaw's had been that afternoon when he had been angry. Behind them, Lottie Wren's mum was in a black dress with knotty stitching and small mirrors on it. Nice, and a bit like some of the things Mrs Gilchrist wore in the summer term. But his parents had won the best and most correct outfit contest for sure.

Mrs Gilchrist shook out her fringe. 'Well, Mr and Mrs Akromah, what can I say? Kwame is our angel. He's sensible, *sensitive*, so polite – the dinner ladies are always banging on about his politeness.' Mrs Gilchrist pretended to be exhausted. 'And the children in our class adore him too. He's got a great, "can do" quality, and gives an excellent example of what good behaviour looks like to some of the less mature ones in the class. He's fab at his number work, wonderful at stories, loves art. A wonderful pupil. Aren't you, Kwame?'

Kwame nodded and sucked his lower lip. He so badly wished Mrs Gilchrist had a megaphone so everyone in the hall could hear.

'He is a credit to you.' She put her palms together. 'Thank you for bringing him to us.'

'Very kind,' Mummy said. 'We are proud of him, aren't we, Akwesi? We know our son he takes schooling very serious, isn't it, Akwesi?'

Kwame tapped his knees. His teacher's words were brilliant but also unsurprising. He knew he was a clever boy and working hard was important: Daddy said if you were Black you had to work four times harder than everyone else – which was true because racism still existed, even though Martin Luther King tried hard to make it stop – so Kwame put a lot of effort into being a clever boy, and Daddy said, if you put effort into things it pays you a dividend. The dividend was gold stars at the end of the week.

As Mrs Gilchrist went on about how super-splendid he was, as he had predicted she would, Kwame's bored and drifting mind came up with questions. The first was about what, exactly, made parenting difficult. Yaw had said it wasn't an easy game, but Kwame wasn't so sure. If you were a parent, you just had to go to your job from nine until five, then come home, cook dinner, be a bit nice, occasionally a bit strict; come up with weird but important rules about what you could say about Yaw and what you couldn't, who you could talk to about him and who you couldn't. You just had to keep on doing that sort of thing, the same tasks, day in day out, for infinity. Simple.

The second question was about why Daddy couldn't sit still. Kwame knew he was fidgeting a bit himself – rubbing at his knuckles, cracking them – because it's strange when people talk about you as if you aren't there. But what was Daddy's reason? As Daddy listened to Mrs Gilchrist with a cold frown, he kept patting the red hanky sticking out of his top pocket over and over again, as if scared it might disappear. Finally, Kwame wanted to know why tonight, whenever Mummy said Daddy's name, Mummy said it like it stung her or like she thought it the worst name ever known to humankind.

Because he was intuitive as well as being sensible and

polite, Kwame understood those questions were probably not the right things to ask and stayed quiet. To his left, Jason Greig's dad – a tiny head in a massive bomber jacket – was switching between listening to Mr Bell and glowering at Jason. Kwame smiled up at Daddy, hoping that might calm things, but Daddy was lifting up his hand to Mrs Gilchrist like the lollipop lady showing the cars who was boss.

'Okay, okay, but now for the business we have to attend. Where does my son fall in the class rank? First place? Or closer to the middle? Is he on track to perform well in these SATs examinations in years to come? Is this one here his exercise books?' Daddy pointed to the stack by Mrs Gilchrist. 'We will peruse them for our assurance.'

'A-kwe-si.' Mummy's jaw became stronger. 'The young woman is singing joys on your son and you won't let her continue? Only for the sake of test scores. Aden? You can't even do a "Thank you, Mrs Gilchrist, for the time you putting in to help our son"? You can't say that? Well, don't worry, I have done it for us now.'

Mummy folded her arms. Mrs Gilchrist played with her fringe. The backs of Kwame's knees heated up.

'Do be my absolute guest, Mr Akromah, and flick through his work. By all means.'

Scanning the pages as if he were searching for something hard to find, Daddy was like a detective. All he needed was a magnifying glass and one of those little hats.

'You'll see, Mr Akromah, that Kwame works very neatly. He also shows he has been listening to what we've discussed as a class, and his evaluations whenever we do an experiment are so thoughtful.' Mrs Gilchrist tapped at a worksheet. 'Here, we were learning about the water cycle.

Kwame's written about droughts and the need to be careful with water because it's –'

'Precious,' Kwame piped in.

'Right! Do you see, how nicely Kwame phrases it in his own words here?' She ran the chewed pink rubber on her pencil beneath his sentences for Daddy to follow.

'Yes, but –'

Trying to be funny, checking the space to the left and right of her chair as if making sure no one was eavesdropping, Mrs Gilchrist began to whisper. 'We don't really rank the kids at this school – it's not the done thing – but, between you and me, if I had to make a call I'd put Kwame at the top – across the board. Every subject. His literacy scores are particularly strong. It's –'

'Akwesi, you see, nothing to worry about.' Mummy's words came out too fast, as if too hot for her mouth; yam nibbled straight from the grill. It was all too hot. If Kwame had his way, when they got back to the flat he would slam doors like Akua did when Mummy and Daddy's rows were at their biggest and they wouldn't listen to her pleading. He would scream and shout at Mummy and Daddy for their behaviour; for their madness more horrible than Melodee's gloomsquirt hatred of love and her swearing; for not letting him collect his shiny praise in peace; praise for storing away until another time, when he needed it to make him feel brighter and better.

Nothing was shiny now, because they were behaving like crazy with their twisted expressions and jitteriness, and Mrs Gilchrist was trying to chuckle it off even though she was nearly drowning. He pressed the heels of his Clarks into the floor, wishing he could throw out a sentence to make everyone do real laughs. The kind of sentence Yaw could chuck to neighbours in the stairwell. But Kwame couldn't think of anything. Maybe he wasn't so smart after all.

'I know, we know,' Mummy was even faster now. 'My son, our son, is a good boy. We have no complaints and neither does this Mrs Gilchrist here. So is seeming all things are tickety-boo, isn't it, Mrs Gilchrist? And isn't it also that my husband is here taking all your invaluable time? My husband' – Mummy rotated her handbag in her lap, then clicked and unclicked it -- 'who is coming on like a big king and boss.'

'I am only showing a interest in the progress of my son. It's not criminal.'

'Is *how* you show an interest, Akwesi. *How* you –'

Mrs Gilchrist's clap – an explosion – shocked the three of them.

'On the whole, I think you can tell I'm jolly pleased with the poppet. I'm supposed to set silly targets but nothing for this chap here. Keep enjoying things, Kwame. Keep making the most of everything we're learning. Are you excited about starting on electricity next week? We're going to make remote-controlled toys – fun, eh?'

'Yes, miss. I've started reading ahead a bit. In our *Encyclopaedia Britannica*, about Thomas Edison. He sounds very interesting.'

'Good job, Kwame.' She spoke softly, like it was only the two of them in the hall. No posters about Comic Relief. No Lottie Wren's younger sisters running between the teachers' desks. No Malvinas struggling to translate Mr Plumstead's words into Polish for her mum and dad.

Mrs Gilchrist swivelled back to Mummy. 'My mind's like

a sieve. Honestly! Quick reminder about parental contributions for the Winter Show.'

'Parental what?' Daddy's frown deepened.

'We're not asking for much at all, really, and we're asking now – plenty of advance warning, and it's obviously optional – but what we want to do is to make some gorgeous costumes for the children, and' – Mrs Gilchrist passed them a letter – 'I'm sure you know that budgets for that sort of thing are tight around here, so we're asking for whatever, whatever parents might be able to offer. Big or small. Of course, we know some families aren't in that position . . . but we thought it best to ask everyone and see –'

'Of course, we will give a donation for the important cause. Donation of at least . . . seventy-five pounds.'

'Daddy!'

'Akwesi, we can't a–'

'Mr Akromah, that's very gen–'

Daddy's laugh was not his own. 'Is to support education, isn't it? So, seventy-five pounds. I will give Kwame a cheque. You've no need to be looking as shocked or sorry, Mrs Gilchrist. Is a promise. And thank you for your time, young lady.'

Daddy shook Mrs Gilchrist's hand firmly and then Mummy got up too. Her movements were slow: the folding of the letter, the clicking-open of her bag, dropping the square of paper into it, clicking it closed. It was as if, Kwame thought, she was saving her energy for something – or like she had no energy left.

When Kwame got home, he stopped in the doorway to the living room. The telly was on – *Fresh Prince of Bel Air*.

Carlton was doing the dance Kwame loved. On the sofa, Yaw had spread out his FUBU jacket and was fast asleep underneath it, exhausted after another shift at the car wash. Dark legs dangled over the sofa's arm. His toes were small. His mouth hung open and his eyelids flickered. What did he dream about?

'Leave him,' Mummy hissed to Kwame, taking off her coat, kicking off her loafers, making her way to the kitchen. But Kwame didn't leave him. He sat on the carpet, close to Yaw's head, so if anyone came in it might look like Kwame was watching the telly, enjoying Geoffrey quietly proving Uncle Phil wrong, yet again. But, instead, Kwame pressed mute on the remote control. He tilted his ear up towards Yaw's quiet breathing and listened.

May 2018

Usually, once the register was done, it took a matter of minutes to walk his tutor group, in single file, to morning assembly. But this Friday morning, this simple practice was slow. As they proceeded through the building, their voices rose. Kwame had to remind them they were supposed to travel to assembly in silence. From the head of the line, he kept turning to glare at them, pressing his finger to his lips. Guilty Brianne or Matt would seem humbled and, satisfied, Kwame would set off again. But, after a few paces, Brianne or Matt would resume their nonsense.

The imminence of the weekend – one set to be a scorcher! – might have explained the kids' restlessness. But, more than a little annoyed, Kwame also knew their excitement was because this was to be Marcus Felix's first address to the whole school. Each time Kwame stopped to hiss a vicious shush in the hope of calming his class, that shrill sound was, he had to admit, as much an instruction to his own curiosity as it was to theirs. After telling Brianne that another peep from her would earn an Infraction, Kwame imagined what it would be like to inspire the thrill Marcus Felix seemed to produce in others. He remembered how rapt and flushed and questioning Edwyn was, in the first term at Durham, when Kwame used to do his anthropological, educating-posh-white-minds thing, explaining Nollywood or his Saturday job at McDonald's. Edwyn

returned the favour and tried to reciprocate, with pontifi-
cations on *The Life of Brian* and tips for identifying different
species of woodland birds. Kwame remembered too how,
try as he might, he could never quite match Edwyn's heady
enthusiasm for this exchange of experiences.

Kwame let Brianne waggle her straw boater under Matt's
nose, let Matt snatch it away and refuse to give it back.

After entering the hall and depositing his crew, he saw
it wasn't only his lot who were agitated. All seven hundred students were yelping, fiddling with their ties, blazers,
regulation purple hijabs, singing that Nicki Minaj one
Hanna and Milo both loved. The hall teemed. At moments
like this, it was hard for Kwame to believe this new school
was still not yet at full capacity – two more years, two more
Year 7 intakes to go. Where would they all fit?

The dinner ladies, TAs, NQTs, secretaries, caretakers, and
Mrs Antwi and her Ghanaian assistants clogged the hall's
aisles too. Kwame stood on the edge of the fray as Head
of Maths and Deputy Head of English tutted on either
side of him. He could see, in the distance, a frenzied Natalie
confiscating a mobile from a Year 8. Head of Behaviour
clapped his hands, a call for order. It worked for three bliss-
ful seconds. Then a brave Year 7 blew a wet raspberry and
was escorted out by the new History teacher. Chatty chaos
reigned again.

The first few bars of Otis Redding's 'Sittin on the Dock
of the Bay' oozed out of the speakers without anyone noticing them. Kwame tuned into the familiar melody when the
voice told of leaving Georgia, heading for Frisco. The students fell into thoughtful whispering as the chorus opened
out once more. Marcus Felix strode across the stage with

footsteps that had, Kwame thought, both a tension and a liquid grace to them. The headteacher was in his shirt-sleeves, and wore a crooked smile. The shirt was fitted, cut close into his armpits, and Kwame could see the beginnings of moisture there. Marcus Felix's tie was a challenging neon green, singing out against the whiteness of the shirt and the darkness of the headteacher's forearms. He was not wearing socks, ankles fashionably exposed above polished brogues.

Marcus Felix lowered his right hand. Otis began to ease off.

'Gosh, I love that tune, folks.' Marcus Felix took in and held a breath, as if the essence of the song were a beautiful scent to be savoured. 'I know it sounds cringey as hell but, do you know what, SLA, I *am* a bit cringey. It's a tune that always calms me down – stills me and prepares me, no matter what. And, real talk guys, it seems like you lot need serenity today? Am I right? I could hear you down in my study! And I swear someone did a fart?' Pockets of un-certain sniggering sprang up across the hall before quickly dying down. 'I suppose, SLA, I wanted to play that song because I needed the mood to be a certain way for our discussion this morning. Because that's what it is, folks: this isn't a lecture, it's two-way, back and forth, me and you, right?'

He paced towards the lectern. Kwame was more than a little sceptical about Marcus Felix's intention for dialogue rather than showboating. But, as the headteacher contem-plated the lighting above the stage as though stargazing, Kwame found his arms falling back to his sides.

'There's a sadness about this song too. Otis is kinda

reflective, kinda bruised by life here. He's taking solace, I think, in the quietness of the world around him cos he's hurt, has been hurt.' He slapped the lectern. It wobbled. There was a new, overstimulated quality about Marcus Felix now. 'But that's not the thing I want you folks to be feeling. What I want you to be feeling is Otis's mellowness. That's the bit we need. The dreamy slowness of the water, the light playing on the water, and the breeze – and all that jazz. Are you feeling the mellowness, SLA?'

This was the kind of 'behaviour' Daddy would say was typical of West Indians – ostentatious, undignified, loud-mouth foolishness. Kwame tried to get Natalie's attention, wanted to test his own ambivalence against whatever reaction she might offer him. But, like most of the others in the hall, Natalie's gaze was on the stage.

Marcus Felix pressed a clicker, and a stock picture of some sliced tomatoes appeared on the screen behind him. 'Yeah, so, item number one. There it is. Any tomato fans up in here?' Eager-to-please form captains shot up their hands. The Year 12 stoner crew slid further down into their seats. Ahmed folded his arms more tightly. 'They love them up in Biology. I confess, I'm not a science man – Business Studies is my thing – so when I went to see a Year 8 class on pollination in the Curie Labs last week, I was out of my depth. Organelles this, carpels that . . . Then I noticed these two boys' – the headteacher checked his notes – 'Abdul and Kean. SLA, the way Abdul and Kean looked after their tomato plants, tended to them with such care. Abdul even spoke to the plants a bit –' The stoner crew thought that was hilarious. DaeQuan and his mandem giggled behind lapels. Marcus Felix's jaw hardened. Without looking behind himself, Marcus Felix took three steps away from the lectern. He stood tall in the shadows at the back of the stage. He waited for a good minute and a half. Kwame stared at the tie, that alarming lime line, until it made his eyes blur. The disturbance in the audience stopped. Marcus Felix approached the lectern again, his jaw loosening with each thud of his brogues. 'As I was *saying*, Abdul and Kean chatted to wilting leaves, gave them words of encouragement. And I was humbled. There is something beautiful about seeing young people nurse fragile things into life with such attention.'

Yaw had done exactly that to Kwame, when he was younger. Nursed – or, maybe, nursed and nurtured him when he had felt that things inside and outside of his tiny body might pull him apart. And Yaw had done it all so effortlessly. Maybe hadn't even known he was doing it. With a bow tie; with a talk and a walk to the library; with a single, pure look.

The headteacher clicked his clicker. A rudimentary Clip Art picture of a knife and fork flashed up. 'Yeah, sorry about the visuals on this one, folks; not my finest hour, I was running short on time, what can I say? But this is about something I saw in the canteen, at the beginning of the week. Listen, I've not been at this school for long, but I've already learned that the puddings in the canteen are *next* level. Hold up, can we give a round of applause to my peoples in the kitchens? They're up in the house today. Let's show them love. Clap, guys!' The dinner ladies did awkward waves. 'Yes! Lap it up, Mrs Gutierrez! Lap it up, girl, you deserve that glory! Yes! Anyway, top of the list of top puddings has got to be the apple pie, right?' The hall debated the claim. Because there was the cherry pie to consider, the baked Alaska, the passionfruit cheesecake – not to mention Kwame's favourite, sticky toffee pudding. 'I was queuing to get my lunch. Ahead of me were two Year 12s. A girl, a boy. Think they'd been at Athletics; they were still in their kits. The boy was given the last slice of apple pie. I could see that they'd both wanted it; the girl's face went all long and disappointed. Without batting an eyelid, that boy – a generous soul, man – split it in half, passed it to her. Wasn't asked to do it, no expectation. And his friend gave him the biggest smile, which, I'm telling you, made my heart levitate.'

Kwame watched Nosheen clutch her hands to her chest. Two rows behind, Princess did something similar.

Marcus Felix pushed the clicker again to produce a smattering of pixelated hexagons. They came together to form an image of a paintbrush. 'You love my special effects, am I right?' No response. 'You'll be pleased to know this is the last one: a symbol representing what I saw in the Art Studio. I nearly wept, SLA.'

Again, DaeQuan and his mandem couldn't contain themselves. Head of Behaviour pointed at them.

'Yeah. I nearly wept, lads. I can admit.' Marcus Felix scratched his ear. 'So Candeece was about to finish the most beautiful still life of a vase, a pile of lemons and some bay leaves. The thing looked so real. Amazing. The missus would have loved it in our front room. I asked Mr Munroe about it, and he told me Candeece had been working on it for weeks. Folks, you could see the effort. The detail. The colours, man.' He did a chef's kiss. 'And – it makes me queasy remembering – as she was putting in the final touches, she turned to get rid of a stupid fly' – Marcus

Felix struck the lectern, and the whole school gasped – 'and she knocked a big ol jar of water right over the piece. Everywhere. I mean, *all over the canvas.*'

Marcus Felix buried his head in his hands. He held it there for a second. Kwame wondered whether, within that dark grip, the headteacher's eyes were opened or closed. This was the difficulty: working out if this were all clever contrivance or total sincerity – a man expressing his truth with admirable expansiveness. The headteacher looked up again, his golden irises aglow. 'But people stepped in *immediately*. Hugs, students coming with tissues, clearing up. People helping Candeece find her old sketches, showing how she might be able to do a new one faster than she'd think. Some of them suggesting how she could even make a virtue of the water-damaged places, sort of make lemonade from lemons' – he winked – 'do a collage, or something' – Marcus Felix consulted his notes again – 'mixed media? And Candeece, bless the child, started off all crestfallen, but within five minutes my girl had dusted herself off and was telling Titus that even though her painting was mash up it was still fifteen times better than his.'

Most of the school – staff, students and, Kwame could see, Candeece and Titus too – erupted into warm laughter. The headteacher stepped to the side of the lectern. He was, as far as Kwame could tell, very pleased with the progress and reception of his performance.

'Point is, when you guys are crashing about the place or you're mucking about in the Common Room or what have you, the default way so many of you behave with one another is hardness. I've seen it. I can see it in this hall even now. Body language speaks loud. And that's what a lot of people think about you in the local area too, you know. That you're tough. Fancy uniforms but hard as nails. Your jokes – I hear them, when you're in the corridors. All eye rolling and cynicism, right? I reckon it's how many of you perceive yourself. Not to be messed with, yeah? I get it. But hardness ain't everything. Folks, the opposite is so much more important. It's your softness that matters. Tenderness, softness' – he bounced on the spot – 'call it whatever. The kinds of gentleness I've been talking to you about on this sunny morning, SLA. That stuff is radical. It is what the old folks out there think you're incapable of, but it's the glue of your community, holds it together. And you do it loads. Quietly. When you think no one's watching, you stop speaking with your chest and take the time to care, SLA. You need to cherish that softness. It will save you in your bleakest hour.'

Someone in the audience muttered, 'It's not that deep, fam, *allow.*' Kwame turned towards the sound. The sentence left no trace.

Marcus Felix was unperturbed, scratched his ear again, took his time. 'SLA, let's be real. We know the reason I'm here. I didn't rock up out of thin air. I'm here because of what happened to Madame Evans. I'm here because this community has suffered the most enormous shock. Maybe it's difficult to admit, to say out loud, but that's what's going on. Something has shaken your foundations, SLA. For the time being, your strongest champion, your pillar, is out of action. She cannot carry you. I bet you lot have got a million and one different things to say about Madame Evans and her way – but one thing is true: she has always got your back, repps this school. 24/7. But she can't do that right

199

now, so here I am. And change isn't easy. This, I know, is a scary moment – and it's a sad one too. So if *now* isn't the time to be gentle with one another, to listen to and care for one another, to let down your guards, then, folks' – Kwame was sure that Marcus Felix was about to turn his body in his direction – 'I don't know *when* that time is.'

To avoid walking straight through their heated conversation about the 'People's Vote', Kwame weaved around the smokers by the Bedford. A group of men polished their Ray-Bans and women in slit skirts clasped Aperol spritzes. The tallest man shouted that, deep down, they knew they'd all be fine either way – in or out, transition period or none. He took another drag on his fag. When the oldest man told them to 'calm down, calm down' in a bad Scouse accent, they broke into cackles that startled Kwame.

He almost felt a pang of regret as he turned on to Fernlea. He too could have been out, chatting slurred shit at Friday-night drinks, basking in a beer garden. Natalie and Barbara the TA had wanted him to come to the Windmill for a quick one – Natalie could not face the prospect of going back to hers for more passive aggression or good old-fashioned aggressive aggression from her lodger. Kwame had said no, done a pouty apology, claimed he had other stuff on.

The problem was that the prospect of sitting slumped on the Windmill's decking for yet more analysis of Marcus Felix and his assembly did not appeal. It had already dominated the school day. There had been Mrs Antwi's passing comment at break time about how Kwame must be so motivated to succeed now the school had its own Obama. And, by the water fountains, Malachi bounding over to

Kwame to share his annoying comparison: 'There's something kinda the same about you and Mr F – do you get me? Not cos you're both Black, I ain't that bait, sir. It's something . . . deeper. Like how you both hold yourself up proper, expect the same from us – something like that?' And Kwame had had to do a theatrical 'telling-off cough' when he overheard Melissa Ng from Year 12 chatting near the Data Hub, going on about licking Marcus Felix's head like a scoop of chocolate ice cream, asserting he was at least ten times fitter than Idris Elba. There had been Deputy Head of English's question at the departmental lunch: why was it, she asked, that the *only* English lesson the headteacher had chosen to observe was Kwame's? Not that she had wanted to be observed herself, she was at pains to say as she wiped ketchup from the corner of her mouth, she was just interested in the headteacher's choice. And, at afternoon break in the staff room, there was no bemoaning the woeful lack of Jammie Dodgers in the biscuit tin. Instead, there was the thrum of conversation about the power of the new head-teacher's personality, and the new headteacher's exciting, undeniable capacity to bring about real transformation – as if power and transformation were always unequivocally good things. Just like Mummy had said when Akua had complained about not getting an allowance as big as her mates', the scratched record needed changing.

'I'll help you with those, don't worry,' Kwame said to the Asian woman labouring up the steps to the flat's letterbox. The droopy leaflets for plumbers in her hands seemed as spent as the woman herself. She scanned Kwame up and down, looked at the smart front door and its big lion's head knocker, then turned towards Hanna's windows to assess the smart shutters and the window boxes overflowing with silvery ornamental grasses. She looked at Kwame again. Kwame smiled and beckoned towards the leaflets until she passed a few over. She descended the stairs, shuffling sideways, down to the pavement.

Sinking to his knees, even more uncomfortably hot now, Kwame placed the flyers to one side and rummaged in his busy rucksack for a couple of minutes, trying to find his keys. He muttered remonstrations at himself and his disorganization. When Kwame retrieved them, he was surprised to see the woman waiting at the bottom of the steps, watching. Kwame waved. She nodded, then moved towards 28, but she kept looking back at Kwame after every step she took. In the communal passageway, Kwame rolled his shoulders, rolled away the sour persistence of that staring, and whatever judgements and misjudgements the woman might have made about him. He would not let those things within him. He would not be bound by that familiar, coldly questioning appraisal.

He leafed through the post and separated out his letters, then Edwyn's. Putting Hanna's envelopes on the sideboard, he let his focus drift towards the Tuke. It fell on the young man's arse. Today, the gap between the boy pressed into the corner of the painting and the young man at the heart of the image – imperious nymph, rising out of the shallows – seemed even more unbridgeable than usual. As austere and still as the central figure was, motion was hinted: he was about to wrap a mauve towel around himself, hiding his bum from view, keeping it all to himself.

To a certain extent, Edwyn's chatting about Kwame's Grindr abstinence during the Easter break had been accurate. Edwyn's championing of Kyle, the *This Morning* runner, was understandable too: it had been ages since Kwame had had a good fuck, been held close, felt the soothing power of intimacy. It had been ages since the biting of his lower lip had made the veins in his temples twitch. Ages since he had seen his fingers do things to his lover's shaft that made their moans harden. Too long since he had squeezed out lube overenthusiastically and it had squirted everywhere, the mess childishly funny. Too long since a lover had bowed forward, and Kwame had guided a waist back towards his own body. Too long since a rhythm was found: a bum bashing back into Kwame's groin, and all the sweat, spit and precum meant that skin on skin made a triumphant slap of sound. Absolutely fucking ages since that wild, final push, that dark and bright instant in which Kwame was clear-sighted and shorn of artifice, utterly present in the tension and strength of his sweating, breathing body. Climbing the stairs, pulling off his maroon lanyard, Kwame only wanted that kind of abandon.

November 1997

Holding his mug of hot Ribena, Yaw's Twi whizzed past Kwame's ears like swooping birds – Si-ka, Ob-or-uni, A-juma. Yaw's voice sounded younger, slipperier than when it spoke English – going high and then low in a flash. The sounds vibrated the air of Yaw's – Akua's – tiny box room, and Kwame imagined the stream of words being strong enough to frighten the daisies on the wallpaper, send them running for safety, up high to cobweb-covered corners.

Kwame knew a few Twi words: sometimes, when Mummy was cooking, Daddy would sit him and Akua in the living room, say it was important to know their culture, make them chant basic phrases that showed respect, especially to elders – Yaa agya, Yaa ɛna, things like that. But the pronunciation was often really hard, even though Daddy tried his best to show them. So Kwame definitely couldn't call himself an expert – which was a bit annoying and he hoped one day he would win that prize.

For now, Kwame blew on his steaming drink and decided he would not ask Yaw for a translation of his words, even though he wanted to know. Because what Yaw was saying might be private – for only Yaw and his father to share. He knew some things had to be private.

Da-yie-ye.

Yaw pressed STOP on the cassette player. The tail of his durag fell forward.

'Ready when you are, Lil' G.'

Kwame sipped his drink, enjoyed its gentle burn moving into his stomach.

Last night at dinner, Daddy had said that in the eighties he too used to record long speeches – about the buses, Brixton rioting, Tottenham rioting, church, Balham Market, Les Dawson – that he sent to family Back Home. The family preferred them to short and expensive phone conversations on crackly lines that cut out at the worst time. Kwame had wondered if the family weren't frustrated they couldn't interrupt to ask the recorded voice questions. Weren't they irritated that things couldn't flow back and forth?

Yaw's hands beckoned. 'Come on, Lil' G. Or have you changed your mind?'

'No, it's –'

Kwame rested the mug on the bedside table. He thought the daisies' petals might fold in on themselves, covering their golden centres, as if they wanted to hide like he did. He was annoyed with himself for hesitating. It was great that Yaw had asked him to be part of this recording for his dad, but now confusion, no, sadness held him back.

'I hope you –' Kwame began, his fingers struggling with the waistband of his drawstring trousers. 'No offence, but aren't you upset or ashamed your father can't read well? Isn't that undignified? Sorry. Because that's why we're doing it, right? You can't send letters because he's an illiterate?'

'*Undignified?*' Yaw laughed like a villain and flopped into his – Akua's – desk chair.

'Undignified' was maybe too strong and might make Yaw force him out of the door and into the passageway. But, blinking, Kwame also knew 'undignified' was the right word. It meant not proper, not right. Mummy muttered it at the Arndale Centre in Wandsworth when white boys with pale skin and red spots spat their chewing gum on to the floor. Daddy whispered it if drivers zoomed by, not stopping to let pensioner ladies pick their way over zebra crossings.

'Tell me, if you hadn't got your all-singin, all-dancin "Consider Yourself" solo, how do you think you woulda reacted?'

'Why?'

'Humour me.' Yaw cocked his head to one side. The earrings flashed. He looked a bit funny, but his face was still like something carved from wood and as special and valuable as precious stones. 'Go on. What would you have done?' The question made a widening feeling in Kwame's tummy. A sort of growing emptiness pushing at his sides. 'I'll tell you what I'm thinking you woulda done, Lil' G: you woulda cried your teeny heart out like a teeny girl. Right?'

'No. Don't –'

'You would! Come on, les be real. Big time bawlin.'

Yaw's words zapped a film into Kwame's brain; Kwame tearing up the cast list, tears winding down from his sore eyes.

'Would that be a *dignified* way to carry on, Lil' G?'

'That's got nothing to do with anything. You're being mean because I said a thing that is hurtful about your father, and I regret that and I am sorry for it. Now you're lashing out. It's not fair.'

'Do I seem' – Yaw leaned back in the chair, pretended to smoke a cigarette and spun around – 'like I'm *lashing* anything?'

'Couldn't you have taught him? Like, every night, by lovely candlelight? Read to him from the Abridged Shakespeare like we had in Year 3? Done a quiz with him after each page to see how much he understood? You could have done it until the words slipped into his mind.'

'My papa can't be taught nothing. He's a big old dude, bro. Those guys ain't about listenin and learnin, those bros *do*. Check it: readin and writin and all that is great. No doubt about it. I love my comics, damn straight you knows I do. Sabretooth is killer, and my man Doc Samson ain't playin. And your ma, your pa, they're so pleased you're coming on like some kind of Einstein. God willing, you gonna use your fat brain to do something special.'

Kwame scratched the back of his neck.

'But, my friend, you gotta know: there are seventeen different ways of skinning a cat.'

'What?'

'I think that's it – Haroun at work says it all the time. Is meaning there's more than one path.'

'Okay.'

'So' – Yaw leaped forward, tapped Kwame's temples – 'because of what's in your headpiece, you'll live your life and get by, get me? My papa, his people were different. Tough. They scratch the land to make a living, boy. Growing coco-yam, plantain. Selling it so they could make a little to eat. Ain't nobody got no time for fooling with your algebra and subordinate clauses.'

'I know all about those, we did –'

'If you've gotta put food in the crying mouths, your headpiece gotta be outta dem books.' He wrinkled his nose. 'So what if my papa wasn't well schooled? He has always worked hard. That matters. Went from the small family farm to the city. Atonsu, you remember?'

Kwame nodded.

'Now he helps build roads, fills in potholes, has the gym I told you about. Saved enough to get my Black ass on a plane from Kotoka and get my papers made up – even if they ain't the straightest around.'

'What's not straight about your papers?'

'Ain't that somethin? Ain't all them efforts somethin? Ain't that *dignified*?'

What Kwame wanted to do next was to crack his knuckles, to make the silence less strange and make himself less embarrassed and defeated. But Yaw hated it when he did that, so Kwame watched Yaw instead: Yaw slid his fingers into and around the edge of the durag. Eventually the thing slumped, Yaw took it off and smoothed it across his lap.

After swigging the last of the Ribena from the mug, Kwame walked over to the cassette player, eyeing it like it was a bomb.

'Lil' G, remember, your chat don't need to be long or nothin. He can't really speak English, so don't sweat it. He just wanna know what you sound like. Cool?'

'Cool.' Kwame pushed in his lower lip. 'Press RECORD, then!'

'Do it yourself! You got working hands.'

Kwame found the red button. He coughed. The tape's two wheels whirred, went round and round, the bigger collecting even more ribbon, the smaller one giving it away.

'Hello.' The word sounded bumpy so he tried again, this time seeing his voice as a muscly black arm stretching up – a black arm topped by a powerful fist, like the ones on Yaw's Afro combs. 'Hello, Yaw's dad. How are you? It is a pleasure and delight to meet and speak with you. Maybe Yaw has mentioned me. In case he didn't fully, I will say one or two things about myself before properly starting. My name is Kwame Aboagye Akromah. I am ten and live in Tooting. I go to Thrale School. I have a sister called Akua, a mummy and a daddy. We don't have any pets, because Mummy refuses to buy a thing that will mean more chores for her. If we *were* allowed to have a pet, I would opt for a rabbit.' A light on the top of the recorder blinked. Kwame checked with Yaw that it was all right to continue. Yaw nodded. 'So, yes, a rabbit. Even though they have red eyes like Hell and the Devil, I like how their noses twitch and how they seem quite frightened of everything, because caring for something needy and making it less scared would give you a warm feeling, I think. I would feed the rabbit old leaves. I would call him Lumiere, after one of my favourite characters from Disney's *Beauty and the Beast*. Lumiere is great because he has some good attributes – he is sensible and loyal and sophisticated. That's all the big stuff you need to know –' Kwame was distracted by Yaw's muffled laugh. He pressed PAUSE.

'Erm, Yaw, if you don't want to take this seriously, I would be quite grateful and appreciate it if you could wait downstairs.'

Yaw did a mime of zipping his lips together. His dimples were deep.

'Thank you.'

Kwame pressed the red button again.

'So I didn't get to say something today. I mean, that

doesn't make sense. I mean, we were doing a wedding at school. A pretend wedding, in the playground. Reece Campbell forced it to happen, because he had seen Lottie Wren and Simon Richardson holding hands, so the law is they have to be in holy matrimony now. So we did a wedding for them near the hopscotch. There was a good choir and it was actually quite nice and Reece seemed very happy with how his plan was coming together, even though everyone only agreed to do it out of fear, obviously, so you could see some of the Year 2 choir people shaking in their boots, because Reece kept saying their singing had better be perfect. Reece chose me – me! – to lead the ceremony because he said I had the right way to be a believable priest. I was supposed to lead the ceremony, and I did for a bit. Like, I helped Lottie and Simon do their forced vows and the rings. But I never got the chance to do my proper sermon in full because the bell went before I could. And it would have been *so good*.' Kwame sniffed. 'I still want to say the sermon speech, so I'm going to. I would have done something along the lines of this. A bit like Mr Plumstead but a bit better. Don't tell him that.'

Kwame filled his chest with another big breath and let it out in a whoosh.

'Dearest and beloved. We are gathered to bring together this young woman, this young man. There are quite a few sad things in the world – like dropping litter and Gerry Adams and bullying – and so it's nice to remember good things can still happen. And what is better than two friends showing they have decided each other are the best? What is better than two friends wanting the world to know how special they think one another are? What is better than their saying they will look after each other, always and forever? That is what Simon and Lottie are doing today.'

Kwame pressed PAUSE.

'Damn, dawg.'

'Is something wrong?' He found that he was smiling. 'I enjoyed that.'

'I could tell. All free flowing and freestyling.'

'Not really.'

'What?'

'It wasn't freestyling. I was trying to remember what Mrs Gilchrist told us about how to use repetition and questions in speeches, because they're effective.'

'What she mean, *effective*?'

'I'm not sure but I think it means the words put emotions into your heart.' He searched the wallpaper again, thought the daisies were moving from side to side. 'But I might be wrong. I'll double-check with her tomorrow and then I can let –'

'Nah.' With one hand, Yaw folded the durag into a square. He brought the thumb and index finger of the other hand together, to make a loose *o*. He shoved the durag through the hole, pulled it out the other side with a tug. 'Is cool, Lil' G. What you explain sounds right. Even if it ain't, it sound nice, how you've put it. Sometimes that's enough. You dig?'

May 2018

Kwame stretched his legs and placed his copy of *Tess* on the essays to act as a paperweight. His movements seemed to trigger Edwyn's shifting too. Edwyn unpeeled grass impressed into his ribcage, a ribcage now expanding as Edwyn inhaled, long and full. 'All gay life is welcome here!' he exclaimed, opening his arms – wide, victorious – before stealing the last of Kwame's raspberries and returning to his phone.

All gay life is welcome here?

Throughout Clapham Common – Poofters' Paradise, as he and Edwyn sometimes called it – there was certainly *a lot* of gay life on display. It was Grindr Live, InstaGays in 3D. Scattered groups loudly discussed rope play and dark rooms here, ranked Penélope Cruz's performances there, popped sparkling rosé elsewhere. 'Yes Sir, I Can Boogie' rang out of someone's speakers.

The most ostentatious specimens were near the fountain, five men in backwards caps freeing themselves of T-shirts, vaping. Kwame noted the detail of their bodies – this one's shoulders almost as broad as Marcus Felix's, that one's juicy calves. He remembered how he had felt in front of the Tuke yesterday . . . he could just send Andrew a little hello text . . . There was an ancient pic of Kwame in only a jockstrap that tended to make Andrew spring into communicative action . . . He watched others settling in now: by the footpath, a group with tight fades dropped Whole Foods bags, moved aside nitrous canisters, negotiated with their French bulldogs and unfolded a tartan picnic rug. Nearer his and Edwyn's spot, blonds with neon bumbags were furnishing each other with Pimm's and complaining about the excess of cucumber in the jug. And, of course, everyone was checking everyone out with flicked glances or sometimes prolonged stares: a square-jawed jogger slackened his pace, tried to catch Edwyn's eye. Kwame looked at the raspberry punnet, then at clouds inching across the sky. He blinked in the sunlight.

All gay life?

The glib phrase made him angry and, despite himself, through the ambient chatter, Marcus Felix's recent provocations webbed in his mind. Kwame was again thinking about the openness the headteacher had encouraged him to find in the classroom, wondered what openness might do to him and for him – then and there. Give a release from anger, offer a peace to ease the feeling hotly climbing through him now?

Edwyn was reaching into Phyllida's old Fortnum's icebox, pulling out the artisanal lemonade he'd been sent by a supplier hoping for a shoutout on *This Morning*. 'Yes Sir' became Kylie's 'Slow'. Kwame sat up, made himself speak.

'It's not true, though. Is it?'

'What?'

'Not *all* gay life is here. Is it? Not fully represented, anyway. Probably not all that welcome either.'

'Eh?'

'I'm the only brown person around, aren't I?'

A rosiness took over Edwyn's cheeks. He drank, handed Kwame a cup too. 'I suppose you are.'

'It's not a wildly unusual situation for me to be in – you know, the whole "only Black in the village" thing – but I notice it. Often. And it's *worth* noticing.'

'Of course. Right.'

'My experience of these places is *really* different to yours.'

There was a childlike quality to Edwyn's confusion now. 'Are you saying that, like, your experience of this place, is . . . is compromised?' He stood, wiped grass from his shins this time. 'Because we can leave, Kwame. Stat. That's not a problem at all.'

Kwame gestured for him to sit. Why should he go anywhere?

'These things deserve underlining, Edwyn, that's all: because you're surrounded by your own, you're here in a way that's different from me. You can . . . show up differently. You can . . . immerse yourself in it more easily.'

'Immerse myself in what, exactly?' Edwyn shook out his headphones, his giggle hesitant and strange. 'I was mostly immersed in my podcast. Prescott got me on to this one. Today, Fearne Cotton is teaching me about how Primal Scream Therapy is making a comeback.' But then Edwyn quietened his silly chatter. He clutched his friend's knee and Kwame was certain it was fear intensifying that grip and making Edwyn lean in closer. 'I, I hear what you're saying. I do. I'm being facetious and shit, because I'm a pathetic dick who can't abide conflict. It's utterly pathetic. I'm pathetic. You're right.'

Behind Kwame and Edwyn, the slimmest blond recalled the last time 'Seth' was going through a break-up: *that* night with the plate-smashing. Wind harassed the essays. The whole Common kept on rippling with life and ease, but

Kwame and Edwyn's tiny patch was an island within it all, the two of them in a doleful silence, Edwyn's green eyes getting bleaker and darker.

'Kwame?'

Always these glimpses of Edwyn's vulnerability, this hinting at his weakness and pain – exactly what happened every pissed time at the Marjoram – could not be borne by Kwame. Because – it was so shameful, the old understanding rising now – Kwame accepted *he* could manage discomfort, could curl beneath duvets or press his heels into the ground. But his friend – veins on his forehead so marked now – his friend just could not.

There was a sensation, a rattling or stirring, under his diaphragm; the body's last attempts to hold on to resolve. Bands of grass pollen dropped through the air: diffuse dots colliding, then running away from each other.

'You're not a dick. And you're not pathetic. I just. Reckon you could be a bit more . . . self-reflective?' Kwame waited as Edwyn considered his arm seriously, pressed the pine-cone tattoo. 'It's annoying. You're even more handsome when you're being all solemn.'

The change was dartingly quick: Edwyn flashing a mischievous smile, the rapid-fire batting of eyelashes. 'Perve. Complete perve. I don't know if you're aware, but I'm seeing someone, so these sorts of advances are actually quite inappropriate?'

'Fuck off.'

'Prescott's a decent guy and considers you a friend, so the fact that you're cracking on to me is bang out of order.'

'If I *deigned* to lay my moves on you, you wouldn't be able to resist. Facts are facts. Don't make me have to remind you about Verity's, if you want to talk about unwanted advances –'

'Prescott's very territorial, so I'd watch out if I were you. You should see what he benches.'

'Oh, don't use fucking gym language like you understand it. So embarrassing, Wyn, seriously.'

A spliff scented the air, and Kwame tried to sink into the relief his friend was enjoying, relief they were back to their galvanizing playing. The rattling within had not entirely lessened, but it was different. Resembled ticking more. A clock steadily counting down, Kwame thought. But he just flexed his arms, kissed the little left bicep. 'Anyway I could take out that massive Canadian meathead if I wanted. No prob. Don't underestimate.'

'The thought of you and Prescott locked in combat is totally absurd.'

'If push came to –'

'You *care*, Kwame. That's your entire and full vibe: care.'

'You'd bloody love it. Me and Prescott fighting over you is your literal idea of heaven.'

Edwyn scrabbled in the icebox again. 'Am I that transparent?'

November 1997

If Mummy goes to Saturday-night prayers at His Luminous Salvation in Mitcham, Uncle Ernest comes round to the flat. Kwame knows the routine for this so well: by the doorway, he says hello to this saggy Uncle man who isn't really related to him and offers to take his coat. Uncle picks Kwame up by the waist and shakes him like David Siddon did to a can of Coke when he wanted it to explode in Simon Richardson's face. Daddy tells his friend how proud he is of his growing little prince. Uncle Ernest agrees that, yes, the boy is growing paaaaaaaaaaa. Then Kwame is banned from downstairs and must stay in his bedroom. There, he is meant to read Roald Dahl and change into his pyjamas. Lights out at eight thirty on the dot.

On this particular Saturday evening, Kwame didn't want to do that. Those were such boring instructions. He had followed them so many times and had got no thanks, well done or anything. The idea of rehearsing 'Consider Yourself' again to pass the time – performing to his reflection in the bathroom mirror, using the container for Yaw's Versace Blue Jeans as a microphone – seemed too sad. Yaw was out, 'chillin with his bros', so Kwame couldn't even knock on Yaw's door and watch him play with the Sega he'd borrowed from Marcel.

About half an hour after Uncle and Daddy locked themselves into the kitchen and started playing their African

CDs, Kwame padded back down the stairs. He moved with exaggerated carefulness, shuffling along the corridor with the smell of Mummy's corned-beef stew getting stronger the closer he got to the men's secret den. Eventually, he sat on the floor by the door with his legs up so that the fly-kicking Power Rangers on his pyjama bottoms were pressed against his face.

Blinking slowly, he heard one of the men scrape a chair across the lino.

'Aboa! Stinking scoundrel! That Maria Frimpong from JSS1 was my first and biggest love. *Big*-gest. We were a rock solid. Like a Winnie and Nelson.' Kwame heard clicking. 'And you, you now telling me she had a love for you also. Same time as me? Wo boa. Rewriting a history book as a fan-ta-sy.'

'Truth hurts, saaaaaaa? What can I tell you, Ernest? In those days, I was a dapper. The ladies' man. My apologies for your tears.'

'My eye is drier than your foot.'

'Ah ah! I use a very good baby lotion on my foot. Is the wife's – εyε fo o! Only ninety-nine pence and the bottle is quite large.'

'Maybe I should use some also.' Uncle Ernest kissed his teeth. Something softly hit the floor. 'Perhaps it can help on these bunions.'

'Come on, put that crusty thing away. Is a cooking and eating place that we sit in. You bring contamination with this, your diseased elephant's hoof! Ewurade!'

'Elephant!'

'Elephant!'

There was clapping, laughing, chair-scraping again. Then silence.

'And the boy? This Yaw. Settling well, is he? Eh? Not too much nosy nosy at the, the –'

'Car wash. We found him something in a car wash. Local. There are many like Yaw there, and you know, everything cash in hand and under table and this sort of thing. So the papers he has no one has cared to look too close or question too much. No problems, no questions, and we thank God.'

'Yes, we thank God.'

Kwame wanted to know how there could be many like Yaw, when he, Yaw, was obviously one in a million, but then the music became lots of exciting trumpets, showing off. Kwame rubbed a thinning patch of carpet, pulled up a loose, red fibre, rolled it between his thumb and forefinger.

'Ey! You remember this one?' Daddy sounded silly and overexcited. 'One of my very favourites.'

'Is a nice one.'

'So good, yes.'

'Always bringing a chill to the spine, this one. Is very nice.'

'Very nice.'

Kwame yawned, made sure to keep it quiet. He pressed his feet against the whiteness of the skirting board. Could watery Mami Wata make herself invisible? If he could make himself invisible, he'd walk into the kitchen so he could check the men's faces, because Daddy's tone had become stiff. Kwame wondered if, underneath it all, they wanted to call the song 'beautiful' rather than nice. Mrs Gilchrist said nice didn't mean anything so not to use it for creative writing.

The problem was, he imagined, Daddy and Uncle could never use the word 'beautiful', because it would be too gentle

for them. Often the things people considered beautiful –
like the friendship bracelets Lottie Wren and Ivy Nelson
wore, or the flouncy dress for the angel on the Christmas
tree at Tooting Library, made by Mrs Farooqi – those things
were designed for girls, women. Kwame cracked one thumb
knuckle, then the other. Who made the rule that forced
men to be excited only about hard lines, shouts, winning
and knocking over piles of blocks? It wasn't fair men
weren't allowed to properly enjoy beautiful stuff – like the
bright dinosaur collage he had made with Yaw. Or how,
when Yaw bit his fingernails while they were watching telly,
he would arrange the white crescents into patterns. Or
how snails' antennae get shy and hide if you touch them.
Kwame's eyes followed the grooves in the doorframe's
wood. He perhaps half understood why, when Mrs Gilchrist
called him sensitive at the Parents' Evening, she had said
it a bit weirdly. And Mummy and Daddy probably weren't
interested in hearing him being described like that, because
it wasn't good or usual for a man or boy to be that way.
And that's why Mummy and Daddy had behaved funnily.
But how could he change who he was to be right?

Kwame yawned again.

'Our Ebo Taylor sounds,' Daddy said, 'better than the
best.'

'Ampa. You can't deny. He is very good.'

Last year, Mrs Gilchrist showed them the sari fabric she
was going to use for the Diwali assembly – deep purple and
all edged in gold spikes, speckled with big stars, tiny stars.
Mrs Gilchrist had turned the fabric this way and then the
other. It shimmered. Lots of the boys didn't care and said
the word 'chapati' into their cuffs. Mrs Gilchrist focused on

the girls, who begged to touch it. Touching wasn't enough. Kwame had wanted to breathe the fabric in, so it became part of him so he would glow too.

It always seemed like you could hang on to beauty only for a second before it disappeared. The birthday cake Anna Mathers's mother baked for the whole class – hundreds of layers, with green icing and delicate flowers – was admired for a minute before it was murdered, sliced into thirty sections. The glittery nail varnish Mummy wore to her work Christmas party was chipped by Christmas Eve. After Mrs Gilchrist had talked about the sari fabric it was soon folded up, put in the dressing-up box and everyone had to start Tidy-up Time.

Kwame turned his attention up to the ceiling, to the spooky cracks near the Pay-as-You-Go electricity meter, up between the doorframe and the wall. Daddy and Uncle were play-arguing a bit more, and there was some sloshing.

'Ernest, Aba! She won't be pleased to see us drinking as much as this. She always calling you a bad influence. Mma no adanse pii.'

'So you are under a thumb? A pussy, pussy, pussy cat? Eh? I should stop speaking the Queen's English to you now, eh? Akwesi? I should only miaow, miaow, miaow for a pussycat.'

'Er-nest.'

'You have called my name in this serious voice for what?'

There was more pouring. Kwame blinked slowly again.

'Cheers.'

'Cheers.'

Kwame started thinking about pussycats miaowing and using their tiny paws to push at a tall wall. A picture came to him: Daddy and Uncle Ernest but with the faces of pussycats. Ginger ones. And they were laughing and miaowing and ignoring all the clumsy elephants marching around them. They pushed at a tall wall. They pushed at a tall wall and their tiny paws were stronger than they looked: soon many cracks appeared across the bricks like the cracks across the ceiling and the kittens tried to push their heads through the breaking gaps. The cracks got bigger and bigger, and things started crumbling. Crumbs were falling. Hundreds of crumbs. Daddy and Uncle Ernest kept on laughing and Kwame's head felt heavier.

He woke up, floating. Arms and neck floppy. He was not folded into the corner by the kitchen door any more. Surprising and so nice that the Catherine wheel of his mind had slowed enough to let him sleep so easily. For a second, his swimmy, blurry eyes struggled to get used to the light bulbs above. Then the back of his head butted something firm but soft. His legs swung and knocked against something hard. Daddy's chest was the first realization, the post at the end of the banister, the second. Daddy was carrying him to bed, taking each step and trembling like Kwame was the biggest weight known to humankind. Daddy wasn't angry or complaining or asking why Mummy was vexed. He wasn't grumbling that extra shifts were often offered to Stuart or Peter first with no explanation. No, Daddy was quietly carrying Kwame to bed. And it was lovely, floating like that. Then Daddy's breathing became serious. He stopped moving. Kwame wanted to say that the arms scooped under his back were powerful and Daddy could go on, and that he had to, and could he be this soft with

Mummy too? Because then maybe Mummy wouldn't do the vacuuming with sad, lazy arms and long, blank stares. Maybe then Mummy wouldn't wring her hands so much, like she was trying to squeeze some last drop of something out of herself. But Kwame's lips were too sleepy to make any of those words. Daddy started again, picking up the pace. Kwame nestled his head closer into the folds of Daddy's shirt and Daddy let him, didn't stop him wriggling at all. Kwame felt himself yawning, his feet dangling. It was so nice to be loose, not to be crunched under a duvet, turning inwards with all the energy he had. It was the loveliest and strangest thing to feel so safe.

May 2018

The corridor was heaving with between-lessons traffic. Clusters of sixth formers knotted by the new posters of the headteacher. They had appeared overnight, plastered on every wall, sometimes almost obscuring student work. The portrait – Marcus Felix with arms folded in an 'I mean business' manner, his smile superior (and also quite leering, in Kwame's opinion) – advertised his new 'Drop-in' sessions. These were, apparently, a chance for off-the-record chats that would help to give the headteacher a 'real flavour' of his 'new community'. The vanity of the posters and the histrionics they were prompting made Kwame nearly kiss his teeth like Princess. He was pleased, however, that amid the fray the distinctive form of Ahmed Hussen was plainly visible.

'Ahmed!' he bellowed. The boy did a hammily slow 180-degree turn, then made his way against the tide of maroon-clad bodies until he reached the entrance of Kwame's classroom. A spot, tipped with yellow, nestled near Ahmed's hairline; he was sucking a lollipop.

'Where were you for my Period 3 class? Your input was missed, Mr Hussen.'

'Had things to handle,' Ahmed sniffed, then moved the lollipop so it sat on his lower lip, tilted his chin upward. 'Personal stuff, innit.' The boy held Kwame's gaze for a second before letting his eyes slide over to and linger on the group of uproarious Year 9s discussing whether Kanye West was actually mad or actually very sane. Because in that moment Kwame could sense Ahmed's defences shifting a little, and felt something shifting within himself too; he wanted to reach out and rub the boy's shoulder. The moment passed almost as soon as it came. 'Don't worry, though, sir. I'll get notes off of Chayanne, innit. She's always got things in order, standard.'

'Yep, good plan to make use of a fellow student as a resource. Great to see you showing initiative.'

'Cool, cool. That it? Can I carry on about my business now?'

'One thing.' Kwame pulled out a stapled sheaf from the stack of papers he held. 'Take this. I know you've been putting it off for a while, so it's a bit of guidance about how to knuckle down and get your revision notes ready' – Kwame flipped a page, pointed at an image of a jaunty pencil – 'and there's stuff about different revision strategies. There's an awful lot to reconnect with for these exams – the "Unseen" paper, the Gothic stuff from last year –' Ahmed kneaded his temples, knuckles edging close to the pimple. Kwame tried a different tone. 'If you look here and here, I've suggested ways of making revision a bit more light-hearted, a bit fun.'

'Mad ting, sir! Revision can never be fun. It's bare *long*. Literally meeting dry stuff that you already know, over and over again? Ain't no freshness. All dem lessons that's been and gone. It's like you're being locked off when you're sitting at your table copying out the same notes, and on the other side of the window the world's actually turning and all dat.'

'Think about it as *looking back* in order to move for–'

'Ahmed! Common Room! Com'e'go! It's a trek from this

block to there and Raheem ain't gonna wait forever. Plus, Tian's there too – she was looking *chuuuuuung* in Period 4. Fam!'

Kwame could not see who it was in the throng who needed his student so badly. Ahmed bounced his rucksack to his shoulder, folded the handout and tucked it into his inside pocket. He sucked the lollipop thoughtfully.

'I suppose, thing with the past is that you can't run from it forever, innit. Too powerful for dat. It's like' – Ahmed nodded to himself – 'like, Usain Bolt-fast. Like, catch you in the end, innit. Like, you try play it' – he bobbed – 'but you can't. Always gonna get you, rise up, play *you*. Gotta face it, not fear it, right?'

'Someone's in philosophical mood.'

Ahmed shrugged. 'Ain't nothin special, sir. Jus runnin my mouth, as per. Seeing whatever wisdom pearls come.'

November 1997

In the damp-smelling Junior Cloakroom, everyone was getting their homework and PE stuff out. It was noisy; some of the boys were playing Slaps and saying, 'Your mum!', and the Year 6 girls with Kookai bags and banned chewing gum were calling them immature. As Kwame and Francis hung their coats on the pegs, they wrestled with their rucksacks to pull out pencil cases, packs of Kleenex. Then the cloakroom emptied and they were forgotten.

This morning, Francis was being extra slow because he was chatting too much, explaining to Kwame what an au pair was. While Francis zipped up his bag again, he talked about how last night his parents had announced that he would be getting an au pair and she was called Ines. She was twenty-one, from Barcelona, and she was going to cook and clean and look after Francis. Francis's mummy told him they needed Ines badly; she would lighten the load now Mummy's interiors business was getting so many orders and so much interest.

'Mummy is going to be in the *South London Press* giving top tips for how to be a businesswoman. So she'll sort of be famous.'

'That's cool, Francis. Well done.'

'Thanks.'

Francis was wearing his Gap hooded sweater with the pocket at the front where you can hide your hands. Kwame usually liked it when Francis wore that top, liked the action Francis made as he slid his hands into the pocket, but today, as Francis went on about how he'd seen a photo of Ines and she was pretty and how his mummy said Ines would help make the wings for his Winter Show costume and teach him some Spanish, Kwame thought it would be great if he could pull the hood over his friend's head, yank the toggles, tie them in a double bow and silence him, like Kenny in *South Park*.

They walked up the corridor together and Francis kept going. Kwame passed his hand over his head. His tight curls were greasy. After Mummy had combed his hair, she'd put in too much Pink Oil and now it was disgusting. He wiped his slippery palm on his trousers.

Francis stopped. 'Who's O – Ol – au – dah. Eq – Eq.' He huffed. 'Olaudah Equ – i – ano?'

'Don't know. Sorry.'

'And what's a a-bo-li-tion-ist?'

The huge display Francis pointed at had been made by Year 6. Mr Bell must have put it up after school yesterday. On the wall, using hundreds of tiny squares of coloured paper, the class had built an enormous mosaic of a Black man. He was wearing a red jacket that looked like something, Kwame thought, you might wear in an old-fashioned army. The man had a proud look in his eyes and puffed-out cheeks. It seemed he had a little ponytail too, which was surprising and sweet.

Kwame knew that if they kept on dawdling they might be late for Register and could even end up with their names in the Red Book. But he had begun reading the thought bubbles circling the picture of the Black man. They were filled with serious phrases:

'*Should they too have been made slaves? Every rational mind answers no.*'

'*But is not the slave trade entirely at war with the heart of man?*'

'Autobiography.' Francis went closer to the board. 'That's a story about yourself. Your own story.'

'Mmm.'

Kwame edged nearer the display too, keeping his hands behind his back. One of the pieces was by Tia Owens. It showed lots of different countries' flags: Ghana's was there, next to Nigeria's and Jamaica's. Another part of the display had a map on it, with thick red arrows stretching from West Africa to America and the Caribbean. Jamie Pritchard had done this one. Beneath Jamie's work, a photocopy of what looked like a weird footprint had been pinned up. The title was 'Below Deck', and Kwame realized the diagram showed a ship sliced open. Packed into that ship were rows and rows of people. Black. Black people. Row upon row upon row. Not a scrap of space. They were all connected by what looked like ropes. Hundreds of people. Like assembly, times a thousand.

'Are they prisoners?'

Francis pointed to the top-right-hand corner of the wall. From there, a large drawing of another Black man stared down at them with the saddest eyes. A thick silver clasp covered his neck and out of its centre a long chain spilled and spilled, and it had been used to make a border for that side of the display. Kwame followed the chain – down, down. In another corner, written on tea-stained and torn paper, was a page with the underlined title 'A Slave's Diary'. Kwame recognized Usman Saluddin's writing. His *a*'s were always wonky.

'*My back stings from the horrible lashings I got yesterday afternoon for picking cotton too slowly. Master says if I ever work so slowly again, I'll get even worse . . .*'

Beneath the entry was a sketchy painting of a white man with a curly wig and a thin snaking thing in his hand. The white man stood tall, but at his feet, three Black figures were squatting on the ground with their heads lowered.

Francis began reading from a nearby poster mounted on green card. 'Olaudah Equiano is an icon. A former slave, he played an, an –'

'Instrumental.'

'Instrumental role in ending the selling of Africans into the slave trade. His writing showed the reality of what millions of Black Africans had to suffer from the sixteenth to the nineteenth centuries, and all because European countries – including Britain – wanted more and more money. Africans were kidnapped from their homelands, turned into slaves and forced to work on cotton and sugar fields. The wealth from these businesses was kept for the white countries while the African slaves lived in terrible con–'

'Conditions.'

'Conditions. Yeah. Thanks.' Francis beamed. 'Leon Sachs did that. It's clever and grown-up, isn't it? Sounds like the *Six O'Clock News* or something.'

Kwame's attention was taken up by the Ghanaian flag again, and then by the photocopy of the squashed-up Black bodies. He imagined the noise: the sea, rocking, slapping the outside of the ship. He imagined how much wailing there was. Wailing Black people asking where they were going, and why them, why had they been taken, why did they deserve it. The whites on the upper deck counting coins, flicking them into their treasure chests, singing loud songs and whacking their whips whenever a Black groan rose from below. It must have taken a long time to get from Africa to America. It must have been the most horrid and dreadful thing ever to be below deck. Did they have light? A bit of candlelight that let the slaves see one another's miserable, dying, angry faces – horrible sights from the worst nightmare – so that maybe they wished there was no candlelight at all.

Why had no one – Mummy, Daddy, Akua, Yaw – told him about any of this? He wasn't a baby any more. Kwame let out a struggling puff of air. Part hiccup, part cough, part burp, part grunt. He'd never made a sound like that before.

He didn't understand why Mami Wata hadn't saved them; taken control of the seas, swirled the water and sent those boats back to where they came from. It didn't make sense that Mami Wata hadn't brewed a storm that wiped away the whites but cradled and carried her own Blacks back to the safe shore.

Kwame turned to Francis, who was bouncing on the spot. He couldn't tell what Francis was thinking or if Francis even cared.

'Leon Sachs might be going to private school, you know. Emanuel, that's what it's called. The school are going to pay him to be there. It's called a scholarship.' The tip of Francis's nose was blushing. 'We better shift it, you know. Mrs Gilchrist will be cross if we're any later.'

Kwame stepped back from the posters, the chains, Olaudah; from the big sign at the top that said HISTORY; from a board doing things to his heart and the soles of his feet that he couldn't explain and didn't like, and he wasn't

sure if the feeling would ever pass. Usually, learning new information was good and made you better, stronger. Kwame
did another one of those weird breaths.

'You all right?'

'Yes. Perfectly fine. And you're right, we ought to hurry.'

'Okay.'

'I think Mrs Gilchrist brought in a new batch of conkers.
I want to get some of the best ones.'

'I forgot she mentioned that. Your memory is top-notch,
pal.'

For the rest of the day he was heavier and sadder. Usually,
about twice an hour, Kwame thought about his worst fear:
that maybe soon Yaw would have to move into a faraway
flat of his own so he could stand on his own two feet and
show his true worth as a man, like Daddy said. But it didn't
seem like that mattered even a tiny bit now. Not one bit.

Even though the bones in his body were telling him
not to bother or try with any classwork, Kwame did all
he could to be on his best behaviour, and he made sure
Mrs Gilchrist knew it. In Art, he complimented Marsela
Krasniqi's self-portrait even though it was messy;
Marsela was a refugee from Kosovo, and Kwame knew
Mrs Gilchrist liked it when people gave Marsela attention. In Maths, Kwame sped through his work so he could
help Matthew add up his fractions. He was careful to show
Matthew the method rather than telling him the answers
outright. When it was time for lunch, Kwame leaped forward to help carry Mrs Gilchrist's pile of exercise books
down to the staff room.

Kwame did all these things, so when Free Time came

around in the afternoon, he would be picked to go on the computer for fifteen minutes. When Mrs Gilchrist called out his name and his plan had worked, David and Reece hissed 'fix' and 'boffin' and 'neek', but Kwame didn't care. While everyone else played Top Trumps or made up dance routines, Kwame settled in front of the monitor as it blinked into life.

The computer had only been installed in September. Everyone in the class – apart from Francis and Lottie Wren who had PCs at home – had stared in silent amazement while Mrs Gilchrist first showed them how to change the font styles and sizes – Comic Sans was friendliest, Times New Roman most grown-up – and how to add borders to their work: daisies, stars, rainbows. When she asked for volunteers to try it out, everyone had taken their time and not wanted to. Kwame could tell they were frightened that if they touched it they'd break it, and their parents would be charged a million pounds to buy a new one. But Kwame, and the rest of Year 5, was less scared now. The mouse sat snug under his palm. He could move the little white arrow almost without thinking. He slid the Encarta CD into the right slot. Clicked, waited, clicked.

The screen began to tell him all sorts of things about the slave trade: why it started, and how it changed Africa forever. There were loads of facts, many of which sounded a lot like Leon Sachs's words outside on the wall. Kwame focused on pictures rather than the information. Pictures of rebel slaves. Pictures of the tools used to punish rebel slaves, angry clamps for mouths. Pictures of the slaves ready for sale, and the whites watching them. He went through close-up images of cotton and sugar cane. He thought about how, every time Uncle Ernest came back from one of his trips to Ghana, he would give Kwame a few hunks of sugar cane to chew. Kwame loved that sweetness, cleaner than any ice pole or Sunny D. He could never enjoy that taste again now he knew what sugar cane used to mean.

There were more of the maps too. Why were the arrows that showed coffee going to Europe and guns going to Africa the same thickness and colour as the ones showing slaves going to America – as if people were like coffee or guns? If Daddy knew the names and stories and could keep on drawing the family tree so that it went back, back, back, Kwame might even one day discover that some of those people on those boats were related to him. And he was a person, not a thing. Not a thing! He wanted to shout at the screen giving him these pictures and making him think these thoughts and tell it that HE WAS A PERSON and NOT A THING!

It frightened him that something from so long ago could, here and now, make his skin itch so much. It was scary to think that if these slaves were his ancestors, then the slave masters could be Mrs Gilchrist's or Francis's distant family members. Perhaps Mrs Gilchrist's and Francis's niceness to him was because of shame for the evil their relatives had done in the past. They were right to feel guilty. They should all be forming a nice queue to bow before him – and all other Black people – to say sorry a million times.

Kwame saw Mrs Gilchrist heading towards him from the Reading Corner, probably to tell him it was Tidy-up Time. He pressed ESCAPE, ESCAPE, ESCAPE until the screen was safe again.

*

234

At home that evening, Kwame let Daddy flick through the channels and didn't care how annoying it was. He let Mummy do her same old impressions of the posh and bossy doctors at work, and laughed quietly. He forced himself to eat all the egusi stew on the plate in front of him, even though his stomach had closed up. He watched Yaw get ready to do one of Daddy's late shifts at the warehouse, picking pink bits of fluff from his beard as he put on his uniform. They all moved around Kwame, showing no sign of anger at the past. How was it possible?

Yaw shouted goodbye into the night as the door slammed behind him. Mummy dipped dirty plates into soapy water, wiped them clear of bubbles, placed them in the drying rack. Daddy concentrated on his calculator, using the back of the BT bill to do his workings. Crouching down to be a good boy, Kwame swept some of the crumbs, hair, more of Yaw's pink-fluff stuff into the dustpan, silently moving the brush around the big splits in the lino.

May 2018

The school day had ended with the best kind of chaos. Kwame had booked out the Performance Space and his Year 7s had practised and presented abridged dramatizations of *Jabberwocky*. The kids had loved the poem, loved the absurdity of its sounds. There were cartwheels, gurning, silly walks and even sillier voices. Kwame had found Nosheen's group particularly entertaining. They insisted on performing last; Nosheen claimed they wanted to 'end things with a proper bang'. They did not disappoint. Nosheen did a very good job of being monstrous. She prowled and stomped; bloodthirsty bellowing filled the hall. Finally, she was slain by the gallant warrior – Michelle, whose version of heroism was standing with hands on her hips and flaring her nostrils. Nosheen's fall to the ground, made even more dramatic by the billowing of her hijab, produced rapturous applause.

In the Windmill's beer garden, Kwame recounted the *Jabberwocky* lesson to Natalie. He even did Salima Rayment's monster's roar: a strange, whinnying sound. Although struggling with inevitable end-of-week exhaustion, the crystalline sunlight and bunting already strung up for the royal wedding encouraged him to be buoyant. Natalie's laughter gave the pink-shirted punters and vapers a show. Softened by booze, Kwame imagined that laugh as a glittering wave, sweeping through the air, seeking him out, pulling him in. He sat back and Natalie wiped at her eyes.

'God, I *love* Salima. Did, did I tell you what her Imaginary Ecotourism project was about?'

Before Natalie could begin, Barbara the TA returned from the bar with their third tray of drinks, an ice bucket and snacks. There was the usual, eager shuffling of ash-trays, empties, carcasses of crisp packets, so the tray could be set down, Barbara controlling her swinging braids with two big pink scrunchies that, apparently, her daughters told her were ugly 'AF', but they were a steal from Primarni so whatever. Kwame rested his lanyard on the table and, as he poured Chablis, Natalie continued talking about Salima's wacky report on sleepovers with bonobos. Barbara loved it all.

It would be quiet at home later, given that Edwyn was away at Laleham with Prescott – the first time Kwame had stayed in the flat by himself since they had moved in in early March. Strange to think of the prospect of increased space and silence, even if it was only for a little while. His parents were popping round for a little tea on Sunday to 'check that Kwame wasn't getting into any trouble', as Mummy put it. Kwame could ask Natalie and Barbara to come over to-night – for pizza or something. Save Natalie from yet more hot-headed conflict with her maddening lodger. Perhaps, as they all stumbled through the front door, there would be collective and saucy appraisal of the Tuke and then they'd steadily work through the cava in the fridge. Or Kwame could message Andrew to stop by the flat instead –

Barbara was attempting to do her much-hyped party trick now – cracking open a pistachio with one hand – but success was not coming. Kwame enjoyed the serious encouragement Natalie provided as Barbara tried again.

'Back yourself, girl. You're a strong, independent woman. Lean into the difficulty.'

The wine was making Kwame pleasantly floppy when he noticed Marcus Felix in the distance, flanked by heads of Behaviour and Progress. He looked towards them, looked away, looked towards them again. Walking through the pergola, each member of the trio had slung a blazer over his left shoulder. The T-Birds had nothing on them. The three examined the packed garden, pointing as if surveying peoples and lands they would soon conquer. Marcus Felix nudged Behaviour in the side, slapped him on the back.

'Brilliant! Fucking genius!'

Unaware of the new arrivals, Natalie toasted Barbara's victory with the nuts and began practising too. Kwame declined to join in. His palms prickled.

He saw that Behaviour and Progress were peeling off, weaving through the crowds in search of somewhere to sit. Adjusting his belt and tossing his blazer over the other shoulder, Marcus Felix headed in the opposite direction, towards Kwame and his colleagues. Kwame reached for a sip of water, then stopped. He poured himself – and only himself – another generous helping of Chablis. Glug, glug, glug to the rim. He took a hard gulp.

'Comrades.' The headteacher stood behind Barbara's chair, patting the back of it. Natalie brushed the piles of shells into a neater heap. They all faced him, squinting in the brightness and nodding hellos. Did Marcus Felix get his eyebrows threaded? They had that sort of shapeliness. 'Gorgeous day for it, eh?'

Kwame averted his gaze from Marcus Felix's sweat-dampened shirt, feeling an uncomfortable and unexpected desire to take it off and bite at the nipples to discover how sensitive they were. Then he would sniff and slowly pass his tongue around the headteacher's armpits, his licking exact as it traced salty skin and grazed scratchy hair. The softness and certainty of it all, and the sensation of surrendering, would make Marcus Felix curl his toes and hum, his cock hardening in Kwame's hand, Kwame's cock hardening too.

Kwame looked down and focused on his wallet's worn surface. A tenner stuck out at an angle. He nudged it into place, then picked at the logo embossed on to the leather. He stopped. He readied himself to join the conversation, couldn't stand the idea that his silence might be read by the headteacher as aloofness or awkwardness.

The headteacher was referring, with a wrinkling of his nose, to the red, white and blue bunting dripping from everywhere.

'My little girl, she bloody idolizes Meghan. Honestly, it's all she goes on about. Her hair this, her dress that.' He threw his hands up, stepped back from imagined criticism. 'Don't get me wrong, what they're doing – Harry, Meghan – what they're doing with making history, I'm here for it. Respect, you know. Re-*spect*. Trust me, I know what it is to be in an interracial relationship and even in the twenty-first century having to deal with a whole lot of – pardon my French – shit for it.' Natalie and Barbara nodded seriously. Natalie made a bid to speak – perhaps of the slurs her parents suffered too, in the seventies, eighties – but the headteacher was in full flow. 'So power to them. Beautiful young people. You know, love is love and all that. And Harry seems like a laugh.' The headteacher turned to face Kwame. 'Bet he's your type,

Kwame, eh? All blue blooded and fancy? Tarquins and Giles and all that.'

'Excuse me?'

Marcus Felix whistled, and shook his head like a plumber about to deliver a hefty bill. 'But that wedding is a pageant celebrating the might of a dead empire. It's dead, man. We should bury it. Not give it CPR at the taxpayers' expense. And, and part of me wants to scream at Meghan to run for the hills; hate to see a sister mixed up in that mad family's craziness. But our role as educators is to remain politically neutral, to guide the youth towards their own conclusions, so –' He mimed zipping up his lips.

'There they are!' Kwame, Natalie and Barbara followed his line of sight to a booth four grinning nurses were leaving. Head of Behaviour was beckoning him over while Head of Progress struggled with a Carling parasol. 'I'd invite you to join, but we're old fogies and you're having a charming time here. I've opened up a tab, yeah? Get your next rounds on me.'

'That's lovely,' Natalie said.

'Very kind,' Barbara said.

'Thanks,' Kwame said.

'It's nothing. I know the hours you lot put in. Kick back, have a nice one. Laters, team.'

When he was settled with his cronies, Natalie rubbed sun cream into her forearms luxuriantly. 'Old fogey? Not in the slightest. I mean, we all *would* – wouldn't we?'

Barbara wriggled. 'Mr Felix? No bloody way. Not for me. I prefer mine . . . lankier?'

'Lankier?'

'Yeah, like, I want to be treated delicately.'

'Boring.' Natalie drained her glass. 'I wanna be thrown around a bit. Nothing fancy. Your classic "pull my hair, slap my bum" situation. I'm a low-maintenance kind of gal. Kwame, wha–'

'Popping to the loo.' Kwame got to his feet, the sun strong on his forehead. 'I'll get another bottle on the way back. Make the most of our Great Leader's generosity.'

He walked past red-faced punters, people in wireless earpieces barking instructions at nothing. Despite its stench, the quietness of the gents' was a welcome relief. Standing at the urinal, as his piss pushed soapy green blocks this way and that, Kwame replayed the headteacher's question. It was infuriating that Marcus Felix could breezily pry, be so personal, make thinly veiled aspersions about Kwame's tastes – because they were both Black? Because that was why the headteacher felt able to be so presumptuous and pally, wasn't it? It was infuriating – completely infuriating – that no one else seemed troubled by Marcus Felix's intrusiveness, his showiness.

Kwame's piss came out with more force, the yellow arc rising higher. What would it be like, Kwame wondered, to get away with the shit Marcus Felix got away with – the strutting, straight man's arrogance, the indifference towards others? To behave as if your actions were beyond reproach? What was it like to move through the world with Marcus Felix's grating casualness – carelessness?

Kwame zipped himself up, grabbed at the stubborn tap and washed his hands, certain that Marcus Felix was outside, enjoying his first pint and bantering with 'the lads', almost certainly not giving Kwame a second's thought.

He assessed his eyes in the speckled mirror's reflection.

Edwyn had said he'd seen something like sadness around them, but Kwame noticed other things now. The person looking back — hostile jaw, hostile mouth — seemed pulled to the point of splintering. A flimsy person, too easily altered. Undoing a couple more buttons on his shirt, he recognized that anger was perhaps the emotion that made you smallest: the kind of advice he'd give warring Year 9s to end playground scuffles. Maybe jealousy had the same effect, Kwame conceded. How shameful and undignified for a thirty-year-old man to be jealous. How ridiculous. He looked at himself again, sucked in his lower lip, coughed. For himself this time, he mimed Salima Rayment's monster roar, turned his hands into two scrabbling claws.

December 1997

'The thing you've got to remember,' Mrs Gilchrist said at their next one-to-one Winter Show rehearsal, 'is the playfulness. Yes?'

Kwame watched Mrs Gilchrist rearrange her position so the body of the guitar sat in her lap more snugly, and so her right hand could hold the guitar's giraffe neck tighter. The small spiral-shaped studs in her ears – much more appropriate than Yaw's – sparkled under the light as she adjusted herself. Kwame wasn't interested in her prettiness today. He wished she would talk to him about the display a few yards away, outside of the Assembly Hall where they were trying to get 'Consider Yourself' right.

She tightened the strings and he waited. It was impossible to know what she could say to take away his shame. Shame because how come he got to go to a nice school and to star in the Winter Show and probably get a fifteen-pound WHSmith voucher – exactly what he wanted – for his Christmas present when, a few hundred years ago, a child who maybe had a face similar to his was sold and beaten? None of Mrs Gilchrist's smiles would make things better. It was probably wrong to think she could help anyway. Kwame might have to figure this out alone. Rebel slaves didn't ask white men to lend them a hand to find their freedom. He cracked three knuckles. Their noise was a tiny electricity.

'What the audience will love you for, Kwame, is if you

give them something that isn't so' – Mrs Gilchrist searched for the best way to finish the sentence – 'square?'

'Square?'

'Square. Yep.'

She put the guitar down again, resting it on the chair, and knelt in front of him. Her smell, as usual, was lovely – lilies, clean bath towels – her messy collection of freckles and her swishy, striped skirt were magical. But Mrs Gilchrist was too close; it made his shoulders stiffen and his head turn to the left, sharply, away from her. Because inside her heart most probably the old blood of a white slave master was still beating and he couldn't think of anything more disgusting.

Outside, other people were having lunchtime fun: Ippa Dippa Dation, What's the Time, Mr Wolf and Red Rover, Red Rover. The thick curtains tried to muffle them, but you could still hear the chanting, and the skipping ropes smacking against the ground. Kwame remembered the whipping. He flinched as Mrs Gilchrist placed one hand on his arm and used the other to draw his wandering chin back to the centre, back to her.

'Hey.'

He tried to look down but her breasts were there, and they were too real and shocking. His eyes stung. Why did he always have to be all filled up with thoughts? He imagined Mrs Gilchrist's hands pushing hundreds of cotton balls into his mouth – one after the other after the other, choking. He did a grunt.

'We can talk as adults, right?' She tapped under his chin. 'Kwame, I know it's not easy when you've got to practise, practise, practise. I know it's frustrating and you want to scream out loud when you don't quite meet the mark. It's tough for someone like you who is used to such . . . constant success.'

Kwame screwed up one side of his face.

'Yes. You're a success machine, my friend. Aren't you? And, between you and me' – she did her thing when she pretended to check there were no spies listening – 'really, I think you're sort of bored by how easily things come to you, most of the time. Which is why I am delighted that you are going to be doing this little number.'

'Why?'

'Why?!' Mrs Gilchrist slapped Kwame's back. 'Because of the challenge. The playing against type. It's brilliant! Brain-box as cheeky chappy! It's –'

Mrs Gilchrist was getting carried away; she was pacing, raising her hands to the ceiling in a hallelujah sort of way – so he decided to sit on the floor and slip off his Clarks. Today's socks had mischievous frogs on them. In the playground a ball thudded.

'Kwame, what is the name of the character who sings this song in the film version of *Oliver*?'

'Artful Dodger, miss.'

'Super. And what does that strange name mean to you? Because it is a strange name, you agree with me?'

'It's a nickname, miss. Often nicknames are beyond the norm because they're private. For friends only.' Like Lil' G, he thought. Like Kraakye, he could have said.

'That's right. And why might the Artful Dodger have been given his special title? How did he earn it?'

Kwame scratched the right corner of his mouth. 'Well, he's a pickpocket, Mrs Gilchrist. So maybe he's good at . . . *skilful* at not getting caught.'

'He's naughty, isn't he? He's sneaky, do you see? Cheeky.'

'Kind of.'

'Kwame Akromah, when are you cheekiest? When do you say – uh uh, I ain't doin that, no sir, uh uh, no damn way.' As she spoke, she waggled her head and waved a pointing finger like Rosa Tate did.

'Umm.'

'When you sing these lines, enjoy them. Let the glint in your eye sparkle. Let it blind people it's so bright. This little thief lives in the most awful of situations – dodging the police, begging for food – but he's able to find a joy in his darkness. And that's how we're using the song in our show too: it's a song about family, about inviting people in, showing them a good time. The good old Artful Dodger knows that to have a good time, maybe you've got to break some eggs, if you catch my meaning.'

'Well –' If a slave broke the rules, he thought, they could be killed. If a slave answered back, they'd get their tongue lopped off. That was a new word he'd learned yesterday from Encarta. 'Lopped'. Also 'maimed'. And 'mutilated'.

Mrs Gilchrist breathed out a plunging breath. 'Embrace the chance to have some fun! Embrace it with everything you've got. You've nothing – *nothing* – to lose. So, from the top. Much looser now, okay? And let's three, let's two, let's bring the house down – GO!'

May 2018

'So for a treat I bought myself that Mary Berry woman's book. That woman is not so funny and big like Edwyn's father. But still I bought her book for some few pounds from Amazon. I have it on my Samsung phone now, that Amazon. Is good. And so I made Mary Berry's Battenberg to try this baking craze.' Mummy picked at the clasp of her thin gold bracelet. 'Is good to try a new thing, wa te? Better than me twiddling thumbs and waiting for your father to come home from work.' Mummy's face sank in on itself. 'This retirement is dull like a dishwater. Don't will yours on too fast.'

'I thought you were doing an over-sixties Spanish class at the community centre? How's that going? Fun?'

His mother shrugged, her shoulders almost as emphatically indifferent as Ahmed's always were. 'So-so. Too many vocab tests.' She sipped her tea, then replaced Edwyn's grandmother's Spode cup in its saucer. The precision of her movements was comical. Parodying her delicacy, Kwame used the teaspoon to cut a scoop out of the pink-and-yellow cake in front of him and pushed it into his mouth. It was eye-wateringly sweet. His stomach became unsure of itself, and for a second it seemed yesterday's hangover might have been revived by the sugar rush. He rested the spoon and smiled in appreciation, knowing that a smile wouldn't be enough.

'Eat more! What are you doing? That's all you are eating? No. *More*. I made three. Two for now and one for your fridge. I have jollof here also, and groundnut stew' – she rattled her Tesco bag – 'for your Edwyn, because I know he likes my jollof almost even more than you. He can eat it when he returns later.' Mummy brimmed with self-satisfaction. 'How is my second son? He is returning to his own mother and father this weekend, me boa?' She nodded. 'That's good. That's very nice.'

On the few occasions Kwame had taken Edwyn to Richmond Court, Edwyn maintained a solemn silence and downturned gaze as Kwame punched in the keycode, walked him into the lift, took him through the flat's narrow passageway and sat him at the uneven, fold-down dining table Kwame knew from childhood. As soon as Mummy loaded Edwyn's plate with her food – gifting Edwyn the juiciest bits of chicken – Edwyn produced the most bountiful praise. It sent Mummy into spasms of false modesty that Daddy regarded with confusion and awe.

His mother pulled back the sleeves of her blouse and reached forward to begin feeding reluctant Kwame the Battenberg herself. 'So come for more cake, eh. Be a good boy.'

The look Daddy shot her was sharp. 'Aba! Let him eat at a pace of his choosing. You want to bring indigestion? Besides, you added too much caster or granulated or whatever honey to the thing.'

'I follow Mary Berry's instructions to the letter. If this is good for Mary Berry, is good for you also. You like it, isn't it, Kwame?'

'It's delicious. But I had a big breakfast.'

'Tell me what you ate. For this your breakfast. Your eyes look sallow and unwell –'

'Cheers.'

'I need to check your diet is balanced. You never give me a chance to call or speak on the phone like your sister does, to monitor these things on a regular basis. Am I lying?'

'I've been super-busy so –'

'So I am doing my backlog of mothering here and now. Tell me of this your breakfast you say you consumed. In a full detail.'

'Every single time, you are obsessed with your son's stomach. Every time. *Ob-sessed.* Is it even your own stomach? No! Is belonging to him! Eh henn. Then leave it be.'

The bristling between them made Kwame hop up to open the window and circulate some air. Just as he had done as a child – thrusting a lauded bit of homework under their noses – as an adult he had new strategies for bringing jollity if an argument loomed. One was to make himself the object of their mutual derision. If he told Mummy about the granola and the shakshuka he had eaten that morning, his parents would screw up their noses at the fancy names of the dishes and tut at the faddiness of Kwame's English palate. There would be an extravagant performance about not being able to keep up with these young people's changing tastes – like when he had explained the concept of Airbnb to them.

He took another bite of cake, would try a different tack today: 'So you're flying to Accra in a couple of weeks, right, Mummy? All set?'

'If I had my own way I would stay here,' she pursed her lips. 'The hassle is too much. New passport and anti-malaria and gifts and new clothes for relatives. And all to see this your aunt, who will only moan for more cash monies. Endless. Why can't we do a WhatsApp call if she wants a face to face? Why can't I do a Western Union transfer if she wants to strip us of our pension? They think we are made of gold here. Am I? Is my top Givenchy? No, it's George from Asd–'

'It's quite chic, actua–'

'Has this your aunt ever asked me about my welfare and well-being? I'm telling you no, never since my feet first touch on the soil of Heathrow.'

Mummy paused and raised her eyebrows at Daddy before neatly cutting herself a pink tranche of Kwame's cake. 'When I am there, when I am back home, all the relatives will be asking me when you will be coming to the village with your baby. Babies, plural, God willing . . . They will say they *loved* meeting Akua's beautiful little ones last year and they will want to know when you will –'

Kwame took a breath and hoped he could do this quickly. 'With all due respect, Mummy –'

'With all due respect,' his father interjected, wrestling himself out of his jacket, 'I have told you, you are no little little boy any longer. You are of age. You will be dead soon if you are not careful.'

'Nice.'

'It will not,' Daddy continued, 'be an extraordinary or out-of-the-blue question for your aunty or your nana to want to know when you will show them your next generation.'

'If they ask, tell them I am a big gay. You have my blessing.'

'So what about gay? Can't gays adopt?'

'Tell them I'm a massive gaylord and I'm not bothered about kids right now, or that having kids isn't going to be straightforward for me. Or tell them I think I'll make a terrible father and I'm not up for it – whatever.'

'Adjei!' Mummy addressed the ceiling. 'It doesn't matter if you think you are going to be good or bad father or whatever. That is not the point here. That is making excuses.'

'Why,' Daddy asked, frowning, 'why on earth would you be a terrible father? Eh?'

Kwame flattened thick marzipan against the china with his fork, pressing the tines hard so they made grooves in the sticky paste. He would not air his real concern: he felt the flimsiness Marcus Felix's repartee had revealed, the flimsiness Kwame had seen as he had watched himself in the mirror in the pub. More than that: he felt that maybe he had whittled away at himself, honed himself so much that there was nothing substantive left. When he was younger, at funerals and christenings in rented community centres, aunties more clucking than Mrs Antwi had gifted him fivers and chucklingly called him a coconut as he spoke. They were not quite right, or at least he understood the analogy differently: the problem was not whiteness or white flesh within him; he worried that inside he was entirely hollowed out. Such a person, a person without consistency and solidity, could not be a home for a new, tiny, helpless child.

Kwame sat up taller in his seat. He turned the fork on its side. 'I just don't think I'll ever necessarily be ready for that. For all of that.'

'Ready?' Daddy tilted his head with a jerk. 'What silliness perfect state of ready are you waiting for? What does ready even look like or mean? Yo–'

'Guys –'

'Guys! And what is guys? We are elders. Nonsense.'

It was increasingly difficult for Kwame to resist defensiveness. He felt a little wild, hot on the nape of his neck, like he could say anything. 'Come on – you aren't really bothered about my estranged relatives being concerned with me and kids, are you? It's *you* who want to know. Right? So ask me yourself.' Kwame tickled Mummy's chin and she swatted him away.

'You think fulfilling your biological obligations is a light thing, Kwame Aboagye Akromah?' Daddy gestured to the pot and folded his arms. 'Bring more tea into my cup before it stews. I don't like it once it has stewed.'

Resting on her elbows, Mummy let the wings of her head tie fall forward. Her face became thoughtful. 'Can't you do like Elton John?'

'What?'

'Like Sir Elton John and his Canadian life partner, David Furnish? Get a surrogacy. You and Edwyn can raise him here, in this his nice flat. The lampshades look expensive. The tiles in the bathroom are sparkling.'

'Edwyn? Mum, how many times? We are not togeth–'

'Or, or even Gibson Bellamy can buy the flat downstairs. Make it a grand big nursery for your little boy? Are you telling me Gibson Bellamy can't do that? I won't believe if you say he can't. The man is able to buy the whole of the road and still have plenty change for his pocket.'

'Okay, so we've decided it's going to be a boy. Cool.'

'Of course, a boy,' Mummy said. 'How can you two men raise a girl? No, is a boy. It must be. And I will come and help you for the first few years. You can make a spare room down there in the new purchased flat for me. With a nice view on the garden. The baby will try to come for my breast milk and find it as dry as Sahara but he will take to the bottle well enough. And so I will take care of things and you can do your teaching and Edwyn can continue his paid drinking, eh? For me is a better project than baking cakes, me boa?'

'Daddy, tell her.'

'No, Kwame, *you* tell her.'

'Anyway, who is down there in that lower flat? That small-small stick insect student girl coming behind us when we arrive? Anyone else? Gibson Bellamy can bring his money wand to wipe her away. And, while he is at it' – Mummy waggled her head – 'he should also wipe off that corridor's painting. Is not a respectful thing to see naked buttocks when you cross the threshold. And I don't like the painting boy's eyes at all. They don't connect with you when you look. Is not nice or right. Take it off. Put up nice flowers instead. Van Gogh's *Sunflowers*. And then give me a grandson, also.' A smile crept across her lips. Kwame half expected her to give him a wink.

Perhaps just three years ago, the weirdness, the wandering nature of their chatting, would not, Kwame conceded, have been possible. The very idea his mother could – in a casually joking way – encourage him towards surrogacy, and that Daddy would be amused enough to nudge her under the table as he was doing now, was beyond farcical.

His parents' rage both immediately after he came out and in the years that followed was stinging. It was a rage – no, a revulsion – that seemed impenetrable. It was unswayed even by Akua's pleading and pity, pity that somehow made Kwame even more furious and hostile too. Because why should Akua have to advocate for him? Why should she have to build bridges just as she had done when they were teenagers and his parents could not control their stupid squabbling? Why did bridges even need to be built because of his saying who he was? And how could his parents do it again – the same intransigence, hardened blankness – exactly the closing-down they'd done after Yaw had left?

Every time Kwame tried to speak to them in the two or so years after he told them he was attracted to men and wanted to be with a man, Mummy's and Daddy's faces quivered and they wrenched the conversation round to June's and Joanna's new teeth. Or Mr O'Shea's carpal tunnel. Anything but *that*. Kwame would never forget Edwyn un-fussily giving him a rent-free room in the old Norwood flat when he had had to leave Richmond Court. Nor would he forget Edwyn's enveloping affection each time he returned dead-eyed and broken-spirited after more failed petitioning of his parents.

So, now, listening to Mummy and Daddy's funny blath-ering on about imaginary grandkids and letting them spin silly dreams about the future felt like an almost impossible delight.

An ambulance outside sent blue across the living-room walls.

Daddy fingered his beard. 'You think your mummy is a bit barmy, isn't it? Eh? Fruit loop.'

'Is not a barmy! Why am I a barmy? I am speaking my mind. I only want a baby to handle and adore. Your sister has done her responsibility, and this your . . . your special circumstances or whatever is making you slow to complete your end of the bargain.' She hugged herself. 'Do you know how sweet and beautiful you were as a baby? Eh? With these funny wispy hairs like you are a half-caste. And you hardly ever cried.'

Daddy nodded. 'Ampa. Sometimes, you will make this grizzly sound – small lion – like you battle against all manner of the world's troubles. Occasionally, few tears. Otherwise, no big weeping tragedies like with some of these babies on Mitcham Road nowadays.'

'Tiny Black angel. So peaceful. And beautiful eyes. Watching on every last little thing so closely.'

Before it closed for the day, Kwame's parents wanted to buy some plantain and kenkey from the African grocer's on Hildreth Street. They were amazed it had not become a café or estate agent, that it had survived the gentrification sweeping through Balham. So Kwame waved them off from his doorstep, watched their stooped forms get smaller as they walked towards the end of Fernlea. Though he wished they'd walk closer together, and that maybe Daddy would offer Mummy his arm, he understood that was not the way they worked. To be honest, Kwame didn't know *how* they worked. He had never, for example, known what conversations or negotiations his parents had between themselves that had lessened their anger about his sexuality and transformed their initial revulsion into tolerance. And it was important to be exact: it was *tolerance*. Perhaps that was all he could hope for. Was there something weak about that resignation? He thought about Daddy at his thirtieth-birthday party: Daddy's illusory but well-meaning aspiration for his son to be boldly striding forward, demanding that the world bend to his will. Kwame kept watching them as they made their slow, measured way up the street. He knew he *should* call them more often, see them more too. He knew he should. But sometimes lingering resentment – really it was hurt, not resentment – about what they had done to him, *and* after what they'd done to Yaw, made him so reluctant. His parents turned the corner by the Moroccan restaurant and disappeared.

'Sunday trains, fucking shit as ever.' Edwyn plonked down his holdall, tossed back his head. 'How goes, dear friend?'

'Soooooo I'm guessing the weekend went like this.' Kwame sat up on the sofa, did a preparatory cough, placed his hands on his knees. 'Because you're often a little basic with these first visits, you probs timed it perfectly so the taxi arrived on the grounds for sunset? So Prescott was agog as the car went round the lake and he saw peacocks doing their thing. And then there was Phyllida being horrified at the new tattoo? Like, mourning the sullying of her darling boy's alabaster?'

'When she saw it she dropped two fat, fat tears. Then she was like, "I want to get one on my thigh."'

'And then maybe forty-five minutes or so after that, like, a couple of Gibson's French 75s in, she was interrogating Prescott about' – Kwame searched the cornices above – 'something like . . . his most *self-destructive act to date* . . .'

'Of course she sat herself next to him at the Friday dinner. Apparently, after doing the "What on earth do you see in my son?" bit, she told him he was handsome *enough* but had an unfortunate chin. And then she asked what secret children he was running away from in Canada. And then Prescott said she went on about the ha-ha for ages

256

and he just nodded and asked her loads of nice questions. She fucking adores him.'

'Obviously she does.'

'But how was Friday pub time with the laydeez?'

'Eugh, don't remind me.'

'What?'

'There was a lock-in at the Windmill.'

'Love that for you, Kwams.'

Kwame's headshaking was grave, but there was a smile on his lips too. 'Wyn, I got so *pissed*. Like, like final year at uni, properly strutting around the bar and offering wisdom to any poor bastard.'

'Exceptional.'

'Ended with me sending Natalie loads of voice notes about her Marina situation after I got home at like four.'

'You and voice notes is never good news. Remember the one to Gina after Rowan's?'

'Let's not revisit.'

'Is that Marina stuff still going on? It's been months.'

'Yep. There's now some complicated stand-off about a broken fridge door.'

Edwyn ruffled his curls. 'Oh my God. Play the voice note. It's the best when you're *that* Kwame.'

'No.'

'What better remedy for Sunday-night blues than to relive your Friday-night rev—'

'Better for whom?'

There was silence apart from the hummed progression of a car somewhere. Edwyn presented his waiting palm for a second before diving forward, snatching the iPhone from Kwame's lap and wriggling back.

'Edwyn Bellamy, you are a special kind of cun–'

Soon enough, Edwyn had pressed in the passcode, searched through the relevant messages, found what he desired. Kwame's voice filled the room.

'The thing is, *Natty bébé*, you've got this light, you know? And every time you embroil yourself – cos it's embroiling yourself, NA-TA-LIE – in the Maaaaaaariiiiiinaaaa shit, yeah? It dims your light? It's the most gorgeous fucking beacon. And you're just letting it fall off – I don't get why you'd wanna do th– Number one: why the fuck does she get to you so much? Like, why the fuuuuck is she eating away at the, at the – why is she under your skin like that? Why is she *under* your skin like that? People can't live their FUCKING lives like that. It's criminal. It's a waste. Are you a wasteman? No. So. She's touching on something deeper, babe. What does that tell you? That's what – yeah – that's the investigation you should be doing now, right now, rather than getting embroiled – it's quite a sexy word, isn't it? Don't get EM-BROI-LED in Marina not watering the cheese plant. Fuck cheese and their plants. Like, that's surface shit. What is it, what's really the tug and the push between you both?'

There was rustling, a scratching.

'Oh, shit the fucking –'

There was more rustling, then a little click.

'Wow.' Edwyn handed back the phone. 'Impassioned stuff. *Bébé*. Erm, what brought that on?'

Kwame paused, frowned. Was it passionate? Was that the right word? It had sounded more volatile. Wilder. The same kind of volatility he'd experienced when chatting to his parents earlier. But with an odd lucidity too. Kwame breathed on the dark surface of his phone, watched his condensation bloom, tried to wipe away oily smears. Strange to think that, in part, Marcus Felix and his insinuations were behind such intensity of feeling, behind the excessive ordering of shots. 'Stressful old end of the week at school. There's lots going on.' The smears on the phone were stubborn and only seemed to change direction under his thumb rather than disappearing altogether. 'I blame the sambucas. And the, the Espresso Martinis too.'

'We've talked about this in the past, Kwame – they're a trashy abomination.'

'Look at the recklessness I get up to when I'm un-shackled and unchaperoned.'

'Yep.' Edwyn played with the remote absent-mindedly. 'You're a liability.'

Kwame watched Edwyn become excited when *Death Becomes Her* was about to start on BBC2. As Edwyn pulled the blinds, Kwame went back to the words of that woozy late-night incendiary. *Why is she under your skin like that? Why is she under your skin like that?* The credits rolled and the question became something else in his mind: pictures of Marcus Felix's hands *on* Kwame's skin. The two of them, pressed against each other. Still but moving in and towards each other. Now other movement: the headteacher's palms, a little roughened, skimmed the length of Kwame's back. Fingers spread Kwame's buttocks; Kwame braced against the initial sharpness, as the headteacher rubbed his asshole. And then the featheriness of a tongue working in tandem with those fingers. Kwame warming, then melting.

On the screen, Meryl Streep was lowering sunglasses, then slowly framing her face with a headscarf. The sound-track – suspicious cellos – made the speakers vibrate.

'I'm obviously not the first to say it but fuck me she is mesmerizing,' Edwyn whispered. '*That's* a legend, isn't it? Eh? Just captivating.'

Kwame felt himself nod, reach for more cashews. He found cool glass: the bowl was empty.

December 1997

In Tooting Library, after school, he sat on the corduroy beanbag Mrs Farooqi kept aside especially for his visits. He wriggled his bottom into the squishiness and crossed his ankles to make it more comfortable. He was trying his hardest to read about birds from the big Dorling Kindersley book on his lap that Mrs Farooqi had recently got in. She wanted his opinion before she gave it to the other girls and boys to try.

So he learned how ostriches have long eyelashes.

And how emus only live in Australia.

And that the little kiwi bird has an excellent sense of smell.

The pictures were pretty, especially the close-ups of feathers: so delicate you wanted to pick them off the page and tickle them against your arm. And the information about how some men birds nursed the eggs was interesting too.

But, really, what was the point of anything now? Learning facts; being excited by the new-book smell; thinking about his posture to keep his singing voice 'beautifully bright' like Mrs Gilchrist had said in their one-to-one. Kwame turned pages of showy parrots and proud toucans. He wanted to know how any of this mattered when the world had shown a bigger, more important, more horrible truth. That when you think you are clear about what badness you have to battle, and you get on with doing that, you actually know nothing. Nothing. Because the world could become a monstrous eagle. If it wanted, it could swoop and press its claws into your sides. It could take you off and drop you somewhere worse. It wasn't fair: he had just been merrily living his life. Waiting to start another school day with Francis, wanting to enjoy the tuck shop at break and the Feely Bag creative-writing task in the afternoon. Then BAM, out of nowhere: the slave trade. BAM, everything dark and lonely forever and ever. He wished he had been prepared for it, but then also knew there was no way to be prepared for something like that. Shifting his weight from side to side on the beanbag, he almost laughed at Akua's idea that he should concentrate on fun.

Falcons can see eight times more clearly than humans.

Falcons are very fast.

When Kwame looked up, Yaw was at the front desk, chatting to Mrs Farooqi. Mrs Farooqi was using her hands a lot as she spoke and Yaw's durag flashed under the lights as he nodded to show he cared what was being said. Yaw made a questioning face, his thin eyebrows coming together, and Mrs Farooqi pointed to the corner from where Kwame watched. And Yaw was smiling, beckoning for Kwame to come over. The smile helped Kwame slope off the beanbag and plod near to the beeping entrance gates.

'Your ma belled me to come get ya.' Yaw squeezed Kwame's shoulders. 'Let's get your things and bust outta here, a'ight? She's doing groundnut stew, man!'

On Mitcham Road, they walked by the shop that sold everything – beach balls, mousetraps, stepladders, special leotards to suck in chubby tummies. They went by steamy

Dallas Chicken, noisy with hungry secondary-school kids who, in their dark uniforms, were like the scavenging crows he'd flicked past earlier. Kwame liked how hidden and small he was inside his own dark coat. The weight of his rucksack on his back was good too, so was the serious treading of Yaw's fake Timberlands. Yaw was chatting about how sick it was that Mummy's okra was never, ever slimy. He talked about how Babou made everyone laugh by doing his terrible breakdance during lunch. But Kwame was struggling to remember the beginning to Tupac's saddest song, when he tells a story about how awful it is to live surrounded by only hate and to have no way out. Yaw had played it to him, with bowed eyes, a few days after he had arrived.

'You quiet today, Lil' G. What's up? Where's my Mr Chat, Chat, Chat?'

'Nothing. I mean, he's here.' Kwame pulled his hand out of a pocket, waved. 'Just. I think I'm just worn out from all the . . . dreaming and excitement. W-winter Show in less than two weeks. C-can you believe how the time flies, Yaw?'

It was a bit of a lie – and really you should never lie. But Kwame couldn't explain exactly how frightened and confused he was, now all he thought about was their ancestors' backs being slashed open and their mouths being clamped shut. He didn't understand how it would ever be possible to feel good again when he now knew that their people had once been so hated – maybe were still hated just as much.

'Yep, it's a total madness. Can't believe imma be celebrating my first Yuletide season wit y'all in just weeks.' Yaw flinched. 'Hold up.'

They stopped outside St Boniface Church, beneath the big, watching rose window. The durag seemed to be

263

irritating Yaw. So Yaw ran his fingers under the fabric's rim and flipped the whole thing off, freeing his hightop for a second. Both earrings were glistening. Yaw started afresh. He draped the shiny black cloth over his head, pulling it back so that his eyes weren't covered. Then he pinched the two flappy legs of the fabric now hanging down either side of his face. With both hands, he pulled those to the back of his head, keeping them perfectly flat. The flappy legs were long, so Yaw was able to bring them back around to his forehead again, before finally tying it all off at the back with a looping bow. Under the bow, the black glow of the left-over cloth spilled down his beautiful neck. Yaw pulled that left and right, patted everything down.

And then they started up again: a smelly bin van rolled by, the 133 let out a handful of crumpled passengers, and Yaw was excited about whether he might have any post at home, a cassette, a reply from his father to their message. But Kwame wanted to rewind, so Yaw could redo his durag. It had felt like an answer to something, or a second when things were clearer, that moment when Yaw had taken black satin and crowned himself with it.

May 2018

On the doorstep, after tying the dressing gown's sash around his waist, Kwame watched Edwyn slide into the taxi that would whisk him to the *This Morning* studios. Earlier, as the two of them had squeezed around the sink to brush their teeth, he had learned that Edwyn's segment on today's show was to come after a 'canine caper', border collies doing a dance to Whigfield's 'Saturday Night'. The dogs would be, Edwyn admitted with hammy gloominess, a tough act to follow. Kwame had commiserated. Moving back into the communal passageway, Kwame plucked a tail of dust that stretched from the Tuke painting's frame towards the perfectly arched foot of the central figure. A smell of almost-burning swept down from upstairs. The toaster pinged.

The early start necessitated by Edwyn's noisy departure was helpful. Kwame had not planned many lessons for the day ahead and so was grateful for the extra hour to think about doing maybe fun, maybe thought-provoking activities with his classes – particularly with his Year 12s. They were about to move from studying *Tess of the D'Urbervilles* in isolation to comparing it with *Mrs Dalloway*, as the exam board had prescribed.

Back in the kitchen, the sound of Kwame's knife scraping at his blackened toast rhymed with the rasp of Prescott's snore. Perhaps Kwame could be personal, revelatory, tell the Year 12s about his own first encounters with Woolf in his second year at Durham, hunched over the desk in the library, puzzled and thrilled. He could say that wrestling with Woolf's iridescent sentences was a much more appealing prospect than another interaction with Harrovians telling him how proud he must be to have 'made it to such a wicked uni, mate'. Kwame plastered the toast with butter and Marmite, crunched it between his teeth.

The doorbell's ringing almost made him drop his breakfast. He wondered what Edwyn might have forgotten. When Kwame opened the door, he did not find a frazzled Edwyn complaining about leaving notes or keys, but, instead, a sweating Marcus Felix, wearing the tightest mint-coloured bodysuit and doing jumping jacks. It was important, Kwame felt, to focus on the headteacher's face – the gently bloodshot but still searching eyes, the exaggerated panting. It was important to avoid looking at the nipples pressing against Lycra, or the bulge between Marcus Felix's legs. The head of his cock – long, tapering – was clearly visible. Kwame started tying and retying his robe's belt, then stopped, fearing the gesture looked camp. He worried his face might be tired or puffy. Blinds in the flats on the other side of the road were being pulled up. A confused seagull was resting on the roof of a Foxtons Mini.

Marcus Felix was beaming. 'Good! You're up. Thought I'd have to hammer at your door, get you a bad rep with the neighbours. So, mentoring! *Empezamos, sí!* Ain't no time like the present. Healthy body, healthy mind. Early bird, worms. Think I'm all out of appropriate clichés now. You got any others to hand?'

'How did you find out where I –'

'Jogged past here the other morning. Saw you, all moody and hunched over, leaving the gaff.' The headteacher made a grumpy face, then beamed again. 'Put two and two together –'

'But you can't just –'

'So do you fancy a quick run around the Common before lessons start? Hey? Got plenty of time. Get the blood pumping. Burn off some frustration.'

Kwame relaxed his stance. 'Who's frustrated?'

'After we've sweated it out, we can toss a few possibilities around, chat about your plans for the 2018/19 academic year? Go on. A quickie. 5K?' Kwame watched Marcus Felix reach around to his back. He swung a little Nike rucksack forward to his chest and produced two bottles from it. They were filled with something vividly pink. 'I've even made you a smoothie. I call this one the Berry Brutal. Shedload of habanero chillies in the mix. Killer, mate. Infernal heat.'

'Sounds revolting.'

'Habaneros are very good for the circulation. My nan's ninety-eight and swears by em. That and a daily dose of Captain Morgan. Or *doses*.'

Kwame's toes gripped the insides of his slippers. The lamp posts out on the street turned themselves off.

'She's a right nutter, though, my nan. Voted to Leave. Can you imagine it, Kwame? She's basically Windrush and she voted to Leave. I was like, Nan, the Leave lot, yeah, they want *you*, want *me*, out of here. They ain't your peoples, Nan. But you know what they're like, the elders.'

Kwame remembered Sunday: the tea, his parents, their complicated stubbornness. He offered a small nod of weary understanding that Marcus Felix seemed to like – until he sniffed again. Coughing, the headteacher turned his head.

The sinews in his neck toughened, his jaw looked ready to shoot. With a grimace, he spat out phlegm. 'Eugh, summer cold or something. Apologies. Not very courteous of me. I'm sorry, bruv.'

The furrowing of his brow changed him. Kwame imagined him as younger, smaller: sent to bed without dinner for swearing during grace. Full of remorse and with a touch of self-loathing.

'Tick tock,' the headteacher said to his Apple Watch.

'I mean, I haven't run for ages, so —'

'So? *So?* You're very good at saying no, aren't you? A master at *gracious* refusal. I need to learn your tricks.'

'I don't —'

'Yeah. You're very good at shutting things down before things have even had the chance to become . . . things. What's that all about? Chat away, bruv — I'm all ears.'

'With all due respect, Mr Felix —'

'Oh, crikey.'

'You seem to have quickly come to very concrete conclusions about what I'm like and what I'm not like.'

'These are all speculations. Punts. But tell me, am I hitting the mark with my suppositions?' The bridge of Kwame's nose itched. 'You scared, Kwame?'

'What?'

Marcus Felix grabbed his left foot and held it behind him to stretch out his quad, leaving his right foot on the pavement for support. His balance, Kwame thought, was very secure.

'Scared an old-timer like me is gonna shamefully whoop your Black arse?'

*

268

Of course, Marcus Felix was always out in front.

Every two hundred yards or so of their run, Kwame did a thumbs-up in response to Marcus Felix's inquisitive, amused glance back over the shoulder. The headteacher often seemed to take this as a signal to accelerate. He picked up his speed and, with head down, teeth gritted, Kwame followed suit, ignoring the protestations of his calves. It was all wrong. The day was too loud in its brightness, the maples they passed too bold in their redness. An army of midges mobilized itself to attack Kwame exclusively.

To begin with, their route – of Marcus Felix's designing – seemed logical enough. They went under the graffitied railway arch, past the ghostly quiet children's playground, up through the Balham bit of the Common, across the building traffic of Bedford Hill, then closer to the lido. But then their course zigzagged and looped. Marcus Felix led them off the main path which other, more sensible runners kept to. They skipped over low railings and found themselves on rougher ground, scratchy patches made shady by hornbeams. Then they circled back to the main path to do the whole route again. Every few minutes, Marcus Felix – hazel irises aglitter – shot one of those curious looks back to Kwame, perhaps challenging Kwame to ask for a breather. There must have been some rationale to Marcus Felix's method, a clever training technique maybe. Or perhaps he was just fucking with Kwame.

Soon Kwame gave in and his body did what it needed to do. Left foot followed right foot, propelled by his arms. He bobbed to avoid low-hanging branches. The neon soles of Marcus Felix's Nikes, the darting shadows of birds and the dancing of sycamores filled his field of vision. Clouds gathered above so the earlier glare was reduced.

Gradually, breathing from the bottom of his lungs and with eyes still fixed on those soles, Kwame came to accept many things. He came to terms with the tightness radiating across his left thigh. He acknowledged that his position as follower came with benefits: the exhausting business of decision-making had been outsourced. He recognized that there was often a sense of care in Marcus Felix's check-up glances. Kwame liked being looked at that way; it encouraged him to lift his chest and lengthen his stride.

They stopped by the weeping-willow-fringed lake. By day it was home to anglers in pursuit of bream. By night its foliage shielded teenagers' furtive fingering. A duck jabbed at roots on the water's edge. Marcus Felix shook off sweat, then clutched his shins. Kwame collapsed on the ground. He was amazed when his phone told him they'd been running for only twenty minutes. He almost said as much to Marcus Felix, but, when Kwame looked up from the screen, the headteacher was engrossed in stretching out his triceps. The sight of exposed armpit hair made Kwame busy himself with getting to his feet, dusting twigs from his bottom and making his way to the nearby bench.

'I. M. Clive Aneurin Montgomery. 1924–2016. Never Forgotten. Your loving Aoife Eilish Montgomery.' Marcus Felix read the weathered plaque on the seat with reverence. Kwame hovered while the headteacher stared at the sign, chest still pumping. 'Being left behind must be unbearable.'

'Mmm.'

They sat.

'Left with nothing but memories.' The headteacher

pulled his smoothies out, offered Kwame one. 'Makes you think, doesn't it?'

'Think about what, exactly?'

'Making sure you do something with your life that matters. Stands the test of time.'

Kwame sipped the drink. '*Wow.*' The tip of his tongue fizzed. He was impressed with his imbuing that single syllable with such sassy incredulity. None of it, however, had been registered by Marcus Felix, who played with the drawstrings of his bag meaningfully.

'What do you think you can do at SLA that will make a positive, lasting change?' Marcus Felix tutted. 'I'm sort of getting ahead of myself.'

A stooped woman yards away was throwing hunks of bread that plopped on the water's surface.

'Do you know what, Mr Felix? That's worth thinking about properly. I don't want to rattle off some bullshit in the heat of the moment. I'd like to sit with it and get back to you.'

It was true that he wanted time. It was truer that the prospect of making Marcus Felix wait appealed. The duck wolfed down a crust, and the headteacher extended his arms, then sat back.

'I know it's happened to you, bruv. Picture the scene, yeah. You're out somewhere. You're minding your jays. You're enjoying a pint. Then some white dude taps on your shoulder and he's like . . .' Marcus Felix stopped to think. 'The white dude's like, "All right, Tyrone! Tyrone, it's been ages, mate." And you have to tell this white dude you aren't Tyrone, don't know Tyrone, don't know white dude from Adam, and so he bes move from you *now*, get me? Then white dude starts making out he's all confused. Or, even better, he tells you you're being "aggressive". White dude scratches his head because we all look alike to them. Ainsley Harriott, Lenny Henry. Then he's more convinced that you definitely *are* Tyrone, you definitely *are*, what you playing at, Tyrone? He tries to put his arm around your shoulder and then you go properly screw face, like *properly* screw face, and the white dude steps back, squints, and is like "Oh maybe you're not Tyrone after all." And he apologizes and goes on about you being the spit and whatnot.' Marcus Felix kissed his teeth. 'I wanna tell whitey what really gets to me is how hard I have fought to be an *individual*. How hard I've worked not to be like anyone else and *to make things different*. I wasn't looking to my dad for a role model – would've been mad. Wasn't looking to no one to show me a route, get me? Wasn't looking to do the same old same old. And I don't want our young people to do that unthinking, self-destructive following either.' He wiggled his hand. 'We gotta carve our own paths. That's what I did. Bet that's what you did too, right? You don't get where you're at, with all your skills, without putting your nose to that grindstone and being your own person. So for a white dude to confuse me with some next brer is the highest of insults. I'm not like anyone, bruv. I'm here to *be* different and *make* things different. End of.'

Kwame smiled.

'What? What?'

'I don't –' Kwame's voice sounded plummier than usual. 'I don't ever go "properly screw face".'

'I know you think you're refined and that, but I reckon I've been treated to your screw face on a number of occasions over the last few weeks. I lie?' Kwame shifted where he sat. The duck was busy again, snapping at a cabbage-white butterfly. He watched the headteacher quickly lick a slither of dry skin on his lower lip and become pensive. 'Can I try another question on you, bruv?'

The startled butterfly dipped and weaved.

'Can't stop you. Go on, go for it.'

'What was it that got you into teaching in the first place? I'm curious.'

Massaging a knee, Kwame recalled the period around his applying for teacher training: having left Richmond Court, trying to feel at home in what felt very much like *Edwyn's* home, reaching out and trying to hold on to something steadying, a job with worth and purpose. He could not do what the rest of the Durham lot had done: try for a place on a grad scheme at an unethical firm where his presence would invariably make colleagues mutter about 'quotas', or sign up for a parentally bankrolled law conversion course. Or drift, like Edwyn did, trying his hand at modelling for life-drawing classes, cheese-making, go-go dancing, waitering, copyediting, a course in Medieval French at the Sorbonne – all while enjoying the fat of Gibson's land.

The duck snapped again, and the dazed butterfly sought sanctuary on a wiry marigold, bringing its wings together, hands in prayer. Kwame thought about the standard answer to Marcus Felix's question that he had reeled off in job interviews. It was a treatise about sharing opportunity and helping to fulfil young dreams. But, as the butterfly opened out one wing, that treatise was supplanted by the image of Ahmed craning over a notepad, face scrunched with concentration. And Kwame thought about starting at Mount Nod Secondary School too, just a couple of years after Yaw had left, and how that had left its deep and strange mark: how carefully he sought acceptance across the board – the skaters, the rude boys, the Asian rude boys, the neeks, girls – getting close enough to all but not so much so that anyone might be able to look at him too much; making sure he was liked just enough, spreading himself thin and making, in none of those groups, a solid home. He thought about being selected, against his will, to be head boy: how often he had been rolled out to smilingly recite a script at Open Evenings. How he was mentioned in the principal's closing address as an example of 'the good' the school could 'do' for each prospective student in the audience. How his stomach had contracted as he listened backstage. Kwame thought about Reece too, hands on his bowed head, facing the wall, fighting against a tear. And, as the butterfly flew again, tracing circles of varying sizes, he imagined a younger Marcus Felix, his screw face locked as he broke from the pack.

Kwame released his knee.

'School can be a really isolating place, at times. I doubt many of our students would talk about it in those terms' – Marcus Felix's scoff was sympathetic – 'but that doesn't mean it isn't true. Even though there's, like, the buzz and the throng of the classroom and the playground or whatever, there are kids who are trapped in this sense that they're lost, alone, like it would be impossible for someone else to get whatever complicated shit they're going through. Because being a child, being a teenager, is complicated shit. So, through what I teach, through how I am with them in the classroom, I want them to know there's more than that darkness? Yes, darkness is there and it's real, and we need to face it, but it's not as all-encompassing as they think. On my best days, when I'm at my most idealistic, yeah, that's what I want to give them.'

They both concentrated on the water. But then a breeze picked up and the butterfly was spun round. Kwame wished the hapless insect a little peace, a single moment in which to settle. Turning to his right, he noticed the headteacher's stare: there was an almost-imperceptible difference to it. Less definition about the corners of his eyes. Kwame's head felt strange. Unfastened, somehow. 'I mean a lot of that is probably projection. It's about me. How *I* was as a kid. Like, back then I experienced the odd period of . . . despair. Times when I thought all good had been taken away. Or, or had abandoned me.'

The butterfly was being forced ever further left by the wind and kept trying to right itself. 'Do they still grab you, Kwame, those moments of despair, as you put it? Or are they firmly in the past now?'

'I'd like to say the latter. And mostly that's true. But there are days when – not days of despair, per se – but times of heaviness when, like, certainty seems utterly, totally absurd.'

The whiteness in Marcus Felix's stubble looked like hundreds of pinpricks of light. 'Isn't there something to be said for a little uncertainty?' He pressed his palms together. The muscles in his arms rolled. 'That's when risk – and reward – can flourish.'

'Why would I – why would I actively welcome risk? Haven't I already got enough to contend with?'

'*Interesting*. Very interesting. What exactly are you contending with, Kwame?'

'I –' There was a new scuff on Kwame's left trainer: a

jagged lozenge across the midsole. What was he contending with? Where to fucking start? With the sometimes silent, sometimes shouted imperatives of a world that, yes, just as the headteacher said, often seemed to squint and squint and squint at him? Or maybe he could begin with those nearest to him: Mummy, Daddy, Edwyn – the way that what they thought of as embracing or bolstering so often felt like the exact opposite.

The morning air continued warming and the silence continued opening out. But the headteacher's gaze remained entirely unchanging, his only movement a little lean forward, and the resting of his cupped hands on his knees. Perhaps it was this steadiness that convinced Kwame that whatever further words might come from his mouth would be gently held and carefully borne, which made him want to speak more.

'There's, there's lots, actually, but there's mostly a lot of contending with myself? You know? My shortcomings? Me stuck thinking about me in the same old same old ways and –' He smiled. 'Suppose I'm getting a bit nebulous and woolly. But then it is six a.m. And you have just tried to destroy my legs and respiratory system, so.'

'Nothing nebulous there at all. I like the way you flow. And I *feel* what you're saying – *I feel you*, fam. It means a lot to me that you've kinda been able to –'

Kwame couldn't believe what was coming from him: the loudest giggle, shrill and vaulting and unstoppable. Marcus Felix could only watch on confusedly as Kwame wiped his eyes, coughed to clear his throat, before making his voice as portentous as Marcus Felix's had just been. Kwame adopted the moody pouting too. '*I feel you*, fam. Nah, I, I *feel* you.'

276

'That, mate, is uncannily on point, you know. Eerily good.'

'I've had ample opportunities for research.' Kwame paused. 'Has anyone ever told you that you chat a lot? I mean, like, *a lot* a lot.'

The blast of shared laughter was the last straw for the butterfly. It gathered its strength, found a distant focus in the willows' leaves, and went higher, higher, higher.

December 1997

In the days before Akua came back home at the end of her first term at Manchester, Yaw's excitement about finally meeting her was everywhere and constant – and a bit annoying, to be honest. Especially at dinnertimes. Yaw was as curious as the stupid cat from the saying. What was Akua into? What singers did she dig? What did she do to chill? Who were her peoples? What was their vibe?

While Yaw kept on asking, Kwame tore off the slightly burnt bits from his oven chips and put them to one side – even though Mummy called that wasteful – and kept what he knew about Akua to himself: Akua was into her collection of big earrings. She liked the R&B singer Toni Braxton a lot; when Akua did chores, she sang that un-break heart-break song in a rumbling voice Kwame supposed was meant to sound mature. Akua's girlfriends – Valeria from 437 as well as Laetitia – sometimes came over. Kwame was only allowed to see them for a brief minute; Akua mostly imprisoned them in her room for secret meetings. In these, because of their loudness, Kwame heard them talk about the trainers they wanted and they repeated boys' names over and over again as if they were witches' spells.

Kwame didn't want to guess whether Akua had changed her style up at Manchester, whether she had become, as Daddy imagined, a druggy punk or alcoholic hippy like all students these days. It was boring when his parents talked about Manchester being very strong for her course and that was why they let her go, and just as dry when Yaw went on about the gift of education – how his life would have been very different if he had been able to start a degree. Instead, Kwame wanted to ask when they would get out the Christmas tree and lights. Also, to tell them that Mr Pauls, the teacher for Year 2, and Mr Plumstead had announced they were going to film the Winter Show and make a video for posterity – a word which Kwame liked the sound of. Plus, Reece Campbell and David Siddon had stopped talking to each other, because David had called Reece's mum a sket when Reece beat him at pat ball. *These* were important topics.

But the last night before Akua got back was a fun one. Not only because the Akua Chat was shorter than usual, but because of Yaw's shining mood: he did not have shifts at the car wash or the warehouse this weekend and so the world, apparently, was his massive oyster. Yaw kept saying he was loving his Friday vibes, clicking his fingers and trying to spin in circles. His balance was quite bad so he kept falling, but everyone liked his efforts anyway. Daddy was doing something with fuses from the broken lamps, Mummy was calling lots of people and talking in rushing Twi. Once he had finished his sheet about earthquakes, Kwame set to work too, helping Yaw move his bits and pieces out of Akua's room.

Because of Yaw's shining mood, because Yaw had rented a famous film from Blockbuster that had Janet Jackson and Tupac in it, and because Daddy agreed Kwame could watch too if they promised to fast-forward through any inappropriate parts, it was easy to pretend bad things hadn't happened or didn't exist. Things like the slave trade, or how much Reece Campbell's sadness after the sket row had unexpectedly made Kwame want to punch David Siddon in the nose until blood cried down over his lips.

They squeezed Yaw's bags into the cupboard under the stairs, rearranging the coffee table, sofa and La-Z-Boy so that Yaw could sleep on it; they had to tighten the La-Z-Boy's tired old screws, which used a lot of elbow grease. Even though Mummy left the room giving Daddy the hardest stare and thudded upstairs, Daddy had a glowing mood too, claimed it was a Lads' Night for real lads only and rewarded them with a Beijing Inn takeaway to eat with the 'movie', as Yaw kept calling it. They had sticky lips and sticky fingers from too many duck spring rolls, sweet-and-sour chicken balls, Kung Pao beef, wiped clean with lemony wipes. Yaw and Kwame sat side by side, cross-legged on the sofa, Kwame clutching his feet as the film called *Poetic Justice* started.

Yaw became obsessed with the screen. You could tell he had probably wanted to see the film forever and ever. The storyline was about two main characters, Lucky and Justice, two names as strange as each other. Lucky was played by Tupac. He was often quite moody and did a lot of scowling, like he had been unfairly told off, but his moodiness was not so bad that you were scared by him – concentrating on his eyes that were clever and slow sent any worries far away. As they watched the movie, you could tell Yaw wanted to marry Justice. Every time she appeared, Yaw talked about how her fineness was 'greater than a princess'. Daddy agreed and clapped Yaw on the back. If Kwame talked about how lovely Tupac's mysterious eyes were, Daddy probably wouldn't be so pleased.

Violence and kissing and love stuff happened quite a lot in the film. Yaw was always skipping the tape ahead past those bits and pressing his hands over Kwame's face to hide the badness. The blindness Yaw created for him in those moments was rough: a palm coming down over Kwame's eyes without warning. The fifth time one of the actors leaned forward with a pouty, wet mouth, the fast and fiery feel of Yaw's scratchy lemon-scented fingertips on Kwame's skin made him very jumpy. Everyone thought that jumpiness showed Kwame's desperation to be included and to see, so they filled his bowl with more buttery popcorn, and told him to bide his time and enjoy his God-given, precious childhood.

It would have been good and dramatic if Akua *had* done her hair like one of those angry punks from Camden. But, disappointingly, when Akua arrived the next morning and stood on the doorstep surrounded by checked laundry bags, she was the same as normal. Maybe a tiny bit taller. And her eyebrows had changed shape, were pointier, and she wore a brand-new puffer jacket – about three times bigger than Yaw's fake FUBU – made from purple fabric that had glitter in it. The jacket – a squidgy cloud that you were hungry to squeeze but absolutely could not – made Akua wide. Kwame worried she wouldn't be able to get through the corridor into the flat she was so big. He realized the thought was an exaggeration and he should control his imagination. Maybe the idea of having to share Yaw with Akua was making him wild. Looking down at his own outfit – the sweatshirt with the clean red, white and blue stripes, his navy trousers with the turned-up bottoms and his black Danger Mouse slippers – made him a bit calmer. He was pleased with his sensible appearance.

Daddy eyed the coat and flared his nostrils like it had the worst smell – fresh dog poo on the shoe or Ravi Akbar. 'So you spending your student grant on such things?' he asked, as he watched Yaw take her luggage upstairs. 'Designer fashions?'

'The colour is interesting, I think. Good to try, to try new things.' Mummy didn't sound as if she believed her own words.

'Oh my days, as *if* it's designer, Daddy. *As if.* It's C&A. And where's my hug, man? Acting like you haven't missed your one and only daughter. Come here, old-timers.' She scooped Daddy and then Mummy into squidgy embraces. The sight of his parents being swallowed up in all that twinkly fabric brought a smile to Kwame's face.

Once released, Daddy and Mummy returned to their shouty talking in Twi and sometimes in English about an aunty back home and her broken roof. Daddy was putting the volume up on *Grandstand* quite loud, even though he knew nothing about football and didn't care about it.

'Glad to see it's still shiny happy people up in here.' Akua was sort of speaking under her breath as she unwrapped herself from the puffer cocoon, but Kwame could still hear her words from where he stood at the bottom of the stairs. 'How's it going, pipsqueak?'

'Erm, if you are referring to me, I don't go by that name.' He placed his hands behind his back and pushed his hips forward. 'But I am doing very well, thank you for asking. Very well. I was doing my vocal warm-ups before you arrived, which I have to do daily, otherwise my vocal cords might crack and perish. I need to take good care of them.'

Akua nodded and pulled Kwame's right earlobe. 'Suppose I'll 'llow you for not replying to my card cos you're still hella cute and hella neeky.'

The memory of the Eevee card made Kwame's face too hot. He flicked his sister away and turned to see Yaw, peering down over the banister. Kwame faced his sister again, wanted to be more in charge of the situation. 'Have you ever done vocal warm-ups, Akua? Is that something you know how to do? It's quite complicated and professional.'

'Oh, yeah, the Christmas play! How could I forget? It's all Mummy and Daddy chat about whenever I ring. You must be nervous. Big pressure, right? Bet you'll be brilliant.'

'Winter Show, actually.' He pushed his hips forward again. 'Winter Show. It's called that because of multiculturalism, Daddy says. So you have to use the right words otherwise you could get yourself into great deals of trouble.'

'Thanks for the advice.'

'That's my pleasure.' He followed her as she headed to the kitchen where she reached into the fridge and drank orange juice straight from the carton, the very same lurgy-spreading crime for which he had had to tell off Yaw a few days ago. She wiped her mouth with the back of her hand, then glugged more, as if she had been walking through deserts for her whole lifetime.

He shook his head. 'Is it hard, then?'

'What?'

'To do Accounting and Economics at Manchester University? It sounds hard. I learned from Mummy it's called a double course. So does that mean you have to do twice as much work as all the other people? No wonder you look like you don't sleep any more.'

'That's not very *gentlemanly* – is it, kraaaaaakye?'

'Don't say it like that. It's kraakye. Not so stretched out, please.'

Yaw appeared in the doorway, stroking his beard like a villain from a cartoon, his studs flashing. 'Accounting and Economics, eh? With a degree like that, heading for top business dollar, I guess? Making your parents paper in some of these Docklands. Right?'

'I doubt it.' Akua slid her purse, keys and silver Discman on the side and yawned.

'Doubt what? Sky's the limit, homegirl.'

'Yeah.' Kwame pulled out a chair for himself and sat. 'Daddy says you have to have big hopes otherwise life doesn't mean anything. Makes sense, in my opinion.'

'Who's dis telling me about the meaning of life? Wow, little bro. Wow.'

After also taking a seat, Akua reached forward and pinched Kwame's left earlobe. This time, the tug was harder. Rubbing the painful spot until it calmed, Kwame thought it was a bit weird – and quite bad manners, actually – that Akua hadn't properly greeted their special guest, Yaw. She was basically paying him no attention at all, like he had done something naughty and the punishment was being ignored.

'To be honest,' she said, 'I can't even think too far ahead. And, plus, the course isn't even the main thing at the moment. It will be when finals come round for sure, but there's tiiiiiiiiiime before that. For now, there's other things that are as important as the qualification and the work. Understan?'

Now speaking fast like she was excited and much younger than eighteen, she told them about the African Caribbean

Society. There weren't too many Blacks at Manchester, but enough that they needed a club and some 'representation'. Yaw nodded as she listed the nights and events they had arranged, the 'mixers' she had been to with 'the crew': Black students born in Handsworth, Toxteth and Tiger Bay, places she hadn't even heard of until a few weeks ago. She took the mickey out of their funny accents; they took the mickey out of hers, and called her posh, which she thought was the biggest joke. She knew it was stupid, but it still blew her mind that there were Black people who lived outside London. They gave each other advice about places in Moss Side where you could get jerk or shitoh, and went to venues where the DJs sometimes played Bashment. Being with Jade and Oyin and that lot, she said, tapping at the table, reminded her of her city and her own girls, and sometimes that was all she needed.

Kwame wanted to ask if it wasn't quite boring to be in a club where everyone was the same colour, because, like Mrs Gilchrist had said, variety was the spice of life and everyone should spice up their lives. But then Akua twisted her hair into a tufty ponytail, passed it through her scrunchie and, in a fake-bored voice, announced she was going to run for president of the society. Pride fluttered in Kwame's belly. He wished he could travel up to Manchester that very second and say catchy slogans or wave banners to convince everyone to vote for Akua, because, if you were going to enter a race, there was no point if you didn't win. Yaw was saying respect, respect, so Kwame nodded hard, so hard that he went a bit dizzy and Yaw instructed him to chill.

'Will you get a special sash, Akua? If you win the presidentship?'

'I hadn't thought about that, Kwame. I'll need to look into it.'

'You should. You really should. You need something so when you are walking down the street in Manchester City Centre everyone can straight away see that you're important and special.'

'Lil' G' – Yaw was laughing, madly, loudly, so that Mummy and Daddy shouted from the living room to check if he was all right – 'you kill me sometimes, dawg. Kill me stone cold and dead.'

'Oh. Oh, sorry.'

Kwame's cheeks went burning hot again, as hot as Mummy and Daddy's conversation on the other side of the wall. He focused on his fingernails. It was bad that some of them were still dirty even though he had had a bath earlier. At least his sweatshirt was good.

'Anyway, *cousin*, I wanna hear everything about you, Mr Yaw.' Akua made the words sound like a cunning plan that could land someone in deep trouble. 'Mr New in Town. How's it going?'

'Me?'

'Yeah, *you*. Coping in this madhouse, are you? Mummy and Daddy can be a bit . . . intense, with each other, can't they?' Yaw frowned a bit, but Akua went on, 'But I'm sure you've found . . . *fun* elsewhere, though? Eh?'

'I'm lovin it here, Akua. Hundred per cent. It's da baddest bomb.'

'Good.'

'I learn my way around the hood real quick. I do my hard labours at the garage. I collect my coins. I got my friends. We hang, we chill –'

'Good. *Friends*. Great that you've made *friends* and settled into our community here in Richmond Court so well.'

'He has.' Kwame leaned forward, was keen to join in. 'Marcel is one of his best pals, I think. We play Sega with him sometimes. Or the two of them play and I watch to learn the ways. They're very fast with the console thing. I hope to gain the skills soon.'

Yaw nodded.

'So there's Marcel. Any other *friends*? No . . . *special* friends?'

Kwame wished Akua would stop doing the stupid cunning voice and the rising thing with her eyebrow. He wanted to tear off the skinny caterpillar and throw it in the bin.

'What?'

'Straightforward question.'

'I – sure.' Yaw's sitting back in his chair did not seem that comfortable as far as Kwame could tell. 'There's a lot of guys at the garage. They've taken me to the pub a few times. That Rose and Crown by the Common? Man, there was a lot of old dudes throwing those darts and whatever, and they seemed to love staring up at me. And, girl, those white guys can drink for real.'

'No lie. You should see some of the medics at my uni. Mad.'

'But, but it's a'ight. I keep myself sensible and straight and narrow. And it's kind of cool to hit somewhere with the guys after a long day of work. They buy me a Guinness cos they like all my chat, so I'm winning, girl. Yeah.' Yaw drummed his fingers on the table. 'Other than that, life is life. All calm, yo. But, like I said, you won't catch me complaining for that one. I already seen a harder life, I can't live that BS no more. I'm fixin to keep things cool.'

'Oh, okay. *No other* friends.' Akua stood up and stretched, spoke through a long, sinking yawn. 'My sources must have been misinformed – and misinformed me.'

She went to the humming fridge, drank more juice and then decided to take the whole carton. On her way up the stairs, she told Mummy and Daddy to shush and not disturb her nap. That was brave, good and helpful, because Kwame also wanted peace and quiet to think of something nice to do that would wipe away the hard confusion adding a hundred years to Yaw's face.

May 2018

After diligent study of several online barbering tutorials, Edwyn had perfected the buzzcut, and Kwame enjoyed having Edwyn do his hair. In return, Kwame helped Edwyn organize his freelance invoices. Kwame had always been satisfied by simple admin tasks. So that's what they did that evening: Edwyn trimmed Kwame's hair while they discussed how it was a bit of a shame there'd been no word about a street party on Fernlea for the royal wedding at the weekend, and also how much they had both been frightened of Julian Clary when they were younger. Edwyn moved the clippers around Kwame's skull with a reassuring tentativeness. He was especially good at neatening Kwame's hairline, painstaking work that required a degree of concentration which made their conversation halting for three minutes or so. After one such stretch of stuttering chat, Edwyn scooped the clippers round to tidy up a patch on the nape of Kwame's neck. When the clippers stopped buzzing, Kwame got ready to stand up.

'No. Wait. A gift for you. Well, more a suggestion than a gift, I suppose. I've been thinking about the blankness, the emptiness.'

'What?'

'Your bedroom. The starkness of the walls. I've found you something. It's cool, you'll like it. There's this website database thing that holds amazing queer artwork. They make and frame prints cheaply. A kind of progressive visual-arts archive. I think they've actually even got some recordings of Milo's early stuff up there, which is kinda cool. But, anyway anyway, the piece I've got in mind for you, dearest *you*, I think it'll be, like, quite a good conceptual counterpoint to the Tuke? See what you make of it. I'll put tea on.' Edwyn passed over his phone, then closed the living-room door behind him.

The image on the iPhone was a Robert Mapplethorpe nude. Set against a grey background, it was a series of four monochrome photographs arranged within one frame. A Black man whose skin glistened was sat on a plinth covered in a white cloth. The man's arms were wrapped around his legs, and his head was pressed against his knees so his face was obscured. He had been photographed from four different angles. Kwame zoomed in on the model's toes, small ears, bowed neck, shoulder blades. The picture was beautiful, but, beyond that, Kwame wasn't sure what he thought of this image of a Black man perhaps distressed or weeping, captured by a white eye. Was he weeping or was this a moment of gentle repose? Or self-preservation? Was this clutching and supporting of himself the model demonstrating he needed no one else?

Kwame thought about what he had said to Marcus Felix about despair, resisting the discomfort at how unguarded he had been. Instead, he wanted the unfolding, unfastening sensation he had experienced as he had let himself falteringly speak – and laugh – at whatever cost, the strange sensation of space being discovered and expanding, the recognition that it was Marcus Felix's urgent listening that had encouraged it. The kettle was reaching boiling point, and Kwame knew that, by the pond, there had been other sensations and movements: the headteacher gently leaning in towards him, a pliable and yearning plant angling itself to find light. There was something loving in the gesture: both in the ease with which Marcus Felix could move away from himself – feeling no loss in that – and in Kwame's allowing the man to reach, ever so slightly, towards him.

The kettle's cry waned. Kwame nudged the mound of hair on the floor with his toes. He zoomed in on the Mapplethorpe image, enlarged a glossy black shin. Part of Kwame was curious to know how, *exactly*, Edwyn perceived this as a counterpoint to the Tuke. But he also didn't want Edwyn's interpretation to impose itself on the image, to fix it or explain it away – which was perhaps the same reason he hadn't told Edwyn – or anyone – about the run with Marcus Felix. It was not cowardly tongue-biting – this felt different. As he waited for his tea to brew, he looked around the living room, filled with Edwyn's trippy wall hangings from Essaouira, green banker's lamps and twinkly decanters. Kwame acknowledged that there was a quiet empowerment in the memory being his and only his, not presented for Edwyn's delight, approval, entertainment, intrigue.

He clicked the blue *x* at the top of the phone's screen. The image receded and a list of 'similar artists' appeared. He didn't recognize any of the names but was surprised to see one was Nigerian. *Rotimi Fani-Kayode 1955–1989.* He clicked. The pictures that sprang up were nudes too, but these were otherworldly, documents of secret rituals or initiations. Kwame scrolled through. Kayode's subjects were all Black men: masked Black men with cocks painted gold; masked Black men nibbling at white fingers; long-limbed

Black men playing panpipes; Black men flanked by huge African masks; Black men with blond Afros sculpted into Mohicans. In one portrait – a double portrait – two Black men were asleep. Kwame stopped scrolling. The men lay across each other, wrapped in a loose embrace. Their arms rested on one another's chests. Their hands hung limp. It seemed a funny thing to say of a photograph but the image seemed wonderfully quiet. Kwame felt almost guilty for intruding on their privacy. To him, it seemed they had removed themselves from everything in order to heal. He zoomed in on the central figure's closed eyelids and lingered there a while before selecting the trolley icon.

December 1997

They played with the sugar paper in front of them. Reece had rolled up his and blew through it. David Siddon had rolled his too and turned it into a threatening bat. Soon enough, the whole class sat up, straight as soldiers, and Mrs Gilchrist jiggled the tray she held like she had good things for sale on it: chocolate-chip muffins or Twixes. Wiggling her hips was another fun touch, as if the non-stop rain outside was nothing to be bothered about and everything was tickety-boo. Mrs Gilchrist rattled the tray again and, like everyone else, Kwame's eyes followed her, light and bright, flitting between the tables. Every few steps, she stopped to concentrate before dipping her hand into the tray. She pulled out a seashell – one for each pupil – then a box of coloured pastels for each table.

As soon as Kwame got his one – a massive pink mouth of a thing, lips spread wide open – he ran his fingers around its spiralled end. He remembered the family day at the seaside in Brighton and how much Yaw had enjoyed the story of it. Had Yaw ever been to a beach? Kwame hadn't asked when they had their chat. If Yaw had been to the seaside, he would have run straight into the wall of the bashing waves without screaming at the coldness. He would have been able to handle it, and probably would have even asked the sea to test him more: Mami Wata would have clutched him in her open arms.

'Lovies!' Mrs Gilchrist shouted once the box was empty, 'I thought to myself: I'd love my lot to do some art with a dash of science today; and I thought: gosh, on a morning like this morning, what better than to bring them some sunshine too? And, Year 5, I scooped up some of the seashells I've collected over the years and I thought we could have a go at drawing them with pastels to bring some gorgeous summery sunlight into our classroom.' She picked up a thin grey shell and spoke to it. 'Such precious things. Clever little houses for protection.' She rested it on the edge of Ravi's desk and started to explain to the class what bivalve and mollusc meant. Kwame stroked the shiny inside of his shell. Melodee would like it – it had so many different types of pink – some hot and fiery and then others much creamier.

Mrs Gilchrist's explanations about bivalves and molluscs were quite confusing. He stopped listening to her and tried, instead, to imagine the animal that had once lived in that glossy cave. Something wobbly and see-through and with one purple eye. The shell obviously hadn't been very good at its job of protecting, he thought, considering that whatever had lived in it was now dead, eaten up by some clever fish that had found a way to sneak in and get what he wanted.

'So some art! Does that sound good, Year 5? I'll do one too, yeah?'

Everyone got on with it, even though, Kwame could tell, no one wanted to. You could see from the slowness with which everyone started, and from the fact no one was jealous Jay and Lottie had been given the nicest shells and newest box of pastels – no one bothered to moan about the unfairness.

Maybe, Kwame thought, rubbing out the squiggle he had drawn for the lip of the shell, people weren't particularly bothered because they were a bit exhausted. First thing in the morning, after Register, it had been poetry reading and writing. Then, after break, Mrs Gilchrist had told them to do a worksheet on the Battle of Hastings. Now, in the hour before lunch, it was art about seashells from her holidays. After lunch, they were doing the first ever run-through dress rehearsal of the Winter Show in the Assembly Hall; the first time the separate solos and sketches and skits were going to be sewn together. Sometimes, the leaping around between the different subjects and things your brain had to do at school made it very exciting. Because Kwame's mind often jumped from one twisty feeling to the next, he was sort of used to it. But sometimes, he thought, rubbing some yellow pastel into his cuff and cleaning it with a lick, it was a bit dizzying. The old chalk dust tasted wrong and bitter. He winced, and Francis slipped him a fruit pastille, which he pressed beneath his tongue, even though sweets were banned. He gave his friend a thumbs-up.

Kwame wasn't even a tiny bit nervous about the dress rehearsal. His promise to himself that he was going to dedicate his performance to slaves who never got the chance to do anything as brilliant as be on a stage under a fancy spotlight wiped away any fears he might have had. He had folded the bow tie Yaw had given him and put it in the top pocket of his shirt as a lucky charm; that would help to keep everything fine too. The pastel was stubby and running out, so he did only a few strokes with it, then added some white and blended the two together, like Mrs Gilchrist had shown them ages ago. The part of the rehearsal he was most looking forward to seeing was Year 2's version of the East 17 song 'Stay Another Day'. It had loud bells in it that made the ending huge. Francis had walked past the Music Room when they were practising last week. He said it was one of the most amazing things he had ever seen in his entire whole life. Mr Pauls had got special seats where the front row was low, the middle a bit higher and the final one even higher, and the class had been arranged on those benches to make those levels look good and professional. And, apparently, the even better thing was the clothes: they were all in matching fluffy, white feathers or something fuzzy that made them round – a class of giant snowballs squashed together.

In fact, when they got to the rehearsal later that afternoon, as he waited to go on and do his bit, the only performance Kwame sneaked forward and peeked around the backstage curtain to see was Rohima's. Her outfit was a robot suit her mum had put together from cardboard boxes. She sang 'If I Only Had a Heart'. Though it always seemed Rohima Begum was quite shy because she never volunteered to read aloud to the class when you had the chance, she must have really listened to Mrs Gilchrist's advice: she had learned how to do projection very well. Since Akua had come back for the holidays, her number-one interests were being on the phone, her massive *Financial Marketscapes* book and going to Valeria's any time there was a hint that Mummy and Daddy might start up their 'antics', as she called them. But even Akua would have stopped in her tracks and paid proper attention to Rohima if she were here. The sounds that came from Rohima's robot body glimmered. They were even more lovely than when Kwame had turned the pink shell so a bit of light slid over it. When Rohima went for the hardest, highest, trickiest notes, she didn't even have to strain; they glided from her.

Kwame could see the mouths of everyone in the audience hanging and their eyes going golden, the more Rohima sang. The pulsing hunger in his stomach was half excitement for when he got the chance to be the Artful Dodger, and half pure happiness at Rohima's soaring voice. On her last note, the audience were bouncing, joyful and wild, and Kwame realized Reece had been at the other end of the curtain, peering too. Reece clapped with so much strength Kwame thought it might hurt or sting to smack your palms together like that. It didn't look nice – or right. Reece turned to Kwame and kept looking at him; he smacked his palms even louder, walking towards Kwame, until he was close enough to clap right in Kwame's face, forcing Kwame to blink. And Reece whooped too, a deep but open and huge whoop from down inside his dark throat. Kwame lifted up his chest and whooped as well, his voice getting louder than Reece's and filling the backstage space, so Reece went louder again. Which meant Kwame had to whoop with even greater strength. Kwame didn't even know why he was doing it, why *they* were doing it, but that didn't seem to matter. They kept on going, for maybe thirty seconds – up, up, up – even after the audience's applause had died out and the next act were due on. Clapping and laughing until they could hear a teacher's cross footsteps coming to find out who was causing all the unnecessary racket in the wings, when the two of them took flight to where they were supposed to be – sitting cross-legged in the shadows – both struggling to catch their breath.

May 2018

Kwame rearranged the chairs in the empty classroom. It was good to do something physical. Good to channel the frustration at Edwyn's blithely announced news that he had 'dismissed' Prescott. Apparently, Prescott was 'an actual angel in human form but hadn't enough depth'.

These out of the blue dumpings of Edwyn's beaux were not unusual. The Robin one was dreadful. The Julian one nearly dangerous. But the first of these – the sudden ditching of Harry – had been, in Kwame's opinion, the most unforgivable. Harry and Edwyn had been together for most of the third year at Durham. Harry had a 'hail-fellow-well-met' delight in being an audience for Edwyn. A Wykehamist with pendulous balls – everyone at St Chad's was aware of his kink for stripping off when pissed – Harry's lisp was as exuberant as his enthusiasm for Catullus' poetry. Kwame remembered how, for most of that final year, Edwyn and Harry told everyone about their summer Interrailing idea. Their sentences sweetly crashed into each other's as they spoke, Harry stepping back so Edwyn could go on. The itinerary was going to be idyllic: seven weeks of hopping between vineyards and parents' friends' places; France, Germany, Austria, Croatia, Greece. The bright beginning of the post-Durham expansion of their love.

Just after they had arrived at Gare du Nord on the first day of the trip, Harry checked directions to the hostel. On the platform, Harry had said that the Rue du Faubourg-Saint-Denis exit was their best bet. And, at this point, Edwyn supposedly had a blindingly vibrant vision of doing the whole trip alone. A test of, and testament to, his self, was how he put it, when he called Kwame later. The prospect of going solo seemed, in that moment, so irresistible and emboldening that, according to Edwyn, it had to be done. So he told Harry as much. He apologized repeatedly, let Harry know he didn't properly understand the urge himself but that was no reason not to go with it: the urge should be followed because it was strong and so had probably been brewing quietly, gaining strength unnoticed for a while. Harry had been agog, Edwyn had left and chain-smoked five fags out on the Boulevard de Denain.

As he had quietly listened to his friend relay this down the phone – Edwyn swinging between lucidity and shrieking – Kwame's feelings had varied. There was real admiration for his friend's wanting to see *What if . . .* There was uncertainty about whether Edwyn might be capable of dropping their friendship just as unexpectedly. And a sense of challenge too: Kwame's internal determination to make sure things didn't pan out that way for him. Kwame had also felt conflicted when, over the course of that summer, Edwyn posted pictures of the trip: skies shockingly blue and Edwyn's smile more quietly content than Kwame had ever known it.

Kwame's response to this discarding of Prescott was much more straightforward: just exasperation. He had grown fond of the Canadian and his presence around the flat. His serious questions from the armchair as he tried to enjoy the ructions on *RuPaul's Drag Race* were endearing, and so was his simple interest in Edwyn's comfort, pleasure and happiness.

Kwame kept on shoving the furniture around brusquely. His Year 12s were to deliver presentations about Virginia Woolf's life and background, and he wanted to create a stage area and banks of seats for the audience, to give the whole thing a greater sense of occasion. Once he had shifted the tenth chair to its new position, he remembered he was on After-school Detention Duty later. The realization made him bang a desk, swear like a trooper. The little outburst was witnessed by super-keen, super-punctual Riya and Andrea. They entered the room with awkward eddying smiles. They continued to look at him suspiciously as they got out their files, despite his lie about his small explosion being caused by the stubbing of his toe, and despite his encouraging patter about their imminent talks.

After-school Detention Duty was dispiriting, not least because it meant leaving the school site a good two hours later than usual. Even more than that, its predictability and obvious inefficiency depressed him. Whenever it was his turn to man the miscreants who had earned one Infraction too many, it was always the same ten or so sat before him. Ranks of Brown and Black boys. Sometimes, there were a few wisecracking girls in the mix, and a couple of white lads with crew cuts. But, in the main, the detention demographic was Black, male. Poor. And, when Kwame walked into the Reflection Room, where detentions were held, on seeing Mr Akromah those boys kissed their teeth and let their faces reflect a bolder version of his own disdain. Their eyes, cheeks and mouths churned up with derision — and homophobia? Curiously like the expressions of locals in the village shop near Laleham whenever Edwyn made Kwame get butter or Rizlas. If he was feeling generous because the last lesson of the day had been a success, Kwame leaned towards understanding those boys. He tried to see how there was parity between him and them. The hostility they displayed in those detentions, that 'hardness' Marcus Felix diagnosed, was a strategy for survival. Kwame's way of being and moving through the world, his prudence, he accepted, was just another.

It had to be said, though, that After-school Detention Duty did sometimes have a fleeting moment of comedy. Mrs Antwi often came in halfway through, to take out the recycling. She'd give the boys the deadliest, the most withering of looks. It made the detainees puppyish. They'd stop chewing their gum and yank their ties straight. Mrs Antwi would pretend she had no awareness of her impact, turning away from the boys to ask Kwame about his parents or pinch his cheek if the mood took her.

It seemed that even the radical presence of Marcus Felix – the school's own 'Obama' – had done nothing to deter or diversify the detention demographic: Kwame was annoyed to see so many of the usual suspects when he arrived at the Reflection Room – including Ahmed. After Kwame had slammed his pile of marking down and told them how disappointing it was that they found it impossible to follow SLA's Code of Conduct, he got them started on Head of Behaviour's essay: 'What Does It Mean to be a Respectful Member of Our School Community?' Then Kwame pointed at Ahmed. He beckoned for him to make his way to the corner near the fake tropical plants students were forbidden to touch. Kwame pulled up a chair, waited.

Ahmed hauled himself from his seat. With a lot of groaning, he sloped forward.

'You finally got your coursework in – great stuff, it was pretty good. You've got your revision notes in order – great stuff again, you did the colour-coding thing I suggested. You're on exam leave . . . so, why oh why are you mucking around and getting yourself into trouble *now*?' Kwame threw up his hands. 'A few weeks! Then you're done with this place.'

'Boss, even a week is like a lifetime in this here hellhole, trust.'

'Keep your nose *clean*.'

'Don't chat about my nose.' Ahmed petted his nostrils. 'It's private property.'

'If you carry on like this they'll ban you from the end-of-year prom, Ahmed.'

'They can bun that prom. Dat ting is gonna be dry and dead so they can do what they want.'

'Why are you always such a prize prat?'

'So fresh and fast with your cusses, Mr A. Do you spit bars? You should you kn–'

'Ahmed, what are you doing here? You're wasting your time, my time. Time is a precious commodity, my friend, don–'

'I called him a prick, innit.'

'Who?'

'Don't even know his name. He don't teach me. Some man, innit. There's so many of you screws it's hard to keep up. Think he teaches Biology or some science ting. Whatever. See how he was all flapping his white coat and pointing his stupid goggles at me like he's important. Must be jokin. He ain't nothin. Tryin to tell me this, that and whatnot.'

'Why would you call a teacher a prick? What did you think would happen?'

'I was mindin my own, yeah. Chillin with my brers by the back of the Humanities block and Sports Hall. By that skip and those massive bins.'

'A lovely spot.'

'I know that's where the white mandem go to smoke reefer, but we weren't even doing none of that haram nonsense. Wanted a couple of minutes away from prying eyes to . . . *be*. What's so wrong with dat? So Mr McWhitey whatever he's called comes all runnin up to us and is like' – Ahmed sat up straight, thrust his nose in the air – '"Excuse me, young man, you'll have to move on. You can't *congregate* here." Then – hear this, Mr A – he starts all shoo shooin me like I'm some rat or some dog for him to be gettin out of the way. Can you believe? And who's *congregatin*? I was literally livin my life. Quietly. Nicely. Why is that a threat to you? Me standin and speakin. What's the problem?'

'Ahmed.'

'So when he turned his back, I turned to my boys and I was like "He's a stupid prick." Standard. Not even the worst thing I could have said about him.'

'All those hours in my classroom and your vocabulary's still in the gutter.'

'Wallahi, I tried, like, to whisper and that, but he must have the ears of dog as well as the face.'

'Ahmed!'

'Cos he spun round like some demon and shouting, "Infraction, Infraction, Infraction!" Blah blah blah. He

was lovin it. You people are obsessed with the whip, man.'
Ahmed sucked in his ample cheeks, then nodded at one of
his peers in the front row, who Kwame instructed to get
on with the essay.

'We've learned an important lesson today, haven't we, Mr
Ahmed Hussen? Someone needs to hone their whispering
skills. Develop greater subtlety.'

'Thing is, like, after he booked me and all that, I did get
it. A bit. Like, maybe he was having a bad day. Off day.
Maybe he's got issues in his home life. Crap kids. Crap wife.
I don't know. Maybe that's why he snapped over somethin
so minor. Problem is, sir, what about if *I'm* having a bad
day when I make a mistake or do something wrong? No
one gives me the benefit of the doubt like I am trying to
give that brer now. No one thinks about why *I* might be
mouthing off or whatever.'

'And were you having a bad day?'

'That's not even the point. Point is, you people don't even
think we've got human emotions. You lot see us as problems to be fixed. End of.'

'Do you actually believe that? Take a moment before you
answer. Really work out whether you believe that's how *I*,
and how most teachers here, treat you and want you to feel.'

Kwame waited as Ahmed contemplated his knees, his
laces, the grey carpet, the shadows the shiny aspidistra cut
across the grey carpet.

'When you put it like that. No, sir. I mean. I guess a lot of
you people are trying your bes but . . . thing is, I, I get so' –
Ahmed jammed his fists against his thighs – 'vex sometimes,
and then I do stuff I know I shouldn't do, but I'm glad when
I've done it, cos then it's like I can move on. Like I've been

freed or something. Like a weight's been lifted. But it ends you up in trouble, and that makes me vex as well. Cos I don't need no one tellin me what I've done wrong and how bad I am. I don't need anyone else tellin me that crap. So then I start sayin what I need to say. And, like, I know it's gonna be the same, wherever I go, uni, job, whatever. I'm gonna mess it up cos I wanna get things off my chest and it's my right to get things off my chest, but I can't even do it in the way you people say is right. I get so sick of it sometimes. And like I, I wanna blow.' He stretched out his large hands, made the sound of a detonation. 'Get me? Do you ever get that way, sir? Like, like full of all mad, *weird* feelings and all you need is, like, some kinda release to empty it out and make you better again. More yourself. Do you ever get that way?'

Kwame struggled to think of a meaningful recent example of anything similar. Ahmed's raised eyebrows were persistent, his desire for understanding touchingly plain. Kwame cast his gaze across the lines of desk-drumming, clock-watching young people, and at the green banners advocating COMPASSION, COMMUNITY and COURTESY that ran under the coving. Ahmed's head hung heavy. His hands contracted slowly until they became fists again: all fingers curled in apart from thick thumbs.

Kwame was surprised to find himself thinking back and recalling his own tinier, more furious fists pounding away during that awful night with Yaw and Daddy. The erratic rhythm of the blows came to him, as did the shocking resistance of Daddy's fat belly – stubborn resistance that Kwame had ignored because all he wanted was to inflict pain as great as the hurt he felt. He recalled knowing, even as a child, that his anger sprouted from a kind of helplessness. As Ahmed flexed his fists again, Kwame wondered if that helplessness had dissipated as time had passed on, or if it had transformed into something else entirely.

'Sir?'

Kwame tapped at his teeth and the sound reverberated dully at the back of his skull. 'Erm, probably, probably not so much now, Ahmed. But, yeah. When I was quite a bit younger than you are, ten or so, there was one time when I, I was so *crazy* and out of control and wanted to tear everything down, that I started laying into my dad. Proper punching and kicking and –' He frowned. 'Think I had to be pulled off him in the end.'

'Mr A! Mr Calm-Calm Mr A? Beating his own dad?' Ahmed couldn't contain his joy. 'Reckless, fam! Didn't you get hardcore licks afterwards? The hellfire *beats* my dad woulda unleashed if I –'

'But whether it gave me a sense of release or made me feel better, is hard to say. To be honest, after I'd done it, I was just *sad*. Disorientated. Scared of myself too. Because it sort of throws you to' – Kwame did a crackling noise to approximate an explosion, louder than Ahmed's was – 'to let loose like that. Knocks you off course a little.' He pressed his palms together.

'Ten is when I came here, sir. To this country. Didn't have a smidge of English. Big change. The biggest, man.'

Kwame nodded.

'Big change, but I was the smallest brer you could ever imagine. Seems kinda nuts to say now cos I'm like the size of you times about five, fam, but, no lie, I was a proper titch, trust. But it's funny, cos even though I'm like eight years on and like a big man of the world now –'

'Really?'

'That little brer is still definitely inside of me. All of his ways. Still playing. Still cheeky. Still just wantin things to be nice and calm. A bit mischievous, innit. Bit of a pussy sometimes too.'

'Ahmed!'

'Still upset cos he was taken from one place that was home and just plonked in some next yard and kinda just left to get on with it, in a way. And that little man, inside me, I reckon he ain't going nowhere. He's always gonna be there. Two twos, I actually kinda like that.' Ahmed shrugged.

'Yeah.' Kwame smiled. 'I know what you mean.'

When he walked into his classroom to collect his rucksack at half six, Kwame was so tired that he almost didn't see them on his desk. Beside the pot bristling with chewed biros, a pile of orange chillies: waxy skinned, lurid against the table's top. He sat in his chair and unstuck the blue Post-it note that accompanied them.

Habaneros. Got a glut. Sharing the love. Handle with care. MF

The headteacher's writing was angular, dashed off. There were splodges of ink and a couple of crossings-out, some of which, Kwame was momentarily certain, masked two little kisses. He laid the note flat again and smoothed it out.

Leaning back in his chair, he picked up the most bulbous pepper by its browning stem. He examined its freckled surfaces with all the attention of a discerning diamond merchant. He pressed its pointy apex against the bridge of his nose, brought it down to the nostrils. Inhaling, through its gleaming coat, he could smell its heat: bright and piercing. He imagined them within him, the particles of that spiky scent mixing with and charging and changing his blood; changing him slowly from within, inch by inch and second by second; and Kwame not resisting but letting it happen, welcoming newness and aliveness.

'Earth to Akromah?' Natalie said from the doorway where she stood, clipboard pressed to her chest. 'Curry night, is it?' She gestured in the vague direction of the desk. 'Where's my invite, eh? Nada. Niente. Rude.'

'What?' He returned the pepper to its heap.

'You all right? Seem . . . far away?'

'I was.' He poked out his tongue. 'Until your whiny, needy voice disturbed me.'

'Cheeky shit.'

'But I am very much here now. Very much here.'

December 1997

Tired after another long shift, Yaw moved slower than a rude zombie with his arms dragging, steps sluggish and durag swaying. But it didn't take long for Kwame to convince Yaw to make his bright idea a reality. That Akua wasn't around to poke her nosy nose in was good too: in the last few days, she'd been nicer and a bit more normal to Yaw, asking questions about Ghana and Atonsu, like Kwame had when Yaw first arrived. Sometimes she still wanted to know how Yaw had been spending his free time, using her creepy secretive voice, and Kwame shot her the icy look Akua used on Mummy and Daddy to get them to behave. It never worked. Mostly, Akua and Yaw chatted in Akua's room. Mummy said it was good that, because they were similar ages, they had much common ground to share. Kwame stood outside Akua's door to listen, arms crossed, and the music was SWV or TLC. Yaw thought Akua's rude comments about Mr O'Shea's smell and Mrs Constanza's big bum were funny and said she was wild, wild, wild. Kwame actually found it annoying that Akua took up so much of Yaw's time, to be honest. It was very inconvenient for him. So it was great that today Akua had gone to Streatham Ice Rink with Valeria to try to be like Surya Bonaly. Even though there was no way either of them could be even one per cent as talented as Surya was, with her beautiful spinning. The flat was nice and quiet and empty. Lovely.

There would be no interruptions as Kwame put his plan into action, helped along by his muttering, six-foot-three sidekick.

Kwame had been thinking about the bivalves, molluscs and shells since he had finished his pastel drawing. Pressing her hands to her cheeks in shock and delight, Mrs Gilchrist had called his picture a masterpiece when she had gone round the class to check everyone's work. It was kind of her to say that, but he didn't fully believe her. When he inspected it himself – comparing it, through a squinted eye, with the actual shell sitting in front of him – it was obvious his drawing was wonky and stretched out, plus, he had made mistakes with the spirally end bit that he couldn't cover up properly. The picture probably deserved only a six and a half out of ten. Although his sketch was a bit sub-perfect for his liking, Kwame had turned the idea of shells being failed houses over in his head. For him, that was the most interesting detail in all that Mrs Gilchrist had said. He wondered if he could make one, a better one – a miniature house.

In the living room, they switched off *Newsround*, Yaw pushed aside the nests of Argos side tables and the La-Z-Boy, moved the Calor gas heater, and took the pouffes and dumped them on Kwame's bed, while Kwame set Henry Hoover – with his scratched-off left eye – to work across the carpet. Then, still following instructions as obediently as a little lamb – as Mrs Ashton sometimes said – Yaw placed four dining chairs in the corners of the room. Trying to be as strong as Yaw was with his courageous and muscly shifting of furniture, upstairs Kwame pulled out the beaten suitcases stacked at the back of his parents' wardrobe. He opened them carefully and took out five of Mummy's oldest but least precious ankaras. Five was a good number: he wanted to give Yaw a range to select from.

When he went back downstairs with his pile, Kwame was amazed and over the moon that Yaw chose the fabric that he most liked too. It was different from Mummy's normal Ghanaian material. Usually, the designs were simple shapes grouped in fun patterns like the tessellations worksheets they did in Infants. But the one that they both preferred wasn't like that: it was covered with hundreds of massive, Technicolor butterflies. The person who had made it had cleverly drawn little dashes to show the direction that the butterflies were heading, to help you imagine their flying and floating.

Together, making sure that the cloth fell evenly on all four sides, Kwame and Yaw poured and draped the fabric on top of the chairs, so it created a ceiling and walls. Kwame clapped, fell to the floor and slid underneath and into their creation. Wriggling so that he lay on his back, he stared at those frozen butterflies above. It was mostly very nice and just what he was after. But the miniature house wasn't brilliant enough. Something wasn't quite right. He scratched his chin.

'How's it looking in there, Lil' G? May I join you in the fly new crib?'

'Not quite yet, please. Final job for you.'

'A'ight. Hit me.'

'Please, are you able to get the little torches from the kitchen? And then switch off the big light when you come back in? I think that'll be good.'

'Yeahyeahyeah! Making it chill and like – what you

311

say – *atmospheric*, like that time when we was collaging dinos like pros?'

Kwame's cheeks warmed. 'Exactly. Yep.'

Lying on his side, placing his hands under his cheek and ear like a pillow, Kwame could hear Yaw's muffled movements – quicker and more eager now – as he searched through the sticky kitchen drawer, and did his gruff version of Tupac's 'If My Homie Calls'. Soon enough, Yaw flicked the switch, then turned on the torches so that two bold circles of light pressed through the fabric and pooled on Kwame's chest. It looked like his heart was glowing. Like Yaw was making his heart glow. For a second, the den wobbled and shook as Yaw crouched and clawed his way in. He lay down next to Kwame.

'Proper cosy lil' cosy cave you built yourself here, Lil' G.'

'*We* built it, Yaw. Joint effort.'

Kwame rolled over again, enjoying Yaw's small and grateful smile. Yaw sighed, drew his long legs up to his tummy, squeezed them in close and started muttering the Tupac lyrics again, saying each and every word as if he had written them himself and believed them completely. His lips were fast, clever, lovely. In Year 4, Olu had once put David Siddon in a headlock which was sort of fair, because David Siddon had said all Black people had disgusting rubber lips, which was evil, stupid and so obviously wrong, as you could see from Yaw's moving mouth now. So softly, petal red, gently shaped, rising and falling. It would be lovely if Kwame could run his fingers around the edges of those lips to memorize their shape. And then, later, if ever he were in a place that had no beauty or seemed unwelcoming – maybe if he had an accident like when Lottie Wren broke her arm and had to stay overnight at St George's, or – he thought with a growing sickness – when he started at secondary school, he would draw it with his finger, doing all the sloping lines, on his palm or on the back of his arm. Then he would not only feel more solid again; he would also be reminded of how magical the world could be.

They still surprised him, thoughts like that: the stuff his mind suddenly made up. Sometimes Kwame's own behaviour surprised him as much as his unexpected thoughts. Like how he had clapped with Reece during the rehearsal, and how easy and brilliant it had been to share a naughty, rule-breaking moment. Kwame could never have predicted that would have come along, or how much he would have enjoyed it. Or how unscary it had been to be so close to Reece. It was interesting, maybe exciting, Kwame supposed, turning so that he was flat on his back again, to surprise yourself like that. The idea that he had inside of him all these possibilities that he didn't yet know about himself made the soles of his feet tingly. But, you had to admit it: the unknown was scary too.

Yaw offered, again, to teach Kwame the lyrics to 'If My Homie Calls' and Kwame, again, said no, said today he'd prefer to listen to Yaw's excellent performance. Yaw shrugged his shoulders a bit, making the carpet bristle, and he continued, firing out the hard-to-understand lines about dopes and locks and underground clowns. Yaw picked up the longer of the two torches and started moving it through the air, like a conductor's baton, in time with the beat of his and Tupac's song, so that light slashed and filled the den. Picking up the other torch, Kwame copied Yaw's actions, meeting every beat as precisely as he met the steps in each and every 'Consider Yourself' practice. Light flicked and bounced. Butterflies burned bright, then disappeared, then were fired up again. Kwame felt that caring for someone with all your heart and with everything you've got filled you up and maybe made you bigger. It probably filled in or improved the bits of you that you thought were empty or wrong. Yaw – a bit out of breath – got to the end of the verse and clinked his torch against Kwame's, as if they were clinking together beers like two grown-up men, a gesture that made Kwame laugh. When Yaw nodded and told Kwame that his vibe and his flow were tight and off the chain, Kwame knew, without a doubt, that Yaw was speaking the truth.

May 2018

The sex was good, but the staying-over bit Kwame could do without. Because Andrew liked – needed? – to be held as he slept. Some might have found it endearing that this six-foot-two fifty-year-old QC liked cuddling. The problem, however, was that Andrew's embraces were more like a form of entanglement – a very punitive form of entanglement. When he was with Andrew, Kwame awoke enmeshed within hairy white arms and legs, and had to work delicate magic to free himself from the net without disturbing it.

Early that morning, with Andrew asleep, he wondered when and how the Rotimi Fani-Kayode print on the wall opposite had become lopsided. He played with the soft folds of Andrew's stomach pressing against his own ribs and then tried and failed to wriggle out from under Andrew's right calf. The first trains rolled through Balham Station. Rain continued to pulse.

Edwyn's occasional description of Andrew as 'Fossil Fuck' was uncharitable and unimaginative, and the poor man had earned that nickname because all Edwyn saw when Andrew visited was a subpar Zaddy. To Edwyn, Andrew was only unruly eyebrows, paunch, dun-coloured fleeces. What Edwyn could never believe, no matter how many times Kwame told him, was how *strong* Andrew could be. Kwame loved that Andrew's touches could turn resolute in a second, and the way Andrew's eyes quivered under their eyelids, just because Kwame had slipped off Andrew's socks. And Andrew's face when the butt plug was pulled out – a giddy mask – was sweet. Most importantly, what Kwame found hard to articulate to Edwyn was that gratitude and generosity were central facets of Andrew's fucking. Central and very addictive facets.

A few months before he had started at SLA, on a blank evening in Edwyn's Norwood place, Grindr had shown a pissed Kwame that Andrew (dtf, nsa, dogperson, discreet, no timewasters, edging, hung) was 3km Away and Online Now. The man's profile was full of funny, bombastic phrasing. He'd written sensible things about finding the 'taxonomies' of top/bottom/vers/sub/dom 'jolly dull' too. In a few of his pictures, he had something of the debonair Bill Nighy about him. So Kwame had invited Andrew round – because why not? The fulsomeness of Andrew's adoration had, at first, taken Kwame aback: rarely had Kwame's boozily garbled one-liners been met with so much approval. No one had ever talked about Kwame's feet with such devotion. Andrew's greed for sucking Kwame off, his ravenous eating of Kwame's arse, the simultaneous sturdiness and gentleness of his arms, made sex with Andrew luxurious respite. Being treated with such attention made Kwame's mind stop turning in on itself. Creeping concerns – Andrew's adoration of his Black skin being sinister or cliché, or Kwame's enjoying white subservience being sinister or cliché – fell away.

Kwame liked that he could message Andrew whenever – just as he had done as he'd left school yesterday, paper bag of habaneros filling his pocket and somehow spurring him on – and, no matter how long it had been since they'd last seen one another, Andrew would soon enough present himself on the doorstep without fuss. There was no need to explore what had happened in their lives in the intervening months. No questions about the paler, indented band of flesh on Andrew's bare ring finger. No interest in the finer details of Kwame's head or heart. So much ease and security both in this routine and in their quietly managed distance. When Andrew was summoned, the two of them would happily drink Edwyn's cast-offs or an expensive bottle of wine Andrew brought over, while Bessie Smith or Etta James provided the soundtrack. Andrew, font of pub-quiz trivia, would share an obscure fact about Bessie's hairdresser or similar. When the time came, Kwame would lie back.

In the indigo of the rainy, early morning, Kwame floated between woozy wakefulness and thin sleep, eyelids heavy, flickering, snapping open, drooping. The dawn appeared and then darkened as eyelids slipped and he heard his breathing slow. How hard it had been, when he was younger, to fall asleep if he didn't know Yaw was home and on the other side of the wall. Kwame passed his free hand through Andrew's hair, over and over, as if to settle that memory, or to soothe himself: silky, greying, light and loose. By day, Andrew slicked it back, but now it spilled over Kwame's palm, spreading, falling like the rainwater gushing outside, no doubt spilling from the broken gutter by his window. Edwyn had been especially lucky that the *This Morning* taxi had picked him up earlier – saved him from a terrible soaking. Water plipped against brick, pavement; hissing as it flowed through pipes, gurgling and glugging as it went. Kwame heard the rumbling of engines on Fernlea and envisaged wheels passing through puddles and sending up sharp sprays, great waves; envisaged water filling drains, overcoming grates, washing everywhere. Wind stirred, then died away. The cosy safety of being indoors protected him from all that; then the melody of aquatic sounds and the gentle consistency of Andrew's purring were disrupted by the doorbell.

'I thought I'd make it weekly. Think Thursdays are gonna be better than Tuesdays for me if we're gonna do this on the regs. If that's all right by you? If, if you're not busy with other things at 5 a.m. on a Thursday morning?' Out on the doorstep, Marcus Felix shivered in his red hoodie and his voice got louder as the rain strengthened. 'I'd planned for us to do a different route today, a more testing one since you aced the Common, but the bloody weather's put paid to that idea. Was fine when I left, but now look at it.'

Kwame's grip on the ajar front door got tighter. He wondered if the headteacher could smell the sex on him. 'Yeah. Cats and dogs.'

Had Andrew rolled over, found the bed empty and got up? Any second Andrew might call out in pursuit of more snuggling before he had to zip off to his chambers. Kwame *could* explain the situation to the headteacher. Spirit of openness and all that. Kwame groped the lock as the headteacher mounted the damp stairs. One. Two. Three. Hands squeezing tighter, his awkwardness about Marcus Felix meeting his hook-up was frustrating, belittling –

'How about next week, Mr Felix? Mmm? I'm up for it then. Totally. So I'll see you. Next week, eh? Well, no' – Kwame reconsidered – 'I'll see you before then, of course. At work, later today. Staff room. Great. Thanks for pop–'

'Different smoothie this time. This one's more crowd-pleasing.' He produced a huge bottle from his rucksack.

'You know that looks exactly like sick?'

'Banana, pineapple, cashew. It's next level, *trust*. My missus is the fussiest eater you've ever met and she guzzles this stuff by the gallon. You'll like it. Bet you twenty.' Marcus Felix frowned at his trainers. 'There's something faintly un-ethical about gambling with a subordinate but –'

'I'll give it a go at school. Break time. Sure it's delicious. But, for now, if you don't min–'

'Kwame, manners! Invite me in. Least till this passes. I'm getting sodden. I'm sure it'll be done in about ten, then I'll be on my merry way if I must. Christ. And after man's given you high-grade habanero?! Liberties.'

Marcus Felix came closer to the door. It might have been the inches of height the man had on Kwame, his stance – strong and upright, despite the rain – or the way he stroked wetness from his beard that made Kwame open the door and move aside so the headteacher could pass. Marcus Felix scanned the Tuke, acknowledging the painting with a nod as if something once obtuse had been made simple. Kwame was invited to lead the way.

The speed and gumption with which Kwame moved for the next five or so minutes was quite something. He hustled Marcus Felix into the bathroom, telling him to towel off before he caught his death, and to change into the tracksuit Kwame pulled off the clotheshorse. While the headteacher was busy, in hot whispers he insisted to a dazed Andrew that he not leave the bedroom until Kwame returned. He promised to explain later, silencing Andrew's irritation with a barrage of forceful licks. When it was clear those weren't enough,

Kwame spat on and slipped his thumb into Andrew's arse until he burbled with pleasure.

Seconds later, washing his hands at the kitchen sink, he agitatedly encouraged Marcus Felix to pour them both glasses of the yellow smoothie, and the French farce of the situation struck Kwame as pathetic. Edwyn would never have done anything of the sort. And why was the fucking hot tap always so fucking slow to get its fucking act together? Kwame sniggered at the falling bubbles disappearing down the plughole.

'What's funny?' the headteacher asked.

'Nothing, nothing. Sorry.'

'It's a *very* nice place you've got here, Kwams. The high ceilings are stunning, aren't they? You're renting, I suppose?'

'Yep, with a friend.' Kwame put slices of rye bread in the toaster. 'I mean, I'm renting off of a friend. And living here with him. Yeah.'

'Flatshare?'

'Sort of.'

'I missed out on all that. All that young, carefree stuff.'

'What?'

'I bet you've done things proper. In the right order.' The headteacher chopped the air with his left hand. 'School. Uni. Job. Teaching? Bish, bash, bosh. Maybe throw a gap year in the mix for a bit of colour.'

'Gap year? You crazy! There's no way my parents would have signed off on' – Kwame prepared to do his most exaggerated Ghanaian accent – 'a year of idle wanderings and nonsense.' The headteacher found the impression funny. Kwame was pleased. 'No. You're right. It was pretty bish, bash, bosh. Very *innocuous* . . .'

He spread butter on to the toast thickly before setting it on a plate and placing it in front of his guest.

'I did it so *wiggly*, man. Stupid. Dropped out of school before GCSEs because my dad went AWOL. It sent me into a tailspin.' His nodding was mournful. 'I messed about. Didn't get myself to uni until I was in my late twenties. Worked in the skankiest call centre to get by. People used to get high in their breaks. Like, fully *licked*. Point is, I, I did that, lived at home with my mum for years, saved every penny. Tight times, but I firmed it. I was, like, maybe thirty-three when I got my own place. Mortgaged to the hilt, of course. You could do that pre-crash.' He rubbed his hands together. 'Kwame, it was the pokiest studio. *Grim*. Lived on my jays. Did my teacher training. Gritted. Grafted. Can't deny it was the making of me, but it meant I never really had that, like, twenties, early thirties *playtime*?' He eyed the fairy lights Edwyn had 'ironically' draped around his wacky water jugs, the full wine racks, the photo of Edwyn and Kwame at a fancy-dress party, Restoration themed. Their towering white wigs couldn't fit into the frame and sweat had ruined their foundation and given them a ghoulish patina. Their grins were red and their pupils enormous. They gripped each other's shoulders, rumpling velvet epaulettes.

'Bet you and your flatmate have great fun here, hey? Mad raves? Perhaps I shouldn't ask . . .'

'Not me, Mr Felix. I'm too' – he copied the headteacher's earlier action, chopping the air with his left hand – 'focused on preparing Schemes of Work and plotting how every one of my students will get top A-stars. That's me. 24/7.'

'Sure.'

'So what if you missed out on a few nights out, or

whatever. You're more than all right now, aren't you? You can't regret where you've *ended up*?'

'What?'

'I mean, your tricky route or however you want to describe it. Seems like it's led you somewhere pretty impressive. You're a success. Family. Headships. Widespread *acclaim*.' Kwame drew out the enunciation of the last word.

'I don't *regret* anything. But it . . . it wasn't easy, that process of moving myself on, getting myself up out of shit.' He spat out the last word. 'I've lost people, let people go, for this *acclaim*. And, thing is, once you get to the top, it ain't the end. Then mans on road, and white mans in their own way are on about how this isn't the place for you, up here. So you have to hold your nerve. Enemies of progress, haters, they abound for us, my friend. I've gotta be on the lookout, else next thing I've been trampled.' Marcus Felix turned his hands into a steeple on the table. 'Sorry. Something about you gets me proper reflective. And – what was it – too chatty?'

Kwame reached for his toast and chomped. 'I see what you're saying, I do. But I cannot stand that "We've got to work twice as hard, we can never relax" stuff my parents fed me when I was growing up. Can't stand it.'

'But –'

'I mean I understand the principle – understand where my parents were coming from with all that toil till you drop stuff. *Totally*. But it was actually such a joyless mentality. Not really *encouraging*, not in the truest sense of the word.'

The headteacher shook his head. 'Might not have been a pretty message, Kwame, and yeah, maybe being on the receiving end of that pressure wasn't nice, but it was real talk, Kwame, wasn't it? It's a privilege to have parents who'll chat like that. And it's worked, hasn't it? You're telling me I'm a success – what about you?'

'Worked to an extent. An *extent*, Marcus.'

'Why?'

'Because there's still' – he picked at the chipped edge of the plate – 'quiet dissatisfaction there. And proper, meaning-ful *success* for me wouldn't be achieving my shiny Advanced Practitioner Teacher Status, or whatever. It would be the absence of that – shadow.'

'That dissatisfaction, bruv, might be the beginning of something. Speak to it. Learn from it.'

'I'm sorry but no – it's not the – it's –' A child outside wailed long strains. 'I don't think it teaches anything at all.'

A door closed.

'Your flatmate leaves for work early? What's he do?'

Kwame's speech accelerated, he fidgeted and fussed. 'Oh, that might be one of the lot downstairs. They're for-ever crashing around.'

'Cool, cool.'

'One of them's got the, er, the most ridiculous name. Ridiculous. Listen to this.'

'Go on.'

'She usually goes by her middle name – Hanna – but her parents actually named her *Artemis*. Can you believe? *Artemis*. Bit much, don't you think?'

'Goddess of chastity and hunting. Yes, I can believe it.' Air passed through Marcus Felix's nostrils in a rush. 'It's what my little girl's called.'

'Oh, I'm – I didn't –'

'God, you're gullible, aren't you?'

'Puerile.'

Marcus Felix stood up, went to the fridge, slathered more butter on his remaining triangle of toast. 'No, our one's got a much simpler name. My wife wanted to go a bit hippy dippy – her parents raised her all New Age. Forest was on the cards for a while. As was Silver. As was Titania.'

'Oh dear.'

'But I put my foot down; said it needed to be something our girl can wear with pride. So she's called Serena, and she is both jewel and demon.'

Marcus Felix slid his phone over. On the lock screen was a grinning, mixed-race girl, her rolling black curls tied with a flowery Alice band. After Kwame had cooed appropriately, his own phone beeped. The message was from Andrew: he'd left the flat, had to dash. He'd evidently discovered the aubergine emoji and had used it a lot. Kwame did a brief smile at his screen, looked away.

'I think Serena's got your forehead.'

'People often say eyes. Forehead is a less obvious one, but I'll consider it, given that you're so perceptive –'

'Successful and perceptive? So much praise, Mr Felix. And all in one short breakfast. I am unworthy.'

'If you say so, Kwame.' The headteacher took another bite of his toast, quickly sucked a bit of butter from a finger. 'If you say so.'

December 1997

The night before the Winter Show, Kwame was pulled out of cosy, glittery dreams in which butterflies as big as countries were swooping in through windows, promising to fly him away to the shiniest place. But Yaw's stretchy shouting from downstairs about how someone had to '*Listen! Listen! Yo, hear me out, please!*' drove into Kwame's ears. Kwame's first woozy thought, as he swam towards wakefulness, was that rooms in Richmond Court were like the boxes of Rohima's outfit. Cardboard boxes stacked on top of each other, walls so thin you could hear everyone's words.

With everything vibrating and his tongue scratchy, Kwame gulped a big gulp of water from the glass on his bedside table. The coolness was shocking for a moment, but it didn't do enough to properly kill the weird fear. Earthquake. Thunderstorm. World War. He turned to the glowing, throbbing Care Bears on the ceiling, as if they could do anything or save him from the banging Twi coming through the floorboards – a lot from Mummy, some from Yaw. It sounded worse than the fight all those months ago before Yaw turned up. Much redder than that. The best thing would be for him to shove his head under the pillow, but Kwame couldn't move. Fear pinned his arms and legs.

Daddy spoke up, louder than Mummy and Yaw, clear, marching through with a giant's anger. Kwame twisted in the duvet. Yaw's screaming was a begging girl's – thin and splitting, like soon there would be nothing of it left. Mummy pleaded a lot too, but then she wasn't pleading at all. Instead, she started demanding, as if she would be in charge in the end and the end was coming soon.

'You must let him explain. Akwesi. A-kwe-si! Is a boy. A boy. And he has made a mistake, me boa? Haven't you? I said HAVEN'T YOU ever made error? Eh? EH? And, and, Akwesi, STOP. AKWESI, STOOOOP OH! Even he can turn things around and make this the making of him, if he has the stomach and heart to try, wa te? He can make himself into a good father. We have to give him a chance – A-KWE-SI.' She did the biggest sigh, like she had never been more tired in all her life.

'Yo, Uncle.'

'Adwoa –'

'Yo, Uncle –'

'Why is it always left to me, Akwesi, why left to *me* to always bring sense and reason and calm into this household? Eh? Do, do you see me doing a fury dance like you doing here? Am I? I could do it, isn't it? But I am not. I am calling for the calmness. Whereas look at you, throwing your calm and collected away. Onyame resɔ me ahwɛ nnɛ.'

'Woman, you have to move from me, I beg. You must let me pass or else. Let me pass. LET. ME. PASS.'

'He, he says the child may not even be – you haven't even open your ears to hear what the boy has to say –'

'Uncle, Melodee be getting around the whole estate. With all the guys. She's been with Marcel and – it's not like –'

Daddy was shouting again. Redder, redder. 'The mother came to me. The mother of this your fancy woman Melodee –'

'She ain't *my* Melodee. That's what – Uncle, I ain't have to stand for this kinda treatment. I ain't tryna be –'

'The mother told me of your sneaking, and her suspecting you two up to no good. She came to tell me. Even as I was sweating and breaking my back in the warehouse, breaking my baaaaaaack in the warehouse, this Melodee is laying flat on hers for you, flat on her baaaaaack. And now look! A teenage pregnancy! Like you trying to become a statistic. You BLACK FOOL.'

'Akwesi Bɔkɔɔ! Ka wo bo to wo yem! Before you do something or speak some words you will find yourself regretting.'

'*Disgrace*. Think I'm working in this country day and night and living in this place for you, this small boy, to come on here and SHIT on this thing because you won't keep your PENIS in its trousers? Saaaaaaa? Trying to trick me? Sneaking around to disgrace those who have sacrificed to help set you on your own feet – you think that is correct? You think is how a man should behave? You know the risks we took? Getting your papers, sorting these things?' There was a thud. 'And now you have shamed us in Richmond Court. SHAME. So, so you came to this country to shame yourself, saaaaaaaaaaa? You will travel that path without my guidance and my roof, boy.'

'Yo, Uncle, I ain't no boy.'

'You think you are a white to be doing this promiscuity? One-night stands? You like one-night stands, is it? And bed-hopping, eh? You want to collect STIs?'

'No need for disrespect. Said ain't no need for you to be playin me like that, I ca–'

'I SAY YOU WILL TRAVEL THAT PATH WITHOUT US!'

'Yo, yo, yo, what the hell? Back the f– I said back *off* me, man. What kindo-madness you doin layin hands on me? I ain't, I ain't even.'

More doors opened and shut, and Akua piped up, telling everyone to cool their beans, asking what the fuss was, until everyone wouldn't stop screaming about babies and Melodee, and Akua swore five times. No one stopped her.

Kwame had to force his arms and legs to do their job. He stepped out from under the duvet and left it behind. He opened the door, just a crack. They were all on the landing. Daddy's pale blue pyjamas were crumpled. Mummy's loosened headwrap dribbled down. Akua had one ear still plugged up with her Discman earphone. Yaw rubbed his crucifix as if his life depended on it, water filling and falling from his downturned eyes. The softness of those eyes – a million times more beautiful than Tupac's – made Kwame wobble.

He flung the door open and ran, growling and throwing his arms towards Daddy's tummy with all his courage. His eyes were screwed shut as he punched. He felt out of and totally in control at the same time, everything pouring from him and him holding nothing back. It was exciting to punch, knuckles bouncy on Daddy's belly, each blow giving Kwame energy to hit again. Kwame thought Yaw was maybe saying something, Mummy too, but the noises were streaky and slower than Kwame's fists and his own screaming – because Kwame could hear his voice, very clearly, tearing and enormous and stronger than any of Mummy and Daddy's stupid rowing. And it was never going to stop, his voice, just like his fists would never, ever stop. He opened a hand flat to slap and thwack. He slapped and slapped and slapped Daddy's arms. He didn't know it was possible for feelings to make it so that nothing could get at you. They were making him so powerful, his straining emotions, roaring and able to do anything. The anything he wanted to do right then was to break whatever he could. Because that's what Daddy was doing, with all his exploding words, breaking someone Kwame loved, forcing Yaw to cry and crumble. And Daddy knew it would twist and cut Kwame to see Yaw like that. And Daddy – probably Mummy, probably Akua too – wanted to hurt and punish Kwame with that sight, because they thought it was not right, it was not right, what was inside Kwame's heart.

And so Kwame went on, even though breathing was harder now. Furious. Angrier than Reece could ever be. His throat burned, his knuckles too. But he didn't care at all because he always cared. He spent every minute of every day caring and never getting the thanks he needed, and now people were trying to hurt what mattered to him, the person who was best and loveliest to him. That wasn't fair or right or good. And all he ever tried to do was to be fair and right and good. He had had enough.

Kwame unclenched his eyes to see Daddy stumbling, tottering – about to fall backwards. Akua steadied him; Mummy and Yaw reached to help too. The words and voices made more sense now. They said, 'Oh! oh! oh! oh! Gyae! Gyae! Gyae!' There was tougher pulling at Kwame's fists, as Daddy kept fighting to get his balance. There was Yaw's amazed and frightened face, which Kwame wanted and desperately needed to beam with pride.

Grunting as he righted himself, Daddy pushed them all aside and picked Kwame up by the waist, squeezing as

Kwame wriggled hard to be free. Daddy's footsteps were big and ploddy but fast too; in seconds, he dropped Kwame back into the darkness of the bedroom. He told Kwame not to leave – *OR ELSE!* Daddy's pointing finger was not interested in listening.

Scrabbling around for the light switch, Kwame wanted to scream again but found he couldn't. And nothing – not the sight of his Moomins poster or the stack of Roald Dahls from the library – could make him feel better and less frightened about how he had just been and what he had just let loose. He pressed his ear to the door, the wood rough against his skin, and he listened to more discussion of Melodee, and then something about responsibility. The quieter closing of doors, Yaw's fading sobbing and Akua saying things would be better in the morning, were the last sounds before a long, whirring silence.

May 2018

At Balham Farmers' Market, though the ground was bone dry and no rain was forecast, wellies were out in force. Kwame always found the whole *rus in urbe* vibe of the place silly. The South Circular thundered close by, but rosy-cheeked children's-book-illustrator mummies and po-faced City daddies dressed as though at their second homes – tweeds, deerstalkers – and wellies of all kinds abounded: rainbowed, fluorescent, bog-standard bog-green ones. Edwyn played his part, in his wax jacket and Hunters, black and shiny as an oil slick.

Loitering between stalls – vegan quiches, ethical lingerie – Kwame flexed his toes within his battered Vans, and the memory of Andrew anointing each one with kisses distracted him. Edwyn was saying something about Tuke as they drifted by a stand selling knitting paraphernalia.

'I think there's something beautiful – poetic – about it,' Edwyn said. 'Don't you?'

'Sure.'

'That's all you've got to say on the matter?'

'What?'

'Have you listened at all?'

'Of course. Your stunning words simply sent me into a momentary daydream.' Kwame reached for a sample of sourdough from the bakery stand. 'Sorry, I'm paying attention now. Go on.'

'I was waiting to get my hair done before going on air and I was twiddling my thumbs, so I did a bit of Googling about Tuke.'

'Okay.'

'He did *hundreds* of nude paintings of men. Ordinary lads. Fishermen. Locals from the seaside town where he lived. Falmouth.'

'Yeah, okay.'

'And he left them all – the models – loads of money in his will. There's something beautiful about that. Like, I dunno, in the 1900s when he was working, I imagine when he was admiring these exquisite male forms, he had no way to say to these men what he thought of their beauty. I bet it festered inside him. That desire. But, you know, in his will, he was able to eventually let those guys know what had been in his heart. And perhaps, of course, money isn't the most romantic of symbols, but I bet those lads understood the message.' Edwyn took a sample of tomato bread. 'It made me think about our painting in the corridor much more in terms of Tuke's longing – Tuke's crushed longing – and maybe it sounds grand or even trite, but sometimes don't you have those flashes of recognition when you're, like, *fuck*.'

'Like fuck?'

'Yeah, like, *fuck*: it's amazing what we've got now, what we, as gay men, are able to do. Here, now. What we're able to *do*.'

We?

We?

Edwyn's empathy on Clapham Common had evidently been temporary.

Kwame pulled at his zip, hard, three times. 'Was Tuke definitely gay? Is it recorded somewhere? I mean, how can we know for sure?'

'I suppose – I mean, I don't think he would have described himself using that exact term, sure.' Edwyn pulled the tomato bread in two. 'And I don't think sexuality is anywhere near as linear as you're implying b–'

'I'm not implying anything. I'm curious about what evidence there was that he wanted to –'

'God, you're in such a funny mood today, Kwame. Weird and prickly and off. Knickers all twisted and wedged right up your cr–'

'Mr Akromah?'

Kwame's surprise and distress on discovering Marcus Felix – wearing a backwards flat cap – a spectacled brunette and a frantic Jack Russell standing behind him, was significant. He worried it might show on his face. If he were a different person, Kwame would have drily said, 'We must stop meeting like this' and enjoyed his archness. But he was not a different person, so Kwame worked his lips into a smile.

'Bruv, you been to the cheesemonger's yet? Round by the espresso cart? Had a nibble of his Berkswell? It's out of this world, trust.'

'Mr Felix. Nice to see you. Didn't have you down as a cheese man.'

'Cheese man?' he asked. A sneeze made the dog convulse.

'I'm the fan, actually,' the woman interjected. Kwame assessed the skin around her eyes and neck, estimated she was about the same age as him and Edwyn. Perhaps a tiny bit older. She hopped forward and waggled her raised arm;

her handbag slid down closer to her elbow. 'If it wasn't for me, he wouldn't know his . . . his . . . Swaledale from his Sussex Slipcote.' She waggled her arm again and thrust out her hand. 'He's being bloody rude and bloody slow this morning – so I'll have to introduce myself. Anastasia Felix. Lovely to meet you. And you're . . .'

While shaking the proffered hand, Kwame noted the pointed pronunciation – Ana-*star*-see-ya – and the boldness of her red lipstick. He told her who he was, and that it was lovely to meet her too. Then there were more jovial, messy introductions: Marcus Felix coiled the dog's lead around his wrist and moved across to shake Edwyn's hand, and Edwyn leaned across to shake Anastasia's. The Jack Russell barked, and Anastasia teased that he was feeling left out, which made everyone chuckle, so Harley was also introduced. That wasn't enough to calm Harley; he kept on yapping so that Kwame grimaced, his teeth set on edge. He couldn't help it: it was a tic from that time, weeks after Yaw had gone, when Marcel's snarling Staffy had chased Kwame up Southcroft, and Marcel's mates had screeched with laughter as Kwame had – breathlessly, legs pumping – tried to find the thing funny, but started screaming as the dog got closer and was told to stop being a fucking girl. Kwame had wondered whether Yaw would have leaped to defend him if he were there, or if he would have cackled and called out 'pussy' like the others.

Kwame concentrated on Anastasia and Edwyn comparing wellies – Anastasia preferred Edwyn's to Marcus Felix's tired pair, but then the five of them had to scoot this way then that to avoid customers with huge woven baskets. The Felixes indicated that their daughter, Serena, was getting her face painted as a mermaid, although neither Anastasia nor Marcus was sure what the distinguishing facial features of a mermaid might be; Edwyn speculated that the child would be doused in a shitload of glitter and the Felixes charged an arm and a leg for it.

A pang passed through Kwame as he observed how naturally the three chatted, how animated Marcus Felix seemed to be by Edwyn's shiny patter. The Felixes' responses to Edwyn's machine-gun enquiries were gracious, good-humoured: given that Madame Evans might be convalescing for longer than expected, they were seeking a local flat to rent and were in the middle of viewings. Yes, estate agents were pushy at the moment. Yes, rental prices did still seem to be mental despite whatever anyone was saying about a Brexit slump.

The three of them gabbled away, with Harley bouncing on the spot, only to be chastised by Anastasia. She once broke from the conversation to dab Vaseline on to Marcus Felix's lips, then stopped chatting again a few minutes later to repeat the application because she was displeased with her initial handiwork. The conversation was fluent, fast, familiar. Edwyn was intrigued by Anastasia's purchases: he admired some purple carrots and a turquoise-coloured Mexican shawl she'd picked up. The Felixes were delighted by Edwyn's recommendation of the natural wine stand, where they would get a discount if they mentioned that Edwyn had sent them. Marcus Felix confessed to being more of a tequila kinda guy. Edwyn went on to enact a bawdy tale about a dodgy old tequila importer he'd once worked with.

Kwame scrutinized the Felixes, wanted a better grasp

of the genesis of their marriage, their history and chemistry, without having to ask them and having to endure what would inevitably be a 'cute' performance as they explained things in worn anecdotes ripe with hetero-smugness. While Harley sat up on his unsteady hind legs and the laughter kept rolling, Kwame tried to imagine the lines Marcus Felix had amused Anastasia with years ago at some bar. What piqued her interest, made her palms hotter? Had her taste for chocolate been long-standing or had Marcus Felix helped her discover it? Perhaps that was not it at all. But, in fact, such a reading might well not just be inaccurate but misogynistic too. Ana-*star*-see-ya may have been the instigator. She might have coursed through a packed dancefloor until she was pressed against her irresistible bit of rough, demanding he bump and grind with her. Kwame expanded his eyes to suggest engagement in the discussion about tequila hangovers and tequila hangover cures. Anastasia squeezed her husband's forearm, triggering the casual interlacing of Marcus Felix's fingers through hers.

Marcus Felix's frequent, sideways glances at Kwame pressed at him, seemed to intimate he should contribute more. Harley's head hung glumly, and Kwame tried to construct a clever gag about the melancholic mutt and Theresa May's lamentable premiership with which he could reintegrate himself into the cut and thrust of chat. But everyone had started checking their iPhones. Edwyn was saying 'Super, not next Saturday evening but the one after, it is' and Anastasia was muttering about the babysitter but then saying 'Amazing' and Marcus Felix was winking and promising they'd all have a 'completely fantastic time'. It became clear that the Felixes had been invited round to the flat for dinner and they had accepted that invitation. There was no time or space for Kwame to question or protest. Serena skipped along to join them; she had opted, in the end, for tiger rather than mermaid, a choice Edwyn informed Serena was wise before telling her she looked stunning, *babe*. And Harley – poor Harley – sat in the midst of it all with a paw over his right eye.

December 1997

Why was the FUBU jacket nowhere to be seen? And the Afro comb with the fist, the Versace Blue Jeans, the box of cassette tapes waiting for recording?

Why was the dinosaur collage – speckled with orange flecks from kontomire – gone from the fridge door?

Why, at the breakfast table, did the whirring silence of last night return, when Kwame asked where Yaw was?

How was it so easy for Daddy to wash his hands at the sink and mutter, 'Gone and probably never coming back. And is a good riddance'?

Why did Mummy stare at her bowl of porridge before adding two shakes of sugar – like everything was normal?

Why did Akua whisper 'Another wasteman' under her breath, and only ask if Mummy had washed her Superdrug uniform?

Why did Kwame pick up his bowl and let it drop to the floor, smashing and spreading sludgy koko on the lino?

Why did Akua get the sponge and dustpan and brush without fuss? How come no one told Kwame off?

Why was the dark under the duvet so friendly?

Why did his arms and legs go limp when Mummy and Akua tried to drag him out from under there, with their threats and their chatter about missing the Winter Show?

Why didn't he care any more?

Why did the image of Mrs Gilchrist's face mean nothing?

And why did Mummy and Akua just say fine, fine, fine, fine, drop Kwame's heavy limbs and leave him in his room?

Why was folding into himself – tighter, tighter – the only possible thing to do?

Why didn't he mind about the arm-long list of people he was letting down?

How did the hours move? How did the time pass?

Why did he not flinch when the phone rang or at Akua's lies down the line about Kwame's tummy bug?

Why did it seem like the lines from 'Consider Yourself' were slipping out of his mind like the tears slipping from his eyes?

Why did standing in front of an audience – or standing at all – seem impossible?

Why did he think he would never be able to stand in front of anyone, ever again?

Why was he crumpling?

Why was considering himself the last thing he wanted to do?

Why could he only *sense* the food, the water being brought?

Why did he brush away the hand that stroked his forehead? Was it because he knew it wasn't Yaw's?

Where were Yaw's hands – and his eyes – eyes starrier than the skies he wanted to float through?

Why did he not care that the light was failing and the night rising?

How did the hours move? How did the time pass?

May 2018

There wasn't very much of the lunch hour left when Kwame decided to call Mummy to say bon voyage before her flight the next day. He turned into his classroom, admired how pristine Mrs Antwi had made his grubby whiteboard and went to the window. The blinds had been pulled down, filling the place with a gloom not suitable for his next lesson – Creative Writing, about zoos today, with the Year 8s. Everyone hated these supplementary sessions that Madame Evans and now Marcus Felix insisted on their delivering over the half-term holidays, so best to make things as bright as possible. Rotating the blind's wand, he let light flood in.

Mummy seemed to be anticipating her trip with an unshifting dread. He asked if there were really no way of her finding anything positive about seeing Aunty.

'Won't it be nice not to be in London for a couple of weeks? I'd love to run away from this country right now.'

A world-weary grumble reverberated down the line.

'You don't know this my sister. Your aunty and I – is never been easy. Why Lord God has sent me such trials remains mysterious.'

Kwame rested his elbows on the ledge. There was another hum at the end of the line, then Mummy began a diatribe about growing up with Aunty Regina in the village. Kwame was well aware of the painful minutiae of these stories, but, not sparing detail, Mummy outlined the viciousness of their childhood fights for the scarce resources – food, love, space – on their family's smallholding.

Four storeys below, in the playground, he could see a group of Year 7s playing an elaborate version of musical statues: participants seemed to be throwing themselves into angular dancing, followed by doing very precise clapping and then freezing in absurd positions. A plump girl with stringy pigtails moved when she wasn't supposed to. Her disappointment was nearly as great as Kwame's when Marcus Felix hadn't turned up for their run earlier that morning.

Kwame had cheerily woken up in time for Marcus Felix's expected arrival, had pulled on the snazzy new Nike kit he had bought for himself, stood out on the doorstep for a good twenty minutes doing stretches and star jumps, nodding at unimpressed, dawn-rising labourers. All to no avail. But if he happened to spot the headteacher between meetings, whizzing around school later that day or later that week, Kwame would not make a fuss, would not question him about his absence. There was no dignity in that. And he would do his very best not to ask him about it at Saturday's dinner, for which Edwyn intended to cook one of Gibson's classic wood pigeon recipes.

After the Felixes had trotted off to see another house, Edwyn and Kwame had continued to peruse the market. This perusal was not without tension. Kwame spent the next thirty minutes doing his best to get his friend to text the Felixes with excuses – he'd need to cancel; the dates wouldn't work etc. A dinner party with his boss and his boss's wife was not, Kwame insisted, raising his voice, what he wanted to do of a Saturday evening. But, of course, Edwyn was unswayable. The Felixes were, apparently, fucking 'incredible' people. And why, Edwyn wanted to know, was Kwame being so weird about it all? Marcus Felix was 'cool', he had such extraordinary 'chutzpah'. There was, Edwyn asserted, only good to be gained from making some older friends who might have refreshingly different perspectives. Their world, 'their echo chamber' – Kwame's, Edwyn's – needed expanding. To argue otherwise was to be a complacent stick in the mud. Edwyn paid a man with muddy fingers for a tranche of Stichelton, and the conversation was moved on to whether Edwyn ought to get his face painted like Serena's.

Mummy's phone clattered. 'Kwame, Kwame. Me, I have to go because Mrs Okolie is shouting about something to do with her key.' There was more clattering. 'Is a shame to cut things short because is always nice to talk to my good son. Oh, and don't worry, Kwame, I will return with gifts for you. Plenty. Maybe even those tiger nuts you liked so much as a child every time we visited? You remember?'

Mummy's laugh climbed as she recalled the time – was he eleven? – when he had eaten great handfuls of the gnarled, stripy nuggets even after they had given him violent stomach cramps. Munching and munching, messy, grainy brown blobs over his chin and cheeks like a repulsive rash. But Kwame didn't laugh with her. She recounted how he had been a monster, mashing fistful after fistful into his face, barely pausing for breath. He watched the Year 7s below drawing things to a close. They collected rucksacks, dawdled. Pressing down hard, dragging with force, he scratched his nail along the sill.

'All the aunties went wild about my excellent appetite, but then got a bit scared and wondered about juju when it looked like I'd never stop and they thought I was possessed.'

'It was a bit mad, Kwame. You have to admit.'

'It was such a weird hunger, Mummy. Deep. I'd never tasted anything as sweet, so delicious. And that texture too. It felt good to just reach out and grab and have. I couldn't see or hear anything beyond the hunger.' He adjusted his grip on the phone and could have told her that the hunger – which was deep but unbalancing too – hadn't just troubled him in that aunties' too-sunny compound as he ate despite queasiness. From the moment Yaw had left, and for months afterwards, that frightening thing like hunger hummed under the surface of Kwame's skin. It was a constant gnawing and needing that he could not name and that felt much bigger than him.

But Mummy's voice on the line was absent-minded, whimsical. 'You, with your fine and funny words. Your fine and funny words.'

Kwame looked down at the playground again. It was entirely empty, entirely still.

June 2018

In an ideal world, to avoid staining his hands a gruesome shade of red, he would have slipped on some Marigolds before prising the beetroots out of their packaging. He couldn't seem to find any under the sink so had to go without. He scooped the dark, sopping balls out of their plastic cell and arranged them beside the Bellamy-branded mandolin.

As if in need of Dutch courage before the act of mutilation, Kwame took three more gulps of limy Vermentino. The mandolin's blade was exciting; threatening in its potential to shred fingertips, and magical in its ability to transform bulbous vegetables into elegant wafers. Back and forth Kwame grated the beetroots, moving against the rhythm of the Mary J. Blige ballad coming out of the speakers. Kwame's hips jerked.

'Turn this up – and top me up too.'

His request was swiftly fulfilled, and Edwyn also poured himself more, before lighting the candles on the table. Kwame watched Edwyn's hips working as awkwardly as his, and noted how the jeans made Edwyn's nondescript white man's bottom even more invisible. They sang bits of the lyrics and continued with their preparations: pigeon breasts were dusted with flurries of salt; the heat on the juniper jus was increased. Kwame squeezed lemons for his dressing, pumping the fruit with a vigour that caught Edwyn's attention. The quickly swallowed booze, the stickiness of the airless evening, the prospect of Marcus Felix putting into his mouth something created by Kwame's hands made Kwame jumpy, strange. It was fun. He discarded the spent fruit.

A thought struck him. 'You checked that they're not, like, allergic to anything – or vegetarian? You did check?'

'Texted him yesterday to make sure,' Edwyn said. 'He was like, "No, we're big-time carnivores," which I found kind of gross, to be honest.'

Kwame threw a handful of pips into the bin. 'Do you reckon they'll dress up?'

'I told them it was casual – although, dear friend, *you* seem to have other ideas.'

'What's uncasual about this?' Kwame freed himself from the end-of-the-pier apron with enormous, bright pink boobs that Gibson gifted them years ago. He did a series of twirls that best showed off his lacy black shirt, leather trousers, black DMs.

'You look very handsome. And it's nice you've made an effort, even though you weren't sure about all this to start with. I do like that you always come round in the end.' Kwame's brow contracted. 'Babe, it's a good thing. A really positive trait, that . . . that flexibility? I think that's a bit of you that's so worth celebrating and foregrounding even *more*, you know?' Edwyn frowned, ran his hands down the shapeless beige thing hanging from his frame. 'Is this *too* chilled? It's too chilled, isn't it? I ought to change.'

The doorbell chimed its twee trill.

'Course they're fucking early. What's wrong with straight people? Will you get it? I'm going to find a different top.

345

Two secs. There's more Vermentino in the fridge. Give them that.' Edwyn sprinted out, kept shouting from the corridor. 'Don't open what they've brought. *Don't*. Whatever it is. It'll upset the balance of things. I've curated the story the wines are telling this evening very carefully. I don't want my narrative fucked with.'

'So lots of sorry, really: super-sorry I missed our last run – emergency meeting with Social Services about a Year 12 that I could not wriggle out of, you know how it goes, bruv. And, and sorry number two is that you'll have to manage with just little old me tonight' – Marcus Felix's eyes and lips were full of remorse – 'and this' – he handed Kwame a bottle of Pinot Noir – 'me and this bad boy.'

The label was spare, the typeface simple. Kwame thought this might mean something promising about the quality of the contents. But he was never sure, was never right about these things. There were so many rules.

'Star's gutted she couldn't make it. Says you boys have got sparkle, which is high praise coming from her. She's not easily won over and you guys did it in seconds.' The head-teacher hung his jacket on the coat stand and smoothed it down. Marcus Felix's woody scent did something to the set of Kwame's shoulders. 'This friend of hers – Sally? Bruv, it's, it's not my place to be chatting someone else's business, but I think Star's worried about leaving her alone tonight, get me? But let me not dwell on that, man. 'S not all bad. It'll be quite fun for it to be just us lads.'

'Is that what you call her – Star?' He showed Marcus Felix the way to the kitchen, forgot that he already knew where it was.

'She hates it. I tell her it's better than "Stasi", which I could have opted for. You go by any nicknames?'

Kwame used his phone to reduce the speakers' noise to a muttering, and he saw that Marcus Felix's shirt had a satiny texture he had not noticed out in the passageway. The candlelight rippled across the material as the headteacher settled. The fabric invited touch.

'Kraakye. My parents and relatives used to sometimes call me kraakye. Sometimes. But, other than that, no, not really. "Kwame" doesn't seem to –'

'Kraa-kye? Kraakye.' The effort with which the head-teacher copied the enunciation was endearing. 'What's that mean, then?'

'It's Twi. Something like our word "gentleman". I spose they used to call me that when I was younger because it was funny for tiny me to have such a grand title.'

Kwame got the white from the fridge, poured, wondered what the headteacher would make of the fact that Kwame had also once been called Lil' G, and had glowed every time Yaw had called him that. 'Take a seat, Mr Felix. Please.'

'And did you like it? That they saw you that way? As a little *squire*?'

'I think I did, yeah.'

'Why?'

'I think I sometimes pretended I found it naff, but it actually made me feel as if I were better than others, than the other kids around me. At school. *Distinctive.* And being distinctive, for the right reasons, mattered to me then. Mattered a lot.'

'And – do you still need that now?'

'Sorry?'

Marcus Felix leaned back in the chair so that his crotch was elevated and prominent. He rocked forward, rested elbows on the table. 'Do you still need to feel special? Or are you free of that?'

Drinking, Kwame let his head gently drop to one side. He considered the fineness of Marcus Felix's eyebrows, the darkness of his skin, his parted lips. Feeling the anticipation and resolve of the headteacher's gaze, Kwame found he was at peace with the pressure of those eyes looking directly into his. The quietness and the whispered breeze passing through the room made it easy for Kwame to believe that the man's eyes were speaking to and coaxing out some buried part of himself. Kwame straightened his neck.

'Are any of us properly free?' he asked, testily.

'Us who?'

'*Us* Bla—'

Edwyn flew into the room – a touch of eyeliner, tight T-shirt, paisley cravat, tighter jeans that gave his bottom more character – and then fretted at the hob. 'Is the jus okay? I thought I could smell burning.'

'That's the heat of our scintillating conversation.' The headteacher enjoyed his quip. 'Good to see you, Edwyn. Thanks for having me.'

'Hi, Marcus, great to see you too. Is Anastasia powdering her nose? Or on her way?'

'She's mortified she can't make it, mate. Apologies. Can't be helped, I'm afraid. But you needn't worry, my appetite is an immense one, so I'll be polishing off her portion. Ain't nothin going to waste around here.' He rubbed his belly. 'Can I be of any assistance at all? Hate to be idle.'

The headteacher was set to work. Edwyn knotted himself

into the questionable apron with the boobs and it caught Marcus Felix's attention.

'I would never, *ever* be able to get away with wearing a thing like that. And yet somehow you manage to carry it off pretty well. Kudos.' He patted Edwyn's shoulder, left his hand there for a second.

'Thanks. I think.'

The fourth, now unnecessary, setting at the table needed dealing with. Trying to adapt to the shifted mood in the room, Kwame moved the chair away and picked up the glasses, plates, cutlery, napkins laid out for Anastasia. He concentrated on carefully opening cupboards and drawers and sliding things into their right places, while Edwyn explained to Marcus Felix what they were eating and asked questions about SLA's health. The headteacher stressed he was 'not about shop talk or bloody Brexit chat tonight'.

Kwame could see the headteacher was taking his tasks very seriously. Hazelnuts were scrutinized. Any deemed unworthy – according to some mysterious criteria – were placed to the side. Intuiting where the saucepans were, Marcus Felix found the necessaries for toasting the nuts and got on with that, while quizzing Edwyn about his necktie and asking to see the tattoo up close. Then the headteacher turned his attention to the thyme. He plucked the leaves with methodical nips and softly laid them on the chopping board, then worked the knife keenly before collecting them into a tidy hill. Edwyn tried to move the conversation to Marcus Felix's own dazzling achievements, but Marcus Felix really didn't want that kind of chat. Instead, he helped himself to a massive handful from the packet of Kettle Chips. Crunching, enjoying the Whitney Houston now playing, he floated over to the fridge, talking about how desperate he was to get a motorbike, didn't care if the missus called it trite and mid-life crisis-y, didn't mind that Edwyn agreed with her too. Marcus Felix floated to the side to fetch his glass, floated around to top everyone up. On his discovery that there was no Vermentino left with which to refresh his own vessel, he shook the empty bottle and stamped his foot; this pretended irritation drew to a close only when Edwyn pulled another bottle from the freezer. After sipping, the headteacher slammed his glass on the worktop. 'Fuck it. Why not? But don't breathe a word in the staff room. It'd ruin my street cred.'

He gestured for Edwyn to come closer, then fiddled with the knot at Edwyn's back. The knot, Kwame soon gathered from the headteacher's struggles, was tough. But, ever gallant, the headteacher pressed on, laughing, whispering something that made Edwyn giggle, shaking his head as he wrestled, until he finally unpeeled the apron from Edwyn's body. Still laughing, the headteacher got into it and, grinning madly, presented his transformed self to Kwame. The pinkness of the boobs was even more alarming than usual.

'I was right, wasn't I? Not my thing at all.'

'Nonsense, headteacher.' Kwame crossed his arms, tried a playful smile. 'You're a vision.'

Marcus Felix drained the last of the Sangiovese. 'And that, my friends, is how I ended up meeting the one and only Prince himself. I will dine out on that story till I'm dead and buried. Bar getting married and Serena's birth, it was hands down the best day of my life. Honestly, even now, *even now* as I'm saying it to you, it's mental. Like it happened to someone else. I mean – Prince! *Prince!*'

'Well, that is, I suppose, what connections and the gift of the gab can achieve sometimes.' Edwyn speared the final slither of pigeon on his plate. 'Access to the starriest of starry stars.'

'This will sound like a mad ting or woo woo or whatever, but it seemed . . . sort of fated. I was standing there, in front of him, and he was messing around with his cape and saying something beautiful but a bit incomprehensible about vibrations. And I nodded. No embarrassment or, or awkwardness about being in the presence of such greatness. Just this sense that, yeah, this was meant to happen. He and I were meant to share the same tiny space, for a bit. And it was cool. *He* was cool. I – I'm going off on one again.'

'Not at all. Fate is real, Marcus. But was it sad that, like, you didn't have a mate there, or Anastasia, to share it with? Or do you reckon that would have diminished the experience a bit?' The jus had made Edwyn's lips slick, shiny. Kwame watched him slowly lick them clean.

'None of my mates are into his stuff. They're all massive Spurs fans most of them, nothing else – but I always linked football to my dad, so I sort of turned my back on it after he went. But I love a live gig. Love seeing bands on my jays. Do it all the time.'

'Ah, a maverick,' Kwame said.

'It's more . . . intimate. Meaningful. People in the crowd look at me with such pity, as if I'm the biggest loser, but I don't care. Flying solo means you don't have to engage in empty pre-performance small talk when you're buzzing and don't wanna waste that high on mindlessness. And you don't have to moderate your own emotions about what you've seen, what you've heard, when you're chatting about it to try to reach consensus.' Edwyn's nod was half-hearted. The headteacher noted its lack of conviction. 'But I take your point, Ed. Would've been, yeah, *different* to connect with someone about that backstage miracle. Might have made it more real, I guess. Any red going spare?'

'Mmm. We'll have the last of this Malbec and then there's something silly and excitable to go with the pud.'

Kwame laughed to himself then coughed. '*Sorry*. Sorry.'

'What?'

'Nothing.'

'Go on, Mr Akromah.' The headteacher flapped his napkin. 'Tell the class. Or it's Detention for you.'

'I was imagining your mate Head of Behaviour letting loose to "Raspberry Beret".'

'Yikes.'

'Exactly.'

'I mean – between you and me, Head of Behaviour's not my *buddy*, per se. We're not tight like that.'

Kwame placed his fork on his plate, then his knife. Would the headteacher ever describe him as a friend? How *did* he describe Kwame to others?

'I respect him,' Marcus Felix continued. 'Good bloke. Peerless leader, don't get me wrong, but no. Not friends. He's a different breed from me.' He paused, became fascinated by the shadows and reflections his glass cast on the tablecloth. 'Truth be told, my circle of associates is pretty small. I seem to have shed pals as fast as I've shed my hair. Guess it's what happens when you move around as much as I have to. Banstead one term, Middlesbrough the next.' Kwame nodded, wavering as the headteacher's voice became more doleful, forlorn. Marcus Felix drank. 'Which is why this evening is so lovely, boys. *Lovely* hanging out with two guys who seem so in tune with one another. Proper *simpatico*. It's good.'

'He's . . . reasonably diverting, I suppose,' Kwame said.

Edwyn lowered his hand and rested it on the table meaningfully. 'I was saying to Kwame earlier that I'm lucky I've got him. I benefit so much from his generosity. I've been through some shitty patches, Marcus. My early twenties were a bit tricky. I'll not bore you with the details and it was like a lifetime ago now, so. But Kwame *listened* throughout. He had his own battles, but he was still able to listen and let me talk my way through my troubles.' Edwyn paused as if unnerved but soon went on, the headteacher increasingly interested in his words. 'I mean, I've always thought that sort of patience is probably what makes him a fucking incredible teacher.'

'Yep. I've had the good fortune of seeing him in action in the classroom, mate. He comes alive up in there. And incredible is exactly right. He, he, gets the kids completely. Hundred per cent.'

'I bet. It's like a beautiful, like a truly fucking beautiful . . . I don't know . . . selflessness that you've got sometimes, Kwame? And you do it without even, even like drawing attention to it or making a fuss or anything. It literally kept me going, that selflessness – still really does.'

It might have been pedantic for Kwame to quibble with Edwyn's memories and praise, to clarify that Kwame's so-called patience was, in fact, more complicated. That patience when they were younger came from a sense that he had been out of his depth in Edwyn's blue period. Edwyn's post-university anxieties about professional success being slow in coming or perhaps *never* coming to him – and the long shadow of his father's accomplishments – seemed too big and feverish for twenty-one-year-old Kwame to comment on. On the occasions when Kwame had tried intervention, Edwyn had batted away those advances with barbed rebuttals which had sometimes almost sent Kwame packing. And yet Kwame had remained, had found something impressive, attractive about the intensity and heat with which Edwyn expressed his suffering. That, really, was why Kwame had stayed and stroked Edwyn's wavy hair, all those nights at Laleham when Edwyn wailed.

'I was just showing a little humanity,' Kwame offered. 'When you needed some.'

'Yes,' Edwyn said. 'Absolutely right. It was exactly that. But it was much more too. It was life-saving. Life-changing.'

Because Marcus Felix was woozily talking about holding your dearest tight; and because, ultimately, Edwyn's words had been an attempt at kindness, Kwame looked up from his plate – smeared with the pinkness of beetroot juices and pigeon blood – and raised a little toast to his friend.

By the time they eventually decided to head to the living room for cognacs, the conversation had become significantly more slurred, punctuated by long yawns. Though unsurprising, it was still disappointing that, almost as soon as they had made their way from the kitchen and each had chosen where they'd sit, Edwyn dozed off. He had promised to re-energize them with a clever trick with their amaretti papers, setting them alight in such a way that made them dance high in the air. Kwame explained to Marcus Felix, rolling the decanter's stopper in his palm, that Edwyn's appearing on *This Morning* three times that week had obviously taken its toll. The headteacher pressed the rim of the glass to his lips, wobbling as he drank deeply.

Clutching his own glass, Kwame could hear Hanna below, her laugh a series of explosive snorts. The playlist moved on to Amy Winehouse and, from his seat in the corner of the room, Kwame found that he was amused by the contrasting physicalities of the men opposite him. Edwyn had curled himself into the armchair, head tucked under, arms wrapping protectively. Meanwhile, Marcus Felix dominated the sofa he had taken, his left leg running across the seats, the other leg outstretched towards Phyllida's Turkish rug, his arm thrust behind his head, trying to prop it up.

Kwame felt his head swaying and circling on his neck. 'I love Amy's voice. The way it's so stained and, like, full of truth? The way that it's so tired of being disappointed – but she's not defeated. There's still always that flare there. That chance of a last attack. You know?'

Amy reached for even more plaintive colours now. Edwyn's snore bubbled, and Marcus Felix's foot tapped the rug with an unsteady rhythm for two bars before stopping abruptly. Kwame watched him slip off his suede loafer, wriggle his toes and then bring that foot into his lap. The headteacher hummed along with 'Fuck Me Pumps'. Rubbing his ankle, he moved the foot so its arch became pronounced. He garbled sentences about what he would give to be able to sing: how much he wished he could sing, how jealous he was of his mum, his sisters, his nana, all of whom had voices you wouldn't believe. How much he had always wanted to sing from the top of his lungs!

Kwame commiserated, drily complimented Marcus Felix's humming, praise which made the headteacher feign embarrassment. Kwame noted how well looked after those bending, flexing feet were. The toes were so exact, the nails uniform. When Amy Winehouse's voice climbed, Marcus Felix released the foot, stretched himself out again and closed his eyes, reclining so the full length of his neck was exposed, waiting. Ready to be kissed. The sinews, the stubble descending from the jaw, the Adam's apple. Kwame rested his cognac glass on the coffee table.

Kwame had slept with more than thirty men, and he reflected again on the fact that only three of them had been Black. Joshua. Abiodun. Aaron. Just three. Each of them a one-night thing. Three very different men, three very different kinds of sex. Joshua: hard, fast, efficient, clearly keen to come, shake hands, leave, continue working his way down his to-do list. Abiodun: more tender, more responsive to even the most subtle shifts of Kwame's body, more interested in slow and sincere kissing. Aaron: with the chafing harness that he kept distractingly readjusting throughout proceedings. Just those three. When Brown faces had flashed up on Grindr, or if – as was so rarely the case – a Black man in a club tried whispering into his ear and winding an arm around his waist, Kwame found that reciprocating didn't come easily. He knew he should probably feel guilty about it, but he did not. It wasn't – Kwame was certain – an aversion that spoke of self-loathing. No. He was always tentative, because, with each of those three

Black men, as distinct and variable and beautiful as those encounters had been, with each there had been a moment – a shuddering and shaky moment – when Kwame had felt too seen. A very particular, very powerful kind of closeness that came with a sense of loss too. A feeling that set him on edge rather than settled him.

There was a thumping sound. The headteacher was tapping the sofa. 'You're so far away. All the way over there, on your own.' He tapped, smiled. 'I won't bite.' He tapped again. 'I'm lonely here on my lonesome.'

Marcus Felix neatened his sprawling limbs, moved up to make more space and tapped again, louder so that Edwyn shuffled in his sleep. The headteacher stifled an apologetic giggle, pressed a finger to his lips. Kwame's subsequent sitting next to him seemed to make the headteacher so exultantly happy. His eyes became grateful, juvenile. Maybe he had been to the pub before dinner?

''S better here, isn't it?' the headteacher asked, seriously. 'With me. With me.'

His breath was rich and heavy with all that they'd eaten and drunk, and, Kwame noticed, the woody scent from earlier was still there, perhaps a little less potent now, a little mingled with sweat. Through the loosened collar, the perfect rod of the headteacher's clavicles was visible. Kwame crossed his legs.

'Well, you've pulled me away from my favourite chair, to be honest. So not best pleased.'

'Such an old man.'

'What?'

The headteacher sat forward with a slump. 'Old man. Cocoa. Warmed slippers. *Favourite chair.*'

357

'Such a lazy and woefully inaccurate misrepresentation of me –'

'*Old fucking man.* Knows what he likes but does he like what he knows? Does he? Kwame?'

As the headteacher leaned closer, a heartbeat drummed behind Kwame's ears. It passed down his jaw and along his tongue. He imagined sliding his tongue into the other man's ear, letting it twist and explore. He tried to look thoughtful. 'Do I like what I know? Probably not, to be honest. Probably not.'

Marcus Felix was trying to touch his temples but nearly poked his eyes instead. 'Plenty of secrets and too much else up in that there head of yours, eh? But you have to ask yourself, mate, how are they even helping you? Pandora bes let em out if she's lookin to actually live a life and not just be movin on, on, on – for what?'

'I should get you a water. Get both of us waters.'

'It's not as bad as all that, Kwame.' He waved his hands and the dim light passed over his silky shirt. 'Stop with all that. No one's watching now. It's just me and you.'

'Two waters coming –'

'I'm compos mentis, blad.'

'*Riiiiight.*' Kwame got to his feet, but the headteacher grabbed his wrist to stop him. The fingers were hot and sure, the downward pull so tight as to be almost painful, but Kwame didn't struggle away.

'Do you reckon it was fate? Kwame? Do you? Your mate Edwyn does, but do you reckon it was fate? I'm asking you.'

Kwame freed himself, enjoying the smarting sensation that remained around his wrist, and raised an eyebrow. 'On

Monday morning when I repeat the stuff you've been going on about tonight you are going to be mortified, *boss*.'

'What I was saying about Prince. Do you think that's how it works? Fate. That it can deliver a person into your life, to make you take stock, to make you look again? Because sometimes you have to snap out of it, get me? Sometimes you have to fix up your vision to make sure it's twenty-twenty, for real. Or do you think that's bullshit? Bullshit, yeah? Do you think that's bullshit, because you see me – well, you *think* you see me – you see me, and think he's a bullshitter of smooth talking and hot air with nice teeth.'

'Marcus, that's not what I think at all. You're an incredibl–'

The headteacher found himself, and perhaps Kwame, hilarious. 'Every time, I'm like, go on, Marky mate. I'm within sniffing distance. I'm like, you're close, Marky mate. Keep at it. You've nearly got him. Uncover him yeeeet! Nearly at blood and bone!'

'What are you even t–'

'Excuse me – I'm the questioner.' The headteacher pointed his thumb back into the centre of his chest, grimaced. His golden eyes flashed. 'Me. And I want to know what I want to know about you, Kwame. *You*. And what I want to know is –' He put his hand up to his mouth, let it flop away, shook his head. 'Shit. I've lost my train of thought entirely. Shit, Kwame. Will you help me get it back?' His eyes expanded. 'Aren't we here to help each other, bruv? Eh?' He winked. 'I'll help you if you help me, mate. Eh? I know you want to.'

'So that's too loud, that's too loud now, please. It's all got too loud and too much,' Edwyn muttered from his armchair. 'I'm the party pooper. *C'est fini*, gentlespoons.'

He stretched, stumbled to his feet, stopped the music and started collecting glasses, bottles, the amaretti papers, so Kwame did the same. And when Kwame turned round to offer Marcus Felix a coffee or perhaps water, once more, the headteacher was sitting perfectly upright, feeding Uber the postcode that it needed.

Dodging the obvious suntraps, seeking out shade, Kwame eventually sat his Year 12s in a circle in the cool patch behind the Sports Hall the following Friday afternoon. Sitting back on his haunches as everyone settled, he let Elise and Estelle's intense conversation about hair extensions – the price of Ukrainian weaves versus Malaysian, the quality of Indonesian versus Russian – continue to become absurdly detailed and technical: he enjoyed watching the awkward interest of the white girls in the class. He let them chatter about how jealous they were of the Year 13s leaving SLA in a matter of weeks. They desperately wanted, they said, to gatecrash the imminent Farewell Dance. He listened to them dream up grand plans for their own prom next summer, while he, again, entertained directionless thoughts about Marcus Felix's yanking of his wrist after dinner; the thrill of being held by him – a stretched and breathless second he would never tell Edwyn about, his brief hope that the pull would melt into gentleness.

Once more, Kwame scrolled through Marcus Felix's messages from Sunday morning. The first was a row of green emojis with cheeks bulging. There were various capitalized claims, followed by battalions of exclamation marks, that he did not remember a thing after pudding. The last was an apology if he were guilty of 'hitting the red too hard'. Once more, Kwame inspected his own replies of breezy hangover sympathy, quickly thumbed while Edwyn had been busy channel-hopping.

Kwame had seen the headteacher at school only two times since the Saturday visit to the flat. At the end of Monday break time, there was a swift passing by in the Languages corridor. Marcus Felix had doffed an imaginary hat before he stopped to adjust a Year 9's tie. Later, in the canteen, distanced by a group of prefects, their shared glance lasted a split second before Marcus Felix's PA signalled that he had to be elsewhere, and sharpish. Directly after both occasions, Kwame had felt it: the sense of evaporated possibility and of something precious being stolen.

Now one of the white girls was asking Estelle about Azonto, and Estelle was telling her that those moves were dusty and dead. When one of the Physics technicians walked past the class with an officious trot and examined the group of students critically, Kwame slipped his phone away and made a show of calling for attention. He handed round sheets on to which he had copied snippets of Virginia Woolf's diaries and letters. He asked the class, in pairs, to explore and comment on the extracts, and to report back ideas in five minutes.

The ease with which he had agreed to have the lesson in the open air – something Madame Evans frowned on – had won him credit. As such, the group set about the work with energy. They huddled, scrunching their faces as they tried to decode. Kwame eavesdropped. Riya kept referring to Woolf as 'Virginia' as if they were old chums. It was a tic which Kwame's tutors at Durham had taught out of him, but that Kwame found charming. Andrea said it was weird and disrespectful reading someone's diary and private letters like this. Melissa Ng thought the way Woolf wrote in her journal was really different from the way she wrote in the novel but couldn't find the right words to explain. Anton was unmoved by Melissa's struggles.

When they came together to talk as a class, trying not to be distracted by the ice-cream van at the school gates, Elise and Estelle were keen to share first. Kwame's agreement that they could begin things made them break into coy smiles. Rather than seventeen, they both looked seven. Seven and, Kwame thought, touchingly eager to be noticed and valued.

'Our quote from Woolf was this one, 30 August 1923. This is what she said. I'll do it in my proper voice cos she was posh. Hold on.' Elise coughed a hearty cough. '"I dig out beautiful caves behind my characters; I think that gives exactly what I want; humanity, humour, depth. The idea is that the caves shall connect, and each come to daylight at the present moment."'

'Nicely read, Elise. And tell us, what are your thoughts about Woolf's thinking there?'

'Can I do something a bit, like, different, sir? You can tell me it's wrong but let me flow with it first.'

'It'll be good, sir,' Estelle piped in. 'I think it's quite clever, to be honest.'

'Such a build-up.'

'It's – I wanted to see if I can take the Woolf thing and link it to Tess.'

'Go on.'

'Like, how I see it is that Tess is kind of a cave. As in, in the book, she's this kind of empty space a lot of the time. Other people try to, like, fill her up with all their ideas and opinions about her. Her parents do it. That Angel Clare as well. And that Alec or Alex or whatever that demon is called, he, like, literally does it when he forces her.'

'Nastiness.'

'All of them,' Elise went on, 'impose themselves on her, in a way. Like she's, yeah, a nothing, blank, bare cave they can make their own.'

'Listen to my girl chat! *Impose* – hear her using that dictionary!'

'They *impose* themselves on her, telling her what she wants to do and what she should be and how she has to run her life. By the end of it, she can't stand it no more and she shanks mans because it's too much. Like she's suffocating or something.' The breeze that came was welcome but whipped up grit, so Elise closed her eyes for a second. 'I'm not sure how that deals with the stuff Woolf said about connecting up and the present, but – yeah. That's what I thought when I saw the sentence. I thought about how Hardy makes Tess seem empty to the reader. And it's sad.'

It was sad. The whole class knew it was undeniably sad. And so, perhaps because they were waiting for Kwame to guide them away from that sadness, his students sat, for a moment, undisturbed by the heat, in silence. But Kwame found he could do no artful redirecting. His breathing slowed until it rasped. He wondered if he might cry, there and then. Did that count as showing the blood and bones of himself?

'You, you all right, sir? Is it really that badly wrong?'

'Elise, no!' He sprang forward. 'No, not at all. It's a completely, completely *brilliant* thought, Elise. Honestly. Well done. Really original, and unexpected. And great.' Kwame pressed his clammy palms together and spoke to the whole class now. 'So can anyone come up with an idea about how we *can* put together Elise's great reading of the quotation and the idea of interlocking caves? It might be hard but have a think. We'll figure it out, together. Two mins. Off you go.'

The class huddled again, flicking through their *Dalloway*s and their *Tess*es, exchanging notes. He swallowed. In the distance, behind the kids' bowed heads, Kwame made out the figure of Natalie running towards him. Her arm was frantic, madly appealing for his attention.

When Kwame and his father arrived back at Richmond Court, Mr O'Shea was on his doorstep, moving his feet in and out of his slippers. As Daddy waved a hello – the gesture more dismissal than greeting – Mr O'Shea's eyes illuminated. He genuflected, and muttered relief that Daddy's fall hadn't resulted in anything more than bruising and a few cuts.

Though disorientated by the corridor's unsparing lighting and too-bright peach walls, Kwame still had the wherewithal to keep firmly supporting his father's weight. Mr O'Shea spoke his spells and Kwame smiled the briefest of smiles, which Mr O'Shea – with his feet still fussing away – took as a prompt to share his version of events. Earlier that afternoon, four almighty thuds had startled him and disturbed the pictures of Mary Anne – God rest her soul – on his mantelpiece. He had knocked on the Akromahs' door many times, and shouted Andy's name to find out what was going on but got no response. He had eventually heard something faint and broken, a whine from the other side of the wood. Oh! It was a good thing that he still had a spare key – it really was! And the blood? The blood was the like of which he had never seen before. Kwame's poor pa was barely moving, scrunched up at the bottom of the stairs. The blood! Mrs Okolie's daughter had come up a while ago to do her best with Dettol and elbow grease. Still such a nice girl. Nice manners. He fished a handkerchief out of his pocket and blew into it with sudden strength.

Kwame's instinct was to take this pause to quickly get his father inside to the sofa; Daddy had turned his face away from Mr O'Shea and the heat of his impatience was almost radiating through his tattered fleece. But, still smiling weakly, even as Daddy muttered about finding the keys himself if Kwame had no interest in getting them, Kwame let the old Irishman go on: how worried he had been when Andy was rushed off to St George's, how the fretting had put him off his gammon and egg tea, weren't neighbours just the most important? Kwame squeezed Daddy's tetchy shoulder and let Mr O'Shea draw the conversation to a close on his own terms – by repeating that Kwame ask him if he needed any help. Granting the courtesy of listening until Mr O'Shea had exhausted himself with chatter was a tiny offering of gratitude Kwame could make to this lonely old man.

On entering the flat, Kwame steered Daddy past the dark soapy patch on the carpet. In the living room, he did his best to position Daddy in the armchair closest to the telly despite Daddy's protesting about not being an invalid.

'That O'Shea,' he said, the ottoman sinking beneath the weight of his legs, 'is so smug.'

'Daddy, he was o–'

'Is smug! I tell you he is smug. And all for what? A silly

mishap mistake that is nothing. And now' – Daddy's swollen cheek caught Kwame's attention again – 'now I bet he is, he is sitting on his sofa laughing to himself, thinking everyone says it is old Mr O'Shea who is near the knackers' yard but they should come to see the Black Methuselah next door. Now he is so old he cannot even do things as simple as to get down the stairs without a disaster occurring.'

Daddy started to wrestle out of his fleece but winced. It took a while but eventually he relented and allowed Kwame to help him remove the fuzzy jacket. Folding it, Kwame tucked away the cuff daubed with red.

'Make sure you text message your mother and sister. Make them know we arrived home safe.'

'Did it as soon as we got out of the Uber, Daddy.'

'And make your mother know she needn't call again tonight. What can she do for me from over there in Accra? Nothing. No. Tell her I am sleeping. We will reconvene in the morning. If we must.'

'Daddy –'

'And when you complete that one, fetch us both tea. The hospital's was an abomination.'

He switched on the widescreen television Kwame always thought was far too large for the small living room. The spot above the telly where Nkrumah had once reigned was, at the moment, occupied by a busy new arrangement of photos: June and Joanna dressed up as unicorns, June and Joanna dressed up as Harry and Hermione.

'Good,' Daddy said, '*News at Ten*. We will see Mrs May. I want to hear what mess she has got into today. If she is not careful, that Rees-Mogg will trounce her to take back control himself.'

'Are you sure you want tea, Daddy? Doesn't it keep you up if you have it past six?'

'Did that doctor tell you my marbles were gone? Did their tests and scans show I no longer know my own mind? No. No, they did not.' Huw Edwards's rundown of the day's events got louder as Daddy jabbed at the remote control's buttons. 'And two sugars not the usual single one. I deserve a small treat. Use the tinned milk also.'

During the cab journey from the hospital, the hot weather had broken. Rain had pixelated the view out of the windscreen. It felt like it would never stop. The driver sang along to Luther Vandross on Smooth FM while Kwame fielded WhatsApps from Natalie, Mrs Antwi, Edwyn, Akua and Mummy, and told them he would spend the weekend with Daddy until he was a bit more mobile. But Daddy said nothing during the journey, even when Kwame relayed to him that whoever was messaging sent best wishes or wished him the speediest of recoveries. Even when he passed on Akua's note that the girls wanted to hug their grandfather and so they'd all pop round tomorrow – her Lloyd was coming too. Once or twice Daddy tenderly pressed the dressing on his face where his cheek had caught the radiator when he had landed at the bottom of the stairs. But that was it. Other than that, only sour silence. So Daddy's current, extensive instructions were, Kwame thought while steam fanned from the kettle, a good sign of returning vigour. Despite Daddy's bossiness, Kwame was still touched – confused, surprised but still touched – when he remembered Daddy had called Kwame and not Akua to be with him through it all.

The bossiness clearly served an important, deeper purpose, and understanding its purpose went some way towards making it tolerable: it made Daddy feel more in control and solid, in an unpredictable world where the momentary mis-placing of feet could land you in a hospital bed surrounded by harassed-looking junior doctors. Besides, Kwame's taking orders, being patronized, making tea – these were all things he could accept. Contemplating the idea that this fall was the beginning of Daddy's dotage was a thought that Kwame was less willing to engage with. He found the peppermint tea which Mummy didn't like much herself but still bought for Kwame's visits, and immersed the teabag in the water, bobbed it around. Outside, the earlier storm had bubbled up again; the navy sky moaned, clapped. The green scent from the mug was almost restorative.

When Kwame brought the drinks and some chin-chins through to the living room, he soon noticed the volume on the news had been muted. The hurrahing MPs on the screen seemed even more absurd. Daddy was sat with his head in his hands, his stubby legs planted wide apart. Even though Daddy had been told to elevate his ankle, the otto-man had been pushed to the corner and lay askew on the old brown rug. Blue light from the telly cast coolness over Daddy's bald patch. Was Daddy dozing? There was none of his usual snoring, the irritable snuffle Mummy had imi-tated almost every morning of Kwame's childhood, but Daddy's chest was rising and falling to a rhythm that sug-gested sleep approached. Kwame's tinkled resting of the tray made Daddy shift. Daddy pressed fingers into the unhurt side of his face. There was a determination about his milky eyes.

'You know the last time I heard your mother cry the way she did, down the line, today?'

369

Kwame did not.

'Around when your Yaw left. Those weeks.'

'He wasn't *my* Yaw, Daddy.' Kwame squeezed a chin-chin. It exploded into crumbs.

'That noise. I never wanted to hear it again. I said to myself, when she did that noise, in those weeks after your Yaw upped and left, I made a promise to myself: I said I would make it my life's mission and purpose to keep that kind of noise from her throat. I said to myself I will never again put her in a situation where the only sound she can make is that crying.' Daddy wrapped one arm around his stomach.

Kwame could not remember Mummy making any such kind of piercing cry. Instead, he recalled other sounds and words from that time. He remembered, about a fortnight after Yaw had disappeared, hearing 'deportation' repeated, the only English word Kwame could recognize in the streams of Twi shouted down the phone night after night. Deportation. Deportation. Deportation. After Kwame begged her relentlessly, Akua had eventually explained what the word meant because no one else would.

In idle moments – waiting his turn to skip in the playground, trying on new shoes with Mummy in Clarks – Kwame's mind would slip into dark imaginings: white men grabbing Yaw's arms with their dirty white hands because Yaw's papers and passport and NI number were not his. Dirty white hands that held Yaw back, searched through his pockets, pulling at his body like they didn't care if it tore or split, as if they didn't know his body was price-less. Maybe, in the tussle, Yaw shouted that he wanted to see his kraakye, his Lil' G, to at least say goodbye. Perhaps

Yaw kept on kicking and spitting and refused to give in, but the white men were too many and too much. Kwame had pictured them bundling him into a van, shoving his head, bundling him on to a plane. Whether that was how things had happened or not, he could not know – Mummy and Daddy would not speak to Kwame about it. They only said, 'Gyae gyae gyae gyae,' and went to work with rumbling sighs if Kwame ever plucked up enough courage to ask them where Yaw was.

The months had turned. Melodee's face got long and tired and hard. She started to wear grey, not pink. Kwame wondered when her baby would come. It never did, and so he had thought sorrow had the power to make a whole baby vanish. Soon enough, Melodee and her mother disappeared from the estate too. No one batted an eyelid. Kwame learned to swallow his questions whole, a great, bitter ball of banku solid in the gullet. The swallowing hurt, but he managed. It was a lesson. On the morning when Kwame understood Yaw was gone, what Kwame knew he would miss – perhaps more than Yaw's beauty – was how Yaw had taken Kwame's small life and made it seem like a twinkling, sparkling thing.

Despite the furrowing of his father's forehead, Kwame was pleased when Daddy appeared to be ready to speak again: his voice made those memories of Yaw less pressing and definite.

'Your mother's tears. The crying. Is hard even to describe. It was, was like is almost killing her to make that noise, but she still had to do it. It crushes me to hear.'

'Are you –'

'Now I made her feel pain again. I know my tripping

was accident, I *know* so don't open your beak to lecture me on that one, wa te? But the point remains she will think of me and what may well come to her mind is the worry she has now. Pain and worry this will happen again. Is my job to protect her from such things. And look at me –' He indicated his split face, his ribs, his ankle. 'How can I protect when –'

'Take it easy, Daddy. She wouldn't want you speaking like this, working yourself up – would she?'

Daddy's eyes drooped. The light from the TV made his face stranger. Wind threw rain against windows: a brittle sound. His laugh held both bitterness and resignation. He looked at his palms. 'That evening of your Yaw's leaving. It was maybe my biggest and worst overreaction. I overreacted out of a fear. Was maybe wrong. I know in my heart was wrong. It was a fear because what would the relatives have said back home when they hear we allowed him to be running around sowing oats when he was supposed to come to this London to better himself, eh? Fear of the anger and the disgrace that would come. And, and fear because your Yaw he had ruined any chance to improve his life because he had tied himself to a child too soon. What was his life to be with a child in tow? At his small age? Big fears, even forcing me to bad words and worse decisions and overreaction. I know to overreact is not a virtue. I know that one.' He looked up. 'But you? Oil to my water, son. You, I fear, live only in under-reacting. And why? The, the strength I used to have when I was your age . . . when I think on what I was doing and forging at that time . . .' The wind, high and thin, seemed to be straining towards speech. 'I think on you. All the time. Keeps me up in the nights, sometimes. I read between your quiet lines. I see what I see. It all gives me pause to reflect. And gives me concern.'

Kwame anticipated another monologue on his being a life that was lived incorrectly. This was exactly why sometimes it was more straightforward to stay at home with Edwyn; more straightforward not to return calls but instead to stay at Fernlea with its evenings of predictable lesson planning or imitating Monica Galetti's steeliness on *MasterChef* — washed down with glasses of Edwyn's latest biodynamic discovery. Kwame squared his shoulders and passed his hands over his trousers. He reached for his peppermint tea and drank slowly. 'Well, Daddy, you needn't be *concerned*. There's nothing to be "concerned" about. Promise.'

'You. You have your good politeness and some clever jokes as if nothing has ever touched you. But a father's knowledge is more. I see is draining. To be a Black man? Yes, is to know struggle and to face challenge every which way you are turning. Anywhere on this world where you find a Black man that is the case. Is a fact. But to be a gay man also? A *gay Black* man?' Daddy clucked. 'To find yourself in places where these whites don't understand where you have come from but they still calling all your shots? And the few Blacks that come your way are thinking on you only as a gay alien that is from some out-of-space planet and not a brother?' Kwame swirled the teabag around in the murky water. 'I say I see you, Kwame Aboagye Akromah. How you, you struggle through it all, in your way. You squeezing my shoulder out there in the corridor is like even you are squeezing yourself, telling yourself to keep cool and calm and proper because that's how you thinking you have to be, isn't it? 24/7. All the moves you have to make. Remember

373

how you used to be with that one, that blonde and annoying one from the Thrale Primary School? To get your gold stars and certificates?'

'Mrs Gilchrist?'

'That woman. I knew what she was having you do. Jumping through hoops even then. I resented her for making you do so. It made me a nutter in those Parents' Evenings. Remember? In her presence, me, I behaved often like I was not right in the head. Because it filled me with rage. How she was. Always making you mind your p's and q's and congratulating you for it. And you did it – so that she, so that people don't see you and treat you as a Black hooligan and ne'er-do-well. Is a hard work to do such a thing. Is *graft*. And, yes, I am proud, in some ways, that you grafted well. Schooling. University. Teacher's training. It means now you are not like some of these, these roadmen Black men types collecting ASBOs and only saying whagwan blad blad on repeat. So I'm also saying I respect it, how you climbed the hill with your own two hands. And with us pushing you a little.'

'Daddy.'

'But, but sometimes my fear is that is putting blinkers on your vision. Eh? Making the way ahead too dark for you to even see for yourself.' Lightning creased the sky. The rain came even more thickly. 'In the old days, in the sorting office, we used to call your kind things like, like sissy. Like fairy. Like poof. We used these words because they sounded like nothing, like a little weak breath of air and because we thought of you people as being weak. I know better now. Maybe when you first told us about your preference for boys and whatever I couldn't see it then, but

374

now I have understood. It took a strength to say what you needed to say to us. Yet you, you do not even know what strength you have, what grit.' Daddy spoke to the palms of his hands. 'I only wish you could put that kind of force and guts into a mission that was not only about keeping yourself afloat. You understand me, isn't it?' Daddy looked at Kwame directly until they both nodded. But then Daddy sighed. 'Maybe I have diddlysquat wisdom to share or offer you. You in a world too different from mine.'

Kwame smiled. 'An out-of-space planet, perhaps?'

'Yes.'

'Daddy, I'm here to look after you. *You*. Okay? So no more worrying about me. Not today. I'm fine. I'm, I'm actually lucky. I've go–'

'Your face? When you speak these small words? Is looking so much like a grey puddle. Not bright with truth.' Daddy sat back in his seat. 'Fine. *Fine*. Lucky. Why? Why should you settle for these small things? Eh? When will you take up your strength and be bold enough to ask the world for what is fairly and rightly yours? Eh? When will you let yourself do that?'

Kwame watched a small bubble hover on the surface of his tea. He remembered how his body had begun to submit when he had run behind Marcus Felix, and how it had loosened even more as they sat and talked by the pond.

'Maybe I don't bother any more because it feels pointless: you ask, you scream, you're disappointed, you feel more stuck.' The bubble blinked and burst. 'But I'm sure I used to know how to do it. That *asking* . . .' He could see it, clearly: making Yaw help him with another collage, telling Yaw how to move the chairs so that their den was the right height, Yaw accepting instruction from his tiny boss with nothing more than the easiest of smiles, as if it were entirely good and right and reasonable that Kwame should have power. 'Lost the habit along the way, perhaps. Forgot how it's done. Not sure.'

'Then now remember, wa te? Perhaps I'm here to help you remember and remind you what has been in you and in your plain sight all along. Help you remember for yourself.'

Kwame fell quiet, waited for his father to say something more. But Daddy was squinting at the telly, neck craning slightly. On the screen, arrows, numbers and a Union Jack spread out from our tiny island and coursed across a map of Europe. Then the arrows retreated or doubled back on themselves. The numbers decreased and the Union Jack icon shrank to a small blue nub.

'We sleepwalking into a historical disaster with this Brexit. Mark my words. The next generation will never forgive us.' Daddy changed the channel to another station that played the earlier clip of celebrating MPs. After Daddy swore – which Kwame usually found funny – he turned off the TV altogether.

The next morning, Kwame was instructed to go down to the corner shop with a tenner to get the *Sun*, loo roll, Fairy Liquid. The reward for his efforts, as it sometimes was when he was a child, was that he could use the change to get a treat for himself. Daddy did much bemoaning of the outrageous cost of Mr Agrawal's substandard stock, and of the fact that the better alternative of Budgens was too far away up the steep hill of Nimrod Road. There was tussling and tutting when Daddy pressed the cash into Kwame's palm, despite Kwame's insistence he'd pay for the shopping himself.

Once Kwame had escaped and was out on the doorstep, he found that the peach walls, softened by the morning light, were more soothing than they'd seemed yesterday. This gentleness was enhanced by the kitsch Snoopy Welcome mat that Kwame noticed lay before Mr O'Shea's flat. He drew his arms around his chest, heard birds out on Southcroft. That morning, Richmond Court smelled the same as it always had done. Years had passed – and, as he noticed whenever he visited, some of his favourite families had long gone: no Marcel, no Mrs Jones at 535 – but, though faces changed, the tribes remained the same. West Africans. Somalis. Jamaicans. Tamils. The smells of their different, connected cuisines left traces on the air. Ginger, garlic, pepper, paprika, cardamom, thyme, cumin, saltfish, sizzling fat, all so much more determined than the other presences wafting around: cigarette smoke, disinfectant, Mrs Okolie's knock-off Elizabeth Arden – and the slightest hint of a spliff? All these unmistakable notes of home. He looked at Mr O'Shea's mat again and smiled at the door nestled nearest to his family's. Like a benevolent landowner surveying his acreage, Kwame spread his arms out. He turned around to also take in the doors of 432 and 434, the two flats opposite, the Johnpetters' old place and the Patwaris', and the frayed wind chime strung in the thin strip of wall between them.

Early in Freshers' Week at Durham, before he had met Edwyn and Milo, there had been a mixer – a welcome drinks event for the Humanities students at St Chad's. Kwame had wanted to stay in and keep working through the reading list he hadn't managed to finish because he had been doing shifts at McDonald's most of the summer. But he had slipped into his new Levis and crisply ironed Gap shirt and made himself go along. It seemed like not showing up would be too loud a statement to make at the outset of his new life. This sense of obligation was a powerful pushing force, but so too was the opportunity for Kwame to continue his important observations of the brave and weird world he had found himself in. What a landscape it was, populated by people who went to private schools: big, square-headed boys who apparently woke up before sunrise to do rowing, and girls who went red in the face because of disagreements about Pulp and Nouvelle Vague films – a term which Kwame had had to look up. At that mixer, there was the prospect of an even greater terror, one that both attracted and repelled: there was the chance *he* would be there, the wan-faced boy with a long, twitching fringe who kept glancing at Kwame eagerly whenever they crossed paths in the library.

At that icebreaker bash, the tall girl with eyebrows like a Tory grandee who lived on Kwame's floor – Elspeth? – cornered him. Swaying, she passed him a frothy cider and attempted to clink her plastic glass against his before listing her A-level results, complete with breakdowns for each module. They were, Elspeth (?) was certain, going to be best mates forever! It would have been cruel, Kwame had reasoned, to puncture the jolliness of this very jolly, very wide-eyed girl, and her subsequent enthusiasm for signing up to Improv Soc and A Capella Soc. Then she held forth about the novelty of living in halls – the cuteness, the adventure of living in such dinky close quarters. Her en suite, apparently, had pongy drains – but she'd soon get the warden on to that. Then everything would be *perfect*. Kwame had sipped the warm drink while sketching a loose two-step move. He tried to find her remarking on the smallness of rooms larger than either his or Akua's or his parents' harmlessly naive.

He decided to take the lift instead of the stairs. He pressed the scratched buttons and thought some of the most taxing *graft* – to use Daddy's term that still lingered – of his younger years had been reframing the kind of detachment he had fallen into during that throwaway conversation with Elspeth. It was not, he convinced himself throughout those years, shameful cowardice. It was stepping back so he could try to reinterpret, try to make something good from – or see something positive in – people's less appealing actions and attitudes towards him. Good preparation for the classroom. The lift's doors slid apart. Stepping in, the thought of school prompted the realization that he had an unmarked stack of Year 7 exercise books in the living room at Fernlea. His frustrated growl reverberated around the silvery cell as he descended.

The problem was that he had fobbed off the kids too many times now. Almost every morning for the last month or so, he had started the day intending to assess Year 7's nonsense stories written in response to *Jabberwocky*. The kids had handed them in, with eager grins, weeks ago. In strict capital letters, at the top of his to-do list, each day he wrote a reminder to get those books seen to. He underlined it several times. And every day, he forgot. Or he regretted setting the slightly pointless task in the first place and couldn't bring himself to engage with the pieces. Or he reasoned he would be keener to look at them the following day. Which, of course, was never the case.

Without fail, Nosheen or Rebecca started their lessons by thrusting up proud hands. They'd ask if Mr Akromah had loved their nonsense tale, if he had laughed at the bit with the banana and hedgehog doing a rap battle. Each time he made his excuses and promised to return the work to his class soon their little faces crunched.

He was well aware that a slightly more prolonged wait for his scrawled commendations was something those Year 7s could certainly survive. And it would be a bit of a pain in the arse to have to trot to Fernlea Road now to collect the work and get it done in time for his next lesson with the kids on Monday. He could now legitimately say family issues had got in the way of work. But, Kwame conceded, adding a Sherbet Double Dip for himself to the pile of goods on Mr Agrawal's counter, he knew what the honourable thing to do was.

So many of those Year 7s still retained their lustre. They were yet to take on Ahmed's views of those in charge as unfeeling automatons with no sense of accountability to students, a view that would no doubt come when adolescence took hold. Michelle, Melvin, Nosheen – that riotous lot whose blazers were too big for them – still looked to Kwame, to Mr Akromah, for the fillip of a compliment as boosting as the ones Mrs Gilchrist had offered him to momentarily still his mind's churning. He knew that tiny gestures, glimmers of praise, made those kids leave the classroom with their chests puffed out, and they walked a little taller as they negotiated corridors and streets run by bigger boys and girls. The way he could make those young people move through the world with a little more pride was not, as Daddy might put it, a 'small thing'. It mattered.

He deposited the newspaper and shopping with his father, explained he needed to dash to Fernlea and promised he would be back as soon as he could. Daddy inspected Kwame over his glasses. 'Make sure you don't eat when you are there, eh? I am planning on having you heat up the kelewele for dinner and it would be good for you to help me finish it all. Okay? And wipe this sugar sugar white dusty something from your lip.'

Kwame gathered his keys from the side table, licked around his mouth: sherbet tingled. 'Cheers, Daddy. Promise, I'll be, like, an hour. Tops.'

'I believe when I see. You will meet your Edwyn and then the two of you will start gabble gabble gossiping like old women and, before you know it, it will be midnight or later.'

'An hour, Daddy. I wouldn't leave you like this for long, would I? Honestly, you'll not even notice I've gone.' Kwame stepped back, checked the living room. 'And you're all right for drinks and things? Until I get back, yeah? You're comfortable?'

'And, also, now I come to think of it, when you return you can help me set up our new iTablet. Or whatever it's called. iBook. We got a deal on one a few weeks ago. Tesco. Good value. But I haven't even dared touch the box because it looks so pristine and clean I'm sure my fingers will crack the screen thing so it has a malfunction and I destroy the warranty.' He flicked through the pages of the *Sun*, then spoke in a more hushed tone. 'And it will be a nice surprise if your mummy comes back and I know how to work it well, so I can teach her the ways.'

'Yes, Daddy. That will be nice for her.'

'Thank you, my son.' He removed his glasses and laid his hands, one on top of the other, in his lap. 'Thank you, my son.'

Turning on to Fernlea, a woman perhaps five or six paces ahead of Kwame tutted and paused the conversation on her mobile. The spaniel fussing at her kitten heels squatted in the middle of the pavement and produced a little mound of orange shit. Kwame stopped too as the woman scanned – left, right, clearly scoping out the possibilities of a quick getaway – and chatted on about tonight's Brixton cocktail plans. It seemed she was ready to dash away and leave her dog's offering on the street. But then she heard – and acknowledged – Kwame's curt coughing. Her smile was tight. She made her excuses to the person on the end of the line and unfurled a Waitrose bag from the pockets of her floaty sundress. She scooped up the small gift her companion had left and rose to full height. With her free hand, she slid her sunglasses down and jutted her chin while holding the offending object at arm's length. The precision with which she moved down the road was funny, matching the dog's prissy gait. Kwame felt a small swell of delight; he'd tell Edwyn how he had protected their ends from the foulest of vandalism.

In the communal passageway, the loudness of the music coming from upstairs was unusual, but the artist responsible for the noise was less surprising. Whenever Kwame was away for a few days, he assumed Edwyn took it as an opportunity to indulge his love of The Smiths. Like Morrissey's problematic politics, The Smiths' particular melancholy didn't chime with Kwame at all. Those tunes left him cold and, frankly, rather bored, while they sent Edwyn into raptures.

Morrissey's questions continued to drift down through the passageway's ceiling rose while Kwame collected a couple of parcels for Edwyn, both labelled with his full name: Edwyn Henry Du Bourdieu Orlande Bellamy. Phyllida had once explained that extravagance to Kwame: a complicated tradition, on Gibson's side, of naming boys after their illustrious forebears – decorated generals and Huguenot visionaries. Childishly, he had lied and responded by telling her that he was from a line of corrupt chieftains because he had wanted to enjoy her scandalized reaction. She hadn't disappointed. Edwyn had enjoyed the ruse too.

Kwame pressed his ear to the largest of Edwyn's packages and gave it a good, curious shake – the rattle of something was just audible over Morrissey's wails but revealed nothing of the contents. He collected letters waiting for him beneath the Tuke.

Today, it was the scrunched length of lilac fabric gathered around the central figure's waist that Kwame fixed on. Perhaps it wasn't cloth at all. It was the remains of a merman's tail, one that had recently been slipped out of. Yes, that slight David was in fact a merman, masquerading as human, sent on to land for some secret mission. The haughtiness of his stance might have been because he was affecting the self-important pose of a human male and going a bit over the top; trying too hard to mimic the lads he had seen on the shore from beneath the waves. Maybe the boy crawling into the frame had witnessed this transformation no one was supposed to see. The central figure's frostiness towards him was a warning: keep your mouth shut – or else. Kwame was pleased he had somehow managed to get himself into a suitably surreal mindset for the marking of homework about vengeful toadstools. He was less pleased by how loudly Morrissey called for the hanging of the DJ.

Bellowing Edwyn's full and florid name, repeating it in different pitches, Kwame made his way up to the kitchen. Breakfast things – a plate glossy with ketchup, pans glossy with oil – were still out. Chairs stood at messy angles. The tap had been left running. Kwame turned it off – and wanted the Morrissey turned off too, so stomped towards Edwyn's bedroom, the source of the racket, and in there Edwyn's bare back faced him. The skin seemed almost translucent.

Edwyn was on his knees, and his arse – pointy, pale – rested on his heels. The hair along his arsecrack and across the sacrum was downy. His spine strict, the wings of his shoulder blades precise and paler still. The back of his head was bobbing, twisting and retracting, his wavy hair scruffy and messed. His thin hands worked up Marcus Felix's flowing torso, climbing over the black nipples, seeking the dark throat.

And Marcus Felix, standing, eyes clamped shut, pressed against the bookcase. The sinews of Marcus Felix's neck seemed to lengthen, become somehow reptilian. It was a brittle moment. On tiptoes. On eggshells. On tenterhooks. Marcus Felix rested his hand on Edwyn's head, on his shoulder for balance, then back to his head, strangely like he was knighting the one working, working, working at his cock. Marcus Felix's closed eyes flicked open and met Kwame's, and Kwame watched Marcus Felix struggle for shocked, almost choking breath, then sink and deflate as he came in Edwyn's mouth. Kwame heard Marcus Felix groan, saw Marcus Felix stumble backwards, shaking the bookcase. Edwyn wobbled too, laughed and turned around. Kwame held his friend's gaze for three heartbeats before placing the parcels on the floor.

While Edwyn and Marcus Felix dressed themselves, quieted the music, barked appeals and pursued Kwame, Kwame glided around the flat. He pulled a few shirts from his wardrobe and some underwear from his drawers. He found himself unable to look at the Rotimi Fani-Kayode print on the wall. He gathered the exercise books from the side table in the living room and stowed them beneath his arm.

Undeterred by Edwyn's attempts at explanation, and pleas for Kwame to calm down, give them a second, Kwame walked to the kitchen, where he located three bottles of muscat 'created' by Edwyn's favourite winemakers: the Carons were two plump sisters who had been captured in expressive line drawings on the bottle. Kwame used his imperfect but still useful A-level French to ascertain from the label that, with its suggestions of white pepper and a little mint, the wine was a charming companion with a unique lightness. He slipped the books and bottles into his rucksack and closed the door behind him with a click.

In the passageway, he stopped to breathe. He could hear Marcus Felix's serious mumblings and Edwyn's conciliatory tones above. The words were indecipherable, but there was a rhythm to the exchange, an ease about the back and forth. He moved to adjust the weight of the rucksack and the bottles clinked sharply. Walking past Tuke's marine lads, he thought it would feel good to pull the painting down. One swift and savage tug. Even better to throw it to the ground and stamp on it, so that its glass shattered and Edwyn would be left with slicing shards. Kwame reached for the Chubb lock. It was uncooperative in his shaking grip. After he yanked the stupid thing so rattlingly that Hanna popped her head out to see if they were being robbed, it finally surrendered.

Because Lloyd had said that, when the time came, he didn't mind driving them home from Richmond Court, Akua was allowed another small glass of Edwyn's wine. After being granted this freedom by her chivalrous husband, Akua clapped like her daughters did when given fivers. Kwame watched her plant sloppy kisses on Lloyd's forehead, while Lloyd continued to mutter at the football highlights on his phone. Spread out on the carpet in their matching Princess Elsa dresses, June and Joanna giggled at their mother's amorousness. They kissed their forearms noisily, until Lloyd shot them a glare. Mournfully, the girls returned to harassing the new iPad. Akua remained upbeat. She collected her empty glass and Daddy's from the table, and shook them at Kwame until he did the honours.

June looked up from the screen. 'You'll be tipsy soon if you're not careful, Mummy, and that's illegal.'

'Where d'you learn about tipsy, girl?' Akua adjusted Daddy's cushions. 'Anyway, we're celebrating life today. Aren't we? Eh? Eh? And it's only a little tipple.'

'Tipple is a funny word,' Joanna said.

'It is,' June agreed.

'Life is precious girls, yeah? And, and your grandad gave us a nasty fright. We're all so grateful and relieved. Very relieved.'

Trying to settle his attention within the living room and

with his family, Kwame observed Daddy's pretended concentration on the yelping on a repeat of *Total Wipeout*.

Fussing with the layers of her skirt, Joanna rose with
poise. 'Can I do a cheers?' She lifted her carton of Ribena
skyward. 'A cheers for Grandad and I hope for two things:
one is that your bashed ankle doesn't hurt too much;
thing two is that the grazings on your face go away before
Grandma comes home from the motherland, because she
won't want to be your friend if you look like a scarred evil
mastermind and no one could blame her for being afraid
of you, even though you're lawfully married. So I hope it
mends fast for your sake. God bless and cheers!'

'Joanna!'

June stood too and patted her sister on the back. 'A good
speech.'

'Thanks for the support.'

'Uncle Kwame, how many marks out of ten would you
give Joanna – if you had to?'

'And do a honest score, please.' Joanna meant business,
her arms were crossed. 'I've got thick skin.'

'Well, something with that level of skill . . . it has to be
at least fifteen out of ten.'

'Uncle Kwame! That's impossible! Fifteen out of ten is
impossible!'

'Yeah, Uncle Kwame, that's impossible!'

The girls bounced around Kwame for a second before
Lloyd shot them another glare and they relented, returning
to the carpet, the tiers of their skirts billowing and making
them look like jellyfish.

'This is one of Edwyn's, I assume?' Akua gestured towards the muscat and pursed her lips. 'Tell him how much

we all enjoyed it, yeah? Did you say there's three bottles of it? That's kind of him. Bet it's expensive. He only drinks expensive stuff, doesn't he? For his job. Although he did have some good deals last week. Nice-looking Merlots. Saw him on YouTube – I subscribe.' She sipped. 'I'm not surprised they got him on *This Morning*. He's got that quality about him, hasn't he? Like, you always want to hear what he's going to say next.'

'I suppose so.'

Perhaps nonplussed by Kwame's tepid response, Akua turned towards Daddy, her hooped earrings twinkling, and asked about the painkillers he'd been given and if he could take time off work. Lloyd winced because, Kwame assumed, of a just-missed goal or overzealous tackle. The girls kicked their feet up in unison.

All this innocent activity, Kwame thought, pouring more wine for himself, was helpful. It stopped him considering his constantly pulsating phone or from replaying what he had seen at Fernlea Road a few hours before. The busyness around him flattened out the rough heat that had been within him since he had walked back from Edwyn's flat, through Tooting Common and past the playground. Striding, stomping, he had sworn at cyclists who tore along pedestrian paths: sworn at himself for thinking about calling Andrew; sworn at himself for the failure to take it all more breezily; sworn at himself for not, perhaps, being turned on by what he had seen; for not maybe being a more daring, 'queerer' kind of gay and suggesting a threesome, for not wanting anything like that. The very idea of it made him even angrier. And all this spitted swearing done in a voice so sharp that pigeons fled, white yummy mummies clutched their children and Black yummy mummies sped up their pace.

What could be done with this anger? Anger that, like Ahmed had said, made you want to explode? Sometimes the rage was a wide belt of tension across his lower back. Right now, it was a current along the jugular. Kwame pressed his knuckles into his neck as Akua attempted to get Daddy to talk about his pension contributions. Daddy fobbed her off, and so Akua placed two plantain chips between her lips so they resembled a beak. The girls seemed to think this was riotously funny. Kwame's neck grew tauter.

However intensely anger existed in his bones and boiling blood, Kwame was still very unsure of the legitimacy of that reaction. He could see that, after all, the historic or emotional claim he might have over Edwyn should not prevent his friend from sleeping with his boss. And Kwame had no hold over Marcus Felix that should stop Marcus Felix from doing whatever he wanted with his body. While there was a sense that it was 'not quite cricket', as Gibson might say, was that enough to justify Kwame's feelings of betrayal? Such a large word. He didn't want to carry that entrapping feeling or to have it sap him any more than he was already sapped. *Betrayal*. He wished there were other, greyer ways he could describe it. A better means of negotiating with his need to bruise or break too. He pulled himself up from the sofa.

'I'm going to get more snacks.'

'We've got everything we need here, Kwame. More than enough. Got plenty, serio—'

But he was already gone, making for the kitchen sink fringed with Mummy's under-watered spider plants and caddies of furry sponges. He stared through the window at the plane trees and the patch of grass below, that square of itchy green, wary cats and stray used condoms. The recognition that Marcus Felix and Edwyn had some relationship from which he was excluded; the proprietorial urge he had towards these two men that now seemed so laughable; the notion that these men would suffer none of the twisting Kwame felt as he worked to relax his jaw; the assumption, his *certain knowledge*, that for Edwyn this would do no harm, leave no trace; the embarrassment – these things all hurt. His hands gripped the edge of the sink. He stood on the tips of his toes.

'You okay?'

He turned to face Akua. There was too much to say.

He sniffed. 'Yeah. Thinking.'

'You know he'll be all right, yeah?'

'Daddy?'

'Yes, *Daddy*, of course. Who else?' She finished her drink, rested it on the side. Something like wistfulness overtook her. 'His problem's the same as all of yours.'

'Whose?'

'Lloyd's, Daddy's, yours. All of you. Same. Bloody maddening, to be honest. Even *you*. Your lot are meant to be enlightened and in touch with your emotions.'

'What?'

'Lloyd, Daddy, you: all *obsessed* with coming across as, like, sorted. Self-sufficient. I mean, self-sufficiency's fine and dandy, but it's kind of overrated, if you ask me. What's the problem in actually having a look at your surroundings and seeing what support is there and making use of it? Isn't that common sense? Rather than depleting your own resources all day, every day.' She tutted at Kwame's slowness on the uptake. 'You lot are *long*. It's always been the same. Daddy not even listening to a word I'm saying. You up in here, grinding your teeth because you're sad something properly dreadful could've happened to Daddy and won't turn to me to lean on. All the time, years of it, me trying to hold things together when Mummy gets cold or Daddy gets cold or you get cold. But everyone acts like *I'm* the nuisance for addressing problems and trying to offer solutions, trying to get you lot together and talking. Why? Cos things'll work out by themselves? BS. Or cos you reckon you can figure a way out of shit by yourself, no help needed, specially not from me. Why? Cos that's what you're supposed to do, right? All tough and proud and strong that. Has that approach worked, though? Is it working for anyone, Kwame?'

'Akua, it's not really like –'

She bit something out of a fingernail, took a breath. 'Before you got back from Edwyn's, Daddy was chatting about Yaw, you know.'

'He was doing that last night.'

'Think the accident's made him a bit . . . reflective. He was going on about the whole madness of the situation, Yaw leaving and everything. I asked him for the four hundredth time if anyone back home ever talks about Yaw. And, and he spoke about it more than he ever has before.'

There was a biliousness at the back of Kwame's throat: having to deal with mental images of Edwyn prising apart Marcus Felix's arsecheeks or a splash of Edwyn's spunk against Marcus Felix's skin; having to deal with everyone bringing up Yaw's fucking name every three fucking seconds, as if that name didn't instantly remind him of his first flushes of a difficult understanding.

He had been so terrified by what he had felt, back then. As Akua turned round to tell Lloyd to watch the girls more closely, Kwame wondered if fear had lived within him, in one way or another, always; if it had been fear, more than anything else, that led him to seek out the kind of protection offered by Edwyn's friendship, the sanctuary offered by the proximity to privilege and a turning of blind eyes that was much safer than the hostilities elsewhere. Had the sheen of Yaw's approval offered, for a time, a kind of unreal protection too? But that was such a partial understanding of how things were, or how things had been. Kwame pressed his heels into the floor.

'Apparently,' Akua continued, 'after Yaw was sent back to Ghana, he tried his luck again. Got to America for a bit. Immigration caught up with him eventually. Then some say he tried that whole backway thing – through the Sahara and then dinghies across the Mediterranean. Dangerous. Madness. Proper madness, man.'

After Yaw had left, amid his parents' silence and under the gaze of the unfazed Care Bears sticker, so many possibilities about what might have become of Yaw coursed through Kwame's mind: Yaw had found himself in another packed and pushy city, washing cars and cracking jokes elsewhere; Yaw was in charge of something, he was suited as he pointed at eager teams who lived to be guided by him; Yaw had married the luckiest and most beautiful woman in the whole wide world; Yaw was on stages, firing out the cleverest rhymes. As he'd grown and the world had clarified around him, Kwame's imaginings lost their gleam: Yaw might be a security guard, stern on the door because so few other doors had been shown to him; Yaw was burying his father, his face even more angular, gouged and thinned with sorrow.

Kwame wondered if Akua could see that his calves and knees were trembling, and that he was tightening his thighs, stomach, lower back – doing all he could to keep still. 'Fuck' was all he could say. 'Fucking hell.'

'Some uncle or whoever thinks he's ended up in Dubai, building hotels. Ask Daddy.'

'I. Don't think I can.'

'Daddy was chatting about the fallout straight afterwards. D'you remember your Christmas show tantrum when he left? Kwame, you literally tore yourself to pieces in your room. Holed yourself up for hours. Wouldn't say a word.'

'I know.' His voice was raised but wavering too. 'I *was* there.'

Akua stepped towards him, shook her head as if to clear its confusion at Kwame's agitation. 'But you're fully adult now. A big man. Can't hide like that because it's more convenient. You get me?'

He laughed, and then his eyes fell on the grainy pool of sediment at the bottom of Akua's glass. He remembered a technical term Edwyn had taught him when he had first started at *Decanter* magazine and they had sent him three burgundies to try: *sous bois*, which Edwyn had explained, as he poured them both generous measures of the first bottle, loosely translated as 'undergrowth'. The phrase alluded, apparently, to the musty hints in the wine Edwyn swilled in the glass. It was, he had said, a term that referred to the taste of deliciously earthy things hidden, concealed deep in the secrecy of the forest floor. Dying leaves. Mushrooms. Truffles. It was their *sous bois* quality that made these wines distinctive and desirable.

Akua put her hand on Kwame's arm. 'Things don't have to be as hard as you make them. Honestly.'

She patted him again, moving him aside, and took her glass to rinse away the silty residue. She dried it with a tea towel, then held it up to the light, and Kwame felt his legs refuse to support him any longer. He ended up on the floor, squatting and crying, wobbly on his heels until he kicked his legs out long. Akua met him down there, her hands more frantic than soothing, her palms wet with water from the tap but then wetter with his tears. When Kwame wiped his eyes with his knuckles, back those tears sprang. So many tears for the desperation of the triers. So many tears for the turning of blind eyes. So many tears for the revelation of hidden things. Kwame inhaled in coughed gulps.

Then there was shuffling and June's and Joanna's alarmed voices rather than Akua's down where he remained. The girls' settling taffeta crunched, and they muttered advice about bright sides and a limerick about silver linings so trite that Kwame had to smile for a moment. Delighted, the girls took that split-second twitching at the corners of his mouth as an easy victory, a job swiftly done. Time to move on. Now Uncle Kwame was their marionette and they set about unravelling his folded form. They tugged his elbows and made him sit up straight, spine flat against the cupboards. Next, they pinned his shoulders back and straightened his dog-eared collar. Finally, with Joanna working harder than her sister, they struggled with his bowed head, lifting and repositioning it, determined to make it face forward.

In the following days, while at Richmond Court and at school, Kwame deleted each of Edwyn's hyperbolic messages. In their various ways, the messages all asserted that Kwame was punishing Edwyn with this prolonged silence. That, apparently, was downright unfair.

Disregarding text messages was fairly straightforward. Disregarding IRL emissaries less so.

Phyllida was the first envoy sent to Richmond Court on Edwyn's behalf. She had arrived, unannounced, on a Friday evening. She brought with her one of Gibson's deluxe hampers. Daddy was thrilled to receive it, looked through its hallowed layers in hushed reverence – even though piccalillis and pâtés were not to his taste. Kwame had enjoyed watching Phyllida as she surveyed the Akromahs' surroundings and worked hard to avoid showing discomfort. She had offered gentle concern about Daddy's accident and remarked on the gloriousness of the recent weather, even if the evenings had been chilly. Discreet enquiries about Kwame's plans to return to Edwyn's flat were made while Daddy praised Kwame's dutiful, if now unnecessary, caring for him. Phyllida's hands gesticulated energetically while she spoke of the depth of Edwyn's sorrowful solitude without Kwame. How gloomy and eerily capacious the Fernlea Road place seemed without Kwame's vital presence! How devoid of life, colour – love! Her pout was both knowing and unsettling. Kwame's favourite part of the whole encounter was when she had finished her tea and he could finally escort her out of his family's home and off his patch. He met her doom-laden words about how Edwyn was under such stress with all the telly stuff with hollow assurances he'd get in touch with Edwyn that very evening. Which, of course, he had no intention of doing.

Then Hanna from downstairs visited. Her gift was less glitzy than Phyllida's: a stack of Kwame's post. She had been more direct in her approach, issued a treatise about forgiveness. Forgiving Edwyn would free Kwame from the negative vibes plainly written across his face. She wondered why Kwame was putting himself through such pain. Wasn't he longing for Edwyn too? Weren't they, like, literally inseparable? Kwame and Hanna had sat in the Rose and Crown and nursed half-pints while the match on the big screen made students rowdy, and she kept telling Kwame that Edwyn hadn't 'been himself'. He had cried at her more than once – and she was sympathetic and was trying but worried she hadn't the tools to help. And Edwyn's drinking since Kwame's departure, she went on, had seemed a little less controlled, a little too loud. He'd almost missed his most recent slot on *This Morning* because he was so hungover. Crunching wasabi peas, Kwame had enjoyed the buzz they brought to his nose. He had scrolled through the new dick pics Andrew sent in advance of their meeting later and showed them to Hanna to distract her. It worked for a while but the frisson soon wore off. Hanna returned the phone and resumed her previous theme, so Kwame went back to nodding and marvelling at the efficiency with which Edwyn had mobilized advocates. But, as Kwame nodded, there were other thoughts too: the fact that it was, perhaps, Kwame's own silence about his *nebulous* feelings for Marcus Felix that had allowed Edwyn to blithely do what he had done; the fact that Kwame had not felt right or safe about even trying to share those nebulous feelings with his best friend spoke volumes; and the difficult recognition that Edwyn's identifying what he wanted and pursuing it until he had it was perhaps the truest source of Kwame's jealousy.

On the following Saturday, Milo was back in town for an opening and so he passed by Richmond Court with iced lattes, eager to take a turn around the Common with Kwame. This turn mostly involved their dodging a ball booted by five-a-side teams while also assessing the talents of these sportsmen – strong calves, nice thick thighs. Intermittently, Milo remembered his evident mission. Between slurps of his drink, Milo made references to Edwyn's caprice being an integral part of his identity. Milo had reasoned, as they passed the tennis courts, that Edwyn perhaps hadn't gone about things with Marcus Felix in the most above-board manner. The verve, however, behind everything Edwyn did was a quality Kwame had long benefited from. Edwyn, the line of argument continued, had to be accepted warts and all. If Kwame *had* to see what Edwyn had done as a heinous betrayal, wasn't queerness an elastic way of looking at the world? One that could accommodate the odd misdemeanour? Wasn't this misdemeanour a product of Edwyn's propensity for self-sabotage? Something originating in the shame all gays grappled with? Conceding that this was having little persuasive effect, Milo too asserted the inherent dignity of forgiveness. Kwame heard each sentence and its implications but was more interested in the tree ahead: studded with a flock of lime-coloured parakeets.

A dog walker lost control of her charges and two Alsatians galloped, barked and startled the birds so that they lifted their wings and darted up, as if the tree were throwing off her leaves in exasperation or celebration, or in a bid to lighten herself. Up the flock soared, this vast and loosening net, a wobbling constellation, a series of advancing and retreating green strikes; expanding and shifting, garrulous and outraged, arching one way and then bending another; a swoop, a dip; spreading, collectively and coherently, tumbling and flitting, curving back on themselves only to accelerate forward, endless and always loosening, tumbling and climbing again.

Kwame could hear Milo's voice creeping up a few decibels as he talked about Edwyn's journey, and –

Kwame stood still.

'Enough,' he said to Milo, his hands making slicing motions. 'Enough.'

Just as he'd asked her to, Amara read the final page of *Mrs Dalloway* aloud, very slowly and carefully, giving her classmates the best chance to track the movements from one observation to the next. As she read, Kwame followed along silently and thought about tweaking the long title of the essay he would eventually set the group on this extract. Kwame couldn't help but feel grateful for this, this peace: for the forty-five-minute duration of a class, there could be no external noise or other considerations. Just the young people sitting in rows in front of him. Just giving those young people at least one new idea, feeling, experience to turn over in their hands.

'For there she was.'

Amara closed the book, rested it on the desk. The muffled sounds of other classes and classrooms seemed folded into a total silence now.

'Can I ask you to read that sentence for us again, Amara? Just once more, please.'

'Okay, sir.' She frowned, flipped to the back of the novel again. 'For there she was.'

'Thank you, Amara.' Kwame planted his elbows on the desk. 'Isn't that final line just so incredibly powerful, Year 12? Isn't it just the most beautiful and perfect and fitting end to the novel?'

Amara blinked. Riya's pen was poised. Estelle drummed her fluorescent orange nails against her folder.

'Because the simplicity really smacks you, doesn't it, Year 12? Shocks you with its contrast. Because we've talked about the effect of the stream-of-consciousness style on the reading experience – that it makes us work and can make us feel lost sometimes.' Kwame smiled. 'Remember what Anton said just before half-term – what was it? Them long-off sentences give you a headache.' Anton dusted imaginary dirt from a shoulder, congratulating himself for this dazzling insight. 'But the simplicity of that final line feels different, more direct than lots of what's gone before. Or at least it does to me.' Kwame moved to the front of the desk, sat on its edge. 'And I love it, that last line, because there's been this build-up to Clarissa's arrival. Sally and Peter have been gossiping away and dwelling in the past for ages and then bam' – he clapped – 'Clarissa appears, delivered to the reader in this clean phrase, with the "for" at the start like it was inevitable or obvious. And it's a line that . . . asserts her presence and her . . . her wholeness, right? Amazing to close a narrative which has taken her apart, over and over again, in that way. And, and, that line so freshly affirms her, like, aliveness, right? There's been so much death death death, and yet we close with a statement, such a bold statement, about *being*.' Kwame kicked his legs forward, looked at the photo of Virginia Woolf on the back of his copy of the novel. 'Mad props to my girl as always.'

'Man like Mr A doing his own stream of consciousness live before our very own eyes, I lie?' Elise said.

Estelle high-fived her, and most of the class laughed too, but Anton was chewing his lower lip. He waited for the laughter to move on. 'It's complicated, though, innit, sir? Cos I agree with everything you're saying. It's a good

401

ending – even if it is kinda annoying cos it's just stops and you're like "What's gonna happen next?" and it is kinda jarring to be left in the lurch. That aside, I rate it, still.' He sniffed. 'But there's even more going on' – Anton tugged the zip of his pencil case – 'in, in my humble opinion.'

'Your opinion needn't ever be humble, Anton. Tell us. Speak.'

'It's the grammar. Yeah, we bes check the grammar more close, innit.'

Kwame smiled. 'Keep going.'

'I mean, like, if Clarissa said, "Here *I* am," in her own voice, like *I* first person –'

'Yes.'

'Like in her own . . . dialogue or whatever, it would be like really strong. But it's kinda weird, isn't it, because it's Peter thinking that line. He like, thinks it *about* her.'

'Okay.' Kwame leaned forward, the table squeaking as he moved. 'So what? Come on, Anton.'

'So,' Anton huffed, 'my brain's getting at something like that big moment of her being herself or whatever is connected to . . . other people?' Anton tapped the table twice, grinned to himself. 'And, like, even throughout the whole thing the novel shows that, get me? Cos it's called *Mrs Dalloway* as if it's just gonna be *her* vibing away. But, actually, in the story, we see bare other characters and they help us know more about her and she's bare linked to their lives. So, yeah.' Anton looked at the clock. 'Who knows if that even makes any sense but at least I've moved time and it's closer to when the bell's gonna ring and freedom's gonna come, innit?'

Towards the end of his second year at SLA, Kwame was asked, as part of his Continuing Professional Development, to sit in on Natalie's meeting with a notoriously challenging parent. Madame Evans thought it would be useful for him to see her in action.

Mrs Conway – mother of Ryan Conway, 8L – couldn't understand why her son had been suspended again. She claimed that *he* hadn't started the fight this time: the school were favouring the other boy involved – Ayden – because he was half Indian, political correctness had gone mad, and Ryan was an innocent victim. No reference to the incriminating CCTV footage nor to the fifteen witnesses who saw Ryan lunge at Ayden and Ayden then protect himself convinced Mrs Conway that anything other than injustice was being visited upon her boy.

Kwame found Mrs Conway a pretty terrifying presence, cracked cheeks reddening as she made her demands about the sacking of the entire senior management team. But what was most memorable about this meeting was Natalie's compassionate composure. Sitting behind her desk, her mouth a steady line, she refused to meet the intensity of Mrs Conway's frothing feeling. Mrs Conway effed, blinded, asked to speak to someone 'properly in charge'. Natalie let the woman exhaust herself and addressed her with even-temperedness, asking Mrs Conway if she'd like water, tea perhaps. But Mrs Conway got to her feet and started pointing, shaking.

Natalie did not flinch. Her tone never rose. She held the woman's gaze and encouraged Mrs Conway to pause again, so they could talk more and next steps could be explained. Natalie's measured approach recognized the frustration this mother felt, but it did not soften into apologizing or back-pedalling. Remaining in her chair as Mrs Conway returned to hers, Natalie continued to stand her ground without exertion or condescension. Together, they figured out the fairest wording of a new Behaviour Contract for Ryan.

In her South Croydon flat the Monday after Milo's visit, as she unboxed and decanted takeaway ramens, Natalie acknowledged the inarguable blandness of George Ezra. She acknowledged too that this had no impact on her desire to shag him – the body wants what the body wants, Kwame! Like the Year 12s Kwame had overheard gossiping near the Data Hub earlier, they were both also a bit confused by the once-demure Head of Music's raunchy new make-over. Kwame added more sriracha to the noodles, ate a mouthful and then started telling her about Edwyn and Marcus Felix.

Just as when Mrs Conway had raved, Natalie was kind and unrufflable. She listened, she poured them both more water. She was the epitome of neutrality as Kwame placed the glass on a coaster.

'So that's where we're at. That's – that's what I saw. That's why I've been at home – *at my parents'* – for a while.' He pressed his palms into his thighs.

'Okay.'

'And you promise you won't – not that it needs to be

404

a secret or anything' – he rubbed his chin – 'I don't even know, maybe it does need to be kept quiet? Anyway, whatever, it'd just be – I haven't told anyone but you. So.'

'You can trust me.'

'Thanks.'

'Fuck. That is *a lot.*'

'Yep. It is.' He leaned into the sofa's chunky arm.

'When I first saw you and Edwyn together, I kinda assumed *you* guys were a thing, on the DL. Or that you were gonna end up as a thing, eventually. You've got this tightness and . . . proper connection.'

'You're not the first to have said that.' The rim of Kwame's bowl was glistening. He smiled. 'He tried to kiss me once – just once, never again. Not a big deal. Some party in Canonbury. The birthday of this girl called Verity. Maybe we were about twenty-three, twenty-four.' Kwame screwed up his nose. 'I can remember the smell of the place. Sewagey. Vegetal.'

'Vegetal? Grim.'

'It was in this really damp basement. God knows what kept dripping off the ceiling and getting into everyone's eyes and mouths.'

'Nastiness.'

'And we were all dancing, like a group of us, and it was great and sweaty and stupid and messy.'

'Gwaaaaan, Kwame.'

'Next thing I know, Edwyn is on me, snogging away, going for my neck, clawing at my shirt. All lips and licking and grabbing my arse and cock. He *was* pretty out of it. Kept talking about how this, how us, was the *pinnacle.* Yeah, kept trying to go in for a kiss, saying how the two of us coming together was *the highest, the heavenliest*... And he was sort of speaking to me, ranting all this confessional stuff, but also not talking to me at all?'

'Okay...'

'It was a bit scary, to be honest. Flattering too, obviously. Bit vindicating as well?' Kwame paused. 'Do you know what I did?'

'What?'

'I pushed him away. Right into the crowd. Some dude fell over. There was this big old ruckus.'

'Drama.'

'I told Edwyn he was *too much*. Screamed it. Over and over. Like, everyone was properly staring. But' – he flicked the bowl, it sang a low note back at him for a second – 'that's not really the point. Edwyn being too much, I mean. Or it feels like it's not even that important, any more.'

Natalie scratched her temple. 'So what – what *is* important, Kwame?'

He gave himself a moment, sipped some water. 'I've spent years, with him, being good and honourable and *dignified* and saintly Kwame. And, sure, that all seemed to require a lot of biting my tongue and that's felt like my fault or gutless or... a weakness on my part. And that's probably exactly what that was. Weakness. But weakness is fucking human and fucking reasonable sometimes, when you're just trying to live. And it's kind of dry and tiring and painful to constantly beat yourself up about this stuff and to always be so expertly attuned to what you aren't doing properly, where you're falling short. So –'

'Babe –'

'But I just... wonder what else there might be, other

than all that. You know? What other ways of doing me, doing life. Ways that I can fully take hold of because I've found them, for myself.' He smiled. 'I'm probably chatting absolute pants and there's nothing new out there and this' – he pointed back at himself – 'is it. So I'd better just button up and get on, right? But I *wonder*, Natalie. I *wonder*. Just like I get the little ones to do when they come up with their cray storytelling nonsense and they're loving imagining . . . *whatever* for themselves.' He sniffed. 'And, and this definitely sounds massive and OTT – but the world doesn't often offer many chances to us, to Black people, to wonder outside of ourselves, you know? We're just not encouraged to do it. So much other shit is thrown our way to reckon with it's hard to . . . to go beyond that, sometimes. So we sort of have to make them for ourselves, those opportunities to think elsewhere and beyond.'

Natalie waved her chopsticks. 'Not one word sounds OTT to me, bro. Not even a single one.'

'So much has been whizzing round my head since, since I saw them together. Like, question after question after question. Sorry.' He shook his head. 'Like, you know how after you have a nap in the day and you get up and everything's sort of wonky and you feel a bit tender and, like . . . *frayed*? That's how it's been, since. Suppose that's why I'm splurging incoherently. I haven't even asked you how yo—'

'Why are you apologizing? For why? No need, honestly. Sounds like you really need to be speaking it out.'

Kwame's cauldron of ramen still steamed. Half of a boiled egg sat in the centre of it all, its golden yolk bright, adamant. 'A question that keeps coming back through the muddle is, is how do I answer the question of myself. Yeah.'

He rolled his shoulders. 'How do I answer the question of myself? I keep thinking about it.'

'Big.'

'Yep.'

'So?'

'So what?'

'How do you? Answer it?'

The egg was a small raft in a soupy sea tangled with noodles. Kwame slid his spoon beneath it, cradled it. 'I want to answer it with my eyes closed. Just to begin with. Listening closer to myself and those voices there and paying actual attention to them and entertaining the possibility that I might trust what I hear. There are so many others, voices, out there. But for just a second – let it be just these voices, the ones inside, in the dark. And then, after that, fast, flick my eyes open to see and let all the light stream in and be with the world.' He didn't mind Natalie's quizzical expression at all. 'Because it's been the other way round, me so super-responsive to *everything else*, everything outside, for so long.' He pressed the edge of the spoon into the yolk, felt his own face become as quizzical as his friend's. 'But maybe that's not right. Maybe there's no answer. Or the answer might change, over time. All the time. Maybe that changing is good. Exciting. Maybe the changing, the ability and freedom to be changeable, is a real privilege and pleasure. Maybe it's amazing that I've even got the chance to weigh up that question.'

'For sure.'

'And I've, I've been wondering what life would be like without my friendship with Edwyn being front and centre. How that would change things. Not because I want to

408

punish him. But because *I* need too much from that friendship, Natalie, because I hide inside it. I keep myself all safe and still in our little thing. I was raised with that imperative. Be safe, keep quiet. Best way to deal with fear. It's, like, in my soil. Everything I do, I've always got a sense – a very innate sense – of a safe limit or edge. And it's not, it's not actually helping me to – sorry. I –'

Natalie got up from her seat, draped an arm across his shoulders, was quiet with him. Her scent was rich with orange blossom and summery idleness. She squinted, then recoiled. 'Mate. You've got sriracha on your ear. Your *ear!* How did you do that? Hold on, I'll get more napkins. And beers as well? I know it's a Monday but I think we're in need. Right?'

'Yeah. Great idea. Thanks.'

Kwame knew there would, in time, be not beer but wine with Edwyn. Maybe a glass of Pinot Meunier. Maybe the whole bottle, then maybe a second. There would be a stop–start conversation in which they took tiny, trembling steps. Edwyn would reach for and hold on to Kwame. Black fingers would intertwine with white, and from Edwyn there would be burnt expressions of regret, pledges, visions of shared futures – but what more could come from going backwards?

Natalie returned with Red Stripes and Kleenex, though Kwame was happy enough with just a swipe of his licked thumb, dealing with the sticky sriracha like Mummy would when he had kontomire on his chin as a child. What he did need to do, however, and what he proceeded to do as the light outside bronzed, was to talk to Natalie about her lodger.

July 2018

'You look *peng*, Mr Akromah. Proper peng.'

'Thank you, Asma. You —'

'Am I allowed to actually say that?' Asma's smile glinted, challenged. 'That you look peng? Now that I'm basically like never comin back to dis dutty school again? Or is it still a safeguardin issue for me to pass a compliment to a teacher? You know how I one hundred per cent like to follow rules, sir.'

Barbara clipped the crackling walkie-talkie on to her pocket and thrust out her hand, the very essence of weariness. 'Asma, can you give us your ticket and move along inside, please? I'm sure you've noticed there are others waiting b—'

'What, miss, what, what, *what*? When a brother is looking fly you gots to appreciate, congratulate, celebrate. Don't you think, miss? Man's looking fly so —'

'Have a wonderful evening, Asma.'

'Thank you, sir. Thank you. At least some people up in here got manners.' She shot the TA a victorious glare through her extravagantly fake eyelashes and ambled towards the Sports Hall.

'She is right, though, Kwame. I don't reckon it'd work for everyone but, it has to be said, the whole teddy boy thing works for you.'

He straightened his black lapels and brushed at the

boxy pink shoulders to demonstrate his self-satisfaction. He tugged at the cowboy tie around his neck and asked Barbara if she knew it was known as a bolo. This was news to her; she enjoyed the word – bolo – and waved a gaggle of prefects in through the doors.

News of the Social Committee's decision that the Year 13 Farewell Dance – only the second in the school's short history – would have a 1950s theme had initially bemused Kwame. He hadn't thought the primness of the period would be the sixth formers' thing. But, as he collected tickets from joyful, soon-to-be SLA alumni, he thought he understood the 1950s choice better. The squalling young folk ahead of him were about to become something different and unknown, out in the big, wide world. As if in preparation, they had slipped into costumes – cinched waists, polished spats – to become unlike their ordinary selves. They were all giddily amazed by the radicalness of their transformation – and by the prospect of whatever it was that might lie ahead for them. He understood that.

It had happened with delicious speed: his telling Natalie he needed somewhere new to live; his suggesting he take over Marina's tenancy when it was up for renewal at the end of July; Natalie's rejoicing and oddly lascivious robot dance at the prospect of their being flatmates, his deeply unskilled twerking; Kwame visiting the flat again to see the room that would be his at the beginning of the summer holidays.

The bedroom was much tighter than his one at Fernlea. Bed, wardrobe, old fireplace and window pressed together and dominated all. That didn't matter; he would make it work. He would find a tiny patch of wall space on which to squeeze in his Rotimi Fani-Kayode print. Kwame noted

411

that, for all her mad and antisocial ways, Marina had some virtues: she had kept a window box in excellent health, a spill of white begonias. He was drawn to that windowsill and the window's calming view of back gardens, patch-worked allotments, the suburban stillness. For a moment, looking down at a couple struggling with bamboo poles, he wondered whether this move was yet another unhealthy evasion; another burying oneself beneath the duvet. But it didn't have that familiar quality at all. The sensation of crunched closing wasn't there this time.

The queue for the Farewell Dance became even more hyperactive when a wasp flew by. Girls sought boys to shield them; the same boys resisted being pressed into service. Ahmed – who was more animated than Kwame had ever seen him, it was sweet – swore he wasn't going to have his prom pics ruined by some nasty bee bite on his face. Fat Titus agreed, a hundred and fifty per cent. As the wasp continued, the queuing Year 13s hopped to avoid it like hot coals tested their feet. Girls used their clutch bags to swat. Candeece swore at it in Yoruba. The hounded thing zipped towards the violet sunset that drenched the evening in an appropriately nostalgic mood. Threat now dispersed, the kids returned to joshing and grooming themselves as if nothing had happened – little mirrors pinged open to check teeth for lipstick and were borrowed to check the straightness of fedoras. They made Kwame laugh. He retrieved a ticket from Bamara and sent him in as the TA tried to contain another swell of noisiness and silliness in the line. He envied the purity and apparent simplicity of their emotions. Their buoyancy seemed, for that evening at least, to be absolute.

Marcus Felix's jumpy voice told them via the walkie-talkie to slow down the flow of entrants because chaos had come: the cloakroom and 'Party Photo Booth' were overstretched; one of the pipes in the loos had burst. Mrs Antwi and some of her cleaners were doing their best to sort it. So Barbara showed her palms to the messy queue and told them to take ten big paces back from the velvet rope barrier. Kwame questioned their ability to count when it was clear they had only taken three steps. The students tutted but soon returned to taking selfies. Marcus Felix made another series of scratchy demands.

In the almost three weeks since Kwame had last been at Fernlea Road, he had done a good job of not bumping into the headteacher — taking the longest route to the canteen so he didn't need to pass Marcus Felix's study, for example. The headteacher hadn't seemed to be exerting any particular effort to find Kwame either. But this evening, the intransigent Head of Sixth Form had seen fit to assign both Kwame and Mr Felix bar-tending duties in half an hour. Kwame ground his heel into the concrete, wondering again if there were some way of wriggling out of that job and knowing, after what felt like hours of attempted bargaining, that there absolutely was not.

There was applause, screechy anticipation in the queue: Kwame and Barbara soon gathered from clamouring voices that Tian and Ahmed were getting ready to show everyone the jitterbug routine they'd got from YouTube. Cos Tian was Ahmed's girl now? All that hard chirpsin bore fruit in da end, fam. And Tian wanted them to do something proper heavy and wicked for the Farewell Dance so they learned some historical moves from the fifties. And everyone knows man like Tian likes to flex and when she sets her mind to something, girl does it, get me? So Ahmed had no choice, had to learn the steps. Sometimes, on a level, it's bes to jus let women run tings. Apparently, there was going to be a bit in the dance where Ahmed lifts and flips Tian over his back. No lie! Ahmed's kinda hench, though, still, so man should be able to firm carrying her, she's only likkle. Apparently, apparently, apparently, yeah, when they tried to do the lift in all their practices, they always ended up with Tian landing smack on the floor, which would be jokes to see live, innit! It's actually badmind to say but you know it would be funny to see, innit?! To be fair, though, if they can pull it offt, imagine, it would be pretty sick, though – innit, miss; innit, sir?

Surveying the glittering Sports Hall, Kwame had to hand it to Year 13's Social Committee: their efforts were impressive. The mocktail bar they had fashioned and the tables where Kwame stood – wooden desks draped in gingham, the fridge from the Common Room covered with little postcards of Rizzo and Dorothy Dandridge – had a sort of charm.

With typical conscientiousness, the overly made-up head girl directed Marcus Felix and Kwame to her meticulous recipe cards. On these, they'd find fool-proof guidance on how to create the range of alcohol-free punches they needed to make over the next hour or so. Her terse descriptions of when to expect their first 'punters' and where to get more soda water if supplies ran low seemed to amuse Marcus Felix. Kwame tried not to eye the headteacher's ensemble too closely, while also doing his best to put to the back of his mind the suspicion that Edwyn might have had a hand in putting the outfit together. The James Dean look – biker jacket, white T-shirt, turned-up jeans, leather boots – a headteacher styled as a rebel without a cause was sort of witty. The smoke machine covered the whole room in murky white. The kids shrieked, thrilled.

'I can't tell you how surprised I am,' Marcus Felix said, tapping one of the studs on his jacket.

'By?'

'How many of them have turned up. Specially with the England game on. At my last place, the Middlesbrough one, the end-of-year disco –'

'The kids'll be up in arms if they hear you referring to it as a *disco*, Mr Felix. They're very particular about it being a "Farewell Dance".'

Kwame turned on the tap to wash his hands. Under the rushing flow, he scrubbed his knuckles with a coarse old sponge – right, left, right.

'At my previous school, the PTA laid on a whole spread and barely half of the kids were there. Thought it was' – the headteacher did air quotes – 'lame. They all went and had an illegal rave in some abandoned industrial estate they'd broken into instead. Fucking nightmare.'

There was an edge to his swearing. The lighting changed. Projections of purple triangles slid up from the floor and crossed the walls.

'Sounds horrendous, Mr Felix.'

'Nice that the ethos here is so much more community-minded and positive. The kids clearly want to mark their time at the school, because this is a place that matters to them. They care about it. That's quite an achievement. One that you and our colleagues can be proud . . .' Marcus Felix tailed off, looking defeated, as if he realized the tinniness of his prospectus-spiel.

The smells of adolescent sweat and the Sports Hall's rubberized flooring were unbearable. Kwame stared at the chopping boards' scratched surfaces, then began peeling spirals of zest from oranges. Ed Sheeran's 'Shape of You' blasted from the speakers. The crowd weren't having any of it, the whole room erupted into dissent. The DJ – sweaty Head of IT – relented and put on some Skepta. It was received with braaaps. Mutiny had been stalled.

'It's . . .' The headteacher poured sugar syrup into a big pink bowl. 'Between me and Edwyn. It's not, it wasn't –'

Over the next minute, Year 13 shouted their excitement as 'Shutdown' played on, and Marcus Felix's mouth contorted. The headteacher tried to laugh once or twice, seemingly at his stuttered silence, at his inability to spin a line, at Kwame's unwillingness to fill the blank. Then the headteacher grasped at air, reaching for something, then tipping ever closer to tears. There was nothing good, Kwame felt in his stomach, about being a bystander to this fight.

'Kwame, it's – I should've – I'm – it's *hard*.' He nodded. 'I've not done anything wrong, yeah? I've not lied. I don't feel *shame*.' His chest drooped. 'But, yeah. It's not easy.'

Kwame found half a lemon and pressed it against the juicer's apex with all his strength. He passed the juice on to the headteacher. Then he did the same with the oranges and gave that juice to Marcus Felix too. He wanted to keep his eyes on his hands' motion: the pushing, the pushing. Kwame was not interested in wrangling about blame and forgiveness. Nor was he interested in the business of

416

playing down or disavowing his pain. And he did not know, exactly, what difficulties the headteacher now searching for the glacé cherries might be referring to. He had woolly ideas but would not stand by those with any confidence. But what Kwame did feel, for sure, was curiosity, bigger than fear or anger or jealousy, about what could be gained or shared or where he might go in conversations with this Black man.

Kwame looked up and saw the agitation with which the headteacher arranged plastic tumblers in white rows. The same tense need for precision he had shown when handling hazelnuts before their dinner. Kwame moved the used fruit halves to one side. They were strange, compressed mouths.

'I believe that, Marcus. That, that it's hard.' Kwame washed his hands. 'I also believe – I know – you'll find a way through it. Or you'll make a new way for yourself. It's what we've always done. It's what we always do.'

Marcus Felix dipped his gaze. He slowly handed Kwame some mint. Kwame placed it on the board, chopped it, passed that over to the headteacher. Then Kwame found almond extract, gave that to the headteacher. They worked without many words. Every now and again Kwame stopped to consult Flora's recipes, to check they were right. Sometimes, he encouraged a bit of deviation – an extra quarter-pint of apple juice here, perhaps some tabasco there. The headteacher was quietly receptive, nodded. He prepared the jugs of Pina Colada and the bowls of 'rum' punch with even more purpose while 'Fix Up, Look Sharp' was on. Theirs was an efficient production line.

'Ready?' the headteacher said to the assembled white cups. 'Ready?' he said to Kwame. And because Kwame really was ready, his smile was controlled but sincere.

The first customer of their shift was Ahmed. He fist-bumped the headteacher, then Kwame. Ahmed called them his bredrins, said he'd tried his best in the exams, had given getting the grades for Brunel his all. His voice lowered as he thanked Kwame for being patient with him even when he had not been able to be patient with himself. Ahmed asserted that Kwame and the headteacher were some of the safe ones, told them to never stop being safe and, doffing his red Stetson and grinning, said he respected them: it was nice that the high and mighties weren't so stuck up they couldn't serve the masses the liquid refreshment they needed. As the headteacher put the finishing touches to the two requested Virgin Mojitos, Kwame congratulated Ahmed on the expertly executed lift and flip he and Tian had performed in the queue.

'Thanks, sir, that's very kind of you.'

'It was amazing, Ahmed! Looked professional. The way she kicked up her legs?! Everyone's chatting about it.'

'I know. I was so scared I was gonna mess it up in front of the mandem but it was lit! Bare people filmed the ting. It's on Twitter now, fam.' Ahmed slowed down. 'All being well it could go viral. That'd give my mum something to be happy about. For once.' He pointed to the ceiling. 'It's in the hands of the universe, I spose.'

They could not have been more different, but something about the brightness and honesty of Ahmed's face then, as he pointed up high, reminded Kwame of Yaw, thinking bigger and beyond, talking about drifting alongside stars, floating in peace. Passing Ahmed his drink, Kwame thought of how, in the fleeting second when Yaw and Ahmed had sent their attention skywards, both young men had been pictures of a willing and wholehearted surrendering to hope. It might be better, Kwame thought, to remember Yaw like that, and in those terms, sometimes.

He rested a yellow paper umbrella in Ahmed's cup. 'If your video clip doesn't get the *mass attention* you're after, I'm sure your mum'd be pleased to just see the video herself? Or maybe you could do a live encore for her. It'd make her day. Do you think you'd be able to manage it again? It really did look pretty difficult.'

Ahmed cocked his head to one side. 'Getting that flip right ain't really about technique or skill or nothing.' He sipped his drink. 'Like – and I know it's easier said than done because of worrying and worrying – but the thing that makes that flip work is that you gotta back yourself while you're doing it. Be like "I got dis." You gotta think, why shouldn't I see myself as being able to do it and getting something right? Why shouldn't I see that?' He wrinkled his nose, placed his cup on the counter. 'Not to be rude or nothing, but can I have a bit more lime in my one, please? Thank you. I like things a bit tangy, a bit sharper.' Kwame handed the drink back to Marcus Felix, who added juice in little splashes. 'Yeah, more, more, more. That's it. Keep going, don't worry, I can definitely handle a bit of sour, sir, trus me.'

After everyone had reflected sagely on the news of England's defeat; after even the kids who had lists of Infractions as long as their arms had asked for snaps with all their 'favourite teachers'; after the head girl stood on the stage and tearily led them in a forced round of the Spice Girls' 'Goodbye'; after the lights came up and the pom-poms suspended from the ceiling looked less enchanting and more bedraggled, the Year 13s formed small clusters. They finalized schemes for afterparties, arranging fleets of Ubers and streaming out through the double doors into twinkling darkness. Skirting the edges of their plotting, Kwame did not pry. It was their time. He claimed it as his time too. He rolled up banners, swept up foil discs, tossed crushed corsages and soggy paper plates into the bin bag at his feet.

It had been a long night.

Mostly, there was quietness, apart from continued tidying, and Natalie's and the NQTs' speculations about getting to the Windmill for last orders. But then Kwame could hear something else: singing. The Ghanaian cleaners out by the recycling were singing in Twi. Lobbing things noisily into bins and tentatively singing, clapping, then laughing each time someone forgot a line or word and they had to start all over again. Mrs Antwi's voice was there, conducting, louder than the rest, clear and sailing between and over the thuds and bangs, pulling together faltering and questioning voices.

Kwame couldn't follow the rhythm that the women seemed to slowly be remembering and to slowly be getting right. He did not know the meaning of the words or the story they had to tell. But, for a moment, that rising sound sustained him. He exhaled.

Acknowledgements

Arts Council England and the Society of Authors provided financial assistance that enabled me to develop this novel. I'm hugely grateful to them for that.

Thanks also to the National Centre for Writing, Spread the Word and the Arvon Foundation for creating opportunities for me to collaborate with and mentor other writers. These experiences so often gave me the spur to move Kwame's story forward.

Alan, your missives were vital in helping me hold fast to what I really wanted this novel to be.

Wonderful, lovely, surprising Theo – thank you for words of encouragement that landed at exactly the right time.

Shout out, of course, to the fam: Olivia, Jenny, Moses and Naima, who bring me so much joy and light. Mum gets a very special mention – again! – for her unparalleled translation work!

Tia, your comments on early versions of the novel were invaluable.

Jane, Richard, Natalie, Jasmin and the whole team at Penguin, I am thrilled by how genuinely and energetically you've all got behind this novel.

Ella, your feedback showed real discernment and sensitivity. I'm so appreciative of the way you immersed yourself in the world of the novel.

Helen, once again you've proven to be the ideal editor

for me. *Ideal.* Working with you has been wonderful – and educative, in lots of ways, too. Thank you for enthusiastic support, for singularly thoughtful reading, for challenging me – and for understanding.

Juliet, you are a treasure. I am incredibly lucky to have you in my corner. I have endless gratitude – and admiration – for your shrewdness and your sanguinity in the face of my momentary panic or self-doubt! It also has to be said that your messages are often some of the most hilarious emails in my inbox. It is absolutely brilliant to be doing all this with you. There is no one better in the biz.

And, finally, the biggest thank-you goes to Patrick, who makes all things seem possible. Patrick, your love is one of the most precious things in my life. Truly, this novel would not exist without your unfaltering belief in me – as a person and as a writer. Thank you for being patient throughout the trickiest bits, for thinking with me, talking with me – and for always holding my hand.